Folktales of China

ited by Wolfram Eberhard

FOLKTALES OF *China*

Folktales
OF THE WORLD

GENERAL EDITOR : RICHARD M. DORSON

FOLKTALES OF
China

WITHDRAWN

EDITED BY
Wolfram Eberhard

FOREWORD BY
Richard M. Dorson

THE UNIVERSITY OF CHICAGO PRESS
Chicago and London

Many of the tales in this volume were originally included in *Chinese Fairy Tales and Folk Tales,* Collected and Translated from the Chinese by Wolfram Eberhard, and translated from the German by Desmond Parsons, published by Kegan Paul, Trench, Trubner, and Company, London, 1937, and by E. P. Dutton Company, New York, 1938.

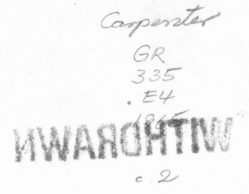
International Standard Book Number: 0–226–18192–8 (clothbound)
Library of Congress Catalog Card Number: 65–25440
The University of Chicago Press, Chicago 60637
The University of Chicago Press, Ltd., London
Revised edition © 1965 by Wolfram Eberhard. All rights reserved
Published 1965. Third Impression 1973.
Printed in the United States of America

Foreword

The relation between the study of folklore and the rise of nationalism is beautifully illustrated in China. In the years following the First World War the sluggish giant, for long a pincushion of the European powers, began to flex his muscles, in the painful awakening that would by the mid-twentieth century lead to a whole new and formidable, even terrifying, personality. Symbol and catalyst of the transformation was the discarding of the classical language which since Confucian times had riven Chinese society between the courtiers and intellectuals, who alone mastered its intricacies, and the vast mass of the peasantry, who spoke the *pai-hua*, the despised common tongue. A movement rapidly developed in 1917, following the publication of articles by the brilliant scholar Hu Shih of the National Peking University, for the nationwide adoption of the *pai-hua* as the vehicle of a truly national literature. Called variously the New Culture Movement, the New Thought Movement, and the New Tide, this literary renaissance aimed at freeing literature from its classical bonds and emancipating the modern Chinese man and woman from the restraints of the past. The acceptance of the *pai-hua* by the popular press and the schools would be one major step toward bringing China into the modern world of the physical and social sciences, technology and mass communications, and power politics.

Within five years the battle had been won, and the incubus of two thousand years sloughed off. The cause for *pai-hua* became identified with the rising spirit of national sensibility. At the Versailles Peace Conference in 1919, the victorious Allies awarded the German-held province of Shantung to Japan; Peking University students staged a stormy protest, the so-called Movement of May 4th, forcing the government to order its delegates to withhold assent. Conscious of their leadership in the New Culture Movement, students and faculty at Peking University issued scores of periodicals in *pai-hua;* book publishers followed suit; political parties saw their advantage, and jumped on the bandwagon; reluctantly, the ministry of education introduced *pai-hua* into the schools.

The future leaders of Chinese Communism zealously endorsed this cause. Ch'en Tu-hsiu, then dean of the college of letters at the university (he was forced to resign in 1919), and founder of the Chinese Communist party, wrote a ringing echo to Hu Shih's proposals in his own article "On a Revolution in Chinese Literature." Ch'en vigorously espoused three fighting principles:

> 1. To destroy the painted, powdered, and obsequious literature of the aristocratic few, and to create the plain, simple and expressive literature of the people;
> 2. To destroy the stereotyped and monotonous literature of classicism, and to create the fresh and sincere literature of realism;
> 3. To destroy the pedantic, unintelligible and obscurantist literature of the hermit and the recluse, and to create the plain-speaking and popular literature of a living society.[1]

Mao Tse-tung was at that time a librarian in Peking University; he would utter similar words at a later date when addressing Communist writers and artists.[2]

The struggle for the adoption of the Mandarin dialects spoken by the vast majority of Chinese peasants as the official language of education and literature brought folklore into conspicuous view. Not only did the vulgar jargon of the people offer a vivid and racy speech, but also it was the language of the popular forms of oral literature which had in the past invigorated classical authors. As he pondered the matter, Hu Shih completely reoriented his

---

[1] As quoted in Hu Shih, *The Chinese Renaissance* (Chicago: University of Chicago Press, 1934), p. 54.

[2] In his now famous "Talks at the Yenan Forum on Art and Literature" in 1942. See *Selected Works of Mao Tse-Tung,* Vol. IV (London: Lawrence and Wishart, 1956), pp. 67–73.

thinking about the history of Chinese literature, and came to the realization that it had undergone a series of renaissances, at those epochs when the literati had reached down and drunk deeply from the wells of traditional folklore. In the arid stretches between, the jaded scholars and poets had lost touch with the vibrant people. Through the centuries anonymous folksongs had inspired the Confucian Book of Odes and the new poetry of the Three Kingdoms and the T'ang dynasty; the songs of dancing girls ushered in the era of Tz'u in the Sung dynasty; folk plays stimulated the high dramas of the Mongol and Ming periods; street reciters of epic tales prepared the way for the celebrated novels which had enthralled Chinese of all walks for the past five centuries. These teeming novels, like the famous *Dream of the Red Chamber,* alone of all literary forms were written in the *pai-hua,* which indeed they had consequently helped to standardize. From Sung times (A.D. 960–1265), professional storytellers and entertainers regaled crowds in the streets; with the development of printing and a literate class of urban shopkeepers came the practice of printing their prompt books (*hua-pen*), first in concise and then in expanded form, in the colloquial language of the stories. From the narrative linking of the *hua-pen* by writers for the people emerged the Chinese novel.

The conscious study and collection of folklore ensued as a direct consequence of the literary renaissance. Hu Shih himself participated in the group at Peking National University which met in 1918 to organize the Folk-Song Collection Bureau. Two years later the Folk-Song Research Society was founded, which in 1922 was brought under the Institute of Sinology at the university. The same year the society began publishing the *Folk-Song Weekly,* whose first issue carried the following editorial statement.

> The aims of collecting folksongs are two: technical and literary. We believe the study of folklore is certainly very important at present in China. Although no scholar has given it attention, and though little can be done by only a few men of limited talents, earnest efforts should be devoted to this study. At least, one should offer some materials for the investigators, or try to attract the interest of others.
>
> Now we collect and print materials to prepare the way for

technical study. This is our first aim. From these sources we may select some good songs in the light of literary criticism and compile them into a selection of The People's Voice. Guido Vitale [a pioneer Italian collector; see p. xxv, below] says, "Based on the folksongs, on the real feeling of the nation, a kind of new national poetry may be produced." Therefore the work is not only to make manifest the hidden light of the people but also to promote the development of the national poetry.

Besides this literary objective, the supporters of folklore research also envisaged social reforms resulting from their labors. The Custom Survey Society, organized at Peking National University in 1923, sought through its questionnaires to learn of existing social conditions and ultimately to remove repressive traditional ideas.

A detailed statement was prepared by the Folk-Song Collection Bureau outlining its objectives. Peking National University invited its professors, officials, and students to contribute, and solicited the assistance of the governments and schools in other provinces. Folksongs reflecting social habits, or with "a deep meaning like proverbs," or about "far-off soldiers, rustics, longing girls and sorrowful women, insofar as they have natural beauty and are not obscene," were to be sought. Any songs circulating among the people since the Sung dynasty were coveted. The instructions to collectors show sophistication in the stress on accuracy, and reveal the special problems of recording in Chinese dialects. Contributors were expected

To annotate the dialect and idiomatic expressions.

To copy the songs as they are, no matter whether they are elegant or vulgar; not to polish the language and not to change the vulgar written characters or colloquial expressions.

To note the sound of the local characters that cannot be found in dictionaries. Transcription in Roman or phonetic alphabet is preferable.

To leave a space for the word that has only a sound, without a character, to note the sound in Roman letters or phonetic symbols, and to annotate its meaning.

To note the society and time in which the songs were or are circulating.

To explain the sentences with bearing on history, geography, and customs of a place.

To write down the tune of a song, if necessary, either in Chinese or foreign symbols.

Between 1922 and 1925 the society received 13,339 songs from seventeen provinces, of which 2,226 were printed in ninety-seven issues of the *Folk-Song Weekly* from December 17, 1922, to June 28, 1925. This period coincided with the height of the New Culture Movement, and young intellectuals turned to the pursuit of folksongs with fervor.

Besides the song texts, the *Folk-Song Weekly* also carried articles on classification and comparative analysis. Both Hu Shih and Tung Tso-pin compared numerous texts of the song "I Have Seen Her through the Bamboo Screen," to show how ten distinct forms had developed from the original one and had absorbed local customs and dialects in thirty-five districts throughout China. A number of sociological studies were also made, particularly by Liu Ching-an, who wrote on "Aunt and Stepmother in Folksongs" and "The Position of Chinese Women as Seen in Folksongs." The concern with social content of folksongs outstripped the hoped-for promotion of a poetic renaissance.

The interest in folksong soon extended to all forms of folk literature. From issue No. 50, the *Folk-Song Weekly* carried articles on such matters as marriage ceremonies; the congee (La-pa-chou) of the eighth day of the twelfth month and its customs; and Meng Chiang-nü, the heroine of a story originating twenty-five hundred years earlier and diffused throughout China in the form of novels, fairy tales, dramas, essays, and poems.

Following the rise of the Chinese National Revolution, initiated by the Kuomintang in Canton in 1925, the Chinese folklore movement split in two. Its founders at Peking moved south to Amoy University, and for several years continued their projects there. But the National Sun Yat-sen University at Canton now took the initiative in folklore research. Its Institute of Philology and History, founded in 1927, endeavored to promote Sun Yat-

sen's nationalism through first-hand investigations. The opening editorial of its *Weekly Bulletin* declared:

> We want to break into pieces all the idols and reject all
> the prejudices in the kingdom of knowledge of the past. We
> want to collect our materials actually—to go to the common
> people to search for their dialects, to the old cultural ruins
> to excavate, and to the different human societies to make in-
> quiry of their customs—to found new studies.

In order to improve the condition of the Chinese people, the
leaders of the national revolution believed it necessary to understand the customs, beliefs, and ideas of the people. Accordingly
the Institute of Philology and History included folklore as one
of its four sections (the others being archaeology, philology, and
history), organized the Folklore Society in 1927, and com-
menced the *Folklore Weekly* (1928–33. Nos. 1–123: a classified index to its contents appeared in the *Journal of Chinese Folklore,* I
[1936], 237–307). The department of folklore established a museum with a Show-Room of Folklore Objects, opened in March,
1928, and exhibited folk costumes, musical instruments, folk toys,
images of gods, and magical amulets. A folklore curriculum
offered courses in Folk Literature and Education, Method of
Studying Legends, Psychology and Folklore, Greek Mythology,
Comparison of Chinese and Indian Tales, Fragments of Yin and
Chou Customs, and Folklore Questions.

Among the ambitious field-survey, research, and training projects of the folklore section, the most successful proved to be the
collection and study of legends and other folktales. Nearly two
hundred tales were printed in the *Folklore Weekly,* and a number of book-length collections were issued in the Folklore Series
between 1928 and 1930: *Canton Folktales* by Liu Wan-chang;
Ch'uan-chow Legends by Wu Ts'ao-ting; *Shao-hsing Folktales*
by Lou Tzu-k'uang and Ch'en Te-ch'ang; *Yang-chow Legends*
by Hsiao Han; *Myths and Legends in the Ch'u Tz'u,* by Chung
Ching-wen; *Discussions of the Tale Meng Chiang-nü,* by Ku
Chieh-kang, in three volumes; and *Superstitions and Legends* by
Jung Chao-tsu, containing a lengthy article on Chinese divina-
tion. Three works in translation introduced Western folklore

techniques and theory: Appendixes B and C in Charlotte S. Burne's *The Handbook of Folklore* (London, 1914), "Question-ary" and "Some Types of Indo-European Folktales," a rudimen-tary finding list, and Lucien Lèvy-Bruhl's *L'Ame Primitive* (Paris, 1927).

The influence of folklore studies extended from Canton to other cities in south and central China—such as Amoy, Fuchow, Canton, Swatow, and Hangchow—where local societies and periodicals were founded. Looking toward national co-operation, the Folklore Society at Canton began issuing the *Journal of Chinese Folklore* in 1936, which ceased after its second number be-cause of the outbreak of the Sino-Japanese War in 1937.[3]

Curiously and incredibly, these activities in collecting and uti-lizing folksongs and folktales, seemingly so modern a technique of folklore science, renewed almost identical methods traceable back to Confucian times. Local officials must have procured songs from the people at that ancient period; Confucius (561–479 B.C.) is said to have selected one-tenth of a harvest of three thousand folksongs and ritual odes for the *Book of Odes* (*Shih ching*). The centralized Han government, which replaced the feudal states in the third century B.C., established a bureau of music to preserve and arrange the secular folksongs as distinct from cere-monial music, sung at community festivals; it also appointed offi-cials to investigate and report on the legends and anecdotes cur-rent in the marketplace. These were analyzed by the ruler and his ministers to judge the mood of the people and the effectiveness of their administration. The folksongs filed and edited in the bu-reau were in time imitated by courtly poets, who divorced the poetic content of the song from its dancing and performing func-tions; the folktales furnished a source for sophisticated writers of fiction in the classical language. Indeed, fiction begins in the Han dynasty from the models of oral tales.[4] Hence the folklore insti-

---

[3] The information on the Chinese folklore movement from 1918 to 1937 is obtained from the valuable account by Chao Wei-pang, "Modern Chinese Folklore Investigation," *Folklore Studies* (Peking), I (1942), 55–76, 79–88.

[4] Evangeline Dora Edwards, *Chinese Prose Literature of the T'ang Period, A. D. 618–906.* Vol. I, pp. 33–35 (London: Probsthain, 1937); Vol. II, pp. 1–4 (London: Probsthain, 1938).

tutes, archives, and field expeditions in China of the twentieth century, with their interest in the social and aesthetic uses of popular song and tale, hark back to long enduring Chinese institutions, alongside which the recently founded European folklore centers seem like Johnny-come-latelies.

Communist elements had already played a part in the Movement of May 4th, in 1919. From 1939, China was caught in the external and internal agonies of the war with Japan and her own civil strife, ending with the proclamation of the Communist People's Republic in 1949. The propaganda possibilities of folklore for Communist ideology, first appreciated in Soviet Russia in 1936, did not long escape the Chinese Communists, who perceived in folklore a splendid opportunity to identify their cause with the great anonymous mass of seven hundred million people. Mao Tse-tung himself was reared among the peasant folk in Hunan province, which he used for his political and military base. Hunan was notorious for its brigands; according to a popular saying, the bandits there were as thick as the hairs on one's head. Associating Communism with the agricultural peasantry rather than with the industrial proletariat—a deviationist principle for which he was criticized—Mao readily looked to folk sources of literature and art in the body of regional songs, tales, and crafts. Popular literature and popular art should support the revolutionary cause. Mindful of his own outlaw past, during which he was the chief target of four "bandit extermination" campaigns launched from Nanking by Chiang Kai-shek, Mao especially promoted the provincial folk legends and folksongs celebrating bandits.

The Communist utilization of folklore required certain adjustments in the methods of European folklore science. These methods were known to the Chinese from the translation of such Western works as Burne's *Handbook of Folklore* and from the lectures of the American scholar R. D. Jameson, who taught at Tsing Hua University in the 1920's and presented the system of the Finnish historical-geographical school in his *Three Lectures on Chinese Folklore* (Peiping, 1932). Terminology too had been borrowed from the West. "Folklore" was first rendered as *min su hsüeh* from 1920 until the founding of the People's Republic, in an attempt to translate the sense of folklore as the study of popular antiquities, in its original meaning when coined by the English antiquary William John Thoms in 1846. The Chinese Communists rejected this term as a capitalist concept, and accepted *min-chien wen-hsüeh,* signifying "literature of the people" (or "folk literature") in oral tradition. Literally, *min-chien* means "amid the people"; *wen-hsüeh* is "literature." *Min-chien wen-hsüeh* is not a completely new term; it appeared in the 1933 edition of the *Chinese Dictionary* (*Tz'u-yüan*), which was published in Shanghai, and was translated as "Folklore." Actually, the phrase with its emphasis on oral tradition and currency is a reasonable approximation of "folklore"; its appeal to the Communists lay in the sense of *min-chien* as "coming from the people."

In the revision of theory, a sharp debate ensued. A transitional figure is Chung Ching-wen, professor of folk literature and folk art in the Catholic University of Peking, and chairman of the folk literature research department of Peking Normal University. In his writings Chung affirmed that folk literature and folk arts originated and developed with the masses of the people during the long process of their social existence and social struggles. Through their powers of artistic creation, the masses have genuinely and fruitfully preserved their own historical record and world view. Chung quoted Gorki as saying that without knowledge of the oral tradition of the people, no one could understand the real history of the laboring class. In analyzing the component elements of folk literature, Chung saw infusions from the literature of the ruling class, from the urban petty bourgeoisie who emulate their masters, from the absurd inventions of Buddhist monks and Taoist practitioners—but these are the poisonous and corrupt additions to the true folk creations.

These ideas, expressed in a selection of Chung's essays on new theories about folk literature and folk art, published in Peking in 1951, seemed to herald him as a doctrinaire Communist folklorist. But Chung refused to follow party dogma. He insisted on separating the scientific study of folklore from its use as socialist propaganda; and he commended the Western techniques of cataloguing variants according to the type-index system, co-operating with ethnologists and anthropologists and faithfully recording and transcribing oral texts. He criticized some articles in the *Journal of Folk-Literature* (*Min-Chien Wen-Hsüeh*) for failing to meet scholarly standards. His own essay, "A Glimpse at the Persian Tales," applied the Finnish method of type and variant analysis of tales as an aid in tracing their routes of travel. The colleagues and students of Chung, prodded by his criticisms, proposed a motion in 1957 to abolish the Communist-dominated Institute of Chinese Folk Literature and Folk Arts in the Academy of Sciences.

Reaction was quick and bitter. "Chung Ching-wen is the salesman of capitalist folklore," stormed Chia Chih, who linked Chung with the imperialists seeking to expand their sovereignty over colonial peoples. Supporting this argument, Chiang Lu quoted an apposite passage in Burne's *Handbook of Folklore* averring that a knowledge of folklore would make possible improved treatment by governing nations of "subject-races under their sway."

The historical fact is that the active scholars in the Folk-Lore Society in Victorian England did influence colonial administrators in Asia, Polynesia, and Africa, who sought to reach a sympathetic understanding of the people they governed by the collecting and probing of native folklore. When "subject-races" progressed from an oral to a literate culture, and read such designations of themselves, they might—as anthropologists have since discovered—find cause for objection, in the vein of Chiang Lu.

In his *Collection of Essays on Folk-Literature* (*Min-Chien Wen-Hsüeh Lun-Chi*) (Peking, 1963), Chia Chih also lashed out at the Finnish school of European folklorists. Their method, he contended, neglected the social setting and artistic values of folktales in order to construct a type index based on their skeletal outlines, stripping the skins and sinews of moving stories. The end result was simply to trace the presumed point of origin of a tale to a particular country. Chia's criticism is not unique; folklorists in Western as well as Eastern Europe have levied these same charges; but in a sense they are irrelevant, since the type index is intended as a tool and not a terminus for the folklore scholar. Chia further attacked Chung's espousal of the European comparative method of motif analysis, which sought to identify similar motifs in international tales but failed to penetrate the fundamental reasons for identity between motifs. Chia would find these explanations in the comparable social conditions in like historical epochs throughout the world, according to the Marxist dialectic. In order to bring to the fore these basic social-historical forces, the Chinese Communist folklorists have developed a technique for processing folktales.

Thus, in his article in the *Journal of Folk-Literature* in December, 1959, Chang Shih-chieh discussed "My Viewpoints about Collecting and Processing." His argument proceeds from the premise that folk literature contains two sets of values: one, the scientific recording of data; the other, the artistic refining of the material for the people. This latter process, aimed at elevating the masses through popularization of collected folktales and folksongs, must precede scientific international research, because of the immediate needs of Chinese society. Chang Shih-chieh offered as an example of this polishing technique his treatment of the story of "Yü T'ung" ("The Fisher Boy").

> An old fisherman earns a bare living by fishing at the Dragon River. One day he sees in the rolling waves a white jade fish jar, which he procures at the risk of his life. An engraving on the jar shows a tiny fisher boy. This fisher boy comes to life and grows; with his fishing rod he hooks the fish engraved on the bottom of the jar, which also become alive. As the fisher boy lifts up the rod, the fish splash on the water. The splash scatters water in all directions, and the water falls in golden drops. When the fisher boy stops angling and returns onto the jar, a spray of gold beans lies all around.
>
> The old fisherman picks up a handful of the gold beans, and heads for the market. Just as he takes out the gold beans to make a purchase, a foreign missionary swaggers by, sees the beans, and questions him. The honest old fisherman tells the missionary all that has happened. Next day the fisherman is brought to the courthouse and accused of having stolen a fish jar from the missionary. After questioning the fisherman, the mandarin decides that the missionary should possess the fish jar. The old man is so incensed that he falls into a faint

and breaks the jar. The fisher boy comes back to life, hooks
the upper jaw of the missionary, and tosses him up in the air.
The mandarin dies of fright.

In processing this tale its collector, Chang Shih-chieh, further
developed the social contrast already weighted in favor of the
humble fisherman as against the foreign missionary and aristo-
cratic judge. In the opening scene, in which the storyteller briefly
treated how the old man obtained the precious jar, the editor
elaborated on the old man's wisdom and courage, to show that
the attainment of a desired end was not a simple or easy matter
but required sterling qualities and heroic effort. Since in the section about the tiny fisher boy's coming to life the narrator had
mentioned that the boy was singing, the collector-editor inserted
an eight-line song, to beautify the narrative. In the next episode,
where the district magistrate rendered his judgment, Chang supplied conversations to expand a point previously made by the narrator, that the fisher boy was dressed in Chinese costume—a peasant touch which shamed magistrate and missionary into silence.
Only when the two brutally exposed their real intent—"simply
want your fish jar"—did the old man faint. Chang claimed that
his method of processing remained faithful to the theme and at-
mospheric details of the story while bringing out more effectively
its central thought. Although he does not say so, Chang may well
have changed the standard folktale figure of a "foreign Muslim
merchant" into the missionary.

Chinese Communist ideology as applied to folktales does more
than sharpen the class struggle between malevolent aristocrats
and foreigners against the virtuous peasant. It seeks to rationalize
and moralize the supernaturalism and magic making of the
wonder tale. Instead of marveling passively at the inexplicable
happenings in these tales, farmers and workers should find in
them guides and spurs to action. In place of the lyric folksong,
singing of lovers trysting by the riverside in the moonlight, people
in Chekiang Province have changed their tune under the regime
of Mao to the joys of digging thousands of tons of river mud in
the moonlight and spreading the mud across their fields. In the
collection *Songs of the Red Flag* (1959) such titles occur as

"Change Your Abacus for a Computer" and "Every Hand's as Busy as Can Be." The text of the latter runs:

> Every lathe is turning with a roar,
> Everyone is on the battlefield,
> Every hand's as busy as can be,
> Every crate of products flashes gold,
> Every drop of sweat is trickling down,
> Every face is alight with a ruddy glow,
> Every wall is covered with red flags,
> Every red graph shoots towards the sky,
> Every heart is joining in the singing,
> Every song's in praise of the Communist Party.

Songs of this sort were intended to honor outstanding workers, channel energies into industrious pursuits, drain off the tensions of communal living, and in general to promote productivity.

In one sense the Chinese Communist use of folklore was anti-folklore—in rejecting and rationalizing away the supernatural elements so prominent in folk expression. In place of the authority of the local gods and demons, the sorcerers and shamans, the party has endeavored to substitute its own voice. Such a publication as *Stories of Not Being Afraid of Ghosts* (Peking, 1961) is unique in the annals of ghost lore; the role of the ghost is reversed and, instead of his terrifying the living, the ghost is effectively routed by the peasant hero. An analogy is then pressed by the editors between supernatural ghosts and the ghosts of imperialism, reaction, false revisionism. These too are bogies and phantoms, which the rational Chinese farmer can dispel with clear thinking; the myth of Western capitalistic supremacy is a ghost that can be laid to rest with the energetic efforts of the workers directed by the party leaders. Thus, the properly presented ghost story can help to raise the level of the people's political understanding.

Similarly, as part of the "wiping away superstitions" movement, the party has aimed to discredit traditional burial customs which hampered their program of land reform. Under the ancient belief of *fêng shui* (wind and water—the name for Chinese geomancy), members of the upper classes sought the help of shamans and diviners in locating propitious burial grounds. The land they purchased for burial was thus unavailable for cultivation, or for telegraph lines, quarries, and roads, which would alter the district lines and disturb the ancestral spirits. At large rallies sponsored by the party in rural areas, the shamans were summoned to perform their geomancy before the people; failing to produce ghosts or spirits, they were obliged to confess that they made their dishonest living through deceptions. The party leaders concluded the rallies with the moral that *fêng shui* was to be found not in haunted graves but in the laboring hands of the folk.

Conversely, the popular traditions which portrayed peasant revolts and uprisings, from Huang Ch'ao's insurgence in the T'ang dynasty to the anti-Japanese war, perfectly suited the party's needs, and were encouraged. They were the stuff of reality not fantasy. Cognizant of his rise to power through a people's revolution resembling bandit revolts of the past, Mao gave status to the study of bandit lore. He himself had accepted the support of bandit forces in his uphill struggle with the militarily superior Kuomintang armies, and pursued bandit tactics in marauding the rich landowners and the service corps of the Nationalist forces to feed his own followers. In the epic Long March of 1934, Mao and his Communist troops retreated from Kiangsi through the vast stretches of western and northwestern China, and swore blood brotherhood with the wild Yi and Lolo tribes occupying the area. When Mao came to power, he stimulated a review and reinterpretation of peasantry insurgence from the late Han to the late Ch'ing dynasties. Successive editions of *Essays on Chinese Peasant Revolts* were published in 1954 and 1955, which drastically revised the accepted attitudes toward banditry. The editors pointed out the misguided and distorted versions of history communicated in documents to court officials by the mandarins, who referred to the righteous revolts of the oppressed peasants as ruffianism and brigandage; hence, the reader must dispassionately analyze these records for their true message.

Even with such editorial advice, the semiliterate peasants could hardly benefit from published documents. The next party move in the resurrection of bandit lore was to institute direct collecting of bandit legends and songs in the outlying districts. In its issue of April, 1958, the *Journal of Folk-Literature* began publishing traditions about the Boxer Rebellion of 1899–1900, collected by Chang Shih-chieh. In these folk annals the valiant peasants heroically resisted the "foreign hairy ones" (*yang mao tze*) and the Manchurian officials. An editorial note called attention to other nineteenth-century rebellions against imperialism and feudalism which had inspired revolutionary folksongs and folk legends, and encouraged folk-literature workers, imbued with political enthusiasm, to collect them diligently. The same call is uttered in the *Szechuan Forest Daily* of January 10, 1959, which pointed out that in revolutionary folktales

> a highly concentrated reflection of the laboring people's thinking and feeling is revealed: their hatreds, their loves, what they oppose and what they pursue. . . . Before the Liberation, many people fought against three great enemies [the Japanese invaders, the Chiang Kai-shek Nationalists, and the United States supporters of Chiang] and toiled with their own labor to create a fortunate prospect for their future. . . . Many of their touching folktales of these revolts are in urgent need of collecting, classifying, and editing. For this reason we think that the notification from the Provincial Propaganda Bureau that everybody takes a part in collecting folktales is timely, necessary, and should be resolutely and thoroughly executed.

From highly trained linguists dealing with the minority peoples to the ordinary man in his home village, the population was enlisted in this self-inventory of its oral history. New cycles of revolutionary tales and songs were soon appearing. In 1959, a year after the announcement of the Great Leap Forward economic program, a volume of *Great Leap Forward Folksongs of the Minority Peoples* was published in Peking. In 1960 and 1962, two books memorialized the Nien Rebellion of the 1860's under the titles *Folksongs of the Nien Army* and *Collection of Nien Army Tales*. By assembling oral military traditions of popular revolts, the Maoists, like socialist regimes in Eastern Europe, have provided a substitute folk history for the national histories written from the viewpoint of rulers.

Consider the thrilling narrative of "How Prince Lu Defeated Li Hung-chang" in the *Collection of Nien Army Tales,* as narrated by Jen Ch'uan-I and processed by Li Tung-shan. The account, running to some fifteen hundred words, is processed in vivid and epic style. Widely known Prince Lu (also Jen Chu or Jen Hua-pang) is the glorious commander of half a million warriors fighting and conquering in the provinces of Anhui, Shantung, Honan and Hupei for the liberation of the peasants. Leagued against him are the mercenaries of the Ch'ing government, the dowager empress of the Purple Forbidden Palace of Peking and her fawning courtiers, and the arrogant governor of Kiangsu Province, Li Hung-chang (1823–1901, regarded in pre-Communist China as a respectable general and liberal reformer), who had dealings with foreign powers. Li Hung-chang procured foreign cannon and troops, and set out to reinforce the "Ch'ing ogres" in their quest for the triumphant Prince Lu. After leading the army of Li Hung-chang by the nose for a year and eight months, Prince Lu confronted him on the bank of the Yellow River in a mighty collision.

> The soldiers led by Li Hung-chang billowed like sea tides toward the garrison gate.
>
> Prince Lu gave a tug at his bridle, and rode to the sloping hills on the left side of the garrison gate. He lifted up a banner pole ten feet long which had been erected on the hill slope. He raised it thrice and swung it thrice from left to right. At once the Nien horsemen from all camps grasped their spears and swords and lined up in single column. The prince lifted up the great banner, and let his horse race forward for several hundred feet. Looking at the Ch'ing ogres, pushing on like ants, he stuck the banner in the ground; his soldiers, who had been spread out in single file, promptly formed a double column. The foot soldiers, equipped with long spears, followed the horsemen; the horsemen were ready with their steel swords. All waited in solemn silence, each resting at his own station.
>
> Behind the Nien army flowed the Yellow River with boisterous breakers and rushing waves. Hearing the roar of the waters behind him, and sighting the Ch'ing ogres in front, Prince Lu waved to his army and shouted:

"Brothers, do you hear? Behind us is the rolling Yellow River. Do you see? In front are the Ch'ing ogres with daggers drawn. What must we do? Look here!"

As soon as he finished speaking, Prince Lu aimed his double-barreled gun at the round gourd atop the pole carrying the big blue banner. "Ping!" Seven fire balls burst from the gourd. In a twinkling, the Nien army erupted like a volcanic explosion toward the enemy position, their swords clashing and clattering in the air.

The Nien foot soldiers brandished their long spears. In front of them Ch'ing ogres wielded sabers. But before they could reach the Nien army, they were pierced by the long spears hurled by the Nien soldiers. One after another, like frogs that had been pinked, the Ch'ing ogres dropped from their horses. In less time than it takes to smoke a pipe, several thousands perished.

Now when the Ch'ing foot soldiers pushed forward for a counterattack, holding up their shields and bending their waists like gadflies, the Ch'ing horsemen were all speared, dead and done for! At this moment, the fighting horsemen on the Nien side maneuvered. Kicking and whipping their horses, they made a detour and wheeled behind the Ch'ing foot soldiers. The Ch'ing ogres were like batter about to be chopped for boiled dumplings. The Nien horsemen whipped out their swords, and behold! the slaughter! "Ka tzu ka tzu"—as though sharp knives were cutting pumpkins. In less time than one needs to finish his meal, the Ch'ing ogres were chopped dead, twenty or thirty thousand of them.

When Li Hung-chang saw that his men had succumbed to Prince Lu's battle array of cavalry and foot soldiers, he hurriedly urged the foreign-gun corps to go into battle.

"P'ing p'ong, p'ing p'ong": the foreign-gun corps fired at the Nien army. At this moment, when he heard the clatter of gunfire, Prince Lu was chasing the fleeing Ch'ing ogres. Reining in his steed, he halted and knocked thrice on its forehead. Strangely, his yellow horse straightened his neck and whinnied endlessly—"Whee whee . . . whee . . . whee whee whee." The rest of the five thousand horses whinnied in like manner. Then each of the horses, as if enchanted, turned its tail southward and its head northward and kicked up its hind hoofs. In a moment the sky became gloomy, the

earth dark. The sun and moon were obscured. The ogreish
soldiers, their eyes blinded with the yellow sand dust, fired
at random.

Thus was Li Hung-chang's foreign-gun corps neutralized
by Prince Lu. Li Hung-chang was so scared that he turned
tail with farts rolling and urine flowing and ran for his life.

This is not typical fairy-tale stuff. Nor does it too closely resem-
ble the legends of the heroic age, from which the Homeric epics
spring, since these concentrate on the single combat, whereas the
modern Chinese text focuses on the movements of massed armies.
Enough of the marvelous hero remains in the figure of Prince Lu
to satisfy the appetite for hero worship, but the freedom fighters
receive their full share of glory. Prince Lu conquers the corrupt
government forces and the foreign mercenaries, not through inexplicable magic and miracle, but by shrewd and clever tactics
which demand the complete co-operation of his men. Rather than
a make-believe wonder tale to idle away a long winter evening,
this is more like a blood-tingling movie script with wide screen
and bright color, in which the sympathies of the listeners are fully
engaged and their energies stirred. Storytelling license has en-
larged to half a million the more likely figure of thirty thousand
troops in the Nien battalions. Historians have recorded the famous battle fought in January, 1867, at Yin-lung-ho, Hupei, but
say that Li Hung-chang did not take command. If the Nien army
was ultimately shattered, there is still substance in Mao's resurrection of the Nien revolt; the defeated Nien remnants surged forth
again in the Boxer Rebellion of 1899–1900, and these successive
blows led to the crumbling of the Manchu dynasty. The guerrilla
tactics employed by the Nien fighters in the 1860's clearly fore-
shadow those adopted by the Communist forces in their conflict
with the Kuomintang.[5]

The Communist utilization of folklore is not entirely to be
shrugged off as fabricated or "processed" propaganda. Western

[5] So concludes S. Y. Teng in his detailed study, *The Nien Army and
Their Guerrilla Warfare 1851–1868* (Paris and The Hague: Mouton &
Co., 1961). He describes the battle of Yin-lung-ho on pp. 184–85. The
so-called Yen-i romance type of popular history, in which the victory of
Prince Lu is written, dates back at least to the Ming period.

folklorists also claim they can beautify tales. Original work has been done, especially with remote minority peoples. Most of the fifty-one ethnic groups inhabiting the mountainous border country of China possess no written language, and so preserve their traditions orally. The party has seen in the collecting and interpretation of their folklore a golden opportunity to penetrate these alien cultures of the Autonomous Regions, embracing nearly half of China proper, and the outlying provinces. Thus, a fieldwork team in the Yunnan area within six months in 1958 accumulated more than a hundred thousand items of folk literature and folk culture; a sampling of 101 tales was published in *Selected Folktales from the Ethnic Groups of Yunnan,* of which several have been translated for the present volume by Professor Eberhard. A general anthology of *Selected Chinese Folktales,* edited in 1959 by Chia Chih, contained 124 stories from thirty-one ethnic groups, on topics ranging from the creation of the universe and the shooting of the suns to the successes of the Communist Party and Chairman Mao. Only forty-seven tales came from the dominant Han culture, the rest being distributed among the minority peoples.

One of the genres previously neglected and now being intensively explored in Communist China is the folk epic, the oral narrative poem of considerable length and antiquity. The Folk-Literature Research Team of Yunnan alone has recorded sixteen folk epics, four of which have been processed and published since 1960. To Western folklorists the nearly extinct form of the folk epic arouses special interest, chiefly because of the prestigious position of the Homeric epics; hence, the excitement at the recording of south Slavic epics in the twentieth century by Milman Parry and Albert Lord, who see in them a continuation of Homeric techniques. The Chinese epics, dealing with events of creation and affairs of gods and kings in ancient times, are of course given the Communist interpretation, praising the freedom-loving, productive, revolutionary spirit of the border peoples under conditions of slavery and feudalism.[6]

[6] For the data in this section I am indebted to Alsace C. Yen, who has generously made available to me his manuscript, "Folklore Research in Communist China," and given me other assistance. He has published

What of Western views on Chinese folklore? Although illustrated volumes of children's fairy tales and of mythology inevitably abound, the report on scientific work in the folktale is brief.

One line of approach taken by Western scholars is through translation of Chinese traditional stories published in the classical and vernacular languages. Two separate forms of such fiction coexisted: the literary story, or *ch'uan-ch'i,* written for the literati in Confucian Chinese by named authors; and the *p'ing-hua,* or anonymous popular-language story, based on the prompt books of paid reciters. Structurally, the vernacular tale betrays its oral origin in repetition and reiteration of episodes and allusions for the benefit of new entrants or at the start of another evening's entertainment.[7] Yet the literary tale too often joins together a sequence of supernatural incidents, and side by side, as in the *Traditional Chinese Tales* translated by Wang Chi-Chen (1944), they do not appear so very dissimilar. Both forms differ from the actual folktale in their degree of stylistic refinement and narrative development and in their reflection of an upper-class milieu.

The second approach—and the important one for the folklorist —is through direct knowledge of oral lore. Before and during the period when Chinese intellectuals were turning their attention consciously to their own folk traditions, the usual run of European travelers, missionaries, legation officials, and private scholars were entering China and examining her ways. The wonders and wondrous beliefs of the Chinese had been transmitted to Europe ever since the historic travels of Marco Polo, but the deliberate search for folklore could not commence until late in the nineteenth century, when the science of folklore had begun to crystallize. In such a work as *The Folk-Lore of China, and Its Affinities with That of the Aryan and Semitic Races* (London and Hong-

---

"Red China's Use of Folklore," in *Literature East and West,* VIII, Nos. 2–3 (1964), 72–86. I also wish to thank Dr. T. K. Cheng of Cambridge University.

[7] These forms are discussed by James R. Hightower in *Topics in Chinese Literature: Outlines and Bibliographies* (Cambridge, Mass.: Harvard University Press, 1953), chap. 12, "Fiction in the Literary Language," and chap. 16, "Popular Language Fiction: the Tale and the Novel."

kong, 1876), N. B. Dennys, who had compiled a handbook of vernacular Cantonese, applied to China the concepts of European folk studies. He knew the recent theories of the philological and mythological folklorists like the brothers Grimm and Max Müller, and the field collections made by his English compatriots at home and on the Continent, and zestfully sought to incorporate the wealth of Chinese lore into the established system. His chosen categories are strictly English: days and seasons, portents and omens, elves and brownies, witchcraft and demonology. Throughout his pages the favorite references are John Brand's *Popular Antiquities,* the cornerstone of English folklore research, and William Henderson's *Notes on the Folk Lore of the Northern Counties of England and the Borders,* first of the English county fieldbooks. Dennys followed a simple technique; he set down an item of Chinese folk belief, and then paraded forth a host of fancied analogies from the Western world, to illustrate his thesis that "a common humanity claims the Chinese and the Saxon."

> As with us there is a sovereign Chinese charm against witches. Sir Walter Scott, in his *Old Mortality,* refers to the popular belief that they can only be shot with silver bullets. A Chinese receipt given in the *Rites of Chow* is as follows: "If you wish to kill this *Shên,* take a certain piece of wood with a hole in it: insert a piece of ivory in the hole, making the form of a cross and throw it into the water: thus the *Shên* will die and the deep become a hill." Certain officers were in old times appointed to "hoot at," "shoot," and "kill" those spirits (*shên*) which were injurious. (P. 90.)

Thus the vastly divergent cultural traditions of West and East are made to seem congruent through a surface resemblance. But Dennys was employing the only equipment at his command, and some universal similarities in folk motifs undeniably exist.

The investigation by Europeans of Chinese folk matter in the vernacular speech imposed of course the task of mastering a formidable tongue. A pioneer collection of compelling interest is the assemblage of street rhymes heard in Peking by a secretary in the Italian legation, who in 1896 brought out *Chinese Folklore: Pe-*

kinese Rhymes, "first collected and edited with notes and translation by Baron Guido Vitale." The translation was rendered in quaint English from the enigmatic Chinese characters; between the Chinese and English texts Vitale sandwiched explanatory notes for the most esoteric characters, notes needed to illumine the customs and allusions taken for granted in the pithy rhymes. Frequently the illiterate rhyme singers could suggest no clue for a word or expression, and Vitale had to guess at the character.

A whole culture bursts into view in these specimens of street literature gathered from the urchins of Peking. Not the courtly class of magistrates and literati and languorous ladies, familiar in the traditional stories from medieval literature, but the noisy throng trampling through the city streets comes to life in these taunts, cries, and little verse-tales. Here are singsong jeers, rich in colloquial imagery, hurled by Peking youths at provincial water carriers with their uncouth dialect; old men defecating in the road; opium smokers pulping their mix for a third and last smoke; greedy eaters of roast dog meat; pork-shy Mohammedans; bald Buddhist priests. Peking boys imitate the cries of various street vendors, hawking such exotic wares as Artemisia annua, lalaqua'r grass, sowthistle and parsley, white stramony flowers and larkspur. They chant rhymes about beggars, imperial wrestlers, cruel mothers-in-law, traveling players, spirits who appear at festivals. One rhyme pictures the complete apparel of a young girl, with her foreign cloth and chignon; another describes a bridal ceremony and its symbolism—often mentioned in folktales—of the phoenix as the bride and the dragon as the bridegroom. A cycle of broad jests about uxorious husbands is glimpsed in one verse, supposedly sung by a small boy about his parents; for punishment the misbehaving husband must kneel down bearing an oil lamp on his head, and suffer the pain from the dripping oil—hence the proverbial saying that a gay fellow has oil stains on his back.

The stuff of legends and folktales is plainly contained within these street verses. One says, cryptically: "At the temple of Pai-t'assu, there is a white pagoda—on the pagoda there are bricks but not tiles—on the pagoda's pedestal a gaping crack appeared—and Lu Pan-ye himself came down to replace it." This rhyme renders a popular tradition about a famous pagoda which had once shown a great crack, threatening its collapse. A strange mason appeared shouting the words, "Mend the big thing." A few days later the crack had closed, and the mark of a mason's trowel was visible. The folk believed that the genius protector of masons and carpenters, Lu Pan-ye (see Tales No. 32 and 36 in this volume) had intervened.

Several rhymes are miniature folktales.

> There was a small baldheaded man, whose name was Kao, who went to burn incense on the first and on the fifteenth. People burn incense to get a son or a daughter. But the baldheaded man burns incense to make his hair grow. After three days the hair was growing, and he burns incense, and dresses the God with a new jacket.
>
> After three days the hair fell off, and he upset the Kuanti statue and placed him against a stand to burn him. But Kuanti, seeing that, was awfully irritated. He took up his great halberd and split the man's calabash (head) into two ladles. (P. 123, No. LXXXVI.)

The moral and ritual implications of this cautionary tale, imbedded in Chinese folk religion, are clear enough: do not abuse the favors of the gods. Another tale-in-rhyme is universal in its mockery of the nagging wife, and follows the structure of a formula tale.

> The old brown woman rolls herself all over the ground, scolding because her husband does not buy cosmetics for her. But when he has bought cosmetics then she does not use it, scolding because her husband does not buy hemp for her. When he has bought hemp, then she does not thrash it, scolding because her husband does not buy a horse. When he has bought a horse, she does not feed it, scolding because her husband does not buy a wardrobe. When he has bought the wardrobe, she does not put her things there, scolding because her husband has not bought a cord. When he has bought a cord, she hangs herself—and frightens her husband to death. (P. 126, No. LXXXIX.)

The *Pekinese Rhymes* first opened a peephole for Western eyes into the steaming, raucous folk culture of the Chinese common people. They intrigued Chinese intellectuals too, who saw in them a source for a national poetry. Vitale tells how his teacher, a literary man, indignantly denied that such rubbish existed, but when the baron placed some dollars within his reach he changed his mind, and eventually procured forty rhymes. In 1901, Vitale brought out a collection of *Chinese Merry Tales* as a first reading book for students of colloquial Chinese.

In the following decades a few other Western scholars made Chinese folklore their province. A magnificent life work undertaken by the French Jesuit missionary Henri Doré was the *Recherches sur les superstitions en Chine,* published in Shanghai in eighteen volumes from 1911 to 1938. Knowing closely the peasants since 1886, when he had come to China at the age of twenty-seven, Father Doré scoured the pagodas and the villages for popular images of Buddhas, Taoist immortals, transcendent spirits, protective deities and patrons of the trades, and stellar divinities. These he presented in grotesque color plates, interspersed among his descriptive commentaries on daily magical practices, the elaborate pantheon of deities and demons, and the popularized religion of Confucianism, Buddhism, and Taoism—the tripartite division of the encyclopedic enterprise. In the course of the work Father Doré reprinted a number of religious legends, Jataka tales, and sutras retelling saints' miracles strewn through the popular sermon literature of Buddhist missionaries and priests. Invaluable though the *Recherches* of Doré are, they do not employ the modern technique of direct field interviews.

The one Western scholar who has made the oral Chinese folktale his specialty is Wolfram Eberhard. Trained in Germany as a Sinologist and sociologist, he engaged in extensive field work in southeastern China in the 1930's and taught on the faculties of Peiping and Peking universities. Familiar with the European system of the tale-type catalogue, through which a national stock of folktales is identified, he constructed an index for the relatively meager hoard of three thousand tales available for China, where systematic field collecting had begun only since the literary renaissance. This index appeared in 1937 as *Typen chinesischer Volksmärchen,* in the well-known Finnish series of the Folklore

Fellows Communications. Here he identified 215 types of
Märchen and 31 types of jocular tales, arranging them according
to such rubrics as "Animals and Human Beings," "Animal or
Spirit Helps the Good Person, Punishes the Evil," "Creation, Beginning of the World," "First Human Being," "Gods and Mortals," "Magic, Magic Treasure and Magic Deeds," "Heroes and
Heroines," and "Stupid People." Within the catalogue he provided a synopsis of the tale type, a list of sources, the names of
variant characters, and historical, comparative, and geographical
notes concerning the tale. In 1941, Eberhard published a supple-
mentary monograph in the same series, *Volksmärchen aus Südost-China, Sammlung Ts'ao Sung-yeh,* which offered the actual
texts of 190 folktales translated into German, corresponding to
many of the tale types he had previously established. This collection was chiefly obtained from schoolchildren in Chin-hua in
Chekiang province, the seat of the aboriginal Yao culture.

Meanwhile Eberhard had brought out, even in advance of his
type index, a volume of texts for English readers, *Chinese Fairy
Tales and Folk Tales* (1937). This collection is a landmark in
the history of Chinese folktale studies. For the first time it presented to Westerners the oral folktale culled from the inaccessible
little books and periodicals where Eberhard's Chinese colleagues
had recorded their field work and from the unpublished texts of
his friend Ts'ao Sung-yeh. Earlier purveyors of purportedly Chinese folktales to Western audiences either had translated art stories which differed considerably in style and purpose from the
true folktale or had Europeanized the Chinese texts. Of eight
hundred humorous tales available to him, Eberhard chose only
twenty-four whose humor could be appreciated by a European.
This clutch of traditional narratives mirrors the bustling world of
the Chinese village peasant and city merchant in a way that, for
example, the much sparer Japanese tales seldom do.

The present edition is a selection from this reader, long out of
print, fitted into the format of the Folktales of the World series.
The tales have been regrouped into more substantive categories;
comparative notes with information about the tales and their
identifying type and motif numbers have been supplied; and half

a dozen new tales have been added from Communist publications, to illustrate the treatment of folktales in Communist China.[8]

Eberhard has encouraged other collectors, notably David Crockett Graham, who published in 1954 a substantial and diversified body of traditions from an aboriginal people in *Songs and Stories of the Ch'uan Miao*. To this volume of rarities Eberhard contributed "Notes on the Connections of the Songs and Stories of the Ch'uan Miao with Chinese Folktales," and prepared the extensive Subject Index. The Ch'uan Miao number 150,000 people, and are ethnically distinct from the Chinese, among whom they live in the mountainous border country of Szechwan, Kweichow, and Yunnan provinces.

This body of work on the Chinese folktale, impressive by itself, is only a part of Professor Eberhard's astonishing scholarship. He has written extensively on the history, society, and literature of China. His *A History of China* (Swiss edition, 1948; English editions, 1950, 1960) is a standard and judicious chronicle. A majestic investigation of the diverse elements in ancient Chinese culture was embodied in *Kultur und Siedlung der Randvölker Chinas* and *Lokalkulturen in alten China* (3 volumes, 1942). Some of this material contributed, with his other researches in the folktale and his personal observations, to the elegant study of *Chinese Festivals* (1952), modest in size but packed with comment on the interweaving of Chinese traditional ceremony, popular religion, folktale expression, social structure, historical change, and regional source. In addition, Eberhard has published specialized monographs on social classes and population movements in medieval China, and on the Chinese novel of the seventeenth to the nineteenth centuries; outside China, he has another corpus of work on Turkish folklore, and has made field trips to Pakistan, Burma, and Formosa from his present base as professor of sociology at the University of California, Berkeley. To Eberhard, folklore is one major strand of the whole civilization.

In recent years the Bamboo Curtain has screened out the would-

[8] Robert J. Adams, the translator and annotator of *Folktales of Japan,* a companion volume in this series, has greatly assisted in the preparation of *Folktales of China.*

be investigators and firsthand observers of China. Yet even from the outside, Sinologists have recognized the high priority given to folklore in behalf of Mao's variety of national socialism.[9] When the new history of modern China is written, folklore will claim attention. As we have seen, the ancient kingdoms of China too paid heed to the social and intellectual energies latent in folksongs and folktales.

RICHARD M. DORSON

[9] Transient journalists have commented on Chinese Communist use of folklore. A writer in the *London Daily Express* for November 16, 1964 (p. 6), Norman Smart, in a story from Peking said that "in Chinese fairy tales the villain is a capitalist, imperialist, or—in Khrushchev's case—a revisionist. Children are taught to bawl these songs and fables at you when you visit the schools. . . . And top of the hit parade is 'Sing a Mountain Folksong for the Party.' "

Introduction

The field of Chinese folklore is still largely virgin soil. Not even the surface has been worked, since folklore studies started late in China. Not until the "literary revolution," after 1917–18, did interest in folklore arise. At that time the reformers hoped to find among the folk the true literature, the true language, the true form, and true subject matter. Folklore, it was thought, would give the key to an understanding of China's earliest history and literature.

Men like Ku Chieh-kang stimulated the collection of tales, and used them to interpret ancient myths recorded in classical texts in fragmentary and varying forms. His interpretations were similar to, but independent from, Marcel Granet's interpretations of ancient Chinese mythology. Ku Chieh-kang traced the development of one folktale (No. 16 in this collection) from present-day oral tradition backward through the short story and dramatic literature into the early classical and canonical literature, not only to show the pattern of change but also to prove that ancient literature contained folk motifs in historicized form.

Other scholars and writers collected folksongs in order to find new forms and new content for modern Chinese poetry. Some of these tried to show that many of the poems in classical Chinese literature had their true origin in folk poetry and were only edited or imitated by scholars. Stimulated by Hu Shih, in his time the most important leader of the new literary movement, students searched through the literature to find all possible remnants of true folklore, such as poetry of aboriginal tribes, ditties, riddles, and proverbs. Encouraged by Lu Hsün, the most prominent writer in the new literary style, others went out and studied folk theater, folk festivals, folk beliefs, and folk art in the hope that some of the elements of these genres might be suitable for assimilation into the new literature and art.

Thus, from about 1920, a number of small groups and associations were founded; they collected whatever they found and published their findings in small and often short-lived journals. The main centers of this activity were, first, Sun Yat-sen University in Canton and, later, Peking National University. But from the middle of the 1920's, owing to the conditions of civil war and political strife, small local groups developed while those main centers faded away. Hangchou, Amoy, Suchou, and Ch'üan-chou had their own small groups of folklorists, and published their own journals and booklets. Few, if any, of these men were trained in folklore, and it would be only too easy to criticize them. For example, they almost never gave the name of the storytellers, often not even the places where the tales were recorded. They seldom told the stories in their original form, but edited their texts. They avoided stories that were, according to their views, immoral and corrupt. However, they collected and published several tens of thousands of folksongs, more than three thousand folktales, many thousands of proverbs and riddles, hundreds of folk plays, and supplied us with a great treasure of folk customs, festivals, superstitions, and medicinal beliefs.

Shortly after the establishment of Chiang Kai-shek's rule, the folklore movement slowed down almost to a standstill. Folklore was regarded as a dangerous field. Whereas Chinese society, it was believed, was quickly developing and was well on the way to becoming more and more rational and scientific, folklorists were accused of keeping alive the superstitious beliefs and attitudes of an era which should not be cherished but, instead, should be allowed to die. Moreover, folklorists—on the basis of their fieldwork in various parts of the country—tended to emphasize local differences, even to isolate local subcultures. Thus folklorists were held to be violating the official dogma of a unified Chinese culture. And because of their folkloristic interpretations of ancient classical texts, they were accused of taking away from the glory of China's ancient past, since, for example, ancient emperors were suddenly reduced to totem animals or mythical heroes.

In the subsequent era—that of the Communists,—it must be

stated that everywhere in the first phases of development, the Communists showed a great enthusiasm for folklore. A number of China's prominent present-day leaders were involved in the folkloristic work of the early 1920's. One of these was the previously mentioned Lu Hsün who, although hardly a true politician, has been claimed by Chinese Communists as one of their best writers. With the establishment of the new regime on mainland China, a new wave of folklore collecting was started. Many books with folk poems, songs, dramas, and tales were published. These books were not compiled by trained folklorists, and they do not constitute scientific source materials for folklorists. According to Chinese Communist opinion, folktales "are concerned with the struggle for production, with the class struggle and all other aspects of social life. Their materials are very wide, their style is variegated, reflecting the wisdom and creative abilities of all laboring people. Such folktales do not only give the reader an education, not only mobilize him, not only give him enjoyment, they also contain valuable materials for our comrades who study folk literature and the social history of our brothers. They also are a rich nutriment for writers, poets and playwrights, with excellent topics for rewriting." (*Yün-nan ko-tsu min-chien ku-shih hsüan,* p. 387.) These books pose difficult problems to the folklorists. Without going into detail, a few points might be mentioned.

The Communist publications are thus far only selections; there is no complete collection of all available tales from one place or from one person. The selections are biased. Stories containing much mythological material and stories praising the emperor, the imperial bureaucracy, or male heroes are largely left out. Tales whose heroes are common people or young women are included.

Within the published stories, changes have been made. This is sometimes, but not always, indicated by the mention of the name of an editor after the name of the man who is supposed to have told the story. As far as can be seen, the editors typically attempt to depict persons of the upper classes—especially the emperor, high officials, and landlords—as bad, cruel, irrational or ridiculous, whereas persons of the low classes—especially landless peasants—are good, warmhearted, helpful, and clever. It is common in these stories for women and girls to take things into their own hands.

Stories collected before the establishment of the Communist regime do not restrict positive moral qualities to the lower classes, and they usually show women and girls in more passive roles, in conformity with the social values and customs of traditional Chinese society.

It can be proved that, at least in folk dramas, whole parts have been deliberately omitted, apparently when the editor was of the opinion that such sections had no educational value. In folktales, this is more difficult to prove, but one cannot help suspecting that it happened in these also.

In collections of folk plays, a large number of dramas were actually created by Communist writers but presented as folk dramas, apparently because they had been acted by folk players. The same cannot be proved for folktales, but there is the suspicion that at least a few stories in the Communist tale collections were created for educational purposes on the basis of existing motifs which were tied together by a plot that illustrated desired social traits. I have included one such suspect story (No. 70). Needless to say, we cannot accept these publications from mainland China without critical inspection, although they purport to contain genuine folkloristic materials. Only when we have parallel texts collected by Chinese before 1948 in China, or by non-Chinese before or after 1948, or reliable texts from neighbors of China, can we judge the degree to which a tale from a Communist publication may be regarded as a genuine tale. This is a tedious job which has not yet been fully done.

Chinese folktales have a long history. Fortunately, a great many tales are contained in the riches of Chinese literature. In most instances, the early writers gave only the barest outline of the tale; in others, they reported the tale as if it were an historical event. No early writer collected tales systematically. Thus we have the time-consuming and almost endless task of going methodically through the whole of Chinese non-political literature in order to find earlier variants of present-day tales. The most promising sources are theater plays, of which there are more than one thousand, and many of which go back to about the fourteenth century. Another rich source are the so-called *pi-chi* (pen notes), collections of notes on an endless variety of topics, written by many authors for the entertainment of friends or simply as personal notes for eventual use. There are thousands of volumes of such pen notes, dating from the eleventh century to the present day. Finally, Buddhist literature is a rich source of tales, especially the sermons of priests and the collections of sermon topics. This source is of special interest because much of the early Chinese Buddhist literature consists of translations from various Indian or Central Asian languages, and the date of translation is usually well known. The earliest forms of many Chinese tales occur in these Buddhist texts; thus we can be fairly certain that the tale is an Indian or Central Asian story which was introduced into China. When a tale is found in one of these texts, it is a valuable discovery because it gives a date before which the story must have been known in India or western Asia (Indian sources are often undatable). It gives us also a date after which the story was known in China, and allows us to study how the story has changed from its first introduction into China to the present time, and which of the imported tales were successful and became Chinese tales and which tales were not accepted. (This matter has not yet been thoroughly studied; interestingly, most of the Indian animal stories were rejected by the Chinese.)

By no means all Chinese tales were introduced from outside the country by Buddhism. Many stories were mentioned in the Chinese literature before the translation of the Indian text in which the same story occurred. It is possible that some of these tales came into China by way of oral tradition and not through books. Some tales were recorded in Chinese texts at a time when, as far as we know, Buddhism had not yet been introduced into China. Some of these tales seem also to be related to Indian or western Asian tales; they may have reached China at the time of the earliest known contacts around 400 B.C. If we leave aside all stories showing affinity with Western stories, many tales remain which have few if any counterparts in the West but which are widespread throughout the Far East. Most of these are creation and mythological tales.

These short remarks may suffice to indicate that China represents an ideal field for a folklorist, if only because he can do research in historical depth—in fact, in greater depth and with better documentation than can normally be done in Europe.

I have refrained from giving all historical data on the tales included in this volume, but I have made reference to some publications in which I have brought together whatever historical information was available to me at the time. All these references are preliminary; further research will, I am sure, produce much richer information. I hope that some day this kind of work will be done by the Chinese themselves, who thus far have not done much in this field.

We do not yet have a satisfactory type index of Chinese folktales. On the basis of some three thousand texts available to me in 1936, I made a preliminary index of tale types. For each tale in the following pages, reference is made to this type index. With further research, a large number of new types may have to be set up and some of my types may have to be redefined.

WOLFRAM EBERHARD

University of California, Berkeley

Contents

I THE ORIGIN OF HUMAN, ANIMAL, AND PLANT CHARACTERISTICS

1	Why Men Are So Bad	3
2	Why Are There Cripples on Earth?	3
3	Whence Came the Ox?	4
4	The Ti-tsang Bodhisattva and the Ox	4
5	Pocket Crabs	5
6	Why Does the Cock Eat the Millepede?	5
7	The Origin of Opium Smoking	6
8	The Origin of the Carrot	8
9	Where Does Rice Come from?	9
10	The Dog and the Rice	9

II LUCK AND GOOD FORTUNE

11	Goldhair Becomes Minister	13
12	A Jar Full of Ants	15
13	The Discovery of Salt	15
14	The Journey of the Silver Men	17

III TALES OF LOVE

15	Faithful Even in Death	21
16	The Faithful Lady Meng	24

17   The Infection   26
18   The Amazing Adventure of a Scholar   29
19   Husband and Wife in This Life and in the Life to
      Come   31
20   The Mason Wins the Prize   33
21   The Stone of the Beautiful Maiden   37

      IV   SUPERNATURAL MARRIAGES

22   The Pretty Little Calf   41
23   The Bank of the Celestial Stream   43
24   The Dark Maiden from the Ninth Heaven   44
25   The Pig That Warms the Ocean   47
26   Why the Horns of Cattle Are Curved   53
27   The Witch's Daughter   55
28   The Marriage of the City Deity   61
29   The Son of the Turtle Spirit   62
30   The Wife of the Monkey   67
31 · The Bear's Husband   68

      V   PERSONS WITH MAGIC POWERS

32   The Magic of the Mason   73
33   The Tale of the Turtle Mountain   75
34   The Geomancer   77
35   The Empress of Heaven   79
36   The Monk with the Bag   80
37   The Festival of Pouring Water   82
38   Kung Yeh-ch'ang Understands the Language of
      Birds   83
39   First Discuss the Price When the Pig Is Dead   86

VI HELP FROM SPIRITS AND DEITIES

40	Lü Tung-pin as the Patron of Barbers	91
41	The Spirit	91
42	The Little People	93
43	The Wang-liang's Magic Cap	95
44	The Fairy Grotto	97
45	Hsiang Meets the Dragon King	98
46	The Wild Goose Lake	100
47	The Bridge of Ch'üan-chou	103
48	The Faithful Official	110
49	The Water Mother	112
50	The Tiny Temple of the City Deity	113

VII KINDNESS REWARDED AND EVIL PUNISHED

51	The Tiger General	119
52	The Gratitude of the Snake	120
53	The Greedy Minister	124
54	The Man in the Moon	125
55	The Gossiping Animals	127
56	The Butcher and the Vegetarian	129
57	Lü Tung-pin Tests the Ascetic	131
58	The Dissatisfied Benefactor	132
59	The Wicked Rich Man Who Was Turned into a Monkey	134
60	The Sacrifice of the Maiden	135
61	The Mynah Bird	137
62	The Helpful Animals	141

63   The Tale of Nung-kua-ma   143
64   Tales of the San Kuan   146
65   The Wishing Stone   151
66   Cinderella   156
67   The Great Flood   161
68   The Story of the Serpent   173

VIII   CLEVERNESS AND STUPIDITY

69   The Mirror   179
70   The Living King of Hell Dies of Anger   179
71   Money Makes Cares   180
72   The Two-Headed Phoenix   183
73   The Donkey in Kuei-chou   185
74   The Rat and the Ox   186
75   Why Does Li T'ieh-kuai Have a Wounded Leg?   187
76   The Mother of Heaven   189
77   The Two Earth Deities   190
78   Chu the Rogue   192
79   The Kitchen Deity   194

Notes to the Tales   199
Bibliography   245
Index of Motifs   249
Index of Tale Types   254
General Index   255

Part I
The Origin of Human, Animal, and Plant Characteristics

· 1 · Why Men Are So Bad

· A LONG TIME AGO in a certain place a man and a dog both died. One of the immortals happened to be passing, and he decided to bring them to life again. He first examined the man and found that his heart had vanished; but the dog's heart was still in its place. So he took out the dog's heart and gave it to the man. He then made a heart out of earth for the dog. Then he said a few spells, and they both came to life again. The dog raised its head and wagged its tail in gratitude. The man, however, not only did not thank his benefactor, he even cursed him.

· 2 · Why Are There Cripples on Earth?

· AFTER P'an-ku, the creator, had made heaven and earth, plants and animals sprang up everywhere, but there were still no men. P'an-ku considered it a grave defect that there was no reasoning being who could perfect and employ other living things, which at the moment were stupid and without knowledge of any kind. He set to work, and for one whole day fashioned men and women out of clay. When they became dry, they were impregnated by the vital forces of Yin and Yang from heaven and earth, and became men.

P'an-ku had made a large supply, which were already partly baked by the rays of the sun when suddenly dark clouds appeared in the northwest and obscured the whole sky. Fearing that his labor might be wasted, the god brushed all the figures into a heap and carried them into the house with an iron fork. But before he had got them all inside, there was a terrific storm and some of the men were damaged. This is the reason why now there are lame, blind, deaf, and other ill people on earth.

·3· Whence Came the Ox?

• IN ANCIENT TIMES man had a hard life and was never able to get enough to eat. Sometimes he ate every third day, sometimes only every fifth or sixth day; so he was always hungry, although he worked day and night. He was really to be pitied.

The emperor of heaven was sorry for men, because they labored ceaselessly without getting enough to eat. He ordered his subject, the ox—that is the ox star in the sky—to go down to earth and say to the people, "If you men are energetic, you can have one meal every three days."

The ox, however, misunderstood his orders; he went quickly down to earth and announced to the people, "The emperor of heaven says you shall have three meals a day and not starve any more." When he returned to heaven and made his report, he was punished for his mistake by being sent down to earth to help men at the plow. "I told you to tell them," said the emperor, "that they should have one meal every three days, but you have now given them three meals each day. Just think of it; men have only two hands and two feet—how can they prepare three meals a day? It is all your fault, and you must answer for it. You must go down to earth and help men plow, so that they will be able to get three meals a day."

The ox, therefore, went down to earth and helped man to farm. The oxen that are now on the earth originally came from heaven.

·4· The Ti-tsang Bodhisattva and the Ox

• IN FORMER TIMES there were no oxen on earth, and man had to plow the fields with his own power. This, of course, was very tiring. The kindhearted Ti-tsang P'usa was sorry for them, and one day he said to Yü huang-ti, "Mankind has such a hard time tilling the fields. Couldn't we send down the ox from heaven to help him plow?" Yü huang-ti considered it for a moment and then said, "No! Men on the earth are not kindhearted. So long as the ox is young and strong and can help them at their work, they will treat it well; but when it is worn out and too weak to plow, they will kill it, eat its flesh, and use its hide." But Ti-tsang P'usa broke in, saying, "Men are really not so bad. I will be guarantor for them. If they kill the ox, eat its flesh, and strip off its skin, I will go down to hell." Seeing how earnest he was, Yü-huang ti granted his request.

At first men treated the ox very well, because it was so strong and could plow so well. But the moment it became old, they slaughtered it, ate its flesh, and skinned it. Although the ox wept bitter tears before its death, men paid no attention to its prayers.

Yü huang-ti was enraged by this news and banished Ti-sang P'usa to hell, where in punishment he had to keep his eyes perpetually closed, except on the thirtieth day of the seventh month. For this reason, men on earth light incense in honor of Ti-sang P'usa on that day.

·5· *Pocket Crabs*

· WE ARE TOLD that in the old days all animals could speak just the same as men. But they were always betraying the secrets of heaven, for which the deities punished them with dumbness. In those days the crab was still round and smooth.

One day a cow was secretly eating rice in a field when a red crab saw it and began to shout, "The cow is stealing rice! The cow is stealing rice!" The cow crossly told the crab to mind its own business, but the crab took no notice and merely shouted louder. This so enraged the cow that she lifted up her foot and stamped on it. The poor crab was squashed flat, and one still sees the mark of a cow's hoof on the shells of crabs.

·6· *Why Does the Cock Eat the Millepede?*

· FORMERLY the cock had a pair of beautiful horns on his head. At that time there was a dragon who was prevented from ascending to heaven by his lack of a pair of horns, and so he offered the millepede as guarantor and borrowed the horns from the cock.

When the millepede came for the horns, he said to the cock, "When you want your horns back, you must call out at dawn, 'Give me back my horns,' and they will be returned at once. You needn't worry." The cock knew how difficult it was to ascend to heaven, and, reassured by the good security, he lent his horns without any more trouble. He also thought he would ask the dragon when he returned, how things were in heaven; and if it was very beautiful, he himself might think of going there one day.

Next morning, at break of day, the cock called out loudly, "Give me back my horns," but although he repeated it over ten times, there was no sign of either the dragon or the horns. The cock went off and complained to the millepede, who quieted him, saying, "If he does not return them this morning, he will certainly do so tomorrow—at the latest, the next day. Just be a little patient, and you will certainly get them back."

The cock waited several days, but although he called out every morning, "Give me back my horns," they never reappeared. He was extremely annoyed at this and ordered all his descendants to eat the millepede at sight. But he has not yet given up hope of getting his horns; he ordered his children always to call out at break of day, "Give me back my horns," because he hopes that the dragon will hear him.

·7· *The Origin of Opium Smoking*

• THERE WAS ONCE a man named Wang Ta, who married a very ugly woman with a face covered with pock marks. After some time Wang Ta could not bear her, and began cursing her and threatening to throw her out. The woman never replied to his curses, for she loved her husband; but in time, when she saw there was nothing to be done about her ugliness, she fell ill. Even then Wang Ta paid no attention to her. Finally, when she felt death was near, she said to him, "All my life you have treated me badly, but after my death you will realize how much I loved you." As she stopped speaking, she died. Wang Ta thought no more about her last words.

About a week later a cowherd came running up to Wang Ta and said to him, "Very strange! There is a small plant growing on your wife's grave." Wang was astonished, and went off at once with the boy to the burial place. There he found a little plant which had just put forth a beautiful snow-white flower. In the middle of the bloom was a small round fruit as large as an ear of rice. Wang Ta went home slowly, deep in thought and rather worried by what he had seen.

That evening he could find no rest. He thought and thought about how brutal he had been to his wife; then he thought of her last words, and finally of the little plant on her grave. He regretted his cruelty, and began to reproach himself for treating her so badly. What could he do if she had turned into a plant to injure him? He lay awake half the night, turning the matter over in his mind, and only toward midnight did he finally manage to get to sleep.

From that time on, the picture of his wife often appeared before his eyes. Not only did he fail to sleep at night, but even during the day he found no peace. Finally he fell ill, and although he sent for the most famous doctors, none of them could cure him. His illness daily grew worse, till he was on the verge of death. Wang Ta had no one to care for him; he had had no children, and his wife, of course, was dead. He lay alone on his bed and groaned in anguish.

Then one evening he had a dream. His wife appeared to him and said, "The little plant by my grave is formed from my soul. No doctor can cure your present illness—only the flower can help you. Tomorrow, go to my grave, scratch the skin of the fruit with a knife, peel it off a little, and let the juice run out. Let this become hard, and then put it in a pipe and light it. If you breathe it in for a long, long while, you will gradually become well." Wang Ta awoke and sat up in bed.

The next morning he got up and did what his wife had told him. Scarcely had he breathed in the smoke when he felt much better, and finally his disease completely disappeared.

Then Wang Ta smoked every day. If he did not smoke at his

regular time, he felt ill at once, just as if he were going to die, and his body felt weak and slack. Now he believed in the final words of his wife. This miraculous balm was the dangerous, destructive opium which so many people now smoke.

· 8 · *The Origin of the Carrot*

· MU-LIEN WAS a good intelligent man, but his mother was very bad. She was a scold and lazy, and did nothing in the house. She thought and talked of nothing but food. She killed many animals, whose bones and skins were heaped up year by year in the garden, till they were almost as high as the little artificial mountain which was part of the garden. Mu-lien often reproached her, but instead of listening to him she cursed him for interfering. He was greatly distressed by her behavior and wept many tears, but he did not know what to do.

One day she became very ill, and said sadly to her son, "I am going to die now, and my soul will be banished to hell by the deity of heaven as punishment for all the living things I have killed." She passed away before she had finished speaking. Mu-lien wept bitterly while he made arrangements for her burial. He invited many famous Buddhist and Taoist priests to read masses day and night in order that his mother might be spared part of her punishment. In this way he used up his whole fortune, but his mother's guilt was so deep that there was no means of saving her. Mu-lien then decided to become a monk and retreat into the mountains to perfect himself.

Later he became a Buddha and went down to hell to save his mother, who had suffered such dreadful punishment that her term was already finished. Mu-lien took her up in his arms and ran and ran until he was too tired to go another step.

It was late in the spring, and tender carrots were sprouting in the fields. Mu-lien lay down to rest by the roadside, but his mother's character was still the same. Having suffered the pangs of starvation in hell, she could not resist the temptation of pulling up a carrot and eating it. Mu-lien knew that, according to the Buddhist canon, his mother had committed a grievous sin, and that he would not be able to rescue her again if the deity of heaven heard of it. In spite of the pain, he cut off one of his fingers and stuck it into the hole where the carrot had been. Later the finger turned into a real carrot. The inside of one kind of carrot is now red as blood, because it was the finger of Mu-lien.

· 9 · Where Does Rice Come from?

· LONG, LONG AGO man had no rice with which to still the pangs of hunger, but had to live from fruits and the flesh of wild beasts. It is true that the rice plant was there, but at this time the ears were empty, and naturally no food could be had from them.

One day the goddess Kuan Yin saw how difficult men's lives were and how they were always hungry. Her compassionate heart was touched, and she decided to help them. One evening she secretly slipped down to the fields and pressed her breast with one hand until her milk flowed into the ears of rice. She squeezed until there was no more milk left, but all the ears were not yet filled; so she pressed once more with all her might, and a mixture of blood and milk came out. Now her task was finished, and she returned home content.

From that time the ears were filled, and man had rice to eat. The white grains are those that were made from her milk, and the ruddy red ones are those that were formed out of the mixture of her milk and blood.

· 10 · The Dog and the Rice

· AFTER THE DELUGE, when the plains had dried up, mankind came down from the hilltops; but there was little to eat, because the old plants had all been destroyed and new ones had not yet appeared. Man was worried about this, but for the moment he lived by hunting. Then the people saw a dog crawling out of a flooded field. On the dog's tail were hanging several bunches of long yellow seeds, which the people planted in the drained fields.

The seeds came up and produced rice crops, and the people had something to eat. For this they were very grateful, and always, before beginning to eat rice, they gave a little to the dog. For this reason too, at the first meal after the new rice harvest, we give the dog its share.

Part II
Luck and
Good Fortune

· GOLDHAIR WAS the nickname of Liu Ta, because his hair was so blond. His parents died soon after his birth, and, having no brothers or sisters, he was brought up by his uncle. When he grew up, he had no desire to study or learn anything, but merely wanted to play. This annoyed his uncle, who from then on refused to give him even a copper. No longer being able to get any money, Liu Ta went to his uncle and said, "Uncle, I want to go away and study. Please give me two hundred ounces of silver." He appeared to be serious, so his uncle said, "I am so pleased to hear that you intend to study. I would even give you three hundred ounces if it were necessary."

Liu Ta took the money and wandered through the land for two years until it was all spent. When his uncle saw him returning empty-handed, he said to him, "Here you are back again. What have you learned in the meantime?"

Knowing that his uncle would ask him this question, Liu Ta had considered the matter, and decided that the best way of preventing his deception being known was to say he was an accoucheur, since who has ever heard of a male midwife? He therefore told this to his uncle, who was horrified at the trade he had learned but could only say, "Good."

Shortly after this, the wife of the emperor had a very difficult confinement. After three days the child had still not been delivered, and the emperor summoned all the midwives in the empire. None of them was able to help. Then the emperor issued an order: "Anyone that enables the empress to bring a living child into the world will be made an official."

This announcement spread abroad, until it reached the village of Liu Ta, where his uncle advised him to go to the palace and try his luck. Liu Ta had no wish to go, but his uncle urged him, saying, "Why did you learn midwifery, if you won't go now?" And Liu Ta thought to himself it could not do any harm to have a try and that after all he might become an official.

On his arrival at the capital, he announced why he had come, and the emperor sent him to see the empress. "This is not difficult," Liu Ta said. "Please buy me a couple of dolls." Then he sat down facing the empress, seized a doll, and said over and over, "Little emperor, come out. Come out quickly, little emperor." He was so ridiculous that, in spite of the terrible pain, the empress was compelled to laugh, and the child was born at once.

The emperor wanted to reward Liu Ta, but all the grandees at court dissuaded him. "He has not rendered any great service," they said. Just at that moment an official informed the Emperor that the ruler of the barbarians had revolted. The officials now all asked the sovereign to entrust Liu Ta with the campaign against them. The emperor said to him, "The leader of the barbarians has revolted; you must go and drive him off. If you succeed, I will give you a post." Liu Ta was far from pleased when he heard that. "How can I fight?" he thought. "If I go out to battle, I shall be killed, but if I stay here, I shall die just the same. I might as well see what turns up." So he said to the emperor, "Agreed, I will go there alone. I don't need one single soldier." The emperor granted his request.

Liu Ta rode off to the battlefield on his horse. From afar off he could make out the ranks of the enemy, and this terrified him so much that he began to shake all over. His terror communicated itself to his horse, which soon became restive and threw him off against a tree. To save himself, he caught hold of a bush, which came up by the roots. The effort made him fall down again, this time into a manure bucket. Fortunately, however, it had a handle, and he lifted it up in his hand. When the barbarians saw a horseman advancing toward them with such an enormous, many-pointed lance in one hand and a huge smoking caldron in the other they were overcome with terror and reported the matter to their king, who immediately ordered a retreat.

Liu Ta returned to the capital and announced to the emperor that the barbarians had retired, but the ministers again prevented his receiving a reward. "He has not done anything remarkable; the enemy retreated of their own accord," they said.

The emperor therefore said to Liu Ta, "I am going to ask you to guess something. If you are successful, I will give you an appointment at once." Pulling out a sack, he continued, "Guess what I have in here!" There being no means of knowing, Liu Ta was in a terrible state and began repeating with a sigh, "Oh, Goldhair! Goldhair!" but the emperor understood "Gold cat," and opening the sack he said, "You are correct. Now I will reward you."

·12· A Jar Full of Ants

· ONE EVENING, a man said to his wife, "On such and such a mountain there is a large tree, and under the tree a jar full of silver coins is buried. On top of the bottle lies a stone. I thought of digging it up this evening, but I prefer to go to bed a little earlier and dig at the first streak of dawn tomorrow."

His neighbor who lived in the next house, heard him say this and rushed off to dig up the jar at once. At the place mentioned he found a large tree, and soon he came upon a big stone, beneath which he found a heavy jar. He put in his hand to feel what was there, but to his horror felt nothing but ants. This made him extremely angry, and, shutting up the jar again, he ran back to the house of the man and the woman.

He climbed on to their roof, and loosened several tiles at a place that was over a hole in their mosquito net. Then he shouted, "You lied to me. Here are the ants for you to eat." He tipped up the jar, but he heard nothing but the clink of falling money. This roused the husband and wife, who said, "How extraordinary! Gold is raining down from heaven." The neighbor caught the word "gold," and, having some doubts, he looked into the jar. Inside there was still one piece of money—the wages for his work.

·13· The Discovery of Salt

· ONCE A PEASANT, who was working in the fields, saw a phoenix perched on a heap of earth by the seashore. A second later it vanished, but the peasant recalled that a phoenix rests only on the site of buried treasure.

In a great state of excitement he began to turn up the earth. After digging for a while, he thought no more of other treasures but rushed home with a piece of earth as quickly as he could, hoping at last to have made his fortune. Then he remembered that people who do not declare treasures to the emperor are punished with death; if anyone heard about his discovery and reported it, his life would be in the gravest danger.

Next morning, therefore, he went to the emperor and said, "Your Majesty, yesterday while at work in the fields I saw a phoenix seated on a mound by the sea. I dug something up, and now I present it to Your Majesty." The emperor looked and looked, but he could see nothing unusual about it, and besides, it had a horrible acrid smell. He became angry, and said, "You dog, you wanted to play a joke on me. You will be executed!" Without delay the unfortunate peasant was beheaded.

This happened in the wet season, when the rain pours down from heaven, and naturally the piece of earth became damp. The moisture ran off it drop by drop, and one day, as the imperial cook was going past with the emperor's dinner, a few drops fell into the food. The cook knew he would get into serious trouble if the emperor discovered it, but there was no time to cook anything else.

At the first bite the emperor realized that the taste was incomparably stronger and better than that of his ordinary fare. "What did you put in the food to make it taste so good?" he asked the cook. "Your servant would not dare to put anything into your food," answered the cook, trembling in all his limbs. "But a few drops fell into it from the piece of earth the peasant brought you some time ago."

The emperor now began to wonder whether the piece of earth was really a treasure after all. He sent for a cup of the liquid and poured it over his food, which was then much tastier than ever before.

Later, many pieces were dug out of the mound. When the moisture from them was dried in the sun, it became white crystals of salt.

The emperor honored the poor peasant who had brought him the salt by appointing his son a high official and giving him great riches. Finally, the old peasant could sleep peacefully in his grave.

· *14* · *The Journey of the Silver Men*

• IN OLDEN TIMES there lived a man by the name of Li. He was so rich that he had eight silver men cast and kept them in his treasury.

His sons and grandsons wasted his wealth, and when it was all gone, they cut a bit off the bottoms of the silver men. Naturally the latter were enraged at this treatment.

One day when they could stand it no longer, they turned into eight young men and went off. They came to a ferry, where they asked the ferryman, "Do you want to be rich, old fellow?" "We poor people are happy if we have enough to eat," answered the old man. "How can we dream of riches?" Seeing that the ferryman had no vein of luck, the silver men crossed the river and continued their journey.

A little later they met a merchant. "Do you want to be rich, brother?" they asked. "If I can earn enough to buy my daily bread, I am content," answered the man. "What's the use of dreaming about riches?" He also had no vein of luck.

Although the silver men asked all and sundry the same question, there was no one who wanted to become rich. Failing to find a resting place anywhere, they eventually returned to the Li house.

On their return to the ferry the boatman recognized the youths as the transformed silver men, because the news of their leaving Li's house had spread abroad. As they were stepping onto the bank and not paying much attention, he seized his opportunity and hacked off one of their fingers with his knife. He found that it really was pure silver, but when he tried to cut off another piece, he saw that they had gone too far to be overtaken. "I have not gained great riches," he said with a sigh, "but at least I have my passage money."

When the Li family saw the silver men coming home, they greeted them with tea and wine, burned incense and paper money, and prayed to them, "Don't run away again. If we do not have the luck to keep you, who has?" And from that time the silver men remained with the Li family.

Part III
Tales of Love

• THE VILLAGE of the Liang family and that of the Chu family were close together. The inhabitants were well-to-do and content. Old excellency Liang and old excellency Chu were good friends. A son was born to the Liang family, who was given the name Hsienpo. Being an unusually quick and clever child, he was sent to the school in the town.

At the same time a daughter was born to the Chu family, who, besides being very clever, was particularly beautiful. As a child she loved to read and study, and only needed to glance at a book to know a whole sentence by heart. Old Chu simply doted on her. When she grew up, she wanted to go away and study. Her father tried in vain to dissuade her, but eventually he arranged for her to dress as a boy and study with Hsienpo.

The two lived together, worked together, argued together, and were the best of friends. The eager and zealous Hsienpo did not notice that Yingt'ai was really a girl, and therefore he did not fall in love with her. Yingt'ai studied so hard and was so wrapped up in her work that her fellow students paid no attention to her. Being very modest, and never taking part in the children's jokes, she exercised a calming influence over even the most impudent. When she slept with Hsienpo, each lay on one side of the bed, and between them stood a bowl of water. They had arranged that whoever knocked over the bowl must pay a fine; but the serious little Hsienpo never touched it.

When Yingt'ai changed her clothes, she never stood about naked but pulled on her clean clothes under the old ones, which she then took off and finished dressing. Her fellow students could not understand why she did this, and asked her the reason. "Only peasants expose the body they have received from their parents," she said; "it should not be done." Then the boys began to copy her, not knowing her real reason was to prevent their noticing that she was a girl.

Then her father died, and her sister-in-law, who did not approve of Yingt'ai's studying, ordered her to come home and learn housework. But Yingt'ai refused and continued to study.

The sister-in-law, fearing that Yingt'ai had fallen in love with
Hsienpo, used to send her from time to time babies' things, swad-
dling clothes, children's clothes and covers, and many other
things. The students became curious when they saw the things,
and Yingt'ai could tell them only that they were the things she
herself had used as a child, which her sister-in-law was now sending her to keep.

The time passed quickly. Soon Yingt'ai and Hsienpo were
grown up. Yingt'ai still dressed as a man, and being a well-
brought-up girl, she did not dare to ask Hsienpo to marry her;
but when she looked at him, her heart was filled with love. His
delicate manner attracted her irresistibly, and she swore to marry
him and none other.

She proposed the marriage to her sister-in-law, who did not
consider it suitable, because after her father's death they had lost
all their money. Against Yingt'ai's will the sister-in-law arranged
a match with a Dr. Ma, of a newly rich family in the village.
Yingt'ai objected strongly, but she could do nothing about it. Day
after day she had to listen to complaints: she was without filial
piety, she was a shameless, decadent girl, a disgrace to the family.
Her sister-in-law still feared she might secretly marry Hsienpo,
and she urged the Ma family to appoint a day for the wedding.
Then she cut off Yingt'ai's school money, which forced her to return home.

Yingt'ai was obliged to hide her misery. Weeping bitterly, she
said good-bye to Hsienpo, who accompanied her part of the
way home. As they separated, Yingt'ai sang a song which revealed
that she was a girl and that she wanted to marry him. But the
good, dense Hsienpo did not understand her hints. He did not see
into Yingt'ai's heart, and tried to comfort her by telling her that
one must return home some time and that they would soon meet
again. Yingt'ai saw that everything was hopeless, and went home
in tears.

Hsienpo felt very lonely without his companion, with whom he
had lived day and night for many years. He kept on writing letters to Yingt'ai, begging her to come back to school, but he never
received a reply.

Finally he could bear it no longer, and went to visit her. "Is Mr.

Yingt'ai at home?" he asked. "Please tell him his school friend, Hsienpo, has come and wants to see him."

The servant looked at him curiously, and then said curtly, "There is no Mr. Yingt'ai here—only a Miss Yingt'ai. She is to be married soon, and naturally she can't leave her room. How could she speak to a man? Please go away, sir, for if the master discovers you, he will make a complaint against you for improper behavior."

Suddenly everything was clear to Hsienpo. In a state of collapse he crept home. There he found, under Yingt'ai's books, a bundle of letters and essays which showed him clearly how deeply Yingt'ai loved him and also that she did not want to marry any other man. Through his own stupidity, his lack of understanding, the dream had come to nought.

Overcome by remorse, he spent the days lost in tears. Yingt'ai was always before his eyes, and in his dreams he called her name, or cursed her sister-in-law and Dr. Ma, himself, and all the ways of society. Because he ceased to eat or drink, he fell ill and gradually sank into the grave.

Yingt'ai heard the sad news. Now she had nothing more to live for. If she had not been so carefully watched, she would have done herself some injury. In this state of despair the wedding day arrived. Listlessly she allowed herself to be pushed into the red bridal chair and set off for the house of her bridegroom, Dr. Ma. But when they passed the grave of Hsienpo, she begged her attendants to let her get out and visit it, to thank him for all his kindness. On the grave, overcome by grief, she flung herself down and sobbed. Her attendants urged her to return to her chair, but she refused. Finally, after great persuasion, she got up, dried her tears, and, bowing several times in front of the grave, she prayed as follows: "You are Hsienpo, and I am Yingt'ai. If we were really intended to be man and wife, open your grave three feet wide."

Scarcely had she spoken when there came a clap like thunder and the grave opened. Yingt'ai leaped into the opening, which closed again before the maids could catch hold of her, leaving only two bits of her dress in their hands. When they let these go, they changed into two butterflies which flew up into the air.

Dr. Ma was furious when he heard that his wife had jumped into the grave of Hsienpo. He had the grave opened, but the coffin was empty except for two white stones. No one knew where Hsienpo and Yingt'ai had gone. In a rage the grave violators flung the two stones onto the road, where immediately a bamboo with two stems shot up. They were shimmering green, and swayed in the wind. The grave robbers knew that this was the result of magic, and cut down the bamboo with a knife; but as soon as they had cut down one, another shot up, until finally several people cut down the two stems at the same time. Then these flew up to heaven and became rainbows.

Now the two lovers have become immortals. If they ever want to be together, undisturbed and unseen, so that no one on earth can see them or even talk about them, they wait until it is raining and the clouds are hiding the sky. The red in the rainbow is Hsienpo, and the blue is Yingt'ai.

·16· *The Faithful Lady Meng*

· THE MENG FAMILY GARDEN and the garden of the Chiang family were separated by only a wall. One year the Mengs planted a pumpkin on their side of the wall, and the Chiangs did the same on theirs. Both plants climbed up the wall, and at the top they joined together and became one plant.

After the pumpkin had bloomed luxuriantly, it developed a huge fruit, which both families wanted to pluck when it became ripe. After a long discussion it was decided that each should take a half; when they cut it open, they found an unusually pretty little girl inside. The two families together looked after her and named her Meng Chiang.

This happened in the reign of the wicked, unjust Emperor Ch'in Shih Huang-ti. He was afraid at this time that the Huns would break into the country from the north and not leave him any peace. In order to keep them in check, he decided to build a wall along the whole northern frontier of China. But no sooner was one piece built than another fell down, and the wall made no progress. Then a wise man said to him, "A wall like this, which is over ten thousand miles long, can be built only if you immure a human being in every mile of the wall. Each mile will then have its guardian." It was easy for the emperor to follow this advice, for he regarded his subjects as so much grass and weeds, and the whole land began to tremble under this threat.

An ingenious scholar went to the emperor and said, "Your method of building the wall is making the whole country tremble. It is quite possible that revolts will break out before it is finished. I have heard of a man called Wan. Now since Wan means ten thousand, he will be enough, and you need only fetch him." The emperor was delighted with this suggestion, and sent for Wan at once, but Wan had heard of the danger and had run away.

Meng Chiang was now a grown-up girl. One clear moonlight night she went into the garden to bathe in the pond. In the joy of the bath she said to herself, "If a man were to see me now, I would willingly belong to him forever, whoever he was." Wan happened to have hidden in a banana tree in the garden and, hearing Meng Chiang's words, he called out, "I have seen you."

Meng Chiang became his wife. While they were happily seated at the wedding feast the soldiers arrived and the heartless brutes seized him and carried him off, leaving Meng Chiang in tears.

In this way she was separated from Wan even before the marriage had been consummated, but in spite of this she loved him and thought of nothing else but him. She was just as attached to her memory of him as other wives to their husbands. Eventually, heedless of the fatigues of the journey, she traveled over mountains and through rivers, to find the bones of her husband. When she saw the stupendous wall she did not know how to find the bones. There was nothing to be done, and she sat down and wept. Her weeping so affected the wall that it collapsed and laid bare her husband's bones.

When the emperor heard of Meng Chiang and how she was seeking her husband, he wanted to see her himself. When she was brought before him, her unearthly beauty so struck him that he decided to make her empress. She knew she could not avoid her fate, and therefore she agreed on three conditions. First, a festival lasting forty-nine days should be held in honor of her husband; second, the emperor, with all his officials, should be present at the burial; and third, he should build a terrace forty-nine feet high on the bank of the river, where she wanted to make a sacrifice to her husband. On these three conditions she would marry the emperor. Ch'in Shih Huang-ti granted all her requests at once.

When everything was ready she climbed onto the terrace and began to curse the emperor in a loud voice for all his cruelty and wickedness. Although this made the emperor very angry, he held his peace. But when she jumped from the terrace into the river, he flew into a rage and ordered his soldiers to cut up her body into little pieces and to grind her bones to powder. When they did this, the little pieces changed into little silver fish, in which the soul of faithful Meng Chiang lives forever.

• *17* • The Infection

• IT IS A CUSTOM in Kuang-tung that each grown-up girl should lie with a man before her marriage. In this way the man who was with her first receives the poison in her body. In a short time he is covered with red spots and great poisonous ulcers, which soon spread and kill him. This custom in Kuang-tung is called "passing on the infection."

In the village of Kao-fu, not far from Wu-shih, lived a man named Ma, who traveled about the province on business. He had no luck, however, and lost all the money he had taken with him. Finally he was reduced to such straits that he no longer had the wherewithal to return home, and there was nothing for him but death.

While begging for money, he reached the house of a rich man whose daughter had just arrived at a marriageable age. Since this girl had not yet passed on the infection, no one wanted her as a wife, which worried the rich man so much that he felt as if a stone were lying on his heart. While he was pondering on his troubles, the beggar appeared. He was at once offered a hundred coins as a reward if he would pass the night with the girl. Ma was delighted, because Shao-hsing people consider the first night with a girl the most enjoyable, but he wondered why a beggar should be offered such a pleasure and be paid for it as well.

The young lady's room was beautifully clean, and its occupant was so far from being ugly that the young man fell in love with her at sight and confessed his passion. She saw at once that he was a stranger fallen on evil days. Not wishing to belong to him, she said in a friendly tone, "You don't come from these parts, and you don't know our customs. All virgins have to give themselves to another man before anyone will demand their hand in marriage. But the man who first possesses the girl soon breaks out in boils all over his body and dies. If the girl does not do it, she herself falls ill. I am warning you because I do not want to be responsible for your death."

At first Ma was worried by the danger, but then he said, "Sister, by forbidding me to do what is necessary, you sacrifice your own life. How could I ever repay you? But, sister, look how miserable and ruined I am; I have no money to return home. Let me stay with you tonight, and then you can marry another man without a qualm." Deeply touched by the moral and noble words of the beggar, the young lady replied, "I cannot accept your offer to die for me merely because you have no money. I want to make a proposal; if you agree, I will give you the money to return home. These are my requests: you must swear brotherhood with me; you must tell me your abode; you must not sleep with me tonight. Then I will soon fall ill, and my father will turn me out of the house, and I can beg my way to you. You must swear to receive me." While she spoke, sorrow overcame her and tears rolled down her cheeks like a broken string of pearls.

Ma agreed to her conditions and, after receiving a large sum of money, he returned to Shao-hsing without taking leave of the rich man. The rich man now thought his daughter was safe from the infection, and he looked around for a suitable match. But a few years later she broke out into red spots which soon became poisonous. Her father was furious, because now he knew she had not given herself to the beggar, and, moreover, girls who catch the disease but remain chaste enjoy an evil reputation. He was not willing to endure the shame, and turned her out of the house, as she had expected he would.

The poor girl was very weak and ill. As she crept along the

streets, she hoped that the god of death would give her his hand.
But then she thought of her adopted brother Ma who was living
in Shao-hsing, and she went on. Being penniless, she had no
choice but to beg her way to the village of Kao-fu. There she
asked for the Ma house, not knowing that Ma had meanwhile
become one of the richest people in the village.

After his return from Kuang-tung, by dint of careful living and
hard work, he gradually saved money, until finally he was prosperous. He often wondered whether or not the maiden in Kuang-
tung who had saved his life and sworn brotherhood with him
had married in the meantime. Had she really fallen ill?

Deep in these thoughts, he walked out of his door just as a
woman with filthy clothes and sores over her entire body was
going by. She asked him, "Please, sir, is there a man named Ma
here?" "There are many," answered Ma; "which one do you want
to see?" "I want to see the one who was formerly a merchant
and lost all his money," answered the beggar woman. "Why do
you want to see him?" asked Ma, "and how do you know he
had troubles in Kuang-tung?"

Then the poor girl told Ma of her misery, and he sighed
deeply and tears coursed down his face. He looked at her and
saw how her beauty had been destroyed as the first cold in winter nips the plants, and he groaned. "My dear sister! Poor sister!
It is all my fault." He led her into his garden. Ma's wife was
kind and treated her very well, since her husband had told her
the whole story. He in the meantime had become quite unrecognizable, for while he had been as thin as a rail before, he had
spread out and was now fat.

Soon the girl's disease became much worse. The open sores had
a disgusting smell, and hot breath rose from her mouth. She
called for Ma, and said to him, "Brother, I fear I am not much
longer for this life. My illness is growing worse. After my death
don't have a great funeral, but bury me simply without much ex-
pense." Ma was overcome by the misery and pain of the girl and,
after promising to comply with her wish, he left her alone.

During the night her mouth became so dry that she was unable
to speak. In her agony she drank everything she found, but she
was still thirsty. Then she saw an old cracked wine jug into

which a fiery red snake had fallen. By no means deterred she swallowed the whole jugful and collapsed on the floor.

Ma became worried about her during the night, and hurried across to see how she was. As he entered her room, there was no sound to be heard. Thinking she was dead, he hurried over to the bed. Soon he found her lying on the floor and, lifting her up, he placed her on the bed.

Because she had drunk the wine and the snake, the ulcers disappeared, and eventually she was cured. Ma took her as his second wife, and they all lived peacefully together for many years.

·18· The Amazing Adventure of a Scholar

· EVERYONE WAS CELEBRATING THE New Year except a certain scholar. He was so poor that he could not even buy firewood, and so he had been sent into the woods by his wife to fetch some. He chopped for a long time but, finding nothing except a few dried sticks, he eventually climbed up to a high peak to look for something better.

On his way down to the valley he came upon a large cave in which a tribe of monkeys were playing. One monkey was just entering the cave with a golden plate piled high with pearls and precious stones. The scholar thought he would try to deceive the monkeys and steal their treasure. He threw a large rock, which terrified most of the animals; but a clever one glanced up and, seeing a man standing on the crag, rushed over and dragged him into the cave. Inside it was very spacious, and in every respect resembled an ordinary palace. The monkeys carried the scholar before a large monkey who was their ruler.

The ruler treated the scholar very well and entertained him for several days. One day the monkey turned into a handsome man and said to the scholar, "This evening we are going to the theater. Do you want to join us?" "To what theater?" asked the scholar. "In the emperor's palace," said the monkey. "That is too far away; how can we get there?" asked the scholar. "Don't bother about that. Just shut your eyes, and when I tell you to open them we will be there." Before the monkey had finished speaking, the scholar found himself in a magnificent theater. There was a large audience composed of the highest officials in the land, but the scholar soon became tired of watching and said to his companion, "What shall I do? I am so sleepy I can hardly keep my eyes open." "All right," said the monkey, "I will show you where you can take a nap." He led him to the women's apartments, into the bedroom of the chancellor's daughter.

Soon the young lady came home from the theater with her maids and went into her bedroom. There she found the man lying on the bed behind the curtains. She was so astounded that for a long time she could not utter a word, but, on looking closer, she saw the stranger's beautiful eyes and realized that he was no ordinary man. She dismissed her maids at once, to prevent their noticing anything and reporting the matter, and then said to the stranger, "Who are you? How dare you get into a young lady's bed!" The scholar nearly fell out of bed at the shock. He hurriedly asked where he was and how he had got there. "This is the palace of the chancellor, and I am his daughter," the young lady told him. The poor man was horrified to hear this, but he decided that his only hope was to tell the young lady everything. She forgave him at once, because they had fallen in love at first sight, and she decided to hide him in the clothes closet.

From that day she kept him hidden and brought him food every day. The maids soon became suspicious, and observed everything through a crack in the door. The news gradually spread through the house, until it reached the ears of her mother, who immediately accused her daughter of improper conduct. But when she saw that the man was both respectable and handsome, she became calmer and ordered her daughter to tell her the whole story from beginning to end. She did not know what to do, but she ordered her daughter to keep the matter secret until she had thought of some plan; it was obvious that sooner or later it would come to the ears of the chancellor.

One evening the mother plied the chancellor with wine until he was drunk, and then said casually, "In such and such a case, what would you do?" She told him the whole story. "There is no difficulty about that," said the minister, "the couple should get married and then everything would be all right." "Do you really mean that?" asked the mother. "Am I accustomed to lie?" asked the chancellor crossly. With this assurance the mother quickly wrote out a statement and gave it to the chancellor, who, being drunk, signed it without a word.

A few days later he heard of the scandal about his daughter, and was so furious that he wanted to kill both her and the scholar. Fortunately, since the mother was able to produce the paper signed by him, he could do nothing about it. Three days later the marriage was gaily celebrated, and a large entertainment was given in the house of the chancellor.

•19• Husband and Wife in This Life and in the Life to Come

• THERE WERE ONCE a husband and a wife who loved each other dearly. One day the wife died. Not being able to forget her, the man at last decided to go in search of her. He had heard people say that the dead become ghosts and live in the spirit land. So he left his home and set out toward this land. After a short while, he came to an inn and asked the waiter which was the best way to the spirit land and how he could find his wife there.

"It is only one day's journey from here to the land of ghosts," said the waiter. "If you go quickly, you can get there and back in a day. When you arrive, go straight to the well. Your wife will certainly come to fetch water, and then you can see her."

The husband followed the waiter's advice and started off the next day. Everything happened as he had been told. He went to the well, seated himself on the edge, and waited. Then he saw a beautiful woman coming for a pail of water. It was his wife, who looked just the same as she had before her death. He called out and took hold of her, but she did not look at him or even raise her head. She behaved like a stranger, filled the pail with water, and returned home.

Sadly and with drooping spirits, the man returned to the inn, where he told the servant how his wife had not recognized him and paid no attention to him at all. "Of course, yesterday I forgot to tell you," said the servant, "return tomorrow and take a small piece of money. When she draws water, throw the coin into her pail. Then she will speak to you."

After a few hours' sleep the man went off full of joy, and waited at the well. Everything happened as he had been told. He threw the money into the pail, and she began to speak to him. She seemed to remember that she was his wife, but she said to him. "Return home. I have become a spirit; we cannot be husband and wife again." She slowly walked away.

The man did not want to let her go, and he hurried after her. As the sun was sinking below the hills, they arrived at a small village. She turned around and said to him, "My dear husband, don't come any farther. In front of you lies my house. I am now married to a ghost who is an official in the underworld. He is very cruel, and if he sees you he will certainly eat you. Please go home now." But the husband could not tear himself away. "Very well," said the woman, "I will conceal you in my house. I will say you are my brother. If he offers you some food, watch to see whether I eat it and then act accordingly. There are many things, poisonous worms and frogs, which you can't eat."

Shortly afterward the ghost arrived. As soon as he reached the doorway, he shouted, "I smell human flesh. I smell human flesh. Who has come to the house?" He showed his teeth and stretched out his claws to search for the stranger. "It's only my brother," explained the wife. "Oh, all right, my brother-in-law. Be quick and get tea and dinner ready." They greeted each other, and the ghost did not eat the man.

Fortunately, during the ten days he spent there, the ghost had to go to the office of the king of the underworld every day, and the man and his wife were able to be alone. But the wife said to her husband, "My dear husband, we can't be married again, and since we can't live here, we had better flee." So one day they ran away.

After traveling for more than ten days, they arrived in the upper world. They stopped outside a house, where the woman said, "I am so thirsty. Wait a moment, I will go in and get some tea. Each of us must take half of this coin." After she had gone in, the man waited and waited, but although he waited till nightfall there was still no sign of her. Feeling very angry, he went into the house and asked the owner whether he had seen his wife, but the man denied it. "But I saw her go in myself," said the husband, very mystified.

Just at that time the owner's wife gave birth to a daughter, and the crying of the little child could be heard throughout the house. The husband refused to go away, and became a workman in the house. It was very strange; no matter who carried the baby, it began to cry; but if the workman took it, the crying ceased at once. Also, no one had been able to open the right hand of the girl since her birth, so great was the strength in her fist.

She grew very quickly. Eventually, when she was seventeen years old, the workman opened her hand; inside lay half a coin, which fitted exactly into his own piece and made a whole coin. They became engaged and were soon husband and wife again.

•20• *The Mason Wins the Prize*

• ONE DAY a magistrate sent for a mason to mend the roof of his house. The magistrate had a very beautiful daughter, who went out with her maid to watch the roof being mended.

The mason fell in love with her at sight, and purposely cut his finger on a tile so that drops of blood fell upon her. When the young lady saw that the mason had wounded himself, she told her maid to fetch a piece of cloth and a needle to bind up his finger. The mason imagined that she had fallen in love with him. When he arrived home, he threw himself on his bed and fell ill, and every day became worse.

His mother, very worried by his condition, asked him what was the matter. The mason replied: "If you promise to do what I ask you, I will tell you; otherwise I must die." The mother promised, and the mason told her how he had seen the daughter of the magistrate and fallen so deeply in love that he wanted to marry her.

His mother said hesitatingly, "How can we arrange that? She is the daughter of an official and will never be willing to marry you." But the son had thought of a plan, which he explained to his mother. "You must take a wooden clapper and beat it in front of the magistrate's gate until someone comes. Tell them that you must see the magistrate himself, and then explain what I desire. You must go there every day until they can no longer bear the noise and will open the door."

His mother took a wooden clapper and went and banged at the door of the magistrate's house. This disturbed the servants so much that they begged her to go away. But she continued knocking until at last they asked her what she wanted. "I want to speak with your master," she said. Although they assured her they could arrange the matter themselves, she insisted on seeing the magistrate in person, until finally the servants, at their wits' end, had to let her in.

When the magistrate came and asked what she wanted, she related the story of her son's passion and illness, and begged him to allow her son to marry his daughter. The magistrate thought the matter over for a moment, and then replied, "That can be arranged, but first your son must bring me three precious things. The first is a pearl from the mouth of a dragon, the second the shell of a turtle spirit, and the third a golden-haired lion. If he succeeds, I will give him my daughter."

The old woman went home, and no sooner had she entered the house than her son was cured. He ran out to meet her, and asked, "Mother, have you seen the magistrate?" "Yes," she answered, "but there is no hope. He wants three precious things: a pearl from the mouth of a dragon, the shell of a turtle spirit, and a golden-haired lion. Only on these conditions will he give you his daughter." "That is easy," said the son. "I will go and get them now."

He started out toward the west, for he thought that such rarities were to be found only in the land of the Buddha in the western heaven. He had been journeying for several days when a dragon suddenly barred his path. He asked the dragon why he would not let him pass, and the dragon replied, "You are on the way to the land of the Buddha in the western heaven. If you promise to ask the Buddha a question on my behalf, I will let you go." "Just tell me what it is," said the young man, "and I will ask him." "You must ask the Buddha why the dragon at such and such a place, who has been morally perfecting himself for over one thousand years, may not ascend to heaven?" The mason noted his words, said good-bye, and continued on his way.

A few days later he was stopped by a turtle spirit, who refused to let him proceed. He begged the tortoise to let him go, since he was on his way to the western heaven. When the tortoise heard where he was going, he promised to release him if the mason asked a question for him. "Of course I will do that," said the mason, "if you will tell me what you want." "You must ask the Buddha why the tortoise at such and such a place, who has been morally perfecting himself for over one thousand years, cannot yet ascend to heaven?" The mason promised to do this, and the turtle set him free.

He went on for nearly a fortnight until he reached a temple, where he went in to rest. On the altar in front of the gods was a golden-haired lion. Since that was exactly what he was looking for, he went up and begged the animal to help him. The golden-haired lion nodded his head in answer, so the young man made an agreement with him to come on the day of his marriage and sit at his father-in-law's table. Then he continued on his way.

At last he arrived at the land of the Buddha in the western heaven, and was granted an audience with the Buddha himself. He asked about the dragon and the tortoise, and the Buddha said, "The dragon cannot ascend to heaven because he has two pearls in his mouth, and all the other dragons only one. If he spits out the superfluous one, he can ascend to heaven. The tortoise cannot ascend because his shell is too rough. If he can change it for another, he can come."

The mason was very pleased with these replies, because he had now found the three precious things he needed to marry the maiden. He thanked the Buddha and set off for home, stopping only to tell the tortoise and the dragon what the Buddha had said, and to receive from the former his shell and from the latter a pearl.

On his return, he at once delivered the two objects to the magis-

trate, and promised to produce the other on the wedding day.
The magistrate could no longer withhold his consent and gave
him his daughter. On the wedding day the golden-haired lion
appeared, and all three presents stood on a table in the guesthall
and were the wonder of the guests.

After the wedding the two loved each other dearly. The husband remained the whole day at home with his wife, and could
not be separated from her for even a quarter of an hour. One day
the wife asked, "Why do you never work?" The husband answered, "Because I cannot bear to leave you." "Then," said the
wife, "I will paint a picture of myself for you always to carry with
you, and you can always look at me, just as if you were really
seeing me."

From that time, when the husband went out he always took his
wife's portrait with him. One day, when he had taken out the
picture to look at it, there came a sudden gust of wind which tore
it out of his hands. Farther and farther flew the picture, until finally it fell into the emperor's palace, where it was found by the
emperor himself.

"Is there really such a beautiful woman?" asked the emperor.
"You must seek her out, and I will make her my wife." The head
eunuch searched high and low, until at last he discovered her
name and where she lived, and brought her to the emperor.
As she was leaving her husband, she consoled him, saying, "It is
not so bad. We will meet again later. In three years come and see
me with a large onion six feet long and a dress made of chicken
feathers, and everything will be all right."

When the wife arrived at the palace, her face became hard as
stone and she refused to smile. When the emperor wanted to visit
her, she told him she was ill. Finally his passion faded, and she
was left alone in her house.

Time passes quickly. Three years went by in a flash. During
this time her husband had sought everywhere for an onion six
feet long, and day and night he sewed the dress of feathers.
When both were ready, he put on the dress and went to the
palace to see his wife, who burst out laughing when she saw him
coming. The emperor noticed her beautiful smiling face and
heard her happy laughter. Half pleased and half surprised, he

asked, "I have not seen you laugh for three years; why do you laugh so much at this stupid man?" Then she answered, "If you were to put on a dress of chicken feathers and carry an onion more than six feet long, I would laugh at you too."

The emperor thought that that was simple, and removed his fine robe and ordered the man to take off his feather dress. As soon as they had exchanged their clothes, the wife called in the head eunuch and ordered him to kill the man with the feather dress. The emperor, in the feather dress, was too terrified to say a word, and was beheaded by the eunuch. Then the mason became emperor, and husband and wife lived happily ever after.

·21· *The Stone of the Beautiful Maiden*

· It is said that the king of the Pai tribes had only one son, whom he loved dearly. When this son wanted to marry, his father called all the daughters of his princes, counts, generals, and ministers into his palace so that the son could select a bride. He looked at the girls for three full days, but he still shook his head and wrinkled his brow because not one of them pleased him.

The prince went to a wise old man and asked his advice. The old man said, "The best flowers blossom in deep mountain canyons; the best girls grow up among the common people. If you look around among the people, you will be certain to find a suitable partner." The prince was very happy, and decided to do what the old man had told him.

All objections of the king were of no avail so that he had to let the son go. Before he set out, the king gave him a slip of paper and said, "All this land under the sky is property of our family, and all people who live on it are our slaves. If anybody pleases you, just attach this slip of paper to the house. The people will then immediately send the girl to the palace."

But when the big eagle circles in the sky, the small quail go into hiding. Whenever the prince came to a village, all the inhabitants ran away and not even the shadow of a young girl was to be seen. For three years the prince searched, but he did not find a suitable partner. Every place he could possibly search he did so, but always in vain. One day he saw a big rock in a village and in his despair he attached the slip of paper to it and continued on his way.

Wherever he went, the big rock with the paper came flying after him. When he walked quickly, the rock was quick; when he took a rest, the rock also took a rest.

The king longed for his son, and waited for him in front of his palace every day. One day he saw him coming, with the big rock flying along behind him. The king was so frightened that he took his bow and arrow and shot the rock. With a tremendous noise it fell down at the foot of the green mountain outside the palace. And the prince fell down too. Later the prince again consulted the wise old man. The old man said, "Mountain goats do not befriend wolves; rats do not marry cats. You are the son of a king. How can common people dare to associate with you?"

Not long after that the king lost sight of his son forever. The prince went to the people, changed his name, hid his origin, and became an ordinary man. The big rock with the paper on it remained forever at the foot of the mountain. Later people came to call it the "stone of the beautiful maiden." You can still see the stone today. It has a hole a few inches deep. It is said that the hole is the mark of the arrow which was shot by the king.

*Part IV
Supernatural
Marriages*

• THERE WAS ONCE an official who had three wives, but none of them had borne him a son. He longed for one very much. One day he had to go away to take up a new post. As he was leaving, his eldest wife said, "When you return, I will offer you gold." The second wife said, "I will offer you silver." But the third wife said, "I will offer you a son." The husband was delighted, but the two other wives were very jealous.

When the third wife really bore a son, the eldest wife tied up her head in a red cloth and bandaged her eyes. The second wife banged a drum so loud that the third wife swooned. When she woke up and asked for her child, the two other wives deceived her. "You did not bear a child," they said; "it was only a horrible lump of flesh." Actually she had borne a beautiful strong son, but while she was unconscious, the eldest wife had thrown it into the lotus pond to drown. Do what she might, the child floated on top of the water and refused to sink. Then the second wife thought of another plan. They collected some straw and grass, wrapped the child in it, and gave the whole bundle to an old water buffalo, which swallowed it at once, much to the satisfaction and relief of the two women.

When the official returned, the eldest wife gave him the gold, the second the silver, but the third wife was ashamed to appear before him. He asked why she did not bring her son to show him. The other two wives explained that she had only borne a lump of flesh and did not dare to appear. When the disappointed husband heard this, he went into a rage and ordered that in the future she must grind rice in the mill as a punishment for the disaster. There she stood and ground rice, and tears ran down her cheeks.

Soon the old water buffalo gave birth to a beautiful, round, glossy calf with golden skin as smooth as satin. Everyone that saw it fell in love with it. The whole day it ran around with its master, rubbed against his clothes, stroked him with its horns, and was very affectionate. The official always gave it some of his food, and the calf bowed its thanks just as if it were a child.

One day when the official was eating dumplings he put a couple into the calf's plate, and said to it, "If you truly understand the human voice and human speech, take these dumplings and carry them to your mother." The calf slowly pushed the plate along with its two forefeet. Everyone thought it would push it into the old cow's stall; instead, it went toward the mill where the repudiated wife was working and dropped it at her feet. Both the official and the wife were very surprised, but the other two wives said to each other, "This pretty little calf is obviously the child in disguise."

Shortly after this the eldest wife pretended to be ill and declared that she could eat nothing except the liver of the little calf. The second wife also took to her bed and declared that she must have the skin of the little calf to cover her. The official wanted to spare his beloved pet, but the eldest wife screamed, "I am going to die, and only the liver of the calf can cure me." The second cried, "I am going to die, and only the skin of the calf can save me." But the official was determined to spare the calf at all costs, and so he let it loose in the hills and bought another calf, which he had killed instead. The moment the eldest wife had eaten the liver, and the second wife had pulled on the skin, they were cured. But the official could not help mourning for his lost calf.

Now a certain young woman named Huang was looking for a suitor. She had it announced that on a certain day, at a certain time, she would throw a colored ball down from her house, and that whoever caught it would become her husband. But strangely enough, the ball did not touch this man or that man but fell straight onto a horn of the little calf. The young lady said with a sigh, "Even a beggar is a man, but to have an animal!" But since she had made the announcement beforehand, she could not break her word.

She hung the wedding robes on the horns of the calf and let it run in front. But no one can run as fast as a calf, and before long the young lady was half a mile behind. She saw it take off the wedding dress beside a large pool of water and then jump in. When she herself arrived at the pool, there was no sign of the calf but only a handsome young man in a wedding robe. The young man signaled to her to follow him, but Miss Huang said, "I can't go with you. I must look for my calf." Then the young man told her he was the transformed calf, and that if she did not believe him she could see the skin lying in the water. The skin was really there, and the young lady was delighted.

The young man led Miss Huang to his parents' house, but when they arrived it was already dark and the doors were locked. He knocked, and called out, "Father, open the door, your son has arrived." But the father cried from inside, "Who is calling me father? I have no son. You must have a mistake." "No," answered the young man, "I have not mistaken the house. I am the child that my mother long ago said she would present to you when you returned home. I was turned into a calf, but now I am a man again." He told everything that had happened to him.

His father was happier than ever before in his life, but at the same time he flew into a terrible rage. He ordered the two older wives to be slain at once, and it was only at the request of his son that he consented to pardon them. He then sent his son to fetch his mother from the mill. From then on, the mill ceased to work and the youngest wife returned to her husband.

•23• *The Bank of the Celestial Stream*

• THERE WAS ONCE a poor young man with only one cow. Because he did nothing but tend his cow, he was known everywhere as the cowherd.

One day the old cow said to her master, "In the stream south of the meadow seven heavenly fairies are bathing. If you go there and steal one of the fairy dresses, you can gain one of the fairies as a bride." The young man did as he was told. All the fairies except one quickly seized their dresses and flew up to heaven. The one who was left behind was called the weaver. She was unable to flee without her dress, and because she could do nothing else, she followed the cowherd and became his wife.

Shortly after, the old cow fell ill. Feeling its end drawing nigh, it said to its master, "When I am dead cut off my skin and fill it with golden sand; then take the ring from my nose and make it into a packet. Carry this always with you on your shoulder, because one day when you are in trouble it will help you." This time also the man obeyed the cow's words.

During the next two or three years the weaver bore the cowherd a son and a daughter. She often asked him where he had hidden her fairy dress. He would never tell her, until one day she asked so often and so caressingly that he eventually betrayed his secret. Then she seized the dress, jumped onto a cloud, and flew away.

The cowherd seized his son and his daughter and flew up to heaven by means of the magic cowhide on his back. The weaver took a golden hairpin and drew a long line to cut off the pursuit. This turned into a broad, raging river. Then the cowherd poured the sand out of the hide into the river, and it formed a big sand bank. But the weaver, seeing herself in danger, took her hairpin and drew a long, celestial river, which successfully impeded the cowherd, who had used up all his sand. He took the ring out of his packet and flung it at his wife, who flung her weaving shuttle in return. Suddenly a white-bearded god appeared, bearing with him an order from the ruler of heaven that they should make peace.

From that time on, each of them has had to stand on opposite sides of the celestial river, meeting only once in the year on the east bank of the stream on the seventh day of the seventh month.

The two stars that are now visible beside the cowherd and the weaver are the ring and the shuttle.

·24· *The Dark Maiden from the Ninth Heaven*

• THERE WAS ONCE a very poor man living all alone in a deserted kiln, who worked when he found anyone to employ him, and otherwise collected firewood in the fields or dung on the roads. Sometimes he earned no money and had to go hungry; at other times he was able to save a few hundred coppers.

At New Year's everyone buys the things he needs for the festival: fish, meat, wine, vegetables, incense, fireworks, inscriptions, and many more things. On New Year's Eve the poor man took 200 coppers out of what he had saved and went to the market. He looked about but could not find anything that pleased him. Finally he saw a picture of a beautiful girl hanging on the wall; this so entranced him that he could not take his eyes off it. "Do you want to buy it?" asked the shopkeeper, and when the poor man nodded, he told him that the price was 600 coppers.

The poor man did not hesitate, but rushed home and took all his savings, amounting to 500 coppers, out of a niche. "If I also use the 200 in my pocket," he thought, "that would make 700, and I can buy two bushels of rice as well." He ran back to the market, bought the picture, and then spent the rest on a bushel of rice and three white cabbage heads, which he took back to the kiln.

Next morning, when everyone was wishing each other a happy New Year, a beautiful picture was hanging up in the old kiln with a large plate of cabbage in front of it. The poor man humbly knelt down and bowed to the lovely woman.

From that day, before every meal and whenever he went out or came in, he used to bow to the picture. Nothing unusual happened for about six months. The picture made him feel very content and soothed him whenever he felt tired.

One day he arrived home exhausted and very hungry, to be greeted, as he opened the door, by the delicious odor of food. He made his bow and went to open the pot, which he found full of steaming hot rice. At first he was too frightened to eat, but eventually he placed an offering before the picture as usual and ate until he was satisfied. In the afternoon he went out to collect firewood, and the food was again ready on his return. He wondered who could have done it.

The next morning he pretended to go and collect dung, but hid instead behind the kiln and watched to see if anyone went in. He waited for a while, but no one entered. Then suddenly he heard someone moving about inside. Creeping up to the door, he peeped into the room. There he saw a beautiful girl standing by the stove making a fire. On the wall there was nothing but a piece of smooth white paper. He was trembling with excitement and did not know what to do. Finally he stepped back, coughed, and then walked noisily up to the door. When he entered the room, the picture of the beautiful girl was once more hanging on the wall, and the pot was full of half-cooked food with a fire still burning underneath.

That afternoon he went out again and waited until he heard light footsteps moving across the room, followed by a soft rattling of the cover of the pot, the noise of water being poured into a basin, the chink of flint and fire tongs, and the wheezing of the bellows. With bated breath he crept up to the door and burst in and, quickly rolling up the picture, he hid it out of sight. When he looked around he saw a beautiful girl standing by the fire. Immediately he went and flung himself down at her feet. He remained kneeling until she raised him up and said, "Since this has occurred, we might as well live together, and then you won't need to be alone so much."

The girl looked after the house so well that their money increased almost as if it grew on trees. After six months they had so much gold and silver that they decided to build a house with halls, pavilions, and terraces, and to fill it with many beautiful clothes and treasures. Here they lived happily together, and everyone that went past wondered, "How strange! Six months ago there was only a deserted kiln here. Who has built this marvelous palace?"

The husband kept asking his wife who she was, but she only laughed and gave him no explanation. Once, when he bothered her too much, she said, half joking, half serious, "I am the dark maiden from the ninth heaven. As a penalty for some sin I committed I was condemned to descend to earth for a few years." But when he asked her for how many years, she did not reply.

Three years passed, and a daughter was born to them, which made them even happier than before. One day, however, the wife became very troubled, as if something unusual had happened, and from that time on she ceased to eat. Fearing that she was ill, her husband wanted to send for a doctor, but she refused to see anyone, and merely asked him casually, "Did you keep the roll of white paper? I should like to look at it again." The husband thought that after living with him for three years and bearing him a child she would no longer want to leave him; so he said no more, but fetched the roll. No sooner had he unrolled it than his wife disappeared and the beautiful girl returned to the paper.

He flung himself down and wept, and his little daughter wept too, but the maiden in the picture did not move. He hung the picture on the wall and worshiped it as before, and later his daughter did the same; but the maiden in the picture never returned to life.

When the old people of the village heard this, they said, "The appointed time that the dark maiden from the ninth heaven was destined to spend on earth had passed, and so she was able to return to heaven."

•25• *The Pig That Warms the Ocean*

• IN A SMALL HUT in a field near the road lived young Baldhead. His parents were long since dead. Every day he cut grass from his two-acre meadow and sold it, and bit by bit he saved enough money to buy a little pig.

Whenever he had time, he played with the little animal, just as if it were a child. Every day he remarked on how big and heavy his piglet was growing; but, strange to relate, after three months, not only had the pig not grown, but its skin had shriveled up like that of an old, yellow-haired mouse. The longer he watched it, the worse it became, until finally he said to himself, "Even pigs won't grow for an unlucky fellow like me."

One day a Muslim treasure seeker came by. At the sight of the little pig he said to Baldhead, "Sell me your pig for one hundred silver pieces." Baldhead was very surprised at the large price offered and, stroking his head, he said to the stranger, "Why do you want to buy my pig? I won't sell it unless you tell me." The stranger answered, "Your pig is a so-called ocean-warming pig. If you place it in a caldron on the seashore, the sea will become as hot as the water in the pot. If the water boils in the pot, the sea will also boil; when the water has all boiled away, the sea will also be dry. You can imagine what treasures there are at the bottom of the sea."

At this news, Baldhead quickly seized the pig and dashed off, calling out behind him, "No, I won't sell it. If you can do such things, so can I." The Mohammedan had to continue his journey without the treasure.

The next morning before crack of dawn, Baldhead put the pig in a caldron, took a few bundles of wood, and went down to the shore. He did everything the Mohammedan had told him, until the water fell several fathoms and sea became full of steam.

Suddenly an envoy of the dragon king shot through the waves. "Stop boiling," he said, "or the palace of the dragon king will collapse." But Baldhead answered, "I am merely cooking my pig. I know nothing about your palace." While the envoy was vainly imploring his pity, suddenly the dragon king appeared in person. "Stop boiling, please," he cried, "and I will give you anything you want."

The sight of the king majestically swaying upon the waves in his ceremonial red dress was too much for Baldhead, and he quickly removed the wood from under the pot, just in time to prevent the pig's being completely cooked. The dragon king then invited him to visit his dominions, and the envoy raised his banner and lashed the waves until they separated and formed a broad road. The three advanced down it to the bottom of the sea, but despite the roaring waves that dashed by on both sides like millions of white eagles, their persons were not even dampened. On their arrival they found a delicious meal already prepared for them.

During the four or five days that Baldhead spent in the palace, he struck up a friendship with a water carrier in the kitchen. One day this man said to him, "On your departure the dragon king will offer you gold and silver. Don't accept it; demand instead the third flower vase on the table." Baldhead made a note of this, and soon after asked for permission to depart. Lung Wang, the dragon king, said to him, "I have no particular treasures to give you, but take that little gourd if you like." "I don't want the gourd," answered Baldhead. "Give me the third flower vase on the table." For a moment the king remained undecided, but then he said, "All right, take it if you want it." Then he ordered a crab general to escort him back to the shore, on which there was no longer any sign of the pig or the caldron.

At home Baldhead placed the vase on the dinner table, and then went out to mow grass. Just before sunset he returned home to cook his evening meal. When he lifted the cover from the dishes, one was already filled with pork and the other with rice. "Who has done this?" he wondered, and called out to ask if anyone was there. However, no one answered, so he sat down and ate his fill.

The next evening when he returned home, the meat and rice were again cooked, but again no one answered his call. The next day he decided to stay at home and watch. He turned an old water container upside down, bored two holes in the bottom, and hid himself inside to watch what would happen. In a short time the flower vase turned into a beautiful maiden, who began to tidy up the house with a smile on her face, and then began to prepare the food. Baldhead waited for his chance, and then sprang out and seized hold of her. "Who are you" he asked, "and why do you cook my food every day?" Blushing as red as a peony, the young lady replied, "I am the third princess of the dragon king. I had turned into a vase and was carried off by you." Suddenly Baldhead felt a tap on his head; a silver plate fell down and beautiful shining coal-black hair appeared all over his head. Then the princess drew a line across the field with her silver hairpin, and immediately a hall and a bedroom arose, more beautiful than you can imagine, in which they lived happily together.

Next door to Baldhead live a wealthy man named Chang. One day as he was coming past with his followers in his sedan chair, he saw a beautiful, big, tall house where formerly there had only been a field. Baldhead led him into the guest hall and begged him to take a seat.

It was just midday, and Chang ordered his cook, who had accompanied him, to go into the kitchen and roast a thrush. In the kitchen the cook saw the princess; the more he looked at her, the more beautiful he found her. He continued to watch her and paid no attention to the bird, with the result that it was burned to a cinder and could not be eaten. "Oh, dear! my master will beat me for this." He ran around in a terrible state, until eventually the princess asked him what was the matter. "My master never eats anything except thrushes," he explained, "and now I have let it burn." The princess took a lump of flour, rolled it to the left and rolled it to the right, and fashioned a thrush, which she gave to the cook. "Take this and roast it for your master," she said. When it was cooked, he carried it into the dining room, and at the first mouthful Chang knew that it tasted much better than ever before. He seized his tobacco pouch and began to belabor the cook, shouting, "Today it was better than you ever cooked before. You were too lazy to cook it well before."

Then the cook knelt down and confessed everything; and since Baldhead was not in the room, he also told how beautiful the wife was. Chang was excited by this news and said, "This evening, take off your clothes and give them to me. I want to see her myself." And that evening, he pulled on the cook's filthy, greasy clothes and, by doing as the cook did, he managed to see the princess.

The next day, before dawn, old Chang sent his cook across to call Baldhead. "You have such a beautiful wife," he said to him. "How can you live on the roadside without a moat? If you don't make a moat around your house within three days, your wife belongs to me." Then he got into his sedan chair and rode away.

Baldhead was so upset that he could not eat, and tears rolled down his cheeks. The princess asked him what the matter was. "Chang has said that if I have not dug a ditch around the house in three days, you must go to him," he explained. The princess knew of a way at once. "Go and buy one hundred garments made of coconut, one hundred hats, and one hundred stakes," she said. "This evening, place the stakes in the field behind the house, and on every stake hang a dress and a hat. Then let the old fool come and see his moat in three days' time." Baldhead carried out her instructions exactly.

Three days later Chang came gaily by, but he was greatly surprised to see a six-foot-wide moat all around Baldhead's house. Anxiously he ran over the little bridge, called for Baldhead, and said to him, "You now have a moat, but there is no water in it. You wife is still not protected. If within three days there is not five feet of water and a dragon in the moat your wife belongs to me." Shaking his long sleeves, he took himself off.

Weeping, Baldhead again went to his wife for advice. "That's easy," she said. "Ask my mother to give you a dragon. Here is a water-diving pearl. Hold it in your mouth, and you can go through the sea as easily as along a street." Baldhead took the pearl in his mouth and went to the dragon palace, but there he discovered that most of the dragons, great and small, had gone off to heaven on a pleasure trip with the dragon king and the third prince. There was only one lazy dragon sleeping in the garden, which Baldhead took and put in the moat. Each time it yawned, it squirted out so much water that the moat was soon filled to the depth of five feet.

Three days later, before dawn, old Change went past and saw the whole moat filled with water. As he came nearer, it looked as though the house was swaying on the waves. The dragon blew up the waves and, shooting out its tail, covered Chang with water. For a moment he remained speechless; then he shouted out to Baldhead, "Now the moat has enough water, but you still lack a hedge of green trees. If within three days you have no grove of trees, your wife belongs to me." And he went off scratching his head.

When the princess heard of Chang's new demand, she said to her husband, "Cut down a couple of trees in the forest and plant them at the side of the moat. In three days you will have a grove of trees." Baldhead took his ax, which had become rusty through lack of use and, going into the hills, he cut down a couple of trees and planted them at the edge of the moat.

At the end of three days old Chang entered Baldhead's courtyard after dinner. There he saw a green wood, already as high as a man, thick and dense. In crossing the bridge, he knocked against a big tree and received a great lump on his head; as he stepped back, he ran a thorn deep into his skin. But when Baldhead came out Chang hid the pain, and merely said, "Now there is a wood, but there are no birds in it. That is too lonely. If within three days the wood is not filled with twittering birds, your wife belongs to me." Then he placed a clod of wet earth on his aching head and went home.

This time Baldhead had no fears. He went and told his wife at once, who said to him, "Buy a few sheets of paper in the street. I will do the rest."

He went off to buy the paper. The princess cut out thousands of birds, blew them into the air, and they flew off with a chirrup into the trees.

On the third day Chang, whose head was still bleeding and aching from his last visit, found Baldhead seated beaming in the shade of the grove. In the branches of the trees thousands of little birds were singing. As Chang started to sit down, he noticed that his head was moist and damp; when he put up his hand, he realized what had happened. Baldhead scolded the birds, "Silly things! Silly things! How can you behave so badly to an old man?" He really intended to say "stupid birds" but had mixed the words up. But old Chang seized his chance and said at once, "You spoke of 'silly things.' Find me some silly things. If you can't bring me some silly things within three days, your wife belongs to me." Then he went to the moat, washed his head like a water fowl, and returned home.

This time Baldhead was very depressed. Going sadly to his wife, he said, "You will have to go to old Chang. This time he wants silly things. Where on earth can they be found?" But the princess only laughed. "I can arrange that," she said. "Go down to the sea and call three times toward the east, 'Silly things,' and they will arrive. They are hidden in a pot. You must tell the old man to remove the cover, and they will then come out." Baldhead went to the sea, and called, "Silly things" three times, and a pot came floating up on the waves. He picked it up and carried it home, and three days later he got into his sedan chair and visited old Chang.

Chang was in the best of tempers, and said to Baldhead, "Well, my friend, be quick and show me your 'silly things.'" "Here they are," said Baldhead. But when Chang saw that he had only brought a pot, he said angrily, "You call that 'silly things'? Hurry up and bring your wife here." But Baldhead said, "Just take the cover off and the 'silly things' will come out." But when Chang did so, a bright flame of fire shot out so swiftly that he was unable to jump back, and all his hair, eyelashes, and eyebrows were singed. At the same time a voice called out of the pot, "Silly thing! Silly thing! Why do you always want the wife of another?" Quickly covering his head, Chang dashed back to the house and never spoke of 'silly things' again.

·26· Why the Horns of Cattle Are Curved

• UP THE HILL, down the hill, at the foot of the hill, there was a stream. In the stream there was water, flowing a thousand miles. Many beets grew on both sides of the stream. Where the beets grew, it was hot. When it was hot, people came to the stream.

In the old time, a Thai girl went to the stream to take a bath. It was very hot, and she was still thirsty after she had taken her bath. She started to drink a handful of water, when a beet drifted down the stream toward her. She picked it up. All its leaves had been eaten off by an animal, but the beet itself was not harmed. She removed the skin and ate the meat, which tasted very good and sweet and quenched her thirst.

After she had eaten the beet, she became pregnant and soon gave birth to a baby girl. When the baby grew up, people liked her very much. When she sang songs, her voice sounded better than the flute of the fairies; when she danced, she outdid the colored clouds in the sky. When old white-haired men saw her in the street, they regretted that they had not been born at the same time that she was, so that they could flirt with her; they were sorry that they could not have black hair again, so that they could ask for her hand. And when young men passed by her, they all wanted to stop and stay near her. When girls saw her, they were afraid that she might take away their lovers and they would be left with no one.

But as soon as the young men learned that she had no father and that her birth was not clear, they all lowered their heads and went on—they would not even stop for half a minute for fear of ruining their reputations. The people in the village said that her ancestry was not clear. The woman all cursed her, saying that she was a bastard, that her parents had met in the night. Whenever the girl heard this, it was as if a monkey were tearing out her heart. Again and again she asked her mother, "Why do I not have a father?"

One day her mother could not resist her pleading any more and told her the whole story. She said, "Your father is very ugly; you certainly will not like him, once you see him."

"Oh no, even if he should be ugly, he is still my father," said the girl in tears.

"Your father is a saintly ox. He ate the leaves of the beet; I ate the root, and so I gave birth to you. The day you were born he told me in a dream that he lived in the midst of the mountains."

"Why did you not try to find him?"

"Ah," the mother said, "I could not bear to leave you alone when I saw how they treated you in the village. Even if I had three sons and two daughters, I would still let them curse and mistreat me."

"Then I will go and search for my father. Tell me, where can I find him?"

"You should take only some beets and go into the mountains. Give a beet to every ox you see, and whichever one eats only the leaves and not the root, that one is your father."

The next morning the girl did what her mother had told her. She went deep into the mountains, to a place far, far away, and there she finally found an ox which ate only the leaves and not the root when she gave a beet to him. She followed him and came to a cave. In this cave there were many supernatural oxen. Now she knew that her father lived in this mountain cave, and she selected a hollow tree next to the cave as her place to live.

When the cattle went away in the morning, leaving lots of dung behind, she cleaned it up. When the cattle returned at night, they were astonished. "Why is it so clean here?" they asked one another. One day her father did not go far, because he wanted to see who cleaned the cave. He found that it was the girl, and so it was on that day that father and daughter first recognized one another.

The girl lived in the hollow tree until fall. Then it became cold, and her father told her to go home. But she did not want to go, and said, "Better I freeze and die in the mountains than to suffer again the curses of the people."

When the ox saw that she did not want to go home, he was determined to build her a house. But how could he build it? He decided to build it out of horn. All the cattle took off their own horns and built a very beautiful oxhorn pavilion to protect her against wind and rain.

The building went up quickly; soon it was almost finished, and only the very top of the pavilion was still missing. A single horn would be enough for this, and so her father shouted, "Enough."

At this very moment, some of the supernatural cattle were just taking off their horns. When they heard his command, they all stopped. There were some who had not yet taken off their horns completely but had already turned, bent, and twisted them. This is the reason why today the horns of some cattle are twisted, turned, and bent, and why there are also some cattle with straight horns.

• 27 • The Witch's Daughter

• In the midst of a range of wild mountains was a small straw hut, where lived an old man with his three sons. Every day the father went out to look for fuel.

Once he met in the wood an aged widow in white clothes, who was seated on a square stone playing chess. Since the old man was a keen player himself, he stopped to watch the game. "Will you play with me?" asked the widow. "Certainly," said the old man. When the widow asked for what stakes they should play, he suggested playing for his wood. But the old woman said, "No, we can't play for wood, because I don't have any wood. How many children have you, though?" When she heard that the old man had three sons, she was very pleased and said, "That is perfect. I have three daughters. If you win, I will send them as brides for your three sons; but if I win, you must send me your sons as sons-in-law." The old man stroked his beard for a while, but finally gave his assent.

He lost each of the games they played, and when the widow got up to leave she said, pointing down into a dark valley, "There is my house. Tomorrow send me your eldest son, three days later the second, and again after three days the youngest." She then departed, and the old man went home, without collecting any more wood, to tell his sons what had happened. How pleased they were when they heard it!

The next day he sent the eldest son; three days later, the second; and on the sixth day he sent the youngest.

As the third son was wandering along, he met an old hermit with a white beard who asked him where he was going. "I am going to be the son-in-law of the widow in the valley. My two brothers are there already," said the youngest son. The hermit sighed and said, "This widow is an old witch. She has only one daughter, with whom she has decoyed many young men and killed them. Your elder brother was eaten by the lion that waits by the outer gate, and your second brother by the tiger that waits by the inner door. You have had the good luck to meet me." Taking an iron pearl from his breast, he continued, "throw this to the lion by the outer gate." Then he gave him an iron rod, saying, "Give this to the tiger by the inner gate. Then cut off a stick from the cherry tree by the stream. When you reach the third door, push the door open with it, and you can enter safely."

The young man took the pearl and the rod, went into the cherry wood to cut off a branch, and after thanking the hermit descended into the valley. Soon he came upon a large high house. At the outer gate he threw the iron pearl to the lion, who began to play with it. At the second door he threw the iron rod to the tiger, who also began to play. The third door was closed tight, but he gave it a push with his cherry stick, and crash! a thousand-pound block of iron fell down and the door opened. If he had opened it with his hand, he would certainly have been crushed to death.

The witch was seated in her room sewing when she heard a noise at the door. She looked out and saw the young man, whom she knew must be the third son of the old man. She wondered how he had passed safely through all three doors, but as he entered she pretended to be very pleased, and said, "You have arrived just at the right time. I have a bushel of linseed that I want you to sow in the field before it rains. When you come back, we will have the wedding."

The young man looked out, and sure enough the sky was full of dark clouds which threatened rain.

He took the bushel of linseed and went out into the field; but the ground was so covered with weeds that he said to himself, "How can one sow this field without a bullock and a plow?" He tried to pull up a few weeds, but soon lay down and went to sleep. When he woke up toward evening, he saw that a herd of swine had turned up the soil and pulled up all the weeds. So he sowed the linseed, thanked the swine for their help, and went back to the old woman.

When she saw him coming, she asked, "Have you finished the sowing?" "Yes," said the young man. But the widow frowned. "You didn't trouble to look at the sky," she grumbled. "How could you sow the linseed? All the clouds are gone, the moon is shining brightly, no rain will fall, and the seeds won't sprout. You must collect them all again, and not one must be missing. When you come back, we will have the wedding."

The youngest son bit his lip, took the empty measure, and went out into the field to search for the seeds. Long he searched, but little he found, though his back ached from the bending. After sadly gazing at the moon, he looked around and saw thousands and thousands of ants, each of which dropped a seed into the measure. In no time it was full, and the son returned to the widow after thanking the ants. When she saw him she asked, "Have you got the seeds?" "Yes," said the son. "Good," she said, nodding. "I am going to sleep now. Tomorrow I will have a new task for you."

The next morning the old witch told him, "I am going to hide. If you can find me, we will have the wedding." And no sooner had she spoken than she was gone.

The son searched high and low but could find no trace of her. While he was looking, he heard a voice call out from the top of the house, "My mother has hidden in the garden. She has turned herself into a half-red, half-green peach that is hanging on a tree against the wall. The green part is her back, the red her cheek. Bite her in the cheek and she will turn back again." The son looked up and saw a maiden in a sea-green dress, with rose-pink cheeks like the half-opened flower of a lotus. He knew she must be the witch's daughter, and, blushing with confusion, he quickly went into the garden.

Sure enough, there on the wall was a peach tree, and hanging on it was a half-green, half-red peach. He plucked it, bit the red side, and flung it onto a stone, whereupon the old woman stood before him with a stream of blood running down her cheek. "Son-in-law! Son-in-law! you nearly crushed me to death," she said.

The son answered, "How could I know you had turned into a peach?" The old woman turned to go, saying as she was leaving, "Bring me a bed of white jade from the palace of the dragon king, and we will have the wedding."

While he was standing in the garden with a drooping head, the daughter came to him and asked what was on his mind. "Your mother told me to bring her a bed of white jade from the palace of the dragon king," he said, "but no mortal can pass through the sea to his kingdom." However, the daughter consoled him. "That is quite simple. I have a golden fork. If you draw a line across the sea with this, a path will form and you can go wherever you want."

The young man took the fork, went to the seashore, and drew a line; and in a flash a road was formed in the waves that led straight to the palace of the dragon king. When he arrived he saw the king and told him that he had come to borrow a bed of white jade. "Certainly," the king said. "In the back palace there are many beds of white jade—just choose one of them." The young man was very pleased and, having selected a bed of white jade, he returned to the widow.

When she saw that he had brought back the bed, she said to him, "In the west, on the mountain of the monkey king, there is a big drum. Bring it back and we will beat it at the wedding." Just as the son was going away, the daughter appeared and asked, "What task has mother given you now?" "I must steal the big drum from the mountain of the monkey king," he said. "I have heard," the daughter told him, "that the monkey king has gone to the western heaven and has not yet returned. Below the mountain there is a lake of mud. If you roll around in the mud like the monkey king, the little monkeys will think you are their ancestor and will bring you to their homes. I will give you a needle, some lime, and some bean oil. These you must take with you, and when danger threatens, throw first the needle, then the lime, and lastly the oil behind you."

The son took the three things, went to the lake of mud below the mountain, and rolled about until his whole body except his eyes was caked with mud. He went quickly up the hill, and all the little monkeys came down from the trees and cried, "Grandfather, you have arrived!" Then they gathered around him and carried him off in a big chest. The son clapped his hands and said, "Your grandfather has come a long way and is very hungry. Quickly, go into the peach orchard and bring me some peaches." Off they ran, as quickly as they could, into the peach orchard with baskets of all sizes.

As soon as the monkeys were gone, the young man jumped down from the chest, seized the big drum that he saw hanging in a shelter, and ran away. He had not got far from the hill of the monkeys when he heard them pursuing him, screaming, "Big black thief! You pretended to be our grandfather, and then you stole our big drum. Wait till we catch you!" The son quickly took the needle out of his pocket and threw it behind him, where it turned into a needle mountain. The little monkeys tore their skin and scratched their eyes on it, but they followed him farther. Then he took out the lime and threw it behind him, where it turned into a mountain of lime. The little monkeys with their torn skin and bleeding eyes stuck to the lime and suffered such terrible tortures that some died, but the rest of them still followed him. Then he threw behind him the bottle of bean oil, out of which the oil poured and turned into a slippery mountain. When the little monkeys tried to climb up, they slipped down again, and so the son escaped and returned to the old woman before the sun had set.

When the widow saw that he had brought the big drum, she said to him, "It is still early in the day. Go into the garden and cut down two hair bamboo sticks, so that we can make a mosquito frame for you." But he thought to himself, "What sorcery is there in the garden?" He plucked up his courage and asked the daughter. "The gardener is a hairy man," she said. "He likes to flay men and eat their fingers. If you try to cut down the bamboos, it will certainly be very dangerous." She took out a coat of coconut and put it on his shoulders, placed ten small bamboo reeds on his fingers, and gave him a two-edged hatchet. "Be quick," she said, "and nothing can happen to you."

The son hurried into the garden, found the bamboo, and cut it down. A dark, hairy man came out of the thicket, seized the coconut coat with one hand, and pulled off the bamboo reeds with the other. Thinking the coat was the skin and the bamboo were the fingers, he began to eat them. In the meantime the son ran away.

When the old woman saw him coming, she asked, "Have you brought the bamboo?" "Yes," said the son. "Good!" said the widow, "But you have not eaten anything all day. Here are some noodles of wheat flour you can have."

The son was really very hungry and, going into the kitchen, he took the cover off the pot. He seized the delicious white noodles in his hands and began to eat them, but soon he felt terrible pains. The door opened, and in came a servant girl with a lamp, who said, "My mistress asked you to join her." He went up to the beautiful maiden. She told the servant to hang the young man on a beam, pull off his shoes, and beat his body with them. After a few blows, ten small snakes fell out of his mouth and crawled about on the floor. The maiden untied the young man and said, "My mother always wants to harm you. She gave you snakes instead of noodles to eat. Now ask her to have the wedding quickly."

The next evening, the wedding actually took place. In front of the hall the drum of the monkey king was beaten, in the room stood the bed of white jade from the palace of the dragon king, and a beautiful mosquito net had been made with the bamboo. Everything was very fine and beautiful. But when they went to bed, there was a broad river flowing down the bed between him and the maiden. His wife said, "This is another trick of my mother's." She looked everywhere, until under the dressing table she found a pitcher of water with a bit of wood floating in it. She took out the wood, threw the water away, and the river vanished at once. Then she said to her husband, "We must flee quickly; my mother will certainly try to do us more harm." Taking a torn umbrella and a cock, she gave them both to her husband, and they fled away in the middle of the night.

The moon was half full and lit up the road in the hills. They had gone but a few miles when suddenly they heard a whirring sound over their heads. The wife took the umbrella, and said, "My mother has sent a flying knife after us. If the knife sees blood, it falls. Throw out the cock, and the knife will kill it." He did as he was told, and the knife vanished at once.

A little later the wife said, "The knife will certainly return. Chicken blood is sweet; human blood is salty. My mother will know that she did not kill us last time. What are we to do?" The son listened carefully, and he soon heard again the whirring of the flying knife. Then he began to cry, and said, "I will sacrifice myself." But the maiden refused. "No, I must die, because I can come to life again. After my death you must carry my body home and buy a large lotus pail to put it in. In seven times seven days I will come to life again." When she had finished speaking, she stepped out and the noise of the knife ceased. The young man saw his bride lying on the ground, her eyes closed, and her face white as a pear blossom, with the knife sticking in her heart and blood pouring out. He wept bitterly and carried her to his home.

It was not yet light in the east when he arrived. He told his father all that had happened, and the father began to weep when he heard how his eldest sons had been killed by the witch. But the son bought a pail, covered up the maiden's body, and watched.

After forty-eight days, he heard loud groans coming from the pail, as if someone was in great pain. Then he thought, "If I don't let her out now, but wait another day, she will perhaps die again." So he took the lid off the pail. The maiden slowly lifted up her head, and said softly, "Why did you uncover me a day too soon? Obviously fate has not intended us for each other." Then her head slowly sank down and her eyes closed. She was dead forever.

· 28 · *The Marriage of the City Deity*

· IN THE TOWN OF CHIEH-YANG there is a custom whereby once a year the images of the deities are carried into the open. On this day altars are erected everywhere, on which offerings are made to the gods, and at the same time plays are performed for several days on end, to provide the gods with the amusement they most enjoy. Sometimes as many as twenty plays are performed on one day, and the excursion of the gods is always a very gay occasion.

One day it was the holiday of the chief deity of the city. His image was carried outside the east gate of the town, where everyone hurried to greet it. Two young girls were standing outside a house door gossiping about this and that, and one of them said, "Look! The old boy is quite handsome. If I knew a young man who looked like that, I . . ." but her sister-in-law interrupted with a laugh and ended the sentence for her, "wouldn't mind marrying him." They were only joking, though, and it did not occur to either of them that it would ever come true.

At the end of the day the god's statue was carried quietly back to his temple, but during the night, when everything was peaceful, he turned into a young man and visited the girl.

The next morning, on awaking from a dream, the girl found a man's black shoe beside her bed. In a great fright she ran off to tell her mother all that had happened. The mother was very worried and said to her daughter, "If he comes again tonight, cut a piece off his coat." During the day a rumor spread throughout the town that the city god had lost a shoe.

That night the girl put a pair of scissors close to the bed. It was already late in the night when she had another dream, so delicious that at the moment of parting she almost forgot her mother's orders to cut off a corner of the stranger's coat. The next morning she heard people saying in the street that the deity of the city had lost a piece of his coat.

Thus it went on from day to day, with the girl becoming daily thinner, for the city god visited her night after night and shortened her rest. Finally, she died and became the companion of the god forever.

For this reason the deity of the city is always carried to Fengwei Hsiang, the home of the girl, and there offerings are made to him, because he is the son-in-law of the family there.

· 29 · *The Son of the Turtle Spirit*

· ONCE UPON A TIME a turtle, who was living in a pond in a nobleman's garden, learned after prolonged study how to change his form at will.

The nobleman had a daughter of rare and unusual beauty, and one day as she was combing her hair at the window the turtle caught sight of her and fell deeply in love. He said to himself; "Since I can turn myself into a human being at will, why should I not become a young man and court this beautiful lady?"

So in the night he climbed onto the bank, turned himself into a handsome youth, and went to her room, where he persuaded her to yield to him. From then on, the turtle became a youth every night and stayed with the maiden till dawn, when he returned to the pond. He left no trace behind him, and even the maiden did not know that he was really a turtle, but thought instead that he was some student from the neighborhood.

At the end of a year the maiden noticed that she was going to have a child. Her mother knew nothing about it until one day on a visit to her daughter she noticed what was the matter. She asked the maidservant who the young man was, but the servant said, "My mistress is very secretive; she remains in her room all day long without going out. But one day, about a year ago, I saw a young man who looked like a student come out of her room. From that time he came every night and went away at dawn." "Is it possible?" cried the mother angrily. "Don't you know where he comes from? How does he get up to her? You have eyes. You must once have seen how he came." "Really, I don't know," said the maid. "Mistress must try to forgive me. He comes and goes without leaving a trace. Sometimes he appears in the wink of an eye, and disappears in the same way." "Then he must be a spirit," decided the mother. "What can be done for my poor daughter?" After a moment's thought she called her daughter to her and said, "The man who comes to see you every night must be a spirit, but I have thought of a plan. When he falls asleep tonight, tie a thread onto his coat, and then wherever he goes we can follow the thread to his abode and decide how to catch him. Don't fail to do this, and tomorrow we will see what happens." Her daughter promised to do as she was told.

That night the turtle came again. The maiden had already hidden a needle and thread under the pillow, and when about midnight her lover fell asleep she sewed the thread onto his coat without his noticing anything.

The next morning the turtle flew out of the window like a bird and vanished in the twinkling of an eye; but the thread flew with him through the window and into the pond in the garden. Then the father said at once, "It can only be the turtle spirit. It must be the one my father put into the pond. But it shall not escape me; I shall kill it."

At once he called for ten workmen and ordered them to scoop the water out of the pond. When it was empty enough to see the bottom, sure enough there was a turtle as large as a round table lying in the mud with the red thread that led to the maiden's window fast in the folds of his skin. "There it is," shouted the father, and he ordered the workmen to carry it up to the edge, where he seized a knife and cut off the turtle's head so that it died. Its remains were cut up in little pieces and thrown into a corner of the garden to rot. After a few months all the flesh was gone and only the bones were left, which no one bothered about.

One day when the maid was walking in the garden, she noticed the white bones, and told her mistress, who wept when she heard about them. She said to her maid, "It is true he was a spirit, but he was still my husband; so how can I leave his bones to lie and rot?" So she gave the maid a little yellow bag to put the bones in and hung it beside her bed.

The son that was born to her in due time naturally bore no love for his grandparents, because he was the son of a spirit. At seven years old he still had no teacher, but he was allowed instead to play about the whole day long.

One day a grave seeker had found an unusually fine burial place for one of the families in the town. According to him, there was a heap of mud in the river near the village. This mound of mud was shaped like a dragon, with a tail, a head, and two horns, just like those of a real dragon, and the sons and grandsons of anyone buried there would certainly rise to high honors. Unfortunately, the current in that place was very strong, and many tales were told of ships that had sunk there, so that no ordinary mortal would be brave enough to swim over and bury the bones.

The rich man consulted the grave seeker, who finally suggested, "If you promise to give a large reward, you will certainly find a man brave enough. We ought to announce that we are looking for someone who can dive well, and reward him hand-somely if he takes the casket over." "That is a good plan," said the official, nodding his head. "We must try that."

He had a notice written out to this effect, except that he wrote nothing about the bones that must be buried there, but only about a treasure, and promised a reward of one thousand pieces of gold and one thousand pieces of silver. Many people read the notice that was posted, but all knew how dangerous the river was and that it would be difficult to find anyone to do it.

One day the son of the turtle spirit was strolling along when he saw a great crowd gathered in one place, and going up he asked what was the matter. "They are looking for someone to dive into the river and bring up a treasure. Can you do that? If you can, you will be given a large amount of gold and silver!" the boys standing by said to him jokingly. "Bring a treasure out of the river and receive gold and silver as well? That is quite simple for me," said the child. "I will tear down the notice." "Better leave it alone," said some older people. "Do you know which river it is? It is the terribly dangerous Li Cha River, where so many people are drowned every year. And a young boy like you wants to dive into it? Go and play and don't come and speak such rubbish here." "But I can do it—you don't need to dispute it," said the boy. Pushing his way through the crowd, he tore down the notice. Then the watchmen seized him and asked, "Surely you are joking when you say you can do it?" "Why should I joke?" the boy replied steadily. "Would I have torn down the notice if I could not do it?" "Well, you must come to our master," said the men. "No," said the boy, "first I must go home and tell my mother; then I will go with you." "Go there first," said the men; "we will wait for you here."

Swift as the wind, the boy ran to his mother, and when he had told her everything he begged her to let him go. His mother thought, "After all, he is the son of a turtle—he ought to be a strong swimmer," And so she said to him, "You can go, but be-fore you enter the water come back to me, because I have some-thing to tell you." The boy promised and went off to the rich man with the watchmen.

When the rich man and the grave seeker saw a seven- or eight-year-old child coming, they were very surprised, but they thought that, having torn down the notice, he must be sure of himself. They sent for wine, and while he drank the rich man said to him, "What we wrote in the notice was not quite the truth. We want to ask you to take the remains of my grandfather and bury them in a favorable spot. Now, in the river there is a dragon formed out of sand, with his mouth always open. I will give you the casket which contains the remains of my grandfather, and you must dive to the bottom of the river and place it in the dragon's mouth. If you can do that, you will receive the promised reward of one thousand pieces of gold and one thousand pieces of silver."

"That is quite simple," said the boy. "I can certainly place the bones in the dragon's mouth." After the meal he took the casket and went home to tell his mother. His mother suddenly remembered the bones of her own husband, and with a smile she took the little bag with the bones of the turtle and gave them to her son, saying, "These are the bones of your father. Take them to the bottom of the river and put them in the dragon's mouth, and hang the other bones on his horns. Don't forget to do this, and don't mix the bones."

The boy promised to follow her instructions and went with the two packets to the river where the rich man and the grave seeker were waiting. The boy called out to them and plunged into the river. Soon he arrived at the bottom of the river. There, sure enough, was a mud dragon more than six feet long, with a head and a tail, and his mouth wide open, as if he wanted to swallow something. The boy took the two packets out of his breast pocket. He threw his father's bones into the dragon's mouth, and hung the bones of the rich man's grandfather on the dragon's horns. Then he shot up again and swam to the bank.

When the rich man and the grave seeker saw that he had returned safely, they knew that their plan had succeeded and they were very glad. They brought him back to their house and gave him dry clothes and delicious food and wine, and when he had finished they sent him home with one thousand pieces of gold and one thousand pieces of silver.

When the boy was ten years old, his appearance suddenly began to change. He was quite an extraordinary young man, and much cleverer than anyone else. Finally, he became emperor, and the son of the rich man was his minister.

• 30 • The Wife of the Monkey

• ONCE A VERY BEAUTIFUL GIRL DISAPPEARED. Her mother was unable to eat or sleep for worry, and went about the whole day asking where her daughter was.

One day she was sitting in the yard bemoaning her loss when a sparrow flew down on the roof and began to twitter. "Dear sparrow," the mother said, "if you know where my daughter is and can lead me to her, I will give you a bushel of roasted beans."

The sparrow agreed. So the mother tied a red string on to the bird's tail as a sign, and they set off on their search. But the bird flew much quicker than the woman and was always waiting for her. Finally, it flew to a cave in the mountains, where it sat down on a stone and chirruped.

A girl came out of the cave, and was much surprised to see the red string on the sparrow's tail. "Where did you get the red string from our house?" she asked. "Your mother gave it to me," said the bird. "She will soon be here herself." While they were speaking, the mother arrived.

"What are you doing here, my child?" she asked. The daughter answered, "I was going for a walk in the village when a monkey came up and carried me off. He will be here in a moment. You must hide, because if he sees you he will eat you up!"

The mother had just time to hide under a jar before the monkey appeared. He sniffed and said, "Why is there such a smell of human flesh?" His wife tried to conceal it from him, but eventually, seeing there was nothing to be done, she told him the truth, "My mother is here but, fearing you would eat her, she hid under a jar." The monkey, however, was very pleased, "Your mother has come?" he said. "Tell her to come out quickly. I want to meet her," and he went and turned up the jar. The daughter said to him, "That is your mother-in-law," whereupon they embraced, and were very happy. The monkey then said, "Today, we have nothing good to eat. I will buy some meat and wine." He went out.

The mother and daughter decided to take this opportunity to run away. First, the daughter told her mother to cook a pot of lime. When the little monkeys saw it, they asked, "Grandmother, what is that?" "It is a good eye medicine," she said, "but it isn't for children." "But we want some," said all the little monkeys. So she covered their eyes with lime, and then said to them, "Go into the sun and let it dry." When it was dry, they could not open their eyes. Then the mother and daughter fled, taking with them all the gold and silver that the monkey had stored away.

When the old monkey came back and saw the little ones could not open their eyes, he asked them what had happened. They told him the whole story. He boiled a great pot of water and told the children to wash their eyes, but afterward there was a red rim around their eyes.

From then on, every morning the old monkey took the children down to the house of their mother. He sat down on the millstone in front of the house, and in a sad voice began to sing his song, "Monkey wife. Monkey wife. It is unnatural to leave your children. Your children weep, your husband is sad."

The girl began to be frightened as well as affected by the tragic song. She evolved a plan with her mother. One night they made the millstone red hot. In the morning the monkey came as usual with his children. When the little ones sat down on the stone, they jumped up with a scream. "What's the matter?" cried the monkey. "I will sit down." He also leaped up with a scream of pain, and they all fled home together. When they looked at each other, all the hair was burned off their buttocks.

They never returned to look for their mother again. From that time, all monkeys have bare buttocks.

· *31* · The Bear's Husband

· ABOUT TWO MILES southeast of my house is the village of Huimin, which the peasants call "Wang P'ing's Homecoming."

In the village nearly all the inhabitants are called Wang, and they tell the following tale about themselves.

Wang P'ing, their ancestor, in his youth went off on a trading journey. One day when he was on the sea a terrific storm sprang up, which drove the ship hither and thither off its course. At last it was driven against a mountain, and Wang P'ing was seized by a bear woman and carried off into the hills where they became man and wife.

Every day the bear woman shut Wang up in the cave and went to look for food. When she came back she told him to pick out what he wanted to eat. Several years passed in this manner, and two children were born to them. The bear woman thought that Wang P'ing was no longer homesick for China, and since it was almost impossible to escape, she finally let him go out and no longer shut him up in the cave.

One day when the bear woman had gone hunting, Wang P'ing wandered down to the seashore with his children. Suddenly he saw a ship on the beach. Finding that the sailors were all Chinese, he told his experiences to them and begged them to weigh anchor as soon as possible.

The sailors did as he asked them, but they were not far from land when they saw a large animal waving and screaming on the beach. Wang P'ing paid no attention at first, but the bear woman jumped into the sea and swam toward the ship. Wang was so terrified that he prayed to the deity of the sea, "God of the sea! Send us a favorable wind. If I escape safely I will build you a large temple as a thanksgiving for saving me, and I and my children and grandchildren will worship you forever." As he finished speaking a wind sprang up, the sailors hoisted the sails, and the ship shot away like an arrow.

On arriving home Wang P'ing built a temple, which still exists in the village; but one cannot decide whether it is the temple that Wang built or another which was built later. In no other place is there, or has there ever been, a temple in honor of the sea deity.

Part V
Persons with
Magic Powers

• THERE WAS ONCE a rich family whose head, Chang Pao, was called by everyone "The Rich." He had two sons and three daughters. The eldest child was fourteen years old, and the youngest only two.

Chang Pao decided to build a new house, and engaged masons and carpenters, who worked for many days till the house was almost finished. Chang's wife was a good woman. She prepared good food for the workmen's daily meal, and as well as meat she gave them spices and sauce and other tasty morsels all cooked together in a delicious stew. The workmen were unusually well treated, but nevertheless the ungrateful brutes considered themselves ill-used and said, "This miserly family won't even give us fresh meat to eat—nothing but old pork and chicken, which no one could stomach." For this reason the masons and carpenters were in a bad humor.

Finally they began to hate their employer and to regard him as their enemy. One day one of the masons decided to call a meeting. He sent some of his companions around to tell everyone to come without fail, since there was something very important to discuss. While they were eating dinner, he sent someone to call them all again. After dinner they all arrived, and the caller of the meeting was elected chairman.

He stepped forward confidently, and said, "I have called this meeting today because our employer treats us so badly. The food is a disgrace. We have worked for many days now without getting any fresh meat. We must revenge ourselves. Think over what we can do." All agreed with him, but after a long time no one had any suggestion to make. "Think a little more quickly," said the chairman, "it is already late." But the men still sat silent, and no plan was suggested, until finally the chairman said, "If you can think of nothing, I will tell you my plan.

"My plan is to build a ship of clay, and to place a boatman on it, with a bamboo pole in his hand, and to fill it with notes and coins. Then we must place the ship over the door, in the eaves of the newly built house, so that it faces outward. In this way the house will have no more luck, and gradually the owners will become poorer and poorer, until finally they will no longer have enough to eat."

When the workmen had heard the plan, they all shouted, "That's what we will do, and you shall carry it out alone." This was what the chairman had intended. Since it was already late, they went home.

Three weeks later the house was finished, and the master mason had carried out all his plans. The masons and carpenters went away to build other houses.

After Chang Pao moved into the new house, not two years passed before he began to have trouble. He was always quarreling or injuring someone, and each time he lost a great deal of money. He and his wife were very worried, but they could not understand why everything went so badly.

At the end of ten years, Chang and his family were as poor as church mice and could scarcely afford three meals a day. Then his eldest son fell ill and died, and one after another of his daughters passed away, until finally he had only the one boy, who had been two years old when the house was built.

That year it was terribly hot—so hot in fact that you could never do without a fan—and many people died. Then Chang Pao died, and his wife and son felt themselves poorer and more lonely than ever.

One afternoon the woman was sitting in the house when suddenly a man appeared outside and cried, "Hallo!" Not having any idea who the man was, she was very frightened. Then he said, "I am old Chen Ts'ai, the master mason who helped to build your house ten years ago."

Now she knew who he was, and since it was dinner time she cooked him some food and gave it to him, saying, "I used to give you finely sliced meat, but now we are so badly off I can only give you tasteless stuff. Please excuse me."

When the mason heard that, he realized that far from treating him badly and giving him bad meat, she had been extremely generous.

After the meal he asked for a ladder, and, climbing onto the roof, he turned the prow of the ship around. "From now on, you will be more successful and will become rich again," he said. Then he went away.

Two or three years later luck returned to the house, and the family became prosperous again.

•33• The Tale of the Turtle Mountain

• NORTH OF CHAO-CH'ING lies the seven star peak, and not far west of that is a hill that closely resembles the back of a turtle, the head of which is formed by several large stones jutting out into the water.

People say that originally there was a turtle living in this mountain and that it opened its mouth every ten years. A geomancer once told a rich man that it was a very favorable grave site, and the man decided to take his advice and bury the bones of his ancestors in this auspicious place. He questioned the grave seeker further, who said to him, "Ten years ago the turtle opened its mouth. This year, on such and such a date, it is due to open it again. If you are seeking a favorable site for the grave of your parents, you must get everything ready on that night, hire a boat, and sail down the river to the turtle mountain. I will arrange the rest." The man was rather doubtful of his proposal, but being superstitious he eventually agreed.

On the day when the turtle was due to open its mouth, the rich man hired a boat, placed the bones of his ancestors on board, and sailed toward the mountain. Despite the evening breeze, the water was as still as glass. Everything was indistinct in the dim rays of the new autumn moon, and the silence was broken only by the splash of oars, mingled from time to time with the rattle of wooden implements and the coughing and low whispering of the crew. There were no other boats on the water, but two lamps were shining in the distance and fireflies danced around. It was a ghostly spot in daylight, but now, with the coffin filled with bones lying in the prow of the boat, it was weird enough to make one's hair stand on end. "Are we nearly there?" asked the rich man. "Not far," answered the geomancer.

On the shore two straw huts could be seen. In the window of each was a lamp which emitted a cold but strangely brilliant light. The boat came to anchor at the turtle mountain, and the geomancer ordered the rich man and all the sailors to keep silence while he carefully watched the turtle's head. The night was piercing cold. The river, checked in its course by the jutting headland, had formed a series of whirlpools, which were sucking at the ship. The waves dashed by on all sides and raced ever more madly around and around.

Suddenly, about midnight, the rich man and the crew were terrified by a noise coming from the turtle's head, but the geomancer quickly ordered them to lift up the coffin and cast it into the turbulent river, where, seized in the maelstrom, it vanished in a flash. The turtle's mouth opened into the water; the moment the coffin sank, the turtle's mouth closed and everything was as before. The waves became quieter, the turtle's head was as usual, the wind died down, and the new moon placidly shone in the western sky. The river became quiet once more, and the coffin had vanished.

The rich man gave a sigh of relief and looked around as if he had just awakened from a nightmare and was wondering where he was. "Everything went off perfectly," said the geomancer proudly. "The coffin is buried, and we can go home." "Where is it buried?" asked the rich man. "Here, of course," said the geomancer. "Now we must drink a bowl of wine to your future luck." "What? You threw the coffin into the river?" "Later you will have good luck. I congratulate you." "Have luck, you rascal! You have stolen my coffin. Thief!" "Do you still not understand?" "Thief!! Give me back the coffin."

The quarrel continued during the whole return journey, and the next day the rich man accused the geomancer before the district judge of purloining his coffin. The judge thought it very suspicious to throw a coffin into the river, and did not understand how the whirlpool into which the coffin sank could be considered a favorable burial site. At length he decided that the geomancer must return the rich man his coffin.

The poor man had no means of escape, but he begged for the loan of the magistrate's magic sword and for a delay of three days, which the magistrate agreed to. Two days later he went back to the turtle mountain, where he mumbled some magic words and with one blow struck dead the magic power of the mountain. The water immediately boiled up, and the coffin reappeared. He lifted it onto the ship and returned it to the rich man, who was overjoyed at seeing it again. When he opened it, he found that the bones had already become covered with golden scales. Now he bitterly regretted his hasty action, but the turtle in the mountain was now dead and could never open its mouth again.

The formation of the mountain, however, is still the same, and the head still juts out into the water.

· 34 ·   The Geomancer

· THERE WAS ONCE a geomancer named Ts'ao living in T'ung-chou. He had two sons. He was an unusually good diviner; whenever he said of a grave that the owners would have few descendants, it was certain that if one made inquiries in the family, they really did have very few children. Or if he said that the owner would be blind, he was blind.

One day he himself became ill, and knew that he was going to die. His two sons knelt down by his bedside and said, "Dear Father, you have always chosen graves for other people, and they have benefited by your choice. Why don't you choose a good grave yourself, so that we can also have a little luck?" The old man replied with a sigh, "Naturally there are favorable sites, but you have no veins of luck." However, since his sons begged him so earnestly, he said at last, "All right. You must try your luck. When I am dead you must not raise a big mound, but wrap up my body in grass ropes and go toward the east. At the place the rope breaks and my corpse falls, you must dig a grave and bury me. Then you must return home and prepare a terrace for the dead. You must place candles there and cover them with a chamber pot. On the house itself you must put a bushel, which must not be touched for seven times seven days. If you do exactly as I tell you, you will both become emperor. But I am afraid that you

will never have such luck, because you will never carry out my instructions." The two sons thanked their father. "Of course we
will do it," they said.

The same day their father died. The two sons secretly fastened
a grass rope to his body and went off toward the east, and at the
eastern sea the rope broke. After they had buried him, they returned home and built a terrace for the dead. There they placed
candles and covered them with a chamber pot, and then they
hoisted a bushel onto the roof of the house.

After seven days the two sons and everyone in the house fell ill.
Their whole bodies and muscles ached as if they were being con-
sumed by fire. There were many clever people in T'ung-chou
who noticed that all newborn children had a strange birthmark.
In the Ts'ao family's garden a clump of strange bamboos suddenly sprang up.

After forty days an uncle paid a visit to the two sons. He was
furious when he saw the chamber pot on top of the candles, and
said angrily, "No wonder you are all ill—you put such a dirty
thing on the terrace of the dead." He took away the chamber pot,
but as he did so there was a red flash and something flew up to
heaven and disappeared.

Now everything was ruined. The illness of the brothers and of
all the household was cured, many of the newborn children with
strange birthmarks died without cause, and the newly grown
bamboos in the garden dried up. When they were later split open,
a small blind child was found in each knot. At the same moment
a famous scholar named Ch'en Shih-hsiao, who was living in
T'ung-chou, became blind.

In the astrological office in Peking a real dragon was seen to
arise in T'ung-chou. It was known that if it grew up and had any
success, it would cause the Manchu dynasty a great deal of
trouble. Therefore people were sent to T'ung-chou to kill the rep-
tile which was lying in the grave of Ts'ao on the seashore. They
first tried by sticking iron and bronze spikes into the sand, but
they could never find the dragon until a scholar said, "The
dragon is already full grown—it lacks only eyes. Bronze and iron
both have a smell, and it can move away. You must use bamboo
staves, and it will be killed."

The next day they did as he suggested, and blood poured out of the ground. Both brothers fell ill and died during that same month.

· 35 · The Empress of Heaven

· ALTHOUGH THE GIRL was only seven years old, she already possessed supernatural powers. Her father and her two brothers were merchants, and each time they were overtaken by a storm during the sea crossing, she rescued them from the waves without anyone's being aware of it.

One day her father and brothers were once more on the sea when a terrific storm sprang up. She felt very troubled at their great danger, and her soul immediately left her body and hurried to their assistance. Being half immortal, she arrived in an instant at the sea, where the waves were breaking as high as the sky.

The ship was pitching and tossing in all directions, and the passengers, pale with terror, thought that their last hour had come. The daughter grasped her brothers in her arms and her father in her mouth and flew over the sea. It made no difference to her whether the sea was deep or shallow. The three castaways saw only a little girl appear through the winds and the waves to save them, and they thought that she was an immortal; they had no idea that she was their own little girl.

Before leaving she had been talking with her mother, who was frightened out of her wits when her daughter broke off in the middle of a word and her body became stiff and cold. The mother thought she had fallen ill, and began to sob and weep, but the girl lay as though she were dead.

After she had called and fondled her for a long time, the girl suddenly said, "Yes." "Wake up, child," said the mother, "I nearly wept myself to death." "Father is dead." "What are you saying?" cried the mother. "Father and my two brothers were overtaken by a terrible storm on the sea, and the ship sank, but my soul hastened over the water to save them. I grasped my brothers in my two hands, and caught my father's clothes in my mouth. But you wept and called for me, until my heart was touched, and I had to answer "Yes," whereupon my father dropped out of my mouth. I would otherwise have saved him, but immediately after his fall he was hidden by the waves, and I could find no trace of him. I managed to save my brothers, but, alas, father is dead!" "Is that really true?" asked the mother. "Yes." "Oh, woe is me, woe is me!"

Soon the brothers came home. Weeping, they clasped their mother in their arms and told her how first their father had been saved and later drowned. The daughter reproached her mother, saying, "You are to blame for the death of my father. Look, my feet and hair are still moist." The mother embraced her children again.

The daughter was sorry for her mother's widowed state and swore an oath never to marry. She tied her hair together and waited on her mother till her death. After her death she became an immortal. She became protectress of merchants and ships on the rivers, and is particularly worshiped by them.

· 36 ·   The Monk with the Bag

• DURING HIS YOUTH the Laughing Buddha lived in a monastery at Feng-hua in the province of Chekiang. Even when eating or sleeping he carried a bag with him, and for this reason the people called him the monk with the bag.

Once upon a time the deity of fire descended to the temple, which in a short time he reduced to a heap of ashes. There being no money with which to rebuild it, the abbot ordered the monk with the bag to collect offerings.

The monk set off with his wooden fish clapper and his bag, and one day he arrived at the house of a widow. She was the owner of a large mountain covered with trees, which had not been felled for more than one hundred years. They were very big now, and the monk begged the widow to give him a bag full of them. Thinking that the monk was making a joke, because, after all, a small bag will not hold many trees, she gave him permission at once.

The monk engaged a few workmen, cut down all the trees on the mountain, and slipped them into his bag. It was extraordinary to see large and small trees vanish into it without a shadow of them appearing inside. It was just like the bottomless cave in the novel *The Monkey's Pilgrimage*.

The widow was horrified when she heard the news and rushed off to the mountain, but every tree had been cut down and there was nothing left but the branches which had been cut off. She thought to herself, "Until now I have lived from the sale of these trees, but with them all cut down I shall soon die of starvation." She knelt down before the monk. "Don't kneel down. I know what you are thinking, but you will have your trees again in three years," he said to her with a smile.

She only half believed his words, but three years later the mountain was really covered with trees as big as before.

Whither did the trees go? The monk had conjured them away to a small well in the temple. Now that the building materials were ready, he did not need to collect any more money, but returned to the temple to supervise the workmen. The temple was to be made bigger than before, and since the time allotted for building was very short no carpenter was willing to undertake it. The monk had to appoint the magician Lu Pan.

Lu Pan ordered his pupils to take the wood out of the well, but they were careless and overlooked one beam, which was to serve as the center pillar. The monk wanted to test Lu Pan, and kneeling down before him, he asked if the building material was sufficient. "Just right," answered Lu Pan, "not too much and not too little."

The work began. When it was almost finished, Lu Pan found to his horror that one beam was missing. Although he calculated again and again, he could not get it right. Having already said that there was sufficient wood, he did not dare ask the monk for any more. The only thing he could think of was to make a center pillar out of the chips of wood that had been scattered about, and, wonderful to relate, it could not be distinguished from a real one.

The monk secretly admired the skill of Lu Pan, and Lu Pan the magic of the monk. Thus the great task was finally completed.

The Festival of Pouring Water

Year after year there is the Festival of Pouring Water.
Let us see who pours upon whom

• THIS IS AN OLD SAYING of the Thai people. From generation to generation to the present day, everybody throws water upon everybody else on this festival day. This is not because it is so hot, nor because people are dusty. What then is the reason? Let me tell you the story from its beginning.

Formerly there was a goblin king who was terribly cruel. If it came to his mind to kill someone, he killed him—he did whatever came to his mind. The earth has four regions, and he wanted to rule over all four of them. He had great abilities. When he was submerged in water, he was not drowned; when he was burned in fire, he did not die. No arrow, spear, or dagger could wound him. From time to time he went out to plunder and to get gold, silver, slaves, and beautiful girls, and nobody dared to stop him. He already had six wives, one more beautiful than the other; but this was still not enough for him, and so he kidnaped a seventh girl. He liked her very much, since she was even more beautiful than all the others.

One night, when he was especially delighted with her, she dared to ask him, "I have heard that you have great abilities, that water cannot drown you, fire cannot burn you, arrows, spears, and daggers cannot wound you. Does this mean that you will live forever on this earth?"

"Not necessarily so, because I too have a weak spot," the goblin king said.

"What are you afraid of, with all your abilities?" she further questioned him.

"This I will tell only you alone," he said in a low voice. "What I am afraid of is that somebody might take a hair from me and strangle me with it."

"You are not afraid of heaven, not afraid of earth. How can you be afraid of a single hair?" she asked even more daringly.

"Do not think a hair is weak. It really can strangle me," he said to her in a low voice.

When she had learned the secret, she thought, "If he really could be strangled by a hair, and if thus we could get rid of the goblin king, this would be fine. We could save many more people from being mistreated by him. I will try to do it." Thus she waited until, after his pleasures, he fell into a deep sleep. Then she pulled a hair from his head, wrapped it around his neck, tied it well, and his head fell off. At this she was filled with joy.

Very soon the head of the goblin king began to roll by itself on the earth. Wherever it rolled, fire sprang up from the earth, and out of the flames numerous ghosts arose. Then the seventh wife became extremely frightened and began to scream aloud. When the other six wives heard her screaming, they all came running. One of them, a very clever girl, quickly lifted the head up. Strangely enough, once the head ceased to touch the earth, the fire and the ghosts disappeared. From then on, they did not dare to lay the head down again for fear it might roll around again. So they carried the head, one after the other in turns, each for a year. As long as the head was not completely dead, blood dripped from it.

Therefore, when after the end of a year one girl handed the head to the next one, everybody poured water over the girl in order to wash away from her body the old blood and also in order to prevent the head from starting fires again.

So it was done once every year. They poured seven times. When every girl had carried the head once, the head finally died. From then to the present day, people pour water over one another, and this is called the Festival of Pouring Water.

· 38 · Kung Yeh-ch'ang Understands the Language of Birds

• KUNG YEH-CH'ANG was a poor man who lived by collecting firewood. With him lived his old mother.

One day, on his way to the phoenix mountain, he saw a number of snakes, both large and small, coming out of a cave and moving about in the most orderly fashion. The last to appear was an enormous golden serpent, which Kung, who had a knowledge of snakes, knew was a snake princess.

The princess and her followers advanced into the midst of the mountains, where she shook her head several times as a sign to the soldiers and all the other snakes to move away. A black snake minister alone remained, and the two glided off into the grass, where they were soon entwined. Kung Yeh-ch'ang was horrified at a mere minister daring to embrace a princess and, seizing his ax, he flung it at the black snake, cutting it in two. At once the sky became dark, and a dark mist rose up and floated away.

The princess had only been slightly wounded by the ax and now, calling for her companions, she slid back to the cave, where she dashed into the presence of the ruling snake to complain of the murder of the minister. The ruler was enraged by the news. "I demand vengeance for the death of my minister," he said, and immediately ordered two snake warriors to go to Kung Yeh-ch'ang's house and bite him to death.

Soon after the snakes had hidden themselves in the bedroom, Kung Yeh-ch'ang and his mother went into the room. Kung sat down on the bed with a sigh, and his mother asked, "What's the matter? Did something go wrong today? If you tell me, perhaps I can help you." Kung replied, "I was cutting wood on the phoenix mountain today when a snake princess appeared with her followers. A shameless snake minister began to fondle her. Actions like this are forbidden between ruler and subject, and so I killed the minister with my ax. The princess was also wounded and fled back to her hole. Don't you think I was quite right, mother?"

Meanwhile, the two snakes had listened to every word of this conversation. When they heard that Kung had killed the minister on very good grounds, they hurried home to make a report. The ruler realized at once that Kung had performed a good deed and, sending for the princess, he swallowed her.

One day Kung again found himself on the phoenix mountain. As he was passing the snake cavern, he saw a huge golden serpent lying in the entrance, holding in its mouth something that looked like a duck's egg. Kung saw that it was really a snake's liver, and said, "If you want to give me the liver, please go back into the cave." The snake did as he was asked, and Kung seized the liver and swallowed it.

As a result of eating the liver, he was able to understand the language of birds. One day, at the end of spring or the beginning of summer, a bird—the soul of the murdered snake minister—perched on a tree in front of Kung's house and sang:

> Kung Yeh-ch'ang, Kung Yeh-ch'ang,
> A tiger has killed a sheep in the hills.
> You eat the flesh
> And I the guts.

Kung understood everything and, going into the hills, he found the sheep's carcass and took it home. But he ate the whole thing, and the bird received nothing.

A few days later a child that had gone into the hills to collect wood was bitten to death by a tiger. The time for the bird's revenge had arrived. He flew to the tree in front of Kung's house and sang:

> Kung Yeh-ch'ang, Kung Yeh-ch'ang,
> A tiger has killed a sheep in the hills.
> You eat the flesh
> And I the guts.

Kung hurried off to search, but instead of a sheep he found only a dead child. As he was standing by the corpse wondering what to do, it began to snow. He looked in vain for a shelter. Since he could find none and it looked as though there was no hope of the snow's stopping he ran home.

The villagers were wondering why the child did not return, and went to look for it. They soon found it lying dead, but they did not see that it had been killed by a tiger. They saw the footprints in the snow, which led to Kung Yeh-ch'ang's house. Although he told them exactly what had happened, they did not believe him but accused him of the murder and led him off to the district magistrate.

No amount of questioning could induce Kung, who kept on repeating the same story, to admit his guilt. Needless to say, the magistrate did not believe that he understood bird language. "I have never heard of anyone's speaking with birds," he said, "and I don't believe it now." Then Kung replied, "If you don't believe me, make five heaps of corn and mix in each heap a salty, or a sour, or a bitter, or a hot, or a sweet substance. Place one heap in the middle and one in each of the four corners. When the birds come to eat, I will translate what they say, and you can see whether I am speaking the truth or not."

The magistrate agreed to his suggestion, and a bird came and pecked at the heaps on the east and the west corners and said, "The east one is sweet, the west one salty." Kung translated these words, and, very surprised, the magistrate set him free.

About seven years later a foreign land sent a strange bird without head or legs. With it came a letter, which said: "If you can feed this bird, our country will send tribute to yours every year; if you fail, we will invade your land and kill you."

The emperor announced at once, "Whichever of my ministers can feed the bird will be appointed earl with a fief of ten thousand families." But none of the ministers at the court could discover the solution.

After a long time one minister, who had formerly been district magistrate, said, "Six or seven years ago I was magistrate in such and such a place. There was a man named Kung Yeh-ch'ang who understood the language of birds. If you send for him, perhaps he will advise something."

The emperor sent an order for Kung to come to court, and a few days later he arrived. After he had made his obeisance, the emperor sent for the bird. Kung listened to what it said, and discovered that it must be fed on red-hot nails and washed in boiling oil.

The bird flourished under this treatment, and Kung was appointed earl with ten thousand families, and his mother was also rewarded. The bird, too, lived happily in its cage.

· 39 · First Discuss the Price When the Pig Is Dead

· THE PROVERB "First discuss the price when the pig is dead" is known all over South Fukien. It is applied to people who do not first think a matter over but only bargain when everything is finished. There is an old story about it, which I will now tell you.

Once upon a time there lived in Ch'üan-chou a Mr. Chin and a Mr. Yi, who were such close friends that they became blood brothers. Unfortunately, Chin fell ill and died, which so upset Yi that he stood weeping beside the coffin of his friend and wanted to end his own life. From then on he thought only of his friend, but there was nothing for him to do.

Hard though it is to believe, the tale of his sorrows reached the underworld, and one night Chin appeared and talked to him in a dream. He told how he had become an official in hell, which made it easy for them to meet; Yi needed only to utter a few magic formulas, and then go to sleep. His soul would then find its way to the underworld, where he could talk with his friend. Then Chin told him the magic words and vanished.

Soon Yi woke with the words still in his mind. He was delighted at the devotion of his friend, and the next afternoon he carried out his instructions exactly. He lay down on the bed, spoke the magic formula, and in a short while found himself in the halls of the netherworld, where his friend was waiting to greet him.

Now that Yi had discovered a means of reaching the underworld, his affection for Chin daily increased, and every day he took a rest and went to meet his friend.

One day Yi's beloved grandson was taking a nap with him. This seven- or eight-year-old child was a good mimic, and when he heard his grandfather's words he copied them exactly and also arrived in the lower world.

Yi was so occupied with his friend that he paid no attention to his grandchild, who wandered around in the halls. The child loved playing, and ran outside to join a crowd of children who were taking pigs' caps off the wall, putting them on, and jumping about. He also took one and began to run about, until he had vanished who knows where!

During his conversation with his friend, Yi quite forgot that his grandson had been with him, and on his return to the upper world he called out to him but could not wake him. The child was as one dead. Suddenly Yi remembered that he had taken his grandson with him to the underworld but midday being past, it was too late to go back for him. I need not tell you what a state the whole house was in.

Yi had to wait till the next afternoon before he could lie down in his bed and visit Chin again. He inquired at once about his grandson, but Chin had to consult the lists of the living and the dead before he had any idea where the boy had gone to.

In these books he discovered that he had been reborn as a pig. The boy had not understood what the other children were doing with the pigs' caps; thinking they were playing with them, he had put one on his head. He had, as a result, been reborn as a pig in Mr. So-and-So's house.

Yi was horrified by this news, and begged Chin to help him. Chin thought for a long time and then said to Yi, "You must return to the upper world and go quickly to Hsing-hua fu. There you must find the house where a sow has just produced thirteen pigs, and you must take one with a white star and kill it. Your grandson will then be able to return to earth as a man."

On his return home, Yi gave orders not to bury his grandson. During the night he went to Hsing-hua fu, where he found the house with the thirteen piglets. When he found the one with the white star, he said at once he wanted to buy it, and then slaughtered it without further ado. His behavior surprised the peasant, but Yi soon arranged the price with him. When he reached home, his grandson had returned to life.

Part VI
Help from
Spirits and Deities

·40· Lü Tung-pin as the Patron of Barbers

· APRIL 14 in the old calendar is the birthday of Lü Tung-pin, and all the barbers in the country sacrifice to him on that day. The custom originated in the Ming dynasty.

The first emperor, Chu Hung-wu, had a scalp disease. Every day he sent for a new barber to come to the palace and shave him, but none of them could do it without hurting him. He had innumerable barbers executed for their failure.

All the barbers in the land were in a desperate state, not knowing what to do. They sent a plea up to heaven; when the Jade Emperor received it, he sent Lü Tung-pin down to earth. Lü Tung-pin changed into a barber, turned his magic sword into a razor, and went to the palace. After he had shaved Hung-wu, not only did the emperor feel no pain, but his disease caused him no more trouble.

At first the barbers marveled at the cure, but gradually they all learned that the man who had shaved the emperor was the envoy of heaven, Lü Tung-pin. They thanked him again and again, and gave him the post of deity of hairdressers.

Ever since, Lü Tung-pin has been worshiped by every barber and is considered the ancestor of the trade.

·41· The Spirit

· IN FORMER TIMES a poor kindhearted man, by trade a fisherman, lived with his family of three in a straw hut on the banks of a river in the middle of a thick forest.

Unfortunately, the fish had been nearly exterminated by the cormorants, and for several days he carried an empty basket home. There was nothing to eat in the cooking pot. His children cried, his wife scolded, but all he could do was to knit his brows.

One night, when the moon had just disappeared behind the

mountains, he was restlessly tossing about in bed. His wife and children were sleeping soundly. Suddenly he seemed to hear a knock at the door. Thinking that no one could be about at such a late hour, he paid no attention, until finally the knocking became very insistent. Having no fear of ghosts, he pulled on some clothes and glanced out of the window near the bed.

The silvery-green disk of the moon was shining through the pines on the western hills, and an icy wind blew in through the window. Going to the door, called out, "Who is there?" "It is I," answered the voice. "I am bringing you fish. Open the door quickly." "Oh, are you Little Number Three?" asked the fisherman, because he had once heard that Little Three caught fish for other people. Since the voice answered his question in the affirmative, he opened the door.

A dwarf, clad in a raincoat and a large straw hat, came smiling into the room with a basket full of fish on his back. He told the fisherman to take out half the fish, and to cook and eat the remainder; on no account, though, must he talk to other people about who had brought them.

Little Three did the cooking himself in the simplest fashion. He used no spices—only salt and oil—but the food tasted delicious. When they had finished eating, he made an appointment with the fisherman for the following night at a certain place to catch fish.

The next morning the fisherman sold the fish, bought some rice, and told his wife that a friend had lent him some money. He sat at home all day and pondered over his experience. When his wife urged him to go out, he merely replied that there were no fish and that it was a waste of time to go down to the river.

Night fell and it was soon time to go. His wife and children were asleep; silently the fisherman took a large fishing basket and went off to meet Little Three. He met him by the wild rocks near the river. The spirit impressed on him the need of following closely and not saying a word and of breathing as softly as possible. The fish could not see Little Three, but if they made any noise the fish would swim away at once. The strangest thing was that the dwarf was able to walk on the water, and he only needed to spit on the soles of the fisherman's shoes to enable him to do the same. Naturally, the fish could not see the fisherman either.

The fisherman did exactly as he was told. He took great

care not to breathe too loudly, and when Little Three caught a fish he took it from him and threw it into the basket. He was kept very busy, and soon became quite out of breath. Before they had gone a quarter of the way, the basket was full; he merely threw the rest of the fish back into the water again, because the spirit went on catching fish without bothering to see whether there was any place to put them or not. A little later they both stepped onto the bank, and shivers ran down the fisherman's spine at the appalling sight of the deep water they had crossed. They returned home, cooked and ate half the fish, and put the other half aside according to the orders the spirit had given.

Every night, except at the time of the full moon, they went out fishing, but the fisherman said nothing to his wife. To avoid all suspicion, he even went fishing during the day from time to time. But he earned so much money that his wife became suspicious, and eventually she discovered everything.

One night she pretended to be asleep and watched to see what her husband would do. She saw him eating fish with another man and then come into the bedroom and go to sleep. She made no sign, but when he had fallen asleep she got up and saw what they had been doing.

The next day she bored a small hole in the plaster wall and watched the two men cooking the fish. She saw how they only cooked half of them, and she thought to herself that if only they could keep the other half they would have food for several days.

She made a plan, and the following night, when Little Three came again and placed the pot on the fire, it suddenly went up in flames. The spirit saw at once that something was wrong and ran away. The fisherman was very angry, but not until his wife came into the room with a smile on her face did he know that the pot had been made of paper.

From then on, the spirit never came to cook and eat fish.

·42· *The Little People*

• THERE ARE MANY people in Ching-ting who own elves, beings that one can hear but not see and that have no shadow. They do all sorts of work for people. If, for example, you are planting flowers, you only need to plant one to show them and they finish the rest of the field. They have a passion for sweeping, so that the houses of people that have elves are always especially clean. When you arrive at such a house and take off your shoes at the door, if there is no dust to be seen when you look round, then you know that there are elves in the house.

Elves are caught in the following manner. You bury at the crossroads two different species of creatures, like millepedes and snakes. Then dig them up several days later and put them in an incense burner, and you will find elves.

Every year they like to eat a human being, and if when their master makes accounts with them on New Year's Eve there is still something owing, he must give them a man. For this reason, on New Year's Eve, if they have broken a cup, their master must pretend they have broken twenty and reckon it against them and tell them to wait until next year for their feast.

If he no longer wants them he can marry them off; but if they refuse to marry, there is nothing to be done. If they consent, he prepares a packet of silver, a packet of powder, and a packet of incense ash—these are really the elves—and drops them in the road. Whoever wants it just picks up the silver. Sometimes people who do not know about it pick the silver up by mistake, and then the elf goes with them. It prefers to live in the cooking pot, and for this reason people who are afraid of elves put a little water into the pot after cooking.

Here is a story about them.

A poor man once found a packet of silver and a packet of powder lying in the road. He knew it was the dowry of an elf, but he wanted the silver and not the imp. He was afraid, however, that it would follow him, and therefore he seized the silver and dashed down to the river, because elves cannot cross the water.

When he arrived at the river, the imp had already climbed onto his sun hat. He threw the hat into the river, and both the hat and its occupant were carried away by the stream. Later the hat was hung on a tree, which withered at once.

The poor man gradually became rich with the silver. One day

he was walking along the river bank with his son when the boy pointed at the withered tree, and asked his father, "Why is the tree withered?" The father told his son the story about the elf. The imp was still in the tree, and when he heard that this rich man was his old enemy, he sprang to the ground, seized his soul, and ate it up.

From then on, the rich man grew thin and yellow, and eventually he died.

•43• *The Wang-liang's Magic Cap*

• THE WANG-LIANG are said to be ogres whose bodies are covered with hair. If they see a human being, they eat him. They live in the midst of hills and cool valleys; so we seldom see them. Some people say that if you see one of them coming toward you, you must hold a stake in front of you, with one point straight against your breast and the other directed toward the wang-liang. This keeps the wang-liang from attacking, but unless you know this way of preventing its approach you are sure to be eaten.

There was once a young fellow named A San, who happened to meet one of these ogres at night. He quickly took a bamboo pole and placed one end against his breast and the other toward the monster. When he did this, the ogre was unable to move and begged to be set free. But A San replied, "I have no intention of letting you go until you give me something."

The monster quickly pulled off a boot and offered it to A San. Knowing that the boot was a coffin, A San refused to take it. Then the ogre asked him, "What do you want?" And A San answered, "I want the straw hat you are wearing on your head." A San knew it was a magic hat, which could make its wearer invisible. Much against its will, the wang-liang was forced to surrender it, and A San set the ogre free and went joyfully home.

From then on, A San wore his magic cap the whole day. One day he stole some things from a fruit stall as he was passing by, but unfortunately a wang-liang saw him and took his cap away. This made him visible to the shopkeepers, who beat him unmercifully before allowing him to run away.

Another man, named A Lin, also caught a wang-liang with a bamboo stick. He demanded the skin on its face, and despite the pain the poor ogre had to strip it off and give it to him. This skin is like a mask, and whoever puts it on is invisible, like the wearer of the cap. A Lin now let the wang-liang go, but one night he met another, whose cap he also took with the well-known trick.

A Lin was delighted with his two treasures, and he also became a thief. He first ordered his wife to steal silver. She put the cap on her head and went into the house of a rich man. Just as she was going to take the money, the man's daughter, who was sleeping in the room, began to cough. Thinking she had been seen, A Lin's wife ran away.

A Lin asked his wife why she had stolen nothing, and she told him about the girl coughing. A Lin said, "What a fool you are! No one can see you. You are too cowardly. This time I will go." And he took the cap and went into the rich man's house, where he stole a lot of valuable jewelry and silver, which he carried back to his house.

In this way he soon became rich, though he still wore his dirty old clothes to lull his neighbors' suspicions.

Every two or three months he stole something. All the rich families lost money and valuables, but no one could catch the thief. One day he hung up the cap on a beam by the fire. His wife, who was nearsighted, mistook it for a bundle of rice straw and shoved it into the fire as fuel. A Lin was furious with her, but luckily he still possessed the mask. Although he had stolen much silver, he had lost most of it again by gambling.

One day, when he had again gambled away all his money, he laid the mask on the table as security, but none of his friends were willing to lend him money on the filthy thing. A Lin said to them, "You must not undervalue this thing. It is a treasure which makes its wearer invisible." When they tried it on and found that, A Lin had not lied, they were willing to accept it as a pledge. But A Lin's luck did not turn. After he had lost all his money, the mask passed into another man's hands.

• MANY YEARS AGO there lived two boys named Liu Ch'en and Yüan Chao who were cousins.

One day they went into the hills to fetch water. It was in the midst of spring, and the hills were carpeted by all sorts of red and green flowers. The boys were so overcome by the beauty of the scene that they put down their pails by the stream and set off for a walk. The country became more and more lonely as they wandered from hill to hill, until the path finally came to an end and they found themselves at the entrance to a cave, with an enormous stone on each side on which two fairies were seated playing chess.

The two boys stood in the mouth of the cave and watched the game without saying a word. At the feet of the fairies a white hare was springing up and down. Much to their wonder, the two boys noticed that each time it sprang up the flowers bloomed at the entrance to the cave, and each time it lay down they faded.

When the game was finished, the fairies looked around at the boys and asked when they had arrived. "A few hours ago," they both answered, and turned to leave. But the fairies said to them, "Stay here in our grotto and don't go home. No one will recognize you." But they did not understand what the fairies meant, and said firmly, "No! No! We must go home." Seeing that they could not persuade them to remain, the fairies gave them each a piece of reed, saying, "If you find everything changed at home, come back here and point the reed at the cave, and it will open."

They took the reeds and returned to the stream by which they had left their poles and buckets. All they found was decayed earth and tall pines growing on each side of the stream, where formerly there had been open ground.

In great perplexity they entered the village, but there they could find no trace of their homes. They asked two old white-haired men whom they saw sitting in a meadow where the house of Liu Ch'en and Yüan Chao was. The two old men replied, "Liu Ch'en and Yüan Chao were our ancestors. We are their descend-

ants in the seventh generation. Why do you young fellows talk
about them in this casual way?"

This was still more confusing, because how could two young
men have descendants in the seventh generation? Perhaps the
white hare jumping about in the fairy grotto represented the seasons, and the afternoon they had spent in the cave had lasted for
four or five hundred years. When the two children heard the
words of the old men, they said, "But we are Liu Ch'en and
Yüan Chao!" This made the old men so annoyed that their
beards waggled to and fro. They called out to other people, who
came up and beat the two boys.

"You young rascals," they cried, "how dare you come and
bother old men!"

The boys fled back to the cave, but the doors were closed tight.
Then they remembered their reeds, but they could not recall
where they had left them. They did not dare to go back and look
for them for fear the people would beat them again. They
knocked and knocked, but there was no answer, and in their
grief they banged their heads against the wall and died.

The ruler of heaven took pity on their sad fate, and appointed
Liu Ch'en the god of good luck and Yüan Chao the god of ill
luck.

·45· *Hsiang Meets the Dragon King*

• OLD HSIANG was very poor. Although he and his family all
worked hard in the field, they often still remained hungry.
Hsiang therefore decided to learn to hunt and fight. Soon he had
learned some tricks of the trade, and as more and more people
joined him, his power became greater and greater. Wherever he
went, he cleared away evildoers and eliminated cruel oppressors
but helped those without food and clothing, so that all the poor
folk regarded Hsiang as their defender. The emperor, however,
looked upon him as a thorn in his side and wanted to destroy
him.

One day Hsiang's maternal uncle, old P'eng, asked him to

come with him to deliver the tax grain to the emperor. Hsiang
had no grain, and so he could not go. Last year the emperor had
seen both of them delivering their grain in the capital; this time
only P'eng appeared. The emperor was astonished, and asked
P'eng what had happened to Hsiang. P'eng replied, "Ha, do you
think he will come? His power is now so great."

So said P'eng inadvertently and half jokingly in front of the
emperor; but the emperor took it seriously, became very angry,
and said, "This is rebellion." Using this as a pretext, he declared
Hsiang a rebel who refused to pay tax grain, and sent a large
army to conquer him.

Hsiang fought a number of battles against the government
army until all his men were dispersed. The emperor's soldiers
hoped to catch him now, but Hsiang was so strong that he ran
from one hilltop to the next so that they could never lay hands on
him. Then they put soldiers on horses all around the mountain,
and encircled it so that not even a drop of water could have
leaked out. When Hsiang saw that he could not escape, he went
into a cave.

When he entered the cave, a cold wind brought a fine fragrance
to him. When he went on, he reached a bright, shiny place. In the
main hall was a man in a splendid dragon gown. The dragon-
robed being looked at him, and, since Hsiang felt that this person
had no evil intentions, he told him the reasons he had entered the
cave. The man in the dragon robe said, "This is the dragon palace, and I am the dragon king. You may stay here for a few
days." Then he ordered his servants to bathe the stranger and give
him fresh clothing, and he served him a lavish dinner.

Hsiang thanked the dragon king and stayed in the cave studying the art of war and magic arts with the king. Hsiang was a
bright man who quickly understood what the king taught him.
After a few days he began to think of father, mother, and sisters
at home, said good-bye to the dragon king, and again put on the
clothes in which he had arrived.

When he left the cave a water carrier saw him, set down his
carrying pole, and ran away crying, "A ghost has come from the
cave." When Hsiang looked at his clothing, he saw that it was in
shreds and that his skin was showing through everywhere. His

hair was like raw hemp that had not been combed. At first he wondered how he could have changed so much in a few days, but then he remembered that a day in the dragon palace is a year among humans. He also wondered how he could face people in this condition. Therefore he went back into the cave. Several times he wanted to go home, but always he was afraid that he would frighten people and he retreated again into the cave.

When his sister heard of the ghost from the cave, and that the face of the ghost looked somewhat like that of her brother, she became sad and tears rolled down her face. She took some clothes and bean cakes, of which her brother was very fond, and put them in front of the cave. Then she called, "Lieh-ko-nai, Lieh-ko-nai! If you are my brother Lieh-ko-nai, take the clothes and eat the cakes and come home with your sister."

After a while she looked again, and Hsiang had put on the clothes and eaten the cakes. Then brother and sister saw each other and, astonished and happy, they embraced and cried. The sister said, "Lieh-ko-nai, after all you are still alive. At home they think that the emperor killed you. Father and mother cried until they were half dead. Let us quickly go home so that they all will be happy."

Hsiang went home, and the parents had their son again; they were happy and sad at the same time, and hot tears rolled down without ceasing. Thus, finally, the long-lost son was reunited with his family.

·46· *The Wild Goose Lake*

• IT IS REPORTED that a man by the name of Chiao lived with his daughter in the village P'o-lo at the foot of Horse Ear Mountain. The girl's name was Sea Girl.

One year there was such a great drought that the people could not live on the products of the fields. Sea Girl and her father went up to Horse Ear Mountain to cut bamboo to make brooms to sell. One day, after Sea Girl had cut a great deal of bamboo, she suddenly saw a shiny lake. The lake was absolutely clear; not a single fallen leaf was on the water. Whenever a leaf fell from any of the trees surrounding the lake, a big wild goose came and carried it away. This was called Wild Goose Lake.

Sea Girl was very glad she had found the lake, and quickly carried her bamboo home. The next day she took an ax and tried to see whether she could make an outlet from the lake to get water for the drought-stricken people. For half a day she walked around the lake. She saw that the lake was surrounded by big mountains, forests, and rocks, but in one place there was a stone gate. She worked a long time on it, but could not open it. This troubled her very much, and she sat down under a tree and tried to decide what she should do. All of a sudden a wild goose came and said to her, "Sea Girl, Sea Girl, you need a golden key to open Wild Goose Lake." Where could she find a golden key? Before she could ask, the goose was gone. Sea Girl walked along the shore until she came to a cypress forest. In the forest were three parrots, whom she asked. "Parrots, parrots, where can I find the golden key?"

The parrots answered her, "Sea Girl, Sea Girl, first you have to find the third daughter of the dragon king." Sea Girl continued to walk along the lake, searching for the dragon king's third daughter. When she came to a pine grove, she saw a peacock sitting on a tree and asked him, "Peacock, peacock, where can I find the dragon king's third daughter?" The peacock told her, "Sea Girl, Sea Girl, you will find her in the canyon of the southern mountain."

Then the peacock flew to the south and alighted in a cinnamon tree. Sea Girl followed the peacock, but when she came to the cinnamon tree she did not see the dragon king's third daughter. Again the peacock on the tree said to her, "Sea Girl, Sea Girl, the third daughter loves songs. If you sing the songs the folk sing, she will come forth." And then the peacock flew away.

Sea Girl began to sing. The first day she sang about the snow flakes on the mountains, but the dragon king's third daughter did not appear. The second day Sea Girl sang about the green grass in the lake, but still the third daughter did not come. On the third day Sea Girl sang about the blossoming flowers on the hills, until the sun disappeared behind the mountains.

Then the third daughter of the dragon king came out of the lake. The dragon king had made a rule that the people of his palace were not allowed to come into the human world without permission. But the third daughter loved folksongs so much, that on the third day she could no longer contain herself and secretly came out of the water. Sea Girl sang even better than she herself and so she greatly admired her.

She asked Sea Girl, "Whose daughter are you? Where do you live? Why do you come to sing here every day?"

Sea Girl answered, "My name is Sea Girl. I live in P'o-lo village at the foot of Horse Ear Mountain. I am searching for the golden key to release the water of Wild Goose Lake to help the drought-stricken people."

The good-hearted third daughter told her, "The golden key is in the treasury of the dragon king, and a big eagle is guarding it. The eagle would kill anybody, except the king himself, who dared to enter the treasury. Only when the king leaves the palace," she said, "is there any possibility of getting into the treasury."

Finally one day, when the dragon king had left, the third daughter took Sea Girl into the palace. Taking turns, they sang songs in front of the treasury. At first the old eagle was asleep and paid no attention to the singing. Soon he awoke and, touched by the music, opened his wings and came to see who was singing. At this moment Sea Girl quickly slipped into the treasury to look for the golden key.

In the treasury her eyes were dazzled. The room was full of gold, silver, and precious stones. If she had taken but one of the jewels, she would have been wealthy for a lifetime. But she thought only of the golden key, and did not care about gold, silver, and riches. She quickly searched through the whole treasury without finding the key. Then in her haste she happened to knock over a big wooden box. When the box fell to the floor, it opened with a bang and out fell a shiny golden key. She took the key and hurriedly left the treasury. When Sea Girl came out, the dragon king's daughter stopped singing and both girls went out to Wild Goose Lake. When the beautiful songs stopped, the old eagle returned to his accustomed place and went back to sleep.

Sea Girl took the golden key and knocked three times at the gate. It opened, and the water streamed out. In minutes all the canals of P'o-lo village were overflowing with water. When the daughter of the dragon king saw that the rush of water would sweep away the whole harvest, she quickly said, "Sea Girl, Sea Girl, the harvest will be washed away." Sea Girl looked back and became frightened. She stopped the water with some straw curtains.

Who would have thought that straw curtains would be so strong that water would only trickle through the seams, after the stone gate was gone? The curtains are still there, but they have become stone curtains by now.

When the dragon king returned, he found that the key was gone and he knew that his third daughter had allowed it to be stolen. He banished his daughter from the palace, and so she went to live on earth with Sea Girl, and both sang together the whole day long. Later the women of all the surrounding villages came together each year on the twenty-second day of the seventh moon to sing songs.

·47· *The Bridge of Ch'üan-chou*

• THE LOYANG BRIDGE lies twenty miles outside the east gate of Ch'üan-chou, just on the borders of the district. It was particularly difficult to build a bridge at that spot, because it is the meeting point of the sea tides and of the river rushing down from the mountains. It is said that evil spirits live in the river, and therefore not only was it extremely difficult to lay the foundations of the bridge but the boat traffic was also very dangerous. There are innumerable tales in Fukien about this bridge, but I will only relate the best known.

When the ruler of heaven wanted to dispose of his carnal body, he considered the entrails to be the vilest part of the human frame. He drew his magic sword, split open his body, and flung his entrails into the Loyang River. But the entrails of the heavenly ruler were still subject to many influences, and they immediately turned into a tortoise and a snake spirit, which were always playing cruel tricks on men in the Loyang River.

Before the bridge was built, everyone had to cross the river by boat. In the reign of the Emperor Shen-tsung (998–1022) of the Sung Dynasty, a pregnant woman from Fuch'ing was once crossing the river to Ch'üan-chou; just as the boat reached the middle of the stream, the tortoise and snake spirits sent a strong wind and high waves to upset it and sink it. Suddenly a voice cried out from the sky, "Professor Ts'ai is in the boat. Spirits must behave decently with him." Scarcely had the words been spoken when the wind and the waves died down. All the passengers had heard exactly what was said, but when they asked each other's names there was no one called Ts'ai in the boat; only the pregnant woman from Fuch'ing belonged to the Ts'ai family. All the passengers congratulated the woman, who was quite bewildered, not knowing whether to believe or disbelieve what she had heard. "If I really give birth to a son who later becomes a professor," she said, "I will charge him to build a bridge over the Loyang."

Several months later the woman named Ts'ai really bore a son, who was named Ts'ai Hsiang. Later, about 1025, he became a professor. His mother told him her experience on the Loyang River and begged him to think of ways and means of building a bridge, in order that she might fulfill her vow. Ts'ai Hsiang was a dutiful son and immediately gave his consent.

At that time, however, there was a law against anyone's being appointed an official in his own province. Since Ts'ai Hsiang was a native of Fukien, he could not become governor of Ch'üan-chou, which is in that province. Fortunately his friend, the head eunuch, conceived a wonderful plan.

One day, when it was announced that the emperor would walk in the garden, the eunuch took some sugared water and wrote these eight characters on a banana leaf: "Ts'ai Hsiang must be appointed official in his home town." The ants immediately smelled the honey and gathered on the characters in vast numbers, to the stupefaction of the emperor, who happened to pass the banana tree and saw the ants drawn up in the form of eight characters. The head eunuch watched him reading them over and over, and quickly wrote out the decree appointing Ts'ai Hsiang to be governor of Ch'üan-chou. The emperor wanted to punish the eunuch when he handed him the decree, but the man excused himself, saying, "The emperor says nothing in jest." Ts'ai Hsiang immediately received the appointment.

On his arrival at Ch'üan-chou, he turned plans over in his head day and night, but the waves of the Loyang River beat so high that no means could be found of fixing the pillars. At length, finding that despite all his learning he was completely at a loss, he decided that the only hope was to implore the help of the gods. He wrote a letter to the dragon king and then asked which of his servants would be willing to go into the sea and deliver it for him.

It happened that one of the servants was a drunkard named Hsia Te-hai, who, mistaking the words for his own name, knelt down and said, "I am Hsia Te-hai. What commission have you for me?" The magistrate nodded his head, and replied, "You must go down into the sea. You have three days in which to deliver this letter to the dragon king. If you fail, you will receive three hundred blows." Throwing the letter to the servant, he left the hall. The poor man was in despair at his plight, but it was too late to refuse and with a heavy heart he returned home.

At first he cursed his luck and cursed Ts'ai Hsiang; but since that did not help him much, he spent all his money on buying wine, and drank and drank until he was quite tipsy. Then he stumbled along to the river, where he planned to end his troubles by jumping into the water. As he arrived at the river bank a stiff breeze sprang up. No longer having proper control of his limbs, he fell down on the beach.

The next morning, as the blood-red sun slowly rose in the east, he was wakened by the crowing of cocks. Opening his eyes, he found himself lying on the same spot by the seashore. When he took the letter out of his pocket, he saw that it was quite different from the one Ts'ai Hsiang had given him. Realizing that a miracle had taken place, he rushed back to the magistrate's residence in high spirits, and told all that had happened to him during the night.

Ts'ai Hsiang opened the letter and saw that there was only the character "vinegar" written on the sheet of paper. After a mo-

ment's thought he understood from the form of the character that
the dragon king had ordered him to lay the foundations on the
twenty-first day at the hour "yu," and he gave orders for all the
necessary materials to be ready at that hour.

Now that the time for laying the foundations had been fixed,
workmen had to be engaged. On the same day eight strange men
appeared and announced that they would do all the work without
payment. Ts'ai Hsiang thought that they were good socially
minded workers and made no further inquiries about them, but
people thought it strange that only eight workmen were engaged
for this enormous work.

The twenty-first day drew near. The tides really seemed smaller
in the river bed, and the workmen got everything ready. For a
few days they did nothing but sit on the ground and play chess.
Everyone thought this too much and urged them to work, but the
eight men merely replied, "It's such a small job. Why make such
a fuss about it? In any case, the hour 'yu' has not yet arrived."

Soon, however, the time came and the river dried up. Suddenly
a whirlwind sprang up at the place where the eight men were
playing chess. Sand and stones were blown in all directions, completely obscuring the sun and the moon, and none of the other
workmen were able to open their eyes. When it became quiet
again, everyone saw that the stone foundations were safely laid.
There was also no trace of the eight workmen who had been
playing chess. It was obvious that they were the Eight Immortals
who had turned into men to help build the bridge.

Although the foundations had been successfully laid by the immortals, the construction of the stonework and balustrading still
remained to be done, and many workmen were engaged to complete the great work quickly.

At that time a monk named I-po, who was one of the fifteen
people on Ts'ai Hsiang's council for building the bridge, gave
him the greatest assistance. Most of the plans and suggestions for
laying out and strengthening the construction originated with
him, and with the help of this Buddhist monk the design was
unusually beautiful.

I-po had one other faculty that caused the people the greatest
astonishment. The workmen at the bridge were so numerous that

sometimes there was not sufficient wood for cooking the food. When this happened, I-po stuck his foot in the stove and the flames shot up and cooked the food in a few minutes.

When the bridge was finished, he changed into an immortal and flew up to heaven. To this day there is a temple in his honor north of the city, where he is worshiped under the name of the monk I-po. The statue is said to be made out of his body, and for this reason the temple is called the temple of the genuine immortal.

Although Ts'ai Hsiang expended his whole personal fortune as well as the donations of the charitable, he found that funds were still not sufficient for the completion of the bridge. Then the goddess Kuan Yin turned herself into a beautiful woman, got into a boat, and sailed up the Loyang River, where she allowed men to throw pieces of money at her. The man who hit her would become her husband, but whoever failed should have their money used for building the bridge. There were many rich young men who thought her so beautiful that money rained onto the ship as thick as snowflakes, but not one single piece touched her. At this moment Lü Tung-pin flew by on a cloud and saw Kuan Yin. He thought he would play a trick on her, and by the help of his magic he caused a piece thrown by a small fruit seller to touch her dress. The little man was overjoyed at winning such a beautiful wife, but suddenly the ship and the woman vanished, to the despair of the little man, who jumped into the river and was drowned.

The money problem now being solved, and the leg of the monk I-po providing sufficient firewood, the workmen were able to return to work. But there were so many people that, although there was enough rice to feed them, there was a scarcity of fish, vegetables, and meat. Kuan Yin heard about this and, through her magic arts, turned the man who had hit her but never received her into thousands of little fishes to serve as the daily fare of the workmen. To this day there is a kind of long, thin white fish in the Loyang River which the people call silver fish.

When the bridge was finished, everyone praised Ts'ai Hsiang; but when the tides were high, the balustrades were still under water and people had to wade over.

Here is a tale about Li Wu, who later rebuilt the bridge of Ch'üan-chou.

About seven hundred years after the death of Ts'ai Hsiang, in the reign of the Emperor Ch'ien-lung (1736–1796), there was a man in the district of Ch'in-chiang of the Li family, who was called Li Wu (fifth) because he was the fifth son.

In his youth he was a ne'er-do-well, always buying things and not paying for them, which made shopkeepers more afraid of him than of a tiger. But there was one butcher who not only made no objection to his debts but even encouraged him to buy more goods. When Li wanted to buy a piece of meat, he only needed to write a receipt and the butcher gave the meat to him at once. Li Wu the lazybones was naturally content with this arrangement, but after it had gone on for some time he began to wonder what the reason was.

One day he again signed a receipt for some meat, but instead of going away he hid himself and watched. The butcher took the receipt and went slowly up to the top of a small hill. There he brushed aside the grass by the temple to the earth deity and thrust the receipt into a grave, at the same time taking out a piece of silver. Then he smoothed down the grass, and went slowly and contentedly down the hill. Li Wu ran to the place and nearly jumped for joy; the grave was filled with pots of silver, one of which was only half full, the other half containing the receipts that Li Wu had given the butcher in course of time.

As he was standing there, a voice called from the sky, "This money belongs to Li Wu. Today you have come, and I, humble spirit, can give up my post." Li Wu understood at once, and carried all the silver back home.

The butcher had discovered this treasure one day when he was passing the temple of the earth deity, whom he had heard saying to his wife, "The silver under the stone belongs to Li Wu, who has still not come for it. I shall have to guard it till my death." When the butcher heard this, he looked about and at length discovered some huge pots, which, however, were only filled with pure water. He knew that the money did not belong to him, but he proposed to make use of it. He used the receipts of Li Wu to produce money from under the stone, because exactly the same amount appeared in the pot as the receipt was made out for.

Now that Li Wu had become a rich man, I do not need to tell you that he opened shops, built houses, and kept a host of male and female slaves. His chief joy was in entertaining guests, and although he may never have had eight thousand guests, like a famous man of old, at least he had a round hundred.

One day, a strange man called K'ang Chin-lung arrived from distant parts. He claimed to be able to discover buried treasures. Perhaps he was also a fabulously wealthy man, but on this occasion he came to test the habits and character of Li Wu. Li Wu was, however, a good judge of character and immediately invited K'ang to be his guest, treating him better than anyone else. He was given basins of gold to wash his face in. Although each time that he washed he threw the golden basin into the lotus pond, Li Wu never uttered a bitter or unfriendly word. After K'ang had been there several months, he disappeared one day without saying good-bye.

Li Wu, it happened, had once insulted some rogue living in the neighborhood. To get his revenge this man accused him of being a bandit, saying that formerly he had been a penniless vagabond, until one day he had become very wealthy. Now his house was always full of guests, and he was obviously planning a revolt. Li Wu's fortune and possessions were confiscated, and he was thrust into a wooden cage and sent to Peking to be tried.

When he passed over the Loyang River in the prison cart, he was soaked through by the high tide that was breaking over the balustrading. He said to the guardians with a sigh, "If I escape with my life, I will raise the Loyang bridge three feet." A stone dealer and a rope dealer that were passing laughed when they heard Li Wu's oath, and they said to him, "You will never escape! But if you return and raise the bridge three feet, we will give you the stone and the ropes for nothing." They had heard of the accusation, and never thought that Li Wu would return alive.

After they had traveled for a long, long way, they arrived at Shantung province, where on all sides they saw fields with stone notices: "Field of Li Wu." They made inquiries, and discovered that they had been bought by K'ang Chin-lung in the name of Li Wu.

When he arrived in Peking, his guilt could not be proved. K'ang Chin-lung made a golden snail for him; the shell was made of gold with a living snail inside. Li Wu presented it to the empress, who was so pleased that she harassed the emperor until Li Wu was declared innocent and sent home.

There he dug up all the golden basins out of the lotus pond, looked after the fields that K'ang had bought for him everywhere, and soon became one of the richest of men.

Then, in order to fulfill his oath, he engaged workmen and raised the Loyang bridge three feet higher. The fortunes of the two traders who had opened their mouths too wide were confiscated for the construction.

· 48 · The Faithful Official

• HSÜAN-CH'ENG lies on the southern bank of the Yang-tzu River. Every year at the golden plum season there was a terrible flood. The people were powerless against this recurrent disaster, and gradually came to look upon it as belonging to the nature of things.

On one occasion during the last dynasty, the deity of the earth appeared to Governor Ch'en in a dream three days before the flood was due, and said to him, "For the past thousand years there have been two iron oxen buried on the summit of Mount Huayang. This year, in the sixth month, they are planning to go down to the sea with the flood. Now I am afraid that if the iron oxen join the river, men and fields and villages will sink beneath the flood and the land will become a great lake. You are governor here, and cannot look calmly on while the people are destroyed; you must do your duty and keep this calamity from occurring. If you knew nothing about it, it would not be your fault; but since I have told you, you must do something. I know in what manner you can save the country, but I doubt whether you are willing to sacrifice yourself."

The governor replied at once, "I am father and mother of my people and am ready to help them. If I can save them, my own life is of no account." "If you really love the people, you deserve the highest praise," said the deity. "The only thing for you to do is to inscribe the names of the people in your district in a book, and when the flood arrives at the town walls you must jump into the water with the book. There is no other means of averting the danger. I beseech you to think over my suggestion." Without further thought, Governor Ch'en agreed to the sacrifice. At that moment he heard the watchman's going and woke to find that it was exactly midnight. His dream was clear before his eyes in the smallest detail.

Soon the cocks began to crow and it became light, and the governor called in his assistants that were on duty. "During the night, two iron oxen have come out of Mount Hua-yang," they announced, "but since they are not running about, we don't think that they will do much harm."

The governor was struck by the news, because it agreed exactly with his dream. He told his experience to the officials, and ordered them to prepare within two days a list of all the inhabitants in the district. The officials worked day and night on receipt of the bad news, and sent the lists to the governor.

On the third day there was a terrible explosion on Mount Hua-yang. Two enormous water dragons broke loose, the iron oxen began to fight, and at the same time the water burst through the dikes and covered the land with a flood several feet deep. The villages and fields on the north soon sank beneath the waves, and within half a day the water had risen to the top of the city wall. Then Governor Ch'en climbed onto the wall, and at the sight of the still rising water he clasped the book in his hand and with one cry sprang into the waves. To the great surprise of everyone, a moment later the flood began to subside and the victorious iron ox and the water dragons vanished.

After the great flood was over, the people of Hsüan-ch'eng built a temple in honor of Governor Ch'en, who had given his life for them. To spread his fame abroad, they offered many sacrifices. The iron ox that had fallen in combat was carried into the town and erected as a memorial. Both the temple and the ox are there to this day.

• MANY YEARS AGO—so many, in fact, that people have forgotten her name—there lived a poor woman. She lived with her old mother-in-law and her little daughter. Because the woman was dutiful, she was always obedient to her mother-in-law and was always kind to her little daughter. But the old woman hated her, and said she was lazy.

One day she said to her daughter-in-law, "All the water we use in the house is brought by water carriers. That is too extravagant. From now on, you can carry the water or you won't get anything to eat."

The poor woman had to do as she was told. Every day, as well as feeding the pigs and the dogs, cooking the food, and mending the clothes, she had to do this hard work. As soon as it was light, she went to fetch water from the distant well. If she had not brought enough, she had to return two or even three times. No woman is strong enough for such work. But even though she lacked the strength she had to do as her mother-in-law ordered; otherwise she received no food and was beaten as well.

One day she could endure this slavery no longer. She put down her pail by the well. Seating herself on the edge, she rubbed her aching and burning feet, and said, "Oh heaven, how wretched I am! The livelong day I have to work, and at the end of it I don't even get enough to eat. Death would be better than such a life." As the thought of suicide passed through her mind, she got up to throw herself into the well.

Suddenly an old white-haired woman appeared, who motioned her back, saying, "Why do you want to die?" The woman was terrified, not knowing where the old crone had come from, but when she saw the kindly, good-natured expression on her face, she lost her fear and told her all her troubles.

"That is nothing to worry about," said the old woman. Pulling out a little wand, she continued, "I will give you a treasure. All you need do when you get up in the morning is to strike the pail with this rod, and it will be filled with water at once. But beware of striking it twice, and don't tell anyone else about it."

The poor woman did not believe that such things existed. But the old woman gave it to her with such sincerity that she began to believe in it, and eventually decided to give it a try. Thanking her benefactress, she returned home. When she secretly tapped the pail, it filled with water in an instant. Now she was very happy, because she no longer had to fetch the water; but she took care to hide the wand and to let no one see it.

Everything went well until one day the mother-in-law became suspicious. She knew her daughter-in-law had to carry water several times a day to fill the pail, but for a long time she had not seen her walking to the well, though the pail was always full. This aroused her suspicions, and she secretly watched her daughter-in-law till she discovered that, instead of fetching water herself, she tapped the pail with a strange stick. The mother-in-law waited until the woman was not watching, and she stole the little rod. Being ignorant of its magic powers, she beat the pail again and again.

Once, twice, thrice—in a flash the water poured out of the pail and covered the house and all the other houses in the whole village. All the rich fields became one big lake.

When the poor woman saw what had happened, she could do nothing, since the old woman at the well had not told her how to make the water stop, and so she was drowned in the flood. The water is still flowing out of the pail—which became a large artesian spring.

Later the people built a temple in honor of the poor woman, and called her the Water Mother.

·50· *The Tiny Temple of the City Deity*

• MANY, MANY YEARS AGO, perhaps even during the Ch'ing dynasty, there was a terrible summer drought at Hang-chou. The sun blazed down the whole day out of a leaden, cloudless sky, the plants hung their heads and dried up, and men were unable to sleep at night because of the heat.

The people prepared to offer prayers for rain. They cleared a place for the sacrifice, where day and night were heard the beating of drums and the clang of gongs and the murmur of the holy scriptures. The people fasted in vain; the sun shone hotter than before, and the sky remained clear. The rice harvest was already ruined. Then the wells dried up, which was even worse. The people burned incense and prayed again, but again their efforts were useless.

Amid scenes of wild excitement the peasants collected in bands of hundreds and thousands, and decided to go to the district governor and demand rain from him. They set off for the governor's residence. They did not wait for permission to enter, but burst past the watchmen in great numbers. The governor soon appeared and asked them what they wanted. "We beg the noble governor to order heaven to send us rain," they shouted. Wanting to avoid further trouble, the governor agreed to help them.

It was a difficult matter—he was no god to conjure up rain at will. Having given his promise, however, he had to find some means. In this sad mood he prepared for bed, but his thoughts were too troubled by the problem for sleep. He got up, washed, and without eating he told his servants to fetch the deity of the city.

Then the living man and the plaster image were placed together on chairs and fastened with chains like criminals. A huge crowd gathered to see the spectacle, since they believed the governor was sacrificing himself for his people. The governor explained, "In this world I am ruler of this province, and in the underworld he is ruler. But since he does not care that men are dying of thirst, I have had both of us placed out in the sun to see which collapses first, his plaster body or my body of flesh and blood." These words were greeted with wild applause.

All day long the governor sat in the sun, but toward evening he retired to bed completely exhausted, and in his dreams the deity appeared to him. "I am a being of the underworld," said the god, "and its concerns are my affair. This world is your affair. I consider it outrageous that you want my plaster body to fall to bits." "It is not my wish alone, but the wish of the whole people," answered the governor. "They are on the point of death, and have begged me to intercede for them. If you would only take the trouble to save Hang-chou, we should be very grateful." "My powers do not extend to making rain," replied the deity. "If you really wanted to help Hang-chou, you could," insisted the governor. But the deity continued to deny his ability in the face of all these protests.

Finally, however, he said hesitatingly, "I really can't send for rain, but if you want, you must . . ." "What must I do?" asked the governor excitedly. The deity was unwilling to explain, but, having already said more than he ought, he continued, "If you succeed in getting rain, you must on no account betray me, or I won't tell you anything." Until the governor had given his word of honor not to mention the deity, he would not say another word. Then he whispered cautiously, "Just before dawn at the fifth watch, you must go alone to Yü-huang Mountain, six or seven miles from the town, where you will see three monks approaching. Let the first monk go by, but seize the second before he can run away. Then make your request, but you must not say it was I who told you."

The governor was so excited after this interview that he leaped out of bed, to the surprise of his servants, who rushed up to find out what the matter was. He could scarcely wait for the end of the next day. The more he prayed for the sun to set, the slower it seemed to move. He went to bed at five o'clock, but rose again quietly at midnight, and crept out of the Ch'ing Po Gate, on the way to Yü-huang Mountain.

When he arrived at the top, he took a short rest after the tiring climb. At the fourth watch, being midsummer, it became quite light. Looking round, the governor saw three monks coming toward him. When they were close, he dashed out and, allowing the first monk to go by, he seized the second by the arm.

"What do you want?" asked the monk. "Why have you seized me without any reason?" For a moment the governor was too frightened to utter a word, fearing lest he might have seized the wrong man. Finally he said, "Noble Yü huang-ti, help my people of Hang-chou. Help us. We are dying of thirst. Save us." "You have really made a mistake," answered the monk; "how could you imagine a simple monk like me to be Yü huang-ti? Stop talking rubbish and let me go." But the governor continued, "Great god, pity the people of Hang-chou. Give us a little rain, or I will kneel down and never get up again," and tears poured down his cheeks like two strings of pearls.

Yü huang-ti's heart was touched by his devotion, and he said, "Get up. Get up. I will look after the rain for you, but on one condition." "Yes, anything," answered the governor, hurriedly drying his tears. "How did you know I was Yü huang-ti?" asked the deity. "I knew that myself," answered the governor. "That is not possible," answered the god. The governor was very troubled now, he thought to himself, "If I don't tell the god, he won't give us any rain; if I do tell him, I shall break my word." Breaking one's word is very bad, of course. And after a long inward battle, he decided his word was less important than the well-being of the people, and he confessed to Yü huang-ti, "The deity of the city told me." "Good!" said the monk. "The rain will appear at once." The governor dropped the monk's arm so as to be able to thank him, but the three monks had already changed into wind, and he had to content himself with making three obeisances to heaven. Then he hurried back to the town, and on his arrival at the Ch'ing Po Gate, rain began to fall. It poured and poured, and the people were overjoyed.

In the evening the deity of the city arrived and bitterly reproached the governor for his betrayal, becoming even angrier when the governor tried to explain that there had been nothing else for him to do. "You deserve death," he shouted, but seeing that the offender was unmoved, he went on more calmly, "but it is too late for regrets. I came today to ask you a favor." "What is it?" asked the governor; "I will do anything you ask. I will never break my word again." "I have been ordered to such and such a place on military service," explained the deity. "I want you to take care of my household. I must depart tomorrow. When the newly appointed city god arrives, I want my family to have some abode, and then they will be content. Good-bye. I shall meet you again in the next life." And he disappeared.

The governor could no longer sleep and, calling his servants, he sent them to look for a house. Finally, they found one with three rooms in the sheep market. In it they placed the deity's wife, his children, and all his household. Today it is called the Tiny Temple of the City Deity.

Part VII
Kindness Rewarded
and Evil Punished

The Tiger General

• THERE WAS ONCE a man whose name was neither Five nor Tiger General, but everyone called him Five Tiger General, for the following amusing reason.

One day this man went into the hills to collect firewood. As he was chopping wood he heard the sound of someone whimpering and crying in pain. Not knowing where the noises came from, he went to look and found a tigress lying beside a cave on the point of giving birth to cubs. Her entrails had come out and were caught in the thorns, which prevented their going back in again. The poor animal was whimpering in the most pitiful way, and gazed dumbly at the man, as if imploring his help. The groans became more and more heartrending, until the man could no longer doubt that she was begging him to help her.

At last he was unable to bear it and rushed home. "Mother," he said, "I have just seen a tiger in labor whose entrails have come out. She is on the point of death. You are an experienced midwife, please go and help her." "This type of birth is very dangerous," said the mother. "If we want to help the beast, the only way to make the entrails go back is to dip them in a bowl of wine."

After they had treated the tiger in this manner, four little tigers were born. The tigress was naturally very grateful. As the old woman was leaving, she jokingly tapped the tigress on the back and said, "Tigress, we are poor people and cannot afford a daughter-in-law. In return for our help, you must bring us a young girl." The tigress nodded its head as if it really understood.

One night, during a terrific snowstorm, a bridal party was crossing the mountain. Suddenly there was a roar like thunder, and five tigers rushed down the hill and closed the path. All the attendants of the bride ran away, and the mother and four tiger cubs carried the bride off to the house of the woodcutter. The man heard their knocking and went to open the door. There he saw, escorted by five tigers, a beautiful young lady. He invited her in, and that same night they celebrated their marriage.

Later the family of the rightful bridegroom heard about this affair and brought a complaint before the magistrate, accusing the woodcutter of stealing their bride. The judge sent for the woodcutter to question him. Although he told the truth, naturally no one believed him, so that his mother had to go into the hills' and beg the tigers to appear as witnesses. The judge had them led into the hall of justice and asked them, "Did you carry the bride to the house of the woodcutter?" All the tigers nodded their heads, and the accused was set free.

Some years later a rebel broke into the land with many wild beasts which none of the generals or soldiers could disperse. The emperor ordered the woodcutter to advance against them with his five tigers. In three days all the wild beasts had been so bitten by the tigers that they fled away and never dared return.

The emperor was very pleased, and accorded the woodcutter the title of "Five Tiger General" and gave him a position on the frontier. From that time the country, which had always suffered from rebellions, had peace.

• 52 • *The Gratitude of the Snake*

• THERE WAS ONCE a child of a well-to-do family. The father unfortunately died soon after the child's birth. The mother, however, carefully looked after their inheritance, and they lived quite comfortably. She sent the child to a school where there was a good teacher, and he was very happy, going there early and coming home late. But, excepting her natural love for her son, the mother was deserted and lonely.

The boy was very kindhearted and friendly toward all living things. He studied industriously, and nearly every day earned his teacher's praise. The teacher commended his work and his kindheartedness. Whenever he found an animal on the point of being killed by another, he always took the trouble to save it and bring it out of danger. He was fond of keeping animals as pets. He put wounded birds into cages, fed them, and looked after them carefully until they were well; then he set them free again.

One day, when he was coming back from school with his books on his back, he found a tiny snake, not more than three inches long, lying half dead and covered with blood in the middle of the road. His kind heart was touched, and he quickly went up and saw that it was not quite dead. He knew that the little snake must have been attacked by some large animal. Pitying the poor thing, he picked it up to look at it. Then he made up his mind to take the snake home. He took his ink box out of his packet of books and placed the little snake inside; then he went home.

His mother was standing by the door, and asked him why he was so late returning. He told her the truth. His mother did not reprove him, but fetched some ointment to put on the snake's wound and hoped that it would soon be well again. From then on, when the boy went to school, he always took the snake with him and was never separated from it. After a month the wounds were healed, and the snake began to show that it recognized him. He kept thinking he ought to let it go now that it was cured, but he could never make up his mind to do so.

Time passes quickly. Several years went by. The little snake gradually became bigger, but it never left the boy. The ink box had become too small for it, and he put it in a large pot. But that also became too small, and then it just fitted into a drawer in his study. Every day when he left for the school, he first opened the drawer and fed his pet, and the snake raised its head to receive the food he put in its mouth. He did this every day, and the snake never harmed him. Only when he brought too little, or forgot to bring it anything at all would the snake stretch its head out of the drawer, as if it were asking for its dinner.

One year it was again the time for the triennial examinations in the capital. The boy was already twenty years old. Although he was still in school, his knowledge was very great. When he heard of the examination, he begged his mother to give him leave to compete. Having received her permission, he chose a favorable day to set out. By this time the snake had become very big; but he took it with him in his luggage on his travels. He packed up all his things, took enough money for the journey, and when the favorable day arrived he took leave of his mother and departed.

In those times, traveling was not convenient. From his home there was no ship or carriage to be hired for the journey. He had, instead, to go on foot over hills and through rivers for more than a month. All this time he was alone, without a single companion. He felt very lonely, because he had never left his village before, and he was terrified at the idea of the long journey.

One day he arrived at a mountain, where he lay down to rest. He looked at the thick forest and the range of mountains, which stretched away as far as the eye could see, and he became very uneasy at the thought that he would need at least ten days to cross them.

While he was sitting on a stone, wrapped in these gloomy meditations, the snake suddenly shot its head out of the basket and stared at him without making a sound. The boy sighed and said, "Dear snake. I have cared for you since the time you were three inches long. Many years have passed, and you have grown big. I am going to the capital to take my examination, and perhaps I shall never return. I must now cross these high mountains and sharp crags all alone, and if I meet a wild beast I shall be lost. My life is hanging by a thread, and if I should die you would be shut up in my bundle of things and would starve to death. I will therefore set you free to hunt for your own food. If heaven permits me to live, you can wait for me and I will pick you up on my way home. Now you can go," and he placed it on the ground. The snake seemed to understand, for it nodded its head and disappeared into the undergrowth.

The student was now alone, and he journeyed on for ten days before reaching a small village on the other side of the forest. There he decided to spend the night, because it was already dark and there was still a long time before the examination took place. But wherever he went, all the inns were filled. He asked a servant the reason, and the man said to him, "Perhaps you don't know that the examination takes place this year, and that all the candidates lodge here on their way to the capital." "Is that the reason?" asked the boy. "What can I do?" "I am very sorry, sir," said the servant, "but really there is no room here. Have you tried the other inns?" "Yes, I have tried everywhere, but I always receive the same answer. Can't you help me?" begged the boy. "It is very difficult," said the servant. "We actually do have one small room, but we never offer it to our guests, because it is haunted. There is nothing else, though." "I am not afraid of ghosts. I will sleep there," said the boy, thinking that after spending so many nights in the open, nothing could frighten him. The servant agreed to give him the room, but refused to take any responsibility. "That is all right," said the boy. "You needn't bother about me." The servant brought his luggage and prepared the bed.

There was not a sound to be heard when he retired to his room. Thoughts of ghosts filled his mind, and he began to feel a little frightened. If anything happened, his life would have been sacrificed in vain. He thought of his home, and of his old mother who was waiting for him. She would weep her eyes out if he never came back. But it was too late for regrets.

The wind whistled outside, and the night was as dark as black lacquer. He sat by his candle, and his past rose up before him like a great flood. He felt depressed and sad, but he was also very sleepy and went to bed, because after all everything is decided in heaven and one cannot avoid one's fate. But his mother—no, he must not think of her any more. Soon he fell asleep.

About midnight he woke up; indoors everything was quiet, but the wind was whistling outside. In the room the candle, dimmed by the dark shadows, was guttering as low as a green bean. He thought to himself that it would not be of much use in an emergency. About two o'clock the wind grew stronger. The glass in the window was making a terrible din, shaking and clattering about. Then the window flew open of its own accord.

The boy woke up in a fright and ran to look out of the window. Outside he saw a dark object, like a large animal flying on the wind closely pursued by another thing. They flew in through the window and stopped by the bed, where they began to fight, one on top of the other in a terrible commotion. The boy sat on the bed and screamed for help, but the noise of battle gradually became softer and then ceased altogether. When he got up enough courage to look down, he saw the two combatants lying tangled together on the floor.

It was not yet light, but sleep was out of the question. He got up hurriedly to investigate. He found a millepede and a snake lying at the foot of his bed, with their teeth locked on each other's throat. When he looked carefully, he saw that the snake was the one he had set free a few days before. He was very sad and shed many tears, but he had the snake buried by the servant and then continued his journey.

Later, he passed the examination in the capital and was made an official in his home town. On his way back he fetched the body of the snake from the inn and took it with him. At home he built a grave for it and made a sacrifice there himself. His mother was overjoyed at his return and chose him a wife. And their life passed in peace and contentment.

·53· *The Greedy Minister*

• ONCE UPON A TIME a schoolboy found an egg lying in the road. He thought it very pretty and, not being sure whether it was a bird's egg or a snake's egg, he carried it along with him and wrapped it in cotton.

A few days later the egg cracked, and a small, thin snake crept out. The boy played with it the whole day long. He loved it so dearly that he never let it out of his sight. He even took it to school, where he played with it secretly during lessons.

Swiftly as an arrow flies the time; day after day goes by. The snake grew a fine skin, and became bigger and bigger until it would no longer fit into the shoe in which the boy had hidden it. But the boy was not afraid and continued to play with it.

One day the teacher noticed him, and said to himself, "What is that boy always doing? Why doesn't he pay attention?" Going down to the boy's place, he found the snake, which reared up angrily at the sight of the stranger. The teacher was terrified by the snake and, keeping his distance, he said in a trembling voice to the boy, "Where did you get that snake?" "I raised it from an egg," answered the boy, "I am not frightened of it; we have been friends for a long time." Then he told his pet to raise its head, and at the sound of its master's voice the snake was no longer disturbed but lifted its head at once. "Drop your head," said the boy, and it sank down again. The teacher said no more, but allowed the boy to play with the snake.

Later, the boy went to the capital to take his examinations, but he could not take the snake with him. As he was leaving, he said to it, "I have looked after you all these years. Please give me a present in return." Then the snake spat up a huge pearl. The pearl gleamed so brightly that it dazzled the eyes. It shone in the dark like the sun, and everything was visible in its light. It was an incomparable treasure. The boy was delighted and, after thanking the snake again and again, he set off on his journey.

He went to the capital, where he took one of the first places in the examinations. Now he was no longer a young student, but a grown-up man and a famous professor. He thought to himself, "It will be best to offer my pearl to the emperor, since then he will make me a high official." He gave it to the emperor.

The result was even better than he expected; the emperor was so delighted with the pearl that the young man was appointed chancellor. But now he was never content. Although, after the emperor, he was the greatest man in the land, he no longer had his treasure. How nice it would be if he could get another! With this idea in mind he asked leave to return home. He wanted to ask the snake for another pearl.

Full of anticipation, he went into the hills where the snake lived. The snake smelled the scent of human flesh and came up, hissing and spitting, to swallow the man. But when it recognized its master, it became quiet again. When the chancellor explained his reason for coming, the snake opened its mouth wide, whereupon the chancellor, thinking it was going to spit out another pearl, quickly stepped forward. However, the snake shot out its head and swallowed the greedy man.

·54· *The Man in the Moon*

• THERE WAS ONCE a young man who loved all animals and living things. One day as he was walking along, he found a swallow that had fallen at the edge of the road. It hopped about, twittering sadly. Pitying the poor bird, the boy carefully picked it up and carried it home. He nursed it with tender care, and after a few days the leg was sound again. To show its gratitude the swallow

made a bow to the boy and then flew off, but shortly it came back
with a yellow pumpkin seed in its beak, which it presented to its
benefactor.

The boy planted the seed in the garden. Day by day the plant
grew stronger and stronger. Hidden among the leaves grew an
enormous yellow pumpkin. When at last it was ripe, the boy
gathered the fruit and split it open. To his great astonishment a
stream of shining gold and glittering silver came flowing out.

The tale of this miraculous occurrence quickly spread through
the countryside, and everyone praised the kindness of the young
man. But there was a very mean child in the neighborhood who
nearly became ill with envy. His mouth watered at the tale of
such riches. He thought he would also rear a little swallow and
get the same reward. It would be easy money. So he knocked
down a swallow that was sitting on the roof, and cared for it as
carefully as the other boy had done. When the bird was cured it
really did bring him a pumpkin seed, which he planted in an
open space in front of the guest hall.

How excited he was when a yellow pumpkin grew underneath
the leaves! But on opening it, he received a terrible shock. Out
stepped a well-dressed old man, with a bill in his left hand, and a
pen and a box of red ink in his right. He wore a pleasant, smiling
expression, and said quietly to the boy, "You wicked child! How
could you be so covetous! But since you worship gold so much,
you can come along with me." Then he wrote something in the
green register, took the boy by the hand, and climbed onto the
runners of the pumpkin, which suddenly shot up like a ladder
into the sky for the two people to climb on. Beneath them the
runners dried up as they passed, so that one could go up but not
down.

Before long they arrived at the Palace of Boundless Cold in the
moon. The roads were made of shimmering jade set in silver, the
palaces were of gleaming gold and agates, everything was so
bright that one could not keep one's eyes open, and so vast that
one could see no end. Still more wonderful were the enchanting
fairies, who danced to the accompaniment of heavenly music.
Their ineffable beauty bewitched the eyes and ears of the boy,
who forgot where he was. After he had looked around for a

while, he asked the old man to take him back again. "You want to return, do you?" asked the old man. "Very well. If you cut down this cinnamon tree here, you can return home; otherwise not." Bringing a silver ax, he handed it to the boy.

In great excitement the boy rushed off with the ax to look at the cinnamon tree, which was made of gold with branches festooned with precious stones and agates. He thought to himself, "If I cut down this tree I can take it home, and then I won't need to work for the rest of my life." He raised his ax and cut a large notch in the trunk, but as he did so he felt a sharp pain in his shoulders. Looking around he saw that he had been attacked by a silver white cock. In a rage he drove it away, but when he looked at the tree there was no sign of the blow he had given it. He gave it another slash, and again the cock struck him. He drove it away again, and once more the cut he had made was not to be seen.

And so it went on and on. He remains there to this day, because the tree never receives more than a single cut before it grows back together again.

If one looks up at the moon on a clear night one can dimly see many trees and people; they are the ones that were in our story of the naughty boy in the Palace of Boundless Cold.

·55· The Gossiping Animals

• THERE WERE ONCE two brothers. The elder had a wife, but the younger had had no chance to marry, since he was a simpleton.

The younger brother sowed a field of barley, but in the whole field only one barley plant came up; it was right in the center of the field. He thought it was so beautiful that he weeded it and manured it several times a day. It grew so well that soon it bore an enormous head of barley, which the simpleton used to fondle and caress all day long.

Unfortunately, just as the barley became ripe, it was carried away by a large bird. This was too much for the simpleton, who pursued the thief, waving his hands in the air, until night fell. Then the bird disappeared, and he was left in the wild mountains, surrounded by howling wolves and roaring tigers. Feeling nervous, he looked around till he found a flat piece of ground, where he clambered up into a tall tree and hid in its branches.

At the foot of the tree brother wolf, brother tiger, and brother monkey gathered. Brother tiger said, "It is so comfortable here this evening. Do tell us another of your stories, brother monkey." The monkey replied, "I don't know any stories, but I have a piece of gossip for you." The wolf and the tiger were naturally intrigued, and the monkey continued, "To the southeast, about fifty miles from here, there is a small village. In it there is a young girl with an unknown disease, which no one is able to cure, and her father has announced that the person who cures her shall have her as his wife. It is really a very simple matter, because the doctor needs only to scratch a little dirt off his spine and make three pills out of it, and the young girl will be cured the moment she eats them."

The tiger and the wolf heaved a deep sigh. "What a pity that we are not men and cannot have such luck!" But the simpleton thought to himself in delight, "There ought to be enough filth on my back for thirty thousand pills." The three animals exchanged some more gossip and then went back into the wood.

The next morning, the simpleton climbed down from the tree, rolled three big dark pills out of the dirt on his back, and set off toward the southeast. He kept on asking the way, until he arrived at the village of the sick girl, where he heard everyone saying, "She is to marry the person who cures her." Then the simpleton produced his pills and gave them to the girl, who was cured at once. Her father was filled with joy, and gave orders to prepare the marriage at once.

While the simpleton was celebrating his marriage, his brother met his death, which came about in the following manner. The elder brother's wife had always loathed the simpleton, but he was strong and could do heavy work, so that on his failure to return she said to her husband, "The simpleton is wandering around somewhere. He ought to come home and do some work." Her husband agreed and went out to search for him. He searched until nightfall, by which time he had arrived at the tree in which his brother had spent the previous night. He also was frightened by the ceaseless roars of the wild animals, and climbed up into the tree.

Brother tiger, brother wolf, and brother monkey soon appeared, and the tiger said, "It is so pleasant here. Do tell us the day's gossip, brother monkey." The monkey replied, "Yesterday someone was sitting in this tree and made his fortune by listening to us. Today we had better make sure there is no one up there before we begin."

When the elder brother heard that, he cowered back and trembled so violently that the branches began to shake, and the animals saw him at once when they looked up. All three of them wanted to climb up and seize him, but the monkey said, "Let me go. Neither of you can climb half so quickly as I."

He jumped into the tree and flung the elder brother to the ground. He called out to the tiger, "Eat him up." But the tiger refused. Then he called to the wolf, "Eat him up." But the wolf refused. As none of them wanted to eat him there, they carried him into the hills. The wolf took a piece, the tiger a piece, and the monkey a piece. Nothing remained of the brother except the head.

• 56 • *The Butcher and the Vegetarian*

• IN P'U-CHIANG there is a proverb: "The butcher gets to paradise; the vegetarian falls into a ditch." If one takes it literally it has little meaning; but if one knows the story connected with it, he will certainly say that it has a profound meaning.

In former times there was a long copper bridge on earth, leading to the western paradise. All good men could cross over on it and become Buddhas and immortals. But later, when Lü Tung-pin was fleeing with Miss White Peony and they were pursued by her brother who was wielding an iron club, he overtook them just as they were crossing the copper bridge. Lü Tung-pin was terrified when he saw the young lady's brother coming, and smashed the bridge with his magic sword. At the same time he swore an oath that no one could ever cross over it to paradise, and this remains true to this day.

Before the bridge was demolished, there was a butcher on earth. He had a debtor who was unable to repay his money and this annoyed the butcher so much that he threatened to skin the man in pursuance of his trade. A passer-by, who heard this remark, asked the butcher how much he was owed. "A hundred cash," the man replied furiously. "Only one hundred cash?" said the stranger. "I will pay it for him."

Very astonished, the butcher asked the stranger, "Is he a relative of yours?" "No." Is he your friend, then?" "No." "Do you know him?" "No. I have never seen him before," said the man. "Why do you want to pay his debt?" questioned the butcher. "I pity him," said the man, "because if you cut off his skin he will die of cold."

Touched by his charity, the butcher thought he also should have pity on his debtor. Without either flaying him or asking for money, he went home, burnt the receipt, and never mentioned the debt again. From then on, he gave up his profession and performed so many good works that he acquired the right to enter paradise.

On his way there he met an old vegetarian, who told him that he had gained the right to paradise through denying himself all meats for forty years. He also was on his way there, and since they were going to the same place they continued their journey together. At dark they arrived at an isolated farmhouse, where they asked to spend the night.

As they entered they were very surprised to see silver tables and golden chairs, red jade teapots and cups of white jade, which completely dazzled their eyes. They thought it must be a traveling palace of the emperor, or at least the country house of a chancellor, but they learned that there was no one in the house except two young widows and four pretty servant girls. The two widows begged them to remain as stewards, and the vegetarian was charmed to comply with their wishes; but the butcher refused, because he did not consider it proper to spend the night alone with the women. He slept on the stone staircase in front of the house. Since it was summer, beyond providing a hearty meal for the mosquitoes, he came to no harm.

The next morning he was awakened by the singing of the birds in the hills, with the warm sun shining on his body. He rubbed his eyes, but the house was no longer there. He was lying in the grass by the roadside. As he stood up he heard a crunching sound, and his hair stood on end at the sight that met his eyes. The vegetarian who had traveled with him the day before had fallen into a ditch and was being eaten by two huge snakes. He did not dare to dally any longer, but went on to the western paradise as quickly as he could.

· 57 · Lü Tung-pin Tests the Ascetic

• ONE DAY Lü Tung-pin changed into a beggar with a festering leg, and went to test a man who had been endeavoring for ten years to become an immortal.

He came hobbling past the hut of the ascetic, and called out, "My foot itches so. Help me! Help me, old man!" The ascetic came out when he heard him, but he nearly fainted at the dreadful appearance of the beggar. "You want my help?" he asked. "That is quite simple. Do you want some food, or clothes, or money? Just tell me what you want, and I will give it to you. I'm not a miser." "No! No!" said the beggar. "Well, what do you want then? Tell me what it is," said the saint. "If, old man, you put your lips to my leg and draw the pus out of the wound, it will become healed at once. I prayed to the gods, and they told me in a dream that you alone could cure me."

The ascetic knit his brows and wondered whether he would be able to do something so revolting. "Can no one save you but me?" he asked. "The gods told me in a dream that you were the only man," answered the beggar. For a long while the ascetic hesitated, but at last he said, "A human life is worth one thousand pieces of gold. I will try." "I will forever be indebted to you," said the beggar. Having made his decision, the ascetic knelt down and thoroughly licked the wound. When he had finished, the leg was quite healed, and a moment later the beggar disappeared. Now

the ascetic knew that he had met an immortal, and he knelt down
on the ground and sent up a prayer of thanks to heaven.

The next day the ascetic himself ascended to heaven as an immortal. There he was able to thank his benefactor for having
made it possible to obtain sainthood.

• 58 • The Dissatisfied Benefactor

• IN A CERTAIN VILLAGE there was a very rich family, the head of
which was always doing good deeds. In summer he bought fans
and medicine to distribute; during the winter he made large
quantities of padded clothes, which he gave to any poor person
suffering from want or cold. He repaired bridges and built roads,
so that innumerable people benefited by his kindness. His fame
spread from his own village to the next, and gradually there was
no one in the whole district who did not respect him for his
charities.

Eventually his renown spread so wide that it reached the ears of
the immortals in heaven. Wanting to test him, one cold winter's
day, two of them transformed themselves into two shoeless, half-
naked beggars and stood outside his house, chattering with cold.
Suddenly, and heaven only knows for what reason, they began
quarreling, and even came to blows.

The rich man, who was seated in his house, hearing the sounds
of combat, quickly went to the door, where he saw two miserable
beggars. He went up and separated them, and then ordered the
servants to bring them clothes, shoes, and socks, and to prepare
some food for them. At the good news the beggars ceased
fighting.

They both purposely ate very slowly, so that the sun went down
and night fell before they had finished. Then they said to the rich
man, "It is dark now, master, and we have no home. Cannot we
stay the night here?" Their benefactor granted their request without any hesitation. "That's quite all right," he said. "Just remain
here. Everything is ready." He sent them off to bed.

The beggars intentionally behaved in the most disgusting manner. They spat all over the bed, and the next morning, after eating breakfast at the rich man's house, they went off without saying good-bye and without expressing their thanks in any way. They thought that their benefactor would certainly get angry with them now and curse them. But he was really a good man; after breakfast, when he did not see the beggars, he merely told the servants to clean up the room and wash the bedclothes, and never said a word against the two strangers.

Just behind his house was a well. One day a maidservant was drawing water when the rich man came by and said jokingly, "How pleasant it would be if the water in the well was wine, but as inexhaustible as water!" The next time the girl was drawing water, she noticed to her surprise that it was yellow in color. At the first sip she knew that it had really turned into wine. She reported the matter to her master, who was even more surprised than she. From then on they began to sell wine, and to sell it much cheaper than the shops.

One day a man came to buy spirits. "Why," he asked the rich man, "do you have no spirits if you have yellow wine?" After the customer's departure, the rich man thought to himself, "How pleasant it would be if the water in the bucket would turn into spirits! We could sell it." While he was speaking, the water in the bucket was suddenly changed. Now they sold brandy and were even richer than before.

One day a man asked them for some grape skins, but the rich man did not know where to get them. The buyer said to him, "You have wine. What do you mean that you have no grape skins? It's merely that you don't want to sell them."

The man went off in a temper, leaving the rich man pondering over the matter. "It is really stupid to have wine but no grape skins. It would be nice if I could have some."

Suddenly he saw the two men who had formerly fought outside his house and afterward had eaten and behaved in such a foul manner. He was greatly shocked to hear them say to him, "It is true that you are kindly and charitable, but you are too grasping. First you had wine, then you wanted spirits, and now you are demanding grape skins. There are no content men in this world. From today the wine and the spirits will vanish, and grape skins will not be available." Just as the man was going to answer, they disappeared. He hurried to the back of the house, but the spirits in the bucket had become water again and the well water had ceased to be wine.

· 59 · The Wicked Rich Man Who Was Turned into a Monkey

• MANY, MANY YEARS AGO there was a rich man living alone with his wife who had never borne him any children. Finally he decided to buy a maidservant.

Although he was very rich, he had a heart of stone and never gave away a farthing in charity. He considered poor people more despicable than dogs, and he not only refused them money and food but also cursed them, shouting, "You should have perished rather than come here." If the beggars did not take themselves off, he drove them away with a stick.

You can imagine how brutally he treated the young slave girl. If anything displeased him he cursed her and beat her, sometimes so badly as to draw blood. The whole day long the house rang with the crack of whips and foul language, and soon all his neighbors nicknamed him the "Cruel One." The maidservant, however, served her master well and faithfully, but when alone she sighed to herself, "Oh, Lord! Why have I come here? What an awful life I have! Will I never have any better luck?"

The saints and deities heard about the cruelty of the man and his wife, and wanted to discover the truth. One of them turned into a barefooted, scurvy-headed beggar, and went to the rich man's house, clad only in a few tattered rags. He called out at the door, "Mother! Master of the house! Help me! Give me something to eat. I am so terribly hungry."

It happened that the old people had gone out and only the maid was at home heating the stove. She used rice straw as fuel, and occasionally there were some grains left in the ears. She had been collecting them for some time, and now she had a bag of more than two thousand grains. So sorry was she for the miserable beggar that she gave him the bag, but she warned him saying, "Take the rice away quickly. My master is a villain. If he sees you there will be trouble, although the rice I am giving you I collected myself." When the immortal saw that she had such a kind heart, he did not go away but gave her a handkerchief. "You must wash your face with this," he said, "but be careful not to let other people use it."

Just at this moment the master and his wife returned. Seeing a beggar, they shouted at the maid, "What have you given to the beggar, slave?" They tried to beat the beggar, who ran away when he saw what they intended, but the poor girl received another dreadful whipping from her master.

She began to wash her face every day with the handkerchief, and her heavy, dark face gradually became whiter and more beautiful. Her master was very surprised, and questioned her closely. She knew she could not keep the matter secret, and therefore told him the whole story. "The only reason why my face becomes white is that I wash it with the cloth that the beggar presented me in return for the rice." When the couple heard this, they shouted at her angrily, "So you did give the beggar some rice! You must give the cloth to us." The servant was very frightened, because the beggar had told her that she alone and no one else might use the handkerchief. But she knew that if she refused she would receive another beating from her master, and so she laid it on her open palms and respectfully handed it to him.

Next morning the old couple both washed their faces with it, hoping to become as beautiful as their slave girl. But as soon as they had used it, their faces and whole appearance changed. Hair grew over all their bodies, and they turned into monkeys. They ran off into the mountains and were never seen again.

·60· The Sacrifice of the Maiden

• IN FORMER TIMES in a village in the Chü district lived forty or fifty families of brick makers, all of whom were quite rich. Living as they did from the manufacture of bricks, they were all very respectful to the deity of the brick ovens. Before building a new furnace they used to sacrifice and ask permission of the deity. When the oven was ready, they used to sacrifice a whole pig and a whole sheep in front of it. If they did this, everything was in order; but if it was not done, the bricks came out yellow or soft, and sometimes even the whole furnace collapsed.

In the village lived a rich man named Ts'ai, who spared neither time nor money to get the whole brick-making business into his hands. He built a large new furnace three miles outside the town. Nothing went according to his wishes; the first time he baked bricks, they remained yellow without being properly fired. He angrily sent for the builders and the workmen to question them, but none of them could find any explanation. Finally an old man suggested consulting a fortune teller. All agreed to this suggestion, and the owner sent for one.

The next day the fortune teller gave the following answer to the questions of the old workman: "It is true that Ts'ai offered sacrifices during the building of the furnace, but he has an evil heart. As a punishment he must offer his daughter alive, and the furnace will be all right."

The old workman reported to Ts'ai what had been said. Ts'ai immediately went to a village one hundred miles away and bought a thirteen-year-old girl for the sacrifice. At the time of a sacrifice there is also a large festival; besides the officiants, many friends and relatives come to take part.

The rich man had a daughter of his own, who as a small child had gone to another family as their future daughter-in-law. Her father now brought her home to be present at the ceremony. She was the same age and hardly distinguishable from the girl he had bought; in fact it was very easy to confuse them if you did not look carefully.

Not wanting the slave girl to be aware of her fate, Ts'ai arranged for her to eat with his daughter on the day before the sacrifice, just like a relative, and to sleep in the same bed.

Nobody in the village, except some tile workers, knew anything about the proposed human sacrifice; they thought the young girl was merely a personal attendant of the master. Ts'ai had told the workmen that when the girl arrived with their food they were to seize her and throw her into the furnace, afterward sacrificing a sheep and a pig. The same evening he told the girl to go to bed early, because the next morning she must rise early to go and call the workmen to breakfast and tell them to bring the sacrifices. The two girls went to bed, but Miss Ts'ai was so excited at the idea of a sacrifice that she thought of it all through the night and never slept a wink.

As it became light, everyone was sleeping except Miss Ts'ai. She quietly opened the door and, in place of the slave girl, went to call the workmen to breakfast. The workmen were already waiting for her arrival. When she reached the furnace, they seized her and flung her inside. Shortly after, when Ts'ai ordered the slave girl to go to the furnace, he was horrified to find no sign of his daughter. He dashed out to the furnace. When the workmen saw him, they shouted, "Everything is done as you said, Mr. Ts'ai." He was overcome by grief, and tears poured from his eyes.

·61· *The Mynah Bird*

• THERE WAS ONCE a plasterer named Liu Shan who kept a very clever mynah bird. Every morning the bird would fly up on the window sill and call with a loud voice, "Big brother! it is morning, it is morning. The sun has risen. How fine, how fine!"

One year the magistrate was having a new house built, and every day the bird followed Liu Shan to the site. Liu Shan would stand high up painting flower designs on the wall, and the bird would stand at his side so that Liu Shan could depict him. When Liu Shan dropped his brush, the bird would fly down and pick it up for him. When Liu was standing on a dangerous spot, the bird would from time to time warn him, "Big brother, be careful! Big brother, be careful!" The craftsmen all loved the mynah bird, and taught it bits of speech and little songs.

One day, just when Liu Shan began to paint a picture of the deities of luck, success, and long life, the magistrate came by and asked Liu, "What does this painting mean?" Liu answered quickly, "This is a picture of the deities of luck, success, and long life." And the bird, very ably, repeated, "Luck, success, long life. Luck, success, long life." The magistrate liked this very much, and asked, "To whom does this bird belong?" Liu said, "To me." The magistrate, smilingly stroking his long five-strand beard, pointed toward the bird, and said, "Come on, I will give you something to eat." Immediately the bird flew toward him. The magistrate smiled and stroked his beard and went away.

The next day the magistrate's housekeeper said to Liu, "The magistrate asks you to send him the bird as a gift. He will make you a gift of ten ounces of silver." Liu answered, "Please go and tell the magistrate that my bird is not for sale." The bird repeated from the beams, "Not for sale; mynah not for sale." The housekeeper went home, smiling coldly.

That year, at the time of the mid-autumn festival, Liu Shan came down with fever. He had to ask the magistrate to advance him five ounces of silver, and he promised to repay it later in the form of labor. Unfortunately, the illness lasted longer than expected. For two months Liu could not work, and so could not repay his debt.

In the winter, when the magistrate moved into the new house, he found that there was a hole in the wall of the eastern hall. He became extremely angry, and immediately sent some soldiers to get Liu Shan, intending to make him pay for his carelessness. The magistrate ordered that he hand over the bird and repay the five ounces of silver. Poor Liu had no money, so how could he repay the magistrate? But he still refused to hand over the bird, and so he was thrown into jail to await punishment.

The bird, who loved its master dearly, searched for him day after day, until one day it succeeded in getting through a broken pipe into the jail and to Liu Shan. Full of joy, the bird flew to Liu Shan and stroked him with its wings. Liu Shan, touched to tears, said, "Mynah, you have reason to be worried about me. Every day the magistrate hangs me up, beats me, and breaks my hands with crossbars, to try to make me give you to him. Brother, I have raised you since you were young. How can I let you go?" The bird could only shake its head and cry, "Ah, ah!" over and over.

From then on, the bird came every day to visit Liu in the jail. It talked to him and tried to console him. But one day a jailer heard the bird talking to Liu. He reported to the director of the jail, who immediately reported to the magistrate. Before the magistrate arrived, the bird was already on the roof, and when it saw that the magistrate had sent soldiers to catch it, it cried, "Wa, wa! You cheat the people, magistrate, but you cannot do this to me," and flew off. The magistrate became so mad that he jumped in anger and gave an order to catch the mynah within three days; otherwise he would punish all the soldiers both high and low. They ran about in the town and outside the town, searching on roofs and treetops, but the bird had long since disappeared.

Again that night the bird came stealthily to the jail to look for Liu Shan. It was happily talking to him when the soldiers caught it—they had closed the pipe. They brought the bird to the magistrate. The magistrate stroked his beard and smiled. Then he said to the bird, "Black mynah, this time you did not get away." The bird sat sadly in the cage and said nothing. This made the magistrate angry, and he said, "What would you think if I were to eat you? Do you want me to broil you or to fry you?" Then the bird said slowly, "Eat me up. Eat me, magistrate. You have been eating human flesh, drinking human blood anyhow. One day they will take your bones and feed them to the wild dogs."

This made the magistrate so angry that he cried out like an exploding firecracker, "Bastard! Bastard! Take this ugly black thing, cut it up alive, and fry it in oil." The cook quickly plucked off the feathers of the bird. Since there was no oil in the kettle yet, he grabbed his big kitchen knife, threw the bird on the block, and then went to pour oil into the kettle. The bird used this moment to struggle free. It shook its wings, but it could no longer fly. The cook was already coming back, so the bird jumped into the sewer pipe.

The poor bird stayed in the sewers for a whole year, picking up a few morsels to eat from the dirty water. Finally, in the spring its feathers grew out again.

One day the bird stealthily crawled out of the sewer and flew away. It began looking everywhere for Liu Shan. Liu, however, had fled from the jail the year before and had hidden himself in the mountains. The bird could not find him, although it searched carefully all over the town. As it flew over the main street, it suddenly heard a loud commotion—the sound of gongs and drums. It sat down on a rooftop to see what caused the commotion. Behold! It was the magistrate on his way to the temple of the chief deity of the city to perform a sacrifice. The bird quickly flew to the deity's temple.

Just when the magistrate lit the incense and offered the offerings, ready to kneel down and perform his prostrations, he heard the deity of the city say, "Today all the people of the whole city accuse you, saying that you are greedy and break the law, committing all kinds of crimes." When the magistrate heard this, his body turned cold. He fell to the floor, beat his head as one beats garlic, and began to howl in a loud voice. The deity spoke again, "If you confess all your crimes in a loud voice, perhaps I can still pardon you. But if you should dare to conceal anything, then your life, you dog, is forfeited." Crying and howling, the magistrate, kowtowing after every sentence, confessed the full story of his crimes. Then he heard the deity again, "Since you have committed so many evil deeds, your life is not worth that of a dog; you shall not be spared. But as I see that you recognize your faults, I will give you only a light punishment for the time being." When the magistrate heard the words "light punishment," he felt better and immediately kowtowed again.

Now the deity told him, "First, you must pull out your beard before my eyes, so that you do not look different from the common folk." Immediately the magistrate plucked out his beard; around his mouth, under his nose, and at his ears he removed all the hairs, not daring to leave even a small one. He had hardly finished when he heard the deity say, "Now, you must perform 365 kowtows in front of me, so that you will know how it feels to make kowtows. Then perhaps in the future you will not make the people perform kowtows in front of you."

Thereupon the magistrate quickly made his kowtows, so that he almost tripped over the deity's altar. When he had completed his 365 kowtows, his head was so bloody and battered that he fainted and lost consciousness. At this moment he suddenly heard a voice from the rafters above him saying, "Magistrate, it is me! Last year you took my feathers; this year I take your beard. Last year you broke my big brother's hands; this day I break your old pig head." When the magistrate lifted his head, he realized what had happened. But the mynah bird was already in the air.

•62• *The Helpful Animals*

• THERE WAS ONCE a poor youth who went to fish in the river every day but was never able to make a good catch.

One day his hook brought up a broken piece of an iron pot. Realizing that it was a treasure, he took it home and hid it in an iron box, which he hung upon a beam.

From that time he daily became richer. One day he engaged as servant a man who had come from beyond a river and beyond a sea. This servant wondered how his master had become so rich, and was sure he must possess some treasure. After a long search he at last found the box hanging on the beam and, secretly opening it during the night, he stole the piece of the iron pot and fled away over the river and over the sea to his own home. Then the young man daily became poorer, and the thief daily became richer.

One day the cat in the young man's house said to the dog, "Master always used to give us meat and rice, and we always got our share of what he ate. Why do we now get only soaked rice?" "Master's treasure," answered the dog, "was stolen by a thief who lives beyond a river and beyond a sea. Since he cannot get it back, we must recover it for him."

The cat agreed to this plan, and they set off. When they arrived at the sea, the dog did not know how to get across; but the cat said, "We cats can always think of a plan. How do you propose to cross?" The dog replied, "We dogs also have plans." Then they both swam across the sea. On their arrival at the river, they crossed it in the same manner.

Then the cat suggested, "Wait here. I will bring you a bone and drink a little fish soup myself, and then we can steal the treasure." They ate and drank, and about midnight the cat crept into the thief's house, went to a mousehole, and asked the mice, "Will you help us to steal the treasure?" "Certainly," answered the mice, "but where is it?" "It is inside the iron box that is hanging from one of the beams," explained the cat. "We must first consult our adviser, who will certainly know of a good plan," said the mice. The adviser was an old one-eyed mouse. It ordered the mice to clamber up the beam and gnaw through the rope that fastened the box.

The noise they made woke the wife of the thief, who asked her husband, "What is gnawing there?" Half asleep the man answered, "How should I know?" But after a while the box fell down with a bang, and she said to him again, "Do get up and see what's the matter." "Oh, go to sleep, it's nothing," said her husband, and turned over.

They were soon deep in slumber. But the mice nibbled a hole in the box, through which one of them crept, took the fragment, and gave it to the cat and the dog. Each of them wanted to carry it, but eventually the cat took it because it did not trust the dog.

When they arrived at the river, the cat took the fragment in his mouth. Halfway across, it slipped out of the cat's mouth and sank to the bottom. The dog scolded the cat, saying, "You said I couldn't be trusted with it, and now you let it fall into the water." The cat naturally had no reply, but it dived into the river and caught a water rat, which, full of terror, asked the cat if it was going to eat it. "No," said the cat, "I won't eat you if you dive to the bottom and bring me back the broken fragment." The water rat agreed to this proposal at once and, diving down, it soon retrieved the fragment. The cat took it again, and they ran on and on until they arrived at the sea.

Then the dog said, "You carried the fragment over the river; I must carry it now." Not wanting to quarrel, the cat allowed the dog to take the fragment and carry it over the sea, but just in the middle the fragment slipped out of the dog's mouth and fell into the water. They swam to a mudbank, where they angrily blamed each other. A fight ensued, during which they were both coated with mud like water buffaloes.

The dragon king, who was sitting in his palace, heard the shouts and sent a messenger to ask what the matter was. He soon learned that they were quarreling about a broken bit of iron. Since the piece in question had just fallen into the court of his palace, the dragon king ordered a servant to return it to them. The cat took it again, and the dog swam behind. When they arrived at their master's home, the cat placed the piece on the table.

When the wife saw the cat, who was as filthy as a water buffalo, she flew into a temper and shouted, "Monster! Now that we are poor, you animals have become as foul as corpses." She gave the cat such a blow that it fell down dead, and then the dog met the same fate. When they were both dead, the treasure returned to the place it had come from—that is to say, the sea.

·63· The Tale of Nung-kua-ma

• A WOMAN WAS once taking some cakes to her parents. On the way she met a man-eating Nung-kua-ma, a monster with a body like a bull, a head like a measure of rice, and sharp teeth and claws. Its eyes gleamed, and its coat was shaggy and thick. The monstrous beast roared with laughter, and said, "Give me all your cakes to eat." The woman said timidly, "I can't do that; they are for my parents." "Good," said Nung-kua-ma, "I will come back this evening and tear your flesh and crunch your bones and eat you up." The woman began to scream with terror. Fearing that men might come and catch it, the monster fled into the hills like an arrow shot from a bow.

The woman was frightened nearly to death. She did not go to her parents, since her heart was beating like that of a hunted deer. She sat in the doorway and wept. To everyone that passed she told her story and begged for their help, but everyone turned pale at the very word Nung-kua-ma and were too frightened even to reply. Naturally, no one could help her, and she began to cry even more.

Finally, a peddler came by with two bamboo baskets on his carrying pole and a little clapper in his hand. He was surprised to see a woman weeping bitterly, surrounded by a gaping crowd, and asked, "Woman, what are your troubles that you cry so bitterly?" Between her sobs the woman replied, "The Nung-kua-ma is coming to eat me . . . this evening." "My dear woman, don't weep," said the old man, "I will give you twenty needles to stick in the door. When the Nung-kua-ma arrives, it will prick itself." The peddler gave her the needles and then continued on his way, beating his clapper as before. But the woman thought that twenty needles would do little harm to the monster, and continued to sit weeping in the doorway.

Then a man arrived who collected swine, dog, and cattle dung, as manure for the fields. Seeing the sobbing woman, he asked the reason. "Don't worry," he said when she told him, "I will give you some dung, which you must stick on the door. When the Nung-kua-ma arrives, it will soil itself and run away." The woman accepted the gift, but she was still not comforted and continued to weep.

A little later a snake catcher came by with a basketful of snakes. He walked slowly along, crying, "Snakes for sale." At the sound of weeping, he also asked for the reason and was told the whole story. Then he said to the woman, "You needn't be anxious. Nothing will happen." But she begged him to help her. He said, "I will give you two big snakes which can climb trees and are terribly poisonous. You must put them in the water pot, because when the Nung-kua-ma comes in with dirty hands, it will certainly want to wash them, and then the snakes will bite it to death. You see you needn't worry." Then he put the two enormous green bamboo snakes into the pot, but after his departure the timorous woman began to weep again.

Next a fishmonger arrived, who saw that the woman's face was swollen with tears. He did not dare to question her himself, but he soon learned from other people what the trouble was. He was sorry for her and, putting three pounds of round fish into the cooking pot, he said, "Don't weep, my woman. Pay attention to me, and you need have no fear. Take this pot with the round fish, but don't put any water in or they won't bite. If the Nung-kua-ma is bitten by the snakes, it will go and wash in the cooking pot. The fish will bite it, which ought to frighten it away at least, if it doesn't finish it off." But when the fishmonger had gone, the poor woman began crying again.

Next an egg seller appeared, calling, "Eggs. Good Fresh eggs.

Eight for ten cents." He also saw the weeping woman, and asked, "Good woman, why are you weeping? It breaks my heart to hear you. Have you quarreled with your husband, or your mother-in-law, or your sister-in-law?" The woman told him her sad story, though she never imagined that such a man would be able to help her. At any rate, it could do no harm, she thought. However, the egg seller said, "Don't worry. Don't weep. I will give you ten eggs to hide in the ashes on the hearth. When the Nung-kua-ma is bitten by the snakes and the fishes, it will try to stop the bleeding with ashes. Then the eggs will burst in its eyes and blind it." But the woman was still frightened and did not stop weeping.

Finally, there came a man who sold millstones and iron goods. When the weeping woman confided in him, he also promised to help her. "I will give you a hundred-and-twenty-pound mill-stone," he said, "which you must hang on the framework of the mosquito netting around your bed. Prop it from beneath, and fasten it to the bar with a wire; and when you hear the Nung-kua-ma coming, cut through the wire, and it will be crushed by the stone." Then he added, "I will also give you an iron tool. If it is still not dead, you can finish it off with that. Now there is nothing more to be done. Just follow the instructions carefully." Now the woman was finally consoled, and she went into the house to prepare everything before evening came.

She lay alone in the pitch darkness, with the iron tool clasped in her hands in case the monster arrived. The first and second night watches went by, but although she strained her ears listening she could hear nothing. The third watch began at midnight. The sky was blue, with scarcely a star to be seen, since the bright moon shone into her room and lit up the floor. A cool, refreshing wind sprang up. She was so tired that she soon fell asleep. Suddenly she heard a noise. It was footsteps, and she knew the Nung-kua-ma had arrived. Hardly daring to breathe, she listened carefully and clasped her iron tool more securely.

"Open the door!" shouted the beast. "If you don't open it, I will eat your bones." With three kicks, it broke down the door. A scream and a curse followed, as it scratched itself on the needles and got the dung all over its hands. "What's all this?" it roared. "You've made me get my hands all dirty, you filthy woman." The door was now open, but it said, "I must first wash my hands. There is time enough afterward." It went across to the water jar. But as soon as it dipped its hands, the green bamboo snakes bit it in the finger and it screamed with pain as the red blood flowed out.

With all its strength, the monster shook off the snakes and then went across to the cooking pot, thinking to itself that the water there must be safe and clean. The moment it touched the water, something else bit it in the finger, which made it cry out even more loudly, "Another of this hag's tricks! I will smash all her bones. But first I must quench the blood at the hearth." While it was burrowing in the ashes, all the eggs exploded and bits of shell flew into its eyes and blinded it. "Damnation!" he cried. "Things are going from bad to worse. I have never met such a woman. I can't stand it."

Now it no longer cared about the pain, but burst screaming into the bedroom in such a fury that it tore off its eyebrows on the door beams, though with its mind full of revenge it did not feel the pain. It bellowed, and threatened: "You filthy old hag! All your tricks can't kill me. Now I am in your room. In a little while, I shall eat you up, bones and all. Only then will I get my revenge." With these words, it grabbed the mosquito netting. The woman cut through the wire with her knife, and bang! The heavy millstone dropped on the beast's head. Its bones were crushed and the blood gushed out like a river. It began to scream in agony, whereupon the woman beat it with the iron tool until it was quite dead.

In this way she escaped being eaten. Instead of being devoured herself, she had killed the monster. She sold it for a great sum of money, and bought everything she wanted.

·64· *Tales of the San Kuan*

• MANY YEARS AGO Mount Yün-t'ai in Chekiang Province was completely surrounded by the sea. On the summit of Mount Ling-chou lived a rich man named Ch'en Kuang-jui.

One day his wife was feeling ill and wanted some fish soup. Ch'en bought a large carp, but as he was preparing to cut it up, the fish suddenly began to weep. This was more than Ch'en could bear, and he ordered the cook to carefully cut off three scales and then put the fish back in the water. The cook prepared a soup with the three scales, and Ch'en's wife was cured.

Shortly after this, Ch'en Kuang-jui found that he had to go south to assume an official post to which he had been appointed. He engaged passage on a large merchant ship, whose captain, however, was the pirate Niu Hung. As soon as the ship had passed the bridge of the nine dragons at the outer headland, the captain threw Ch'en into the sea and tried to compel his wife to live with him. Naturally the wife was disgusted with his proposal, and she contrived to be left in peace by telling him that she was expecting a child. Niu Hung, however, masqueraded as Ch'en Kuang-jui and took up the post with Ch'en's wife.

The wife of Ch'en was actually expecting a child, and after three months a son was born to her. Fearing that the cruel Niu Hung would harm her child, she wrapped it up in red and white silk and placed it in a wooden pail. She then bit her finger and wrote a letter in her own blood, which she hid in the pail, and dropped the child into the river. From that time she pretended to be ill, and refused to live with Niu Hung.

The monk in the temple of the Golden Mountain had risen early and was watching the waves dancing on the river when suddenly he heard the soft crying of a child. The sound gradually came nearer, until he saw something dark being driven toward the mountain by the waves. The crying seemed to come from this floating object. He went down to the foot of the mountain and here he saw a child, wrapped in red and white silk, lying in a wooden pail. He carried it up to the temple, and when he saw the letter written in blood he knew where the child had come from. He put the letter away and kept the little castaway as his disciple, giving him the name of T'ang-seng [floating monk] because he had floated ashore.

When T'ang-seng was fourteen or fifteen years old, all the little temple novices used to mock him. "Floating monk! Floating monk! Man without name or family!" they cried. T'ang-seng wondered whether he really had no parents, and one day, being no longer able to bear the uncertainty, he ran to ask the monk. The monk gave him the letter written in blood, from which he learned that he belonged to the Ch'en family, that his father had been thrown into the sea by Niu Hung, and that his mother was still living, but living in shame. Tears came into his eyes, and he wept over the misfortunes of his parents. The monk comforted him. "Your father is not really dead," he said; "he is now in his old home in Mount Ling-chou." The monk was a supernatural being, and knew everything that had happened. T'ang-seng dried his tears at the welcome news, and took leave of his teacher on that same day. He thrust the letter into his pocket, and went in search of his parents. He carried with him a wooden fish clapper.

For ten long years the wife of Ch'en continued to feign illness, but her longing for her husband and child finally ended by making her a real invalid. For several days she heard someone beating a wooden fish clapper outside the garden wall. Every beat of the clapper went straight to her heart. She said to her maid, "Go to the garden gate and see who is beating a clapper." The maid came back to tell her that it was a fifteen-year-old monk. For some reason the woman pitied him and told her maid to let him in. The monk knelt down before her and said, "Are you not the wife of Ch'en?" She admitted that she was, and asked if he wanted alms. The monk shook his head and produced the letter. At the sight of this, the woman began to weep, for she now knew that the young monk was her son.

T'ang-seng told his mother how he had become a monk on the Golden Mountain, and how he had discovered where she lived, and at last he told her that his father was not dead. This report made his mother so happy that she immediately ceased crying. She was afraid, though, that Niu Hung would discover her son and injure him, and therefore she told him to go and find his father and ask him to send a request to the emperor to have Niu Hung arrested.

T'ang-seng took leave of his mother and went across the sea and over the hills, beating his wooden fish clapper until he arrived at Mount Yün-t'ai.

We must now return to Ch'en Kuang-jui. After he was thrown into the sea by Niu Hung, a young man carried him off to the crystal palace, at the same time continually thanking him for saving his life. Ch'en asked him why he called him his savior, and the young man answered, "I am no other than the third son of the dragon king. I had turned myself into a carp and gone for a swim in the sea, but I was caught by a fisherman and sold to you. Did you not save me then?" The young man took him to the dragon king, who knew already that Ch'en had saved his son's life. He was very friendly to him, and kept him in the crystal palace for ten days.

Ch'en gradually began to feel homesick and wanted to return home. The prince said to him in secret, "Don't accept gold and silver from my father, but ask for the little box on the table." Ch'en went to the dragon king and asked leave to depart, and though the king pressed him to stay he remained firm. Then the king sent for gold and silver, but Ch'en merely shook his head, until the dragon king asked him what he wanted. "I want the little box on the table," he said. The king did not seem very pleased at this request, but since Ch'en was the savior of his son, he could not very well refuse him.

The third prince escorted him up to Mount Yün-t'ai, and then took leave of him and returned to the dragon king. Ch'en went back to Mount Ling-chou, and on arriving home he opened the little box. Inside he found three flowerpots, which turned into beautiful laughing maidens. One said, "I am the eldest daughter of the dragon king." The second said, "I am his second daughter." The third said, "I am his third daughter." They all three became Ch'en's wives, and two or three years later they each bore him a son.

Encircled by the sea on Mount Yün-t'ai, Ch'en knew nothing of the outer world. He often thought of his former wife, but did not know whether she was alive or dead. One day, when he was sadly thinking of her, T'ang-seng appeared, beating on his wooden fish clapper. From him Ch'en learned that his wife was still alive, and that the pirate Niu Hung was administering his post in his name. Needless to say, Ch'en was infuriated by this news, and he engaged a ship on the same day to go to the capital and make a report to the emperor. With the soldiers he was given, he went to the south and killed Niu Hung.

He took his wife back with him, and the nine people lived together in the greatest happiness. There is still a palace called Harmony, built in memory of Ch'en, standing on this point. Formerly the palace was in Ling-chou, but after it had been burned down three times, it was rebuilt at this place. T'ang-seng, however, was a monk and could not always live with his family. Hiring a boat, he left Mount Yün-t'ai and traveled about the world.

Being grandsons of the dragon king, the three sons of the princesses all wanted to be appointed princes by Chiang Tzu-ya at the investiture of the gods. The eldest son said to the youngest, "Brother, go and see if the old man has also given us an appointment." The youngest son went to Chiang Tzu-ya, who appointed them to be the three officials (San Kuan), and without delay the youngest son took the place of honor as inspector of heaven.

After a while, when his brother did not return, the eldest said to the second brother, "Brother, go and see what has happened to our younger brother." The second, however, also learned that he had received a post as inspector of the waters.

Seeing that his brothers did not return, the eldest son finally went himself. He saw his youngest brother in the post of inspector of heaven and his second brother as inspector of the waters, and only the post of inspector of earth was still vacant. He ought to have received the post of inspector of heaven, but his brother was already seated in it, so in ill-humor he took the only one remaining. Later the people built a temple on the outer cape in honor of the three brothers, and one can see that the eyes of the inspector of earth are still red with anger.

After his death, Niu Hung thought of nothing but injuring the descendents of Ch'en Kuang-jui. Before many years had passed, he was reborn as excellency Chin.

He deceived the emperor, saying, "The people of Yün-t'ai are becoming so overbearing they will certainly soon rebel. I beg you to transport them to the interior and set a watch on them." The emperor believed his minister, and sent orders that all the inhabitants of Yün-t'ai were to be moved into the interior. The three officials received no more incense and, to avoid starvation, moved to Shansi.

Eighteen years later the emperor permitted the people to return to their homes, and the officials were given their sacrifices again.

·65· *The Wishing Stone*

• THERE WAS ONCE an old man with three sons, but the sons had never learned anything and sat around all day doing nothing.

One day the old man called his sons to him and said, "Year by year I grow older. You are more than twelve years old, but you never went to school to learn a trade, and after my death you won't be able to feed your families." Then the boys answered, "We will go to work tomorrow." They made a plan that they would meet again in three years' time. Their mother cooked a great bowl of rice, which they all ate together, and the remains she gave to her sons for the journey. Then they went to sleep.

At midnight the eldest son got up, rubbed his eyes, went to the bowl, ate some mouthfuls of rice, and set off along the broad highway.

When the second son awoke, he saw that his brother had already left and, quickly jumping up, he ran to the fire, gobbled up some food, and followed his brother along the road.

The sun was already shining on the straw roof of the cottage before the third son awoke. "The others have already gone," he said. "I had better be off." He hurried across to get some food but, not fancying the rice water left in the pot, he did not eat it but ran out of the back door and went along the byway.

The third son wandered along for two days and two nights, until he came upon a troop of men with small gongs and drums. He went nearer and saw that it was a theater company. He stood quite still watching, until the audience had gone away and the drums and gongs had ceased to beat. After a time one of the players said to him, "What are you waiting here for?" "Nothing," answered the third son; "I would like to learn to be an actor." "You can stay with us if you like," said the man. "We will teach you to play the second clown."

In this way the third son joined the troop. He wore a costume, twanged the guitar, and jumped and danced about until his clothes were worn to tatters. Everyone who heard his songs and his playing said, "How beautifully he plays!"

He traveled all over the land, and like a flash the three years went by.

One day, at the thought of his old mother, he threw himself on the ground and wept. Then he thought of his brothers, who were waiting for him at the meeting place, and he wondered why he had not returned. He took his guitar, pulled on his tattered old trousers, and traveled day and night toward his home.

After two days he arrived at the shores of a great sea and could go no farther. On all sides were high waves and clouds, and there was not a single ship to be seen. The rollers were breaking continuously over the sandy beach, and he felt so sad that he wanted to cast himself into the sea. First, however, he took out his guitar, plucked the strings, and began to play such a sad melody that the tears coursed down his cheeks. He was thinking of his parents, and with these thoughts in his mind he strode singing into the sea.

Suddenly, he heard a call like a human voice and, looking up, he saw before him a messenger of the dragon king with his wave-dividing banner. The envoy said to him. "My master, the dragon king, is enchanted by your song. He begs you to come down to his kingdom and sing something before him." When the third son agreed to follow him, he raised his banner and beat the waves, which parted before them, leaving a broad road for them to walk upon.

The dragon king was delighted to see the singer, and asked him, "Was it you who were singing so exquisitely on the beach? You must be very hungry now, so please drink a little wine and have something to eat." In a flash, crab servants appeared and placed delicious-smelling dishes before him. Being very hungry, the young man ate everything without even noticing what it was. After the meal he began to sing so wonderfully that the dragon king stroked his beard in pleasure, and at the end the dragon prince ordered him to appear before him.

The third son remained three days in the Dragon kingdom, but then he thought of his parents and wanted to return home. The dragon prince asked him anxiously, "Are you not happy here?" "Of course, I am happy," said the third son, "but when I think of my mother I become sad." "I understand," replied the prince. "Tomorrow you can return home. If my father wants to give you gold and silver, don't accept it, but ask for the precious stone that I wear on my breast. If later you are in difficulty, you need only to ask the stone for something and it will appear."

The next morning, as the third son was taking his leave, the dragon king said, "I will give you silver." "I do not want silver," said the third son. "Then I will give you gold." "I do not want gold," said the young man. "If you do not want gold or silver, what can I give you then?" said the king. "I want the jewel that the prince is wearing on his breast," said the third son.

For a long time the dragon king remained wrapped in thought, but eventually he turned to his son and asked, "Are you willing for him to have it?" The prince gave his assent at once and, removing the stone, he put it in his friend's hand. Then two messengers of the dragon king escorted the third son back to the beach, from where he rushed off to the meeting place at which his brothers had been awaiting him many days.

A few days later they arrived home. Their mother had almost wept her eyes out longing for her sons. But when she heard of their return, her sight was restored and she soon saw her sons standing before her. Then they went in to their father, who had become much more wrinkled in the meantime. He asked them, "Eldest son, what trade have you learned?" "I became a coppersmith," answered the young man. "Good. And you, second son, what did you learn?" "I am a silversmith," answered the second son. "Good. Last born, what did you become?" "Father, I became an actor." When the parents heard that their son had become nothing but an actor, they were so incensed that they lost control of themselves. It was not long before they died of indignation and sorrow.

In the next three years the three brothers married, one after the other. One day the eldest wife said to the second, "Our youngest brother-in-law does nothing the livelong day and never earns a farthing. Since his brothers burned his guitar, he only bangs on a bench and makes a frightful din, with the result that our children can't sleep. We ought to divide the inheritance; otherwise the third son will eat up all we have." "Yes, we must do that," said the second wife.

When the third son heard of the division, he took a couple of poles, a few bundles of straw, a big caldron, and two broken plates. Calling his wife, he went over to a small uncultivated piece of ground, not more than an acre in extent, where he inserted the poles, laid the straw on top, and in this manner built a house, in which he lived with his wife. Every morning he went into the hills to gather wood, and they lived from hand to mouth.

Later, the cold northwest wind came and blew against the straw hut, and the autumn rain beat against the doors. The third son could no longer go out and collect wood; he lay on his bed the whole day and looked into the cooking pan, which contained only water. From time to time he drank a little to warm himself and then rubbed his hands.

Suddenly he remembered the wishing stone of the dragon king, and he called to his wife, "What would you like to eat? What about some fish and some roast? Choose whichever you like." His wife was still in bed, but now she turned over and resettled the straw on her legs. "Don't make such silly jokes," she grumbled. "If only we had a bowl of bean curd to eat!" But her husband asked her again, "Don't you want any fish or meat?" But she paid no more attention and, after cursing him for being a fool, turned over and went to sleep.

He, however, secretly rubbed the stone, and said "Dear stone, we do so want a bowl of bean curd and some fish and some meat." In a flash, a spirit appeared, with a dish of bean curd in his left hand and a dish of meat and fish in his right. Putting these down on the ground, he said, "Poor devil! I hope it tastes good," and disappeared.

The third son woke his wife and gave her the bean curd, which she gobbled up in a moment; then he offered her the fish and the meat. She was still suspicious, but when she looked at the plates, they were piled high with delicious fish and fat pork. She seized them and ate as much as she could, until the fat ran down her clothes.

Afterward she asked her husband, "When did you buy this food? Or did you steal it?" Slowly and carefully he pulled the wishing stone out of his pocket. "I didn't buy it," he said. "I got it from the stone. Anything I ask for I can get."

Then the woman cried, "If you possess such a treasure, why

don't you ask it to build us a beautiful house? Our old hovel is soon going to fall down." So he grasped the stone firmly, and said, "Dear stone, build me a beautiful big house." Immediately a spirit appeared, and said, "Poor devil! Enjoy living in it." And from then on, the man and his wife lived in a wonderful tiled house.

One day the eldest brother had to climb onto the roof to mend the tiles, and from there he saw his youngest brother clad like a prince, riding through the village on a stallion. He quickly ran down and said to the second brother, "Come and look. Our brother has turned robber; he has stolen a horse, and obviously means to attack us."

When the youngest son arrived at the house of his brothers, dismounted, and knocked at the door, no one opened it. Finally, he heard his elder brothers shouting, "You wretch! You villain! You never do any work, and now you have become a thief." But the youngest son explained, "I have a wishing stone; why should I rob others? Look at the large house, over there among the trees, which belongs to me."

Filled with curiosity, the brothers looked in the direction indicated, and sure enough, there was a beautiful house in the wood, gleaming like silver in the sun. The sight of this persuaded them to open the door and let their brother in. "What is your wishing stone?" they asked eagerly. "I need only to ask for something, and it is there," explained the brother. "Can't you lend it to us for two days?" begged the two elder brothers.

The third son took the stone out of his pocket and put it on the table, where it fell in two pieces, one of which he gave to his eldest brother, putting the other back in his pocket. They talked a little longer, and then he went home.

The eldest brother shut the doors and began to stroke the stone. "Stone, stone, I want great riches," he said. Immediately the spirit appeared with a heap of gold. "Poor devil! I hope you enjoy it," it said. But the brother frowned, and said angrily, "I own fields and have enough to eat. Next time, don't call me poor devil."

While he was speaking, a great gust of wind blew through the house, the money disappeared off the table, and the spirit sprang into the air and vanished. The half stone flew away out of the window.

Meanwhile, the third son was seated at his meal. The half stone came in through the window and, after circling around a few times, it joined the other half, which had flown out of his pocket. Then both halves fluttered off like two butterflies and slowly sank beneath the sea.

66 · *Cinderella*

• THERE WERE ONCE two sisters. The elder was very beautiful, and everyone called her Beauty. But the younger had a face covered with pock marks, so that everyone called her Pock Face. She was the daughter of the second wife, and was so spoiled that she was a very unpleasant girl. Beauty's real mother had died when Beauty was very young. After her death she turned into a yellow cow and lived in the garden. Beauty adored the yellow cow, but it had a miserable existence because the stepmother treated it so badly.

One day the stepmother took the ugly daughter to the theater and left Beauty at home. Beauty wanted to accompany them, but the stepmother said, "I will take you tomorrow if you straighten the hemp in my room."

Beauty went off and sat down in front of the stack of hemp, but after a long time she had only divided half of it. Bursting into tears, she took it off to the yellow cow, who swallowed the whole mass and then spat it out again all neatly arranged piece by piece. Beauty dried her tears, and gave the hemp to her mother on her return home. "Mother, here is the hemp. I can go to the theater tomorrow, can't I?"

When the next day came, her stepmother again refused to take her saying, "You can go when you have separated the sesame seeds from the beans."

The poor girl had to divide them seed by seed, until the exhausting task made her eyes ache. Again she went to the yellow cow, who said to her, "You stupid girl! You must separate them with a fan." Now she understood, and the sesame and beans were soon divided. When she brought the seeds all nicely separated, her stepmother knew that she could no longer prevent her going to the theater. However, she asked her, "How can a servant girl be so clever? Who helped you?"

Beauty had to admit that the yellow cow had advised her, which made the stepmother very angry. Therefore, without saying a word, she killed and ate the cow. Beauty had loved the cow so dearly that she could not eat its flesh. Instead, she put the bones in an earthenware pot and hid them in her bedroom.

Day after day, the stepmother would still not take Beauty to the theater. One evening, when the stepmother had gone to the theater with Pock Face, Beauty was so cross that she smashed everything in the house, including the earthenware pot containing the cow's bones. Whereupon there was a loud crackling sound, and a white horse, a new dress, and a pair of embroidered shoes came out. The sudden appearance of these things gave Beauty a terrible start, but she soon saw that they were real objects. Quickly pulling on the new dress and the shoes, she jumped on the horse and rode out of the gate.

While she was riding along, one of her shoes slipped off and fell into the ditch. She wanted to dismount and pick it up, but could not do so; at the same time she did not want to leave it lying there.

She was in a real quandary, when a fishmonger appeared. "Brother fishmonger, please pick up my shoe," she said to him. He answered with a grin, "With great pleasure, if you will marry me." "Who could marry you?" she said crossly. "Fishmongers always stink." Seeing that he had no chance, the fishmonger went on his way.

Next, a clerk from a rice shop went by, and she said to him, "Brother rice broker, please give me my shoe." "Certainly, if you will marry me," said the young man. "Marry a rice broker! Their bodies are all covered with dust."

The rice broker departed, and soon an oil merchant came by, whom she also asked to pick up her shoe. "I will pick it up if you consent to marry me," he replied. "Who could want to marry you?" Beauty said with a sigh. "Oil merchants are always so greasy."

Shortly a scholar came by, whom she also asked to pick up her shoe. The scholar turned to look at her, and then said, "I will do so at once if you promise to marry me." The scholar was very handsome, and so she nodded her head in agreement. He picked up the shoe and put it on her foot. Then he took her back to his house and made her his wife.

Three days later, Beauty went with her husband to pay the necessary respects to her parents. Her stepmother and sister had quite changed their manner, and treated them both in the most friendly and attentive fashion. In the evening they wanted to keep Beauty at home, and she, thinking they meant it kindly, agreed to stay and to follow her husband in a few days.

The next morning her sister took her by the hand and said to her with a laugh, "Sister, come and look into the well. We will see which of us is the more beautiful." Suspecting nothing, Beauty went to the well and leaned over to look down. At this moment her sister gave her a shove and pushed her into the well; then she quickly covered the well with a basket. Poor Beauty lost consciousness and was drowned.

After ten days the scholar began to wonder why his wife had still not returned. He sent a messenger to inquire, and the stepmother sent back a message that his wife was suffering from a bad attack of smallpox and would not be well enough to return for some time. The scholar believed this, and every day he sent salted eggs and other sickbed delicacies, all of which found their way into the stomach of the ugly sister.

After two months the stepmother was irritated by the continual messages from the scholar, and decided to deceive him by sending back her own daughter as his wife. The scholar was horrified when he saw Pock Face, and said, "Goodness! How changed you are! Surely you are not Beauty. My wife was never such a monster. Good Heavens!" Pock Face replied seriously, "If I am not Beauty, who do you think I am then? You know perfectly well I was very ill with smallpox, and now you want to disown me. I shall die! I shall die!" She began to howl. The tender-hearted scholar could not bear to see her weeping, and although he still had some doubts he begged her forgiveness and tried to console her. Gradually she stopped weeping.

Beauty, however, had been transformed into a sparrow, and she used to come and call out when Pock Face was combing her hair, "Comb once, peep; comb twice, peep; comb thrice, up to the spine of Pock Face." The wicked wife answered, "Comb once, comb twice, comb thrice, to the spine of Beauty." The scholar was very mystified by this conversation, and he said to the sparrow, "Why do you sing like that? Are you by any chance my wife? If you are, call three times, and I will put you in a golden cage and keep you as a pet." The sparrow called out three times, and the scholar brought a golden cage to keep it in.

The ugly sister was very angry when she saw that her husband was keeping the sparrow, and so she secretly killed it and threw it into the garden. It was at once transformed into a bamboo with many shoots. When Pock Face ate the bamboo shoots, an ulcer formed on her tongue, but the scholar found them excellent. The wicked woman became suspicious again, and had the bamboo cut down and made into a bed. When she lay on it, innumerable needles pricked her, but the scholar found it extremely comfortable. Again she became very cross and threw the bed away.

Next door to the scholar lived an old woman who sold money bags. One day on her way home she saw the bed and thought to herself, "No one has died here; why have they thrown the bed away? I shall take it." She took the bed into her house and had a very comfortable night.

The next day she saw that the food in the kitchen was already cooked. She ate it up, but naturally she felt a little nervous, not having any idea who could have prepared it. For several days she found she could have dinner the moment she came home. Finally, being no longer able to contain her anxiety, she came back early one afternoon and went into the kitchen, where she saw a dark shadow washing rice. She ran up quickly and clasped the shadow round the waist. "Who are you?" she asked, "and why do you cook food for me?" The shadow replied, "I will tell you everything. I am the wife of your neighbor the scholar and am called Beauty. My sister threw me into the well; I was drowned, but my soul was not destroyed. Please give me a rice pot as head, a stick as hand, a dish cloth as entrails, and firehooks as feet, and then I can assume my former shape again."

The old woman gave her what she asked for, and in a moment

a beautiful girl appeared. The old woman was delighted at seeing such a charming girl, and she questioned her very closely about who she was and what had happened to her. She told the old woman everything, and then said, "Old woman, I have a bag which you must offer for sale outside the scholar's house. If he comes out, you must sell it to him." And she gave her an embroidered bag.

The next day the old woman stood outside the scholar's house and shouted that she had a bag for sale. Maddened by the noise, he came out to ask what kind of bags she sold, and she showed him Beauty's embroidered bag. "Where did you get this bag?" he asked, "I once gave it to my wife." The old woman then told the whole story to the scholar, who was overjoyed to hear that his wife was still alive. He arranged everything with the old woman, put a red cloth on the ground, and brought Beauty back to his house.

When Pock Face saw her sister return, she gave her no peace. She began to grumble and say that the woman was only pretending to be Beauty, and that actually she was a spirit. She wanted to have a trial to see which was the genuine wife. Beauty, of course, knew that she herself was the real bride. She said, "Good. We will have a test." Pock Face suggested that they should walk on eggs, and whoever broke the shells would be the loser. Although Pock Face broke all the eggs, and Beauty none, Pock Face refused to admit her loss and insisted on another trial.

This time they were to walk up a ladder made of knives. Beauty went up and down first without receiving the tiniest scratch, but before Pock Face had gone two steps her feet were cut to the bone. Although she had lost again, she insisted on another test—that of jumping into a caldron of hot oil. She hoped that Beauty, who would have to jump first, would be burned. Beauty, however, was quite unharmed by the boiling oil, but the wicked sister jumped into it and did not come up again.

Beauty put the roasted bones of the wicked sister into a box and sent them over to her stepmother by a stuttering old servant woman, who was told to say, "Your daughter's flesh." But the stepmother loved carp and understood "carp flesh" instead of "your daughter's flesh." She thought her daughter had sent her over some carp, and opened the box in a state of great excitement; but when she saw the charred bones of her daughter lying inside, she let out a piercing scream and fell down dead.

·67· *The Great Flood*

· IN A MOUNTAIN VILLAGE lived a woman and her son. She was more than fifty years old; her son, Chou Ch'eng, was exactly nineteen. They were very poor and earned their living by collecting firewood.

Every morning Chou Ch'eng hung his ax on his carrying pole and went into the mountains. Every day by mid-day he collected a large load of firewood, which he would take into the town to sell. With the money he received he would buy some rice and go home, where his mother would have dinner ready for him. He would put down his stick, and while he ate the meal he would tell his mother all that had happened during the day. By the time he had finished it would be nightfall and time to go to bed. The next morning he would go out for firewood as usual, and his mother would cook the rice bought the day before, eat some of it, and keep the rest for her son. In this manner the days went by.

One day Chou went to the hills as usual. His mother had finished dinner and was mending his clothes when she heard the loud clang of a gong ceaselessly beating outside. Putting down the clothes, she went to the door to see what it was, and there she found an old beggar monk. She said to him, "We are poor people and have no spare rice. You must go elsewhere." "Lord Buddha! I am so hungry," said the monk. "Please give me the rice you are saving in the pot."

The woman was frightened when she heard this, because the rice pot was standing in the house and he could not know what was in it. Fearing he might be a saint, she said to him, "The rice in the pot is really for my son. But if you are very hungry, I will give you half of it. Please wait a moment." She went back into the house, put half the rice into a bowl, and brought it out to the monk.

While he was eating he said to her, "I have something important to say to you. When your son Chou Ch'eng comes home, tell him to return to town and buy some sheets of paper and some flour, prepare some paste, and then stick some straw and the paper together to make a boat. When the eyes of the two lions in front of the big temple in the village become red, you must both get into the boat, because the land here will disappear and the town will be covered by a large lake. But remember this: if you see sparrows, ants, or snakes swimming in the water, you may save them; men or wolves, however, you must on no account assist. Do you understand?" Then he went away.

The woman looked up at the sun and, calculating from its place in the sky that her son would soon return, she went into the house, poured the rest of the rice into a bowl, and then went out again to watch for his coming. Since there was no sign of him, she went in again and tidied up the clothes that she had mended; when he still did not come, she went and stood at the door.

The sun was slowly sinking behind the hills in the west. The birds, who had already retired to their nests, were singing their bedtime songs. She became tired from standing by the door, and was worried and anxious about her son.

Only when it was almost dark did she see him coming, and she felt as if a load had been lifted from her heart. She saw that he had a bag on his stick, and was pleased that he was bringing the rice. "Hurry!" she called out. "Why are you so late today? After dinner I have some news for you." "I have already eaten," answered the son. "As I was coming home from the hills today, I met an old man who wanted to buy all my wood. He didn't ask the price, but wanted me to carry it back to his house, which was more than thirty li [about ten miles] away.

As I put down the load, I saw a delicious-looking meal standing on the table, which the old man invited me to partake of. At first I refused, but he insisted on my eating, and being very hungry, I did take some. Afterward, I was afraid he would give me no money, but in the end he gave me twice as much as I ordinarily receive. When I told him that I had to go into town to buy rice, he suggested that I should buy a bushel of rice from him, and he gave me much more than usual." Chou Ch'eng pointed to his bag.

While they were talking, they went into the house. After putting down the bag, he asked his mother what had taken place at home during the day. She told him all about the beggar monk who had urged them to make a boat of straw and paper, but her son was skeptical and asked her, "How can a paper ship carry people?" "That's not our business," replied the mother. "This monk was really a saint, because otherwise how could he know you were called Chou Ch'eng and that there was still some rice in the pot?" Usually Chou agreed with his mother, but this evening he thought she was wrong.

However, the next morning Chou went into the town to buy the things and then came home to paste the ship together. Meanwhile, his mother washed the rice and cooked one pot full, and then another to serve as provisions on the boat. By midday the boat was ready, and Chou ran off to the temple to look at the lions' eyes; but seeing them as white as usual, he went home. Then he went again, but still there was no change to be seen. He returned again and again, until his mother said to him, "It is too late for them to become red today. Wait until tomorrow."

During the night neither could sleep well, and they got up long before the sun rose. Chou rubbed his eyes and ran off to the temple, while his mother packed the clothes and put them into the boat together with the rice, a pot, a bowl, a basin, and a sieve, not even forgetting the old bed.

Again and again the son went to the temple, but the eyes were still not red. In the evening, as he was running there again, people asked him why he continually went there. Chou called out to them, as he hurried by, that he was going to see if the lions' eyes were red. Two young wags heard him say this, and thought to themselves, "What a fool Chou is! How can the lions' eyes become red? Let us paint them ourselves and see what he does."

When Chou Ch'eng went once more, and this time saw that the eyes were red, he rushed home to tell his mother the news, helped her into the ship, and then went on board himself. Scarcely were they inside, when they heard an appalling crash, and on opening their eyes again, they saw nothing but water all around. Their craft, however, was floating on the water just like a real ship, perhaps even quieter. However, it had no rudder and went wherever it wished.

Chou was so horrified that he could barely utter a word. But his mother kept on murmuring, "So many people have met their death. What a disaster! The saint told me that if we saw a sparrow, a snake, or an ant swimming about, we could save them, but not a man or a wolf."

Just as she spoke, a swarm of ants came by, and when they were near enough, she fished them out with the sieve. Then a snake appeared, and Chou rescued it and put it in the boat.

It was nearly evening, but although it was near autumn it was not at all cold. So they sat in the boat and looked into the water and up at the sky. Then they saw a sparrow fly by and prepare to settle on the boat; but, seeing people on board, it became frightened and flew up and down without daring to alight. Chou called out, "Sparrow, come down and I will save you." But the sparrow only flew up higher, on and on, until it became exhausted and fell into the sea. But it fell not far away, and Chou was able to reach it with his hand and rescue it.

Suddenly the ship began to shake. Chou, looking around, saw a white wolf clutching the side and preparing to jump in. Chou wanted to knock it off and began to beat it, but the wolf kept jumping up, until at last Chou's mother called out, "Let it come in, my son. Poor wolf; after all, it is also a living thing." Chou ceased to hit the wolf, and it sprang into the boat.

After a while a man came swimming by, quite exhausted, and Chou asked his mother what he should do. "Of course, save him," she said. "Since we have saved a wolf, we can't very well let a man drown." The ship moved in the direction of the man, and Chou put out his arms and pulled him into the boat. He soon recovered enough to thank Chou for saving his life. He asked his name and the name of his mother, saying at the same time that he was called Wu Yi and that, of his family of five people, all except he, who could swim, had been drowned. "Don't talk so much, Chou," his mother said. "Hurry and give him an old coat to change into and then let us eat."

While they were eating, Wu Yi continued, "I cannot thank you enough for rescuing me, and as a small recognition I should like to call you 'Elder Brother,' but I don't know if this idea would please you." Before Chou had time to answer, his mother said,

"That is a good idea. But as Chou is much younger than you, he must call you 'Elder Brother.'" So Wu Yi knelt down before the mother, and Chou accepted him as his blood brother. They found so many things to talk about that they quite forgot their desperate plight.

It had become dark, and on all sides the sea stretched out to the horizon. There was no wind, but the ship sailed along without the three persons feeling any danger. Chou fed the animals they had saved, and then they went to bed.

Next morning when they woke up, the sun was high in the sky and the boat was lying on the shore. Chou jumped ashore and looked around, but there was no sign of men—nothing but mountains and hills. He carried his mother from the boat, and Wu Yi helped him to take off their belongings. The small animals ran off, but the wolf ran backward and forward, as if it wanted to remain with its rescuers.

They chose a nice spot on the island, and built themselves a house of straw and stone to live in. They still had a little rice, and so they did not suffer from hunger. Then Chou discovered that there was a town thirty li away. He and Wu collected firewood, which they took into the town and sold, thereby gaining enough for their livelihood.

One day, when Chou had just felled a large tree, a thick black cloud came up from the northwest. Chou thought to himself, "In fairy tales such black clouds are always evil spirits. I will give it a blow with my ax." As the cloud came roaring and blustering by, with all his might he hurled his ax into the air. When the ax fell down again, it was covered with blood.

The cloud sped away toward the southeast, and Chou pursued it with his weapon. After chasing it for about five li, he saw it disappear under a stone, which, he found on going nearer, was concealing something. With a great effort he managed to lift it up, and underneath he saw a dark hole stretching into the earth.

He carefully replaced the cover and, after marking the spot, took up his ax and returned to where he had left Wu Yi. "I have been searching everywhere for you," said Wu. "Where have you been?" "I was right about the dark wind cloud," answered Chou. "There was a spirit in it, which I wounded with my ax. Look!

There is still some blood on it." "Oh, don't bother about that," said Wu Yi. "It is almost dark, and we must be getting home. Mother will be waiting at the door."

Noticing that his brother was in an ill humor, Chou said no more but stuck his ax in his belt and took the load of wood. Since it was already late, they went straight home without going into the town.

When they got near home, Chou was surprised not to see his mother standing at the door. When he looked closer, he saw the wolf eating something. Yes, the wolf he had rescued from the water had killed and eaten his mother. With a roar he raised his ax and dashed out the wolf's brains, but his mother was dead. They both wept.

Wu Yi was the first to recover himself, and said, "Don't weep, brother. She is dead, and all our tears won't bring her to life again. Let us carry her into the house, and tomorrow we can sell our wood and buy a coffin to bury her in." Chou wiped his eyes, and they both carried the body into the house. They began to weep again, and went to bed without eating anything.

The next day Chou stayed with the body, while Wu Yi went into the town, sold the wood, and bought a miserably cheap coffin. They placed the body in it and buried it in a beautiful spot. Then they began to collect firewood again.

One day Chou went to town to sell wood. At the town gate he put down his load and rested a while. A crowd of people were standing in front of a red notice on the gate. Being unable to read, Chou asked an old man what it was all about. The old man answered, "On such and such a day, the daughter of His Excellency Wang was carried off from the garden by an evil spirit in a cloud. The man who finds her will receive 10,000 ounces of gold, and if he is over twenty and under thirty she will become his wife."

When he heard this, Chou remembered his experience a few days earlier. But before saying anything, he wanted to go home to ask his brother's advice. He took his load, went into the town, found a purchaser for the wood, and then went home.

He told Wu Yi the contents of the red notice, and asked him if he would accompany him and climb down into the spirit's cave. "Of course I will go with you," Wu said. "If we don't find her, we are no worse off. If we do find her, we shall become rich and have a wife."

Next morning Chou went into the town. When he had found the house of Excellency Wang, he said to the doorkeepers, "Please tell His Excellency that I am here. I know where his daughter is hidden. I want to return her."

The doorkeepers informed their master that a man had come who claimed to know where his daughter was hidden. Wang sent for him at once, and asked him his name, where he came from, and what he knew about his daughter. Chou told him his name, and said, "One day while I was collecting wood on the eastern hill, a dark storm cloud came up from the northwest. As I had always heard that dark clouds were evil spirits, I decided to try to wound it with my ax. When the ax fell down again, it was all bloody. I pursued the cloud to a hole in the hills which was covered by a stone. All this occurred on the same day that your daughter was stolen."

"If you are telling the truth, then she is lost beyond hope," said Wang in despair. But he became more cheerful when Chou said he would climb down the hole and look for her. "Go there at once. Do you need soldiers or weapons?" he asked. "No." said Chou. "Only a basket and a long chain and a few bearers with a chair to bring your daughter back."

Excellency Wang ordered everything to be prepared, and Chou sent a messenger to his house to tell Wu Yi all that had happened. Then he thrust his ax into his belt and set forth. Outside were gathered fifty or sixty people sent by Wang and a large crowd of sightseers. Chou and Wu led the way, followed by the whole crowd.

Spurred on by their excitement, they soon arrived at the spot. Chou said to Wu, "Brother, fasten the chain to the basket, and tie the bell to the other end. I will then get into the basket, and you must let me down. If I pull the chain, the bell will ring and you must pull the basket up again at once." Then Chou tightened his belt, grasped his ax, took the stone cover off the hole, climbed into the basket, and was let down into the hole.

The farther down he went, the broader the hole became, until, about thirty or forty feet down, he touched bottom. As he was coming down, everything was dark below and bright above; now everything was bright below and dark above. He sprang out of the basket and looked around. The place was like a garden; beautiful trees and flowers such as he had never seen before were growing everywhere. The ground was covered with such perfectly mown grass that he hardly dared walk on it. To the west, he could see an artificial mountain. Although it was light, there was no sun in the sky.

Chou did not waste time looking at all these wonders but, grasping his ax, he set off in the direction of the artificial mountain. From there he would be able to see everything. Before he reached it he heard a terrible noise and, turning around, he saw a stone house among the trees. With great care, he peeped through the door, and there he saw an ogre asleep in a chair. It had a gray-blue face, red hair and a red beard, and huge lips, through which two great tusks protruded from its mouth. It was wearing a long, old-fashioned black robe and black trousers, beneath which could be seen a black foot covered with golden hair. On the foot was a great bleeding wound. A bowl of hot water stood on the ground beside it, and on its left sat a beautiful young maiden, with a pale and tragic face, who was continually wiping the sore with a sponge and hot water.

Chou coughed slightly, until the maiden heard him. She motioned him to go a little to the side so that the ogre should not see him, and then she went out to him. Chou asked her, "Are you not the daughter of Excellency Wang?" "Yes," she said, "but why have you come here?" "I am looking for you," he replied. "Oh!" she sighed, "the ogre is so dangerous. It has seven heads, and if one is cut off another grows at once. A few days ago it was wounded in the foot by a woodcutter, and I have to wash the wound. At the moment it is sleeping."

Just then, there was a rumbling sound and the ogre awoke. The girl signaled to Chou to hide in the woods and, returning to the spirit, she continued to wash its wound with the sponge. The ogre rolled its eyes and roared, "I smell human flesh." "But, Master," cried the maiden, "I have not been here long. Perhaps I still smell of human flesh." Satisfied by this, the ogre went to sleep again.

Chou silently ran back to the entrance, tugged the chain to have the basket let down, and then climbed into it and was rapidly pulled up.

"The maiden is there," he told the excited people, "but the spirit is very dangerous. It has seven heads, but I will find a way to dispose of it." Then he said to Wu, "When I have killed the spirit I shall send the maiden up first, and then come up myself." Wu nodded, but already an evil plan was forming in his mind. Chou, however, suspected nothing and let himself down once more.

When he arrived at the bottom, he grasped his ax, crept through the woods to the door, and listened until he was sure the ogre was asleep. The girl was still washing the wounded foot with hot water. When she glanced up, he showed her the ax and she nodded assent. He crept up behind the ogre and cut off one head, but immediately a new one grew, which he also cut off; only after the last head had fallen was there any blood. "Now it is dead," said the maiden, "but why did you take such risks for me?"

Chou told her everything, and she said to him, "As one never knows what may happen to one, I will give you a token." Taking a golden clasp from her hair, she broke it in half and gave Chou one of the pieces. "This is your token," she continued, "and three years is the appointed time, after which it is no longer good."

Chou hid the clasp in his clothes and, leading the maiden to the basket, he shook the chain. Wu knew that the maiden would come up now, and he quickly pulled the chain. Yes, she was very beautiful. The maidservants that Wang had sent led her to the litter and stood around her.

Then Wu called out, "Quickly! Close the hole! The spirit is coming!" The people had turned to look at the maiden, and did not remember that someone was still in the hole. Now they all ran up and helped Wu fill up the hole and then, amidst rejoicing, they returned to Wang's house.

Wang had no sooner seen Wu than he said, "This is not Chou Ch'eng. He was at most twenty years old, and you are more than thirty. How dare you pretend to be Chou!" Then Wu answered, "Chou asked me to come instead of him, but I will bring him." He went out, wondering to himself what he could do and whether he would have to go out and collect firewood again.

Chou was waiting for the basket to descend again, when sud-

denly a shower of sand and stones poured down and nearly killed
him. Then the stones stopped falling, but there was no sign of
the chain; he saw that the hole had been closed. Sighing, he
thought to himself that his end was near, because nowhere could
he find another exit from the cavern. "Whether the hole has been
shut or not does not matter, because I cannot get out without a
basket and chain. I can only await my death." He wandered aim-
lessly about, until suddenly he saw a little white dragon sitting on
a pedestal swishing its tail. Seeing it fastened with a nail, he went
up, and pulled the nail out to let the dragon get down, and said,
"We are companions in sorrow."

Meanwhile, he had become very hungry, because he had eaten
nothing the whole day. He sat down on a stone to see what the
dragon would do. It came to the stone he was sitting on, licked it
with its tongue, then wriggled back to the grass, curled up, and
went to sleep. Chou was very hungry, but there was nothing to do
except lie down and try to sleep.

When he awoke, he was still hungrier. Day and night were the
same, and therefore he did not know how long he had slept. The
little dragon wriggled up again, licked the stone, and then went
back to sleep. Wondering why it did this, Chou decided to try it
himself. The moment his tongue touched the stone, his hunger
and thirst left him. He was delighted with this discovery, because
now his most pressing need was solved. He licked the stone, slept,
and admired the flowers and trees. In this manner the time passed
without his knowing.

One day when he was fast asleep he heard someone call his
name. He was very surprised, since he could see no living thing
except the dragon, which was lying at his feet. "Did you call
me?" Chou asked the dragon. "Yes, I did. I want to repay your
kindness," it replied. "Tomorrow is the day on which I fly up to
earth." "What day is tomorrow?" asked Chou. "Tomorrow is the
second day of the second month," said the dragon. "Punctually at
midday I fly up, and can take you with me." "How can you know
that tomorrow is the second day of the second month?" asked
Chou, "and how do you know when it is noon? You cannot see
the sun here." "I can feel it," replied the dragon. Without saying
another word, it hurried off.

Chou, naturally, was overjoyed. He decided to take home a bit of the stone that allayed hunger and thirst. Although he hacked at it with his ax until his arms ached, he could not break off even the tiniest piece. Seeing it was hopeless, he went for a walk in the garden, then licked the stone for the last time, and went to sleep.

When he awoke, the dragon was lying by his side. "Is it time to go?" he asked. "Yes," said the dragon, curling itself up. "You must get on to my back, shut your eyes, and not open them again until I tell you. Hold my horns tightly." Then Chou heard a clap of thunder, and the wind whistled in his ears. "Open your eyes," said the dragon a moment later. Chou found himself falling gently into a heap of grass, outside the town of Excellency Wang.

When he learned in the town that Wang's daughter was not yet married, he went to the house and announced his arrival. But he had been so long in the hole where there was no sun that his skin had turned a dirty yellow color, and his clothes were hanging in rags. Believing him to be an impostor, Wang greeted him in a distant manner, but he did not venture to send him away.

Instead, he thought of a difficult test, and said to Chou, "Although you say you are Chou Ch'eng, I cannot recognize you. Perhaps my daughter could do so, but first I shall set you a task. If you can do it, you may see my daughter." Chou asked hesitatingly what the task was. "I have two bushels of beans," said Wang, "There are two kinds—one is yellow; the other, black. The two kinds are mixed, and you must separate them in half a day." Then he called the servants and, ordering them to lock Chou up in an empty room, he gave him the beans.

Chou did not dare refuse, but he was very depressed, and thought, "This is a clear refusal of the wedding. But why does he set me such a hard task if he does not want the marriage to take place?" After looking at the beans, he lay down to sleep, since it was impossible to separate them. Then a flock of sparrows appeared; some picked out the yellow beans, others the black, and soon they were all divided.

At dusk the servant returned. When he saw the beans already separated and Chou sleeping peacefully on the ground, he called out, "Mr. Chou, how did you complete the task so quickly?" Chou woke up to see the servant standing in front of him and the beans nicely divided into two piles, but he was careful not to utter a word, because he had no idea who had divided them. The servant, however, thought he was in a bad temper, and went off laughing to inform his master of what had happened.

When Wang heard of it, he mixed a bushel of rice with a bushel of corn and ordered Chou to separate it during the night. Chou, however, was so angry that he decided to do nothing but lie down and go to sleep. Then many, many, ants came and divided the seeds for him, so that when he awoke he saw that the task was done. He could scarcely believe his eyes, and wondered to himself what spirit was helping him.

In a short while the servant arrived, saw the rice and corn divided, and went to tell his master. Wang did not believe it and went in person to see the two heaps, but not a single seed was in the wrong place.

However, he set one more task. In the west room of the treasure chamber there were ten bars of gold. If Chou could carry them into the east room, Wang would take him at once to his daughter; but if he failed, Wang would have him executed. While Chou was being led to the treasure chamber, he was quite happy, because he thought it would be easy to take ten bars of gold from one room to another. To his horror, he found them more like pillars than bars. Each one was ten times as heavy as anything he could move. He thought to himself, "Well, I shall certainly have to die this time, but at least I shall sleep first." While he was sleeping, snakes came and rolled the bars, one after another, into the east room, so that when Chou woke up he saw with delight that all the gold was already moved. "Certainly some god is helping me," he thought.

Then he asked to be brought before Wang. "I have fulfilled all the tasks that you gave me," he said. "Now you must fulfill your promise without giving me any more tasks."

Wang first went to the treasure chamber to see if the bars had really been moved. When he saw them all in the east room, he thought, "He certainly must be Chou Ch'eng. If he had not been so strong and wise, he would never have managed to kill the evil spirit." But to Chou Ch'eng, he said, "It is possible that you are the real Chou Ch'eng, but I have no means of deciding. First, my daughter must see you."

Then a maidservant led him to the door of the ladies' apartments, and told him to wait. Through pearl doorhanging, marvelous perfumes were wafted toward him, making his senses reel. From inside he heard a voice ask, "Have you the token?" He took the half of the golden clasp out of his breast pocket and gave it to the maid. The daughter compared it with her own, and then ordered the maids to take Chou to the guest rooms and inform her father.

Wang led him to the bath, and when he was washed, he gave him a beautiful gown. He sent for the calendar and, seeing that the next day was favorable for weddings, he decided that they should be married at once. There is no need to tell what a sumptuous room Chou was given and what a marvelous bed he slept on.

Next day, all the relations, friends, and guests were there; great trumpets blared, and everyone was very happy. The bride and bridegroom made their obeisance to heaven and to earth and then went into the bridal chamber. When they both had drunk many cups of wine, and all the servants and other people had left them, his wife asked him softly, "Beloved, why did you come so late?" Then Chou Ch'eng told her everything that had happened since their separation. How incalculable is the course of life!

They went on talking for a long time, till suddenly they heard shouting and screaming in the court. The young wife called to the maid, "Autumn Scent, what is the matter?" "A thief fell down from the chimney and was killed," replied the maid.

Chou went out to see, and the maid led the way with a candle. Outside in the courtyard the torches shone as bright as day, and Chou saw that the dead man was his blood brother Wu Yi.

Chou no longer had to collect firewood, but lived happily ever after.

·68· *The Story of the Serpent*

• IT IS SO LONG AGO that I have forgotten in what district the lotus pond was in which every year the lotuses bloomed red in

May and June, bigger than the head of a man. The strangest thing was that they rose above the water at night and sank down in the morning. No one knew what the explanation was, but anything that was placed on them went under with the flower.

At that time a monk heard about this lake and spread the report, "This lotus flower is connected with the western paradise. It is a lotus throne such as the Buddhas of the three ages have. If virtuous people sit on this seat, they can go straight to heaven."

A few days later all the men and women in the town had heard this report, and everyone more than sixty years old seated himself on the lotus flower and went to the western paradise.

Three or four years passed, and no one knows how many old men and women had traveled to heaven on the lotus. The mother of the district governor became sixty years old at this time and, having heard these tales from her maids, she decided to go to paradise herself. She said to her son, "My son, I am just the same as other women. They can all ascend to heaven; being now sixty years old, I have decided to go there tomorrow and not waste any more time on earth. I hope that you will lead a virtuous life and prepare for the world to come. If I see your good life from the western paradise, it will be a great comfort to me."

The official was horrified at his mother's decision. He had heard the reports about the lotus pond from the maidservants. He said to his mother, "You cannot believe such stories, Mother. Don't think any more about it, I want to keep you with me for a long time yet, and I won't let you go."

His mother was very angry when she heard this. "You want to be district administrator, but you don't yet know how to look after your own mother. All sons, daughters, and wives rejoice when their old parents attain paradise, but you want to hinder me. You are a most undutiful son."

Quickly the official answered, "Forgive me, Mother. Do as you will. I will prepare some food for you and order all the things that you will need in the western paradise." But his mother cut him short. "I don't need anything," she said. "In the western paradise one is in the realm of the Buddha and needs nothing to eat. I will take only some incense and a staff—nothing else. Order the litter. I want to leave tomorrow at dawn."

The official withdrew but, after thinking the matter over for a long time, he formed a plan. He ordered his servants and employees to fill a great number of sacks with gunpowder and quicklime. During the night he loaded them onto two ships and sailed off to the lotus lake. The lotus flower was standing several feet above the water, and he poured sack after sack into it. The flower opened and shut, and then sank into the water, carrying the gunpowder and quicklime into the western paradise.

The next morning the official arrived with his sons, his daughters, and all his relations, to escort his mother to the western paradise. On their arrival at the lotus lake, the people collected around and said, "The lake has been turned into a big river by an enormous serpent." The official at once ordered his servants to catch the snake and cut it open.

After they had hacked away for three days and three nights, they brought out bushels of heads and innumerable buttons off the clothes of the old people. The gunpowder and the quicklime were still burning. Everyone now knew that this enormous lotus flower was the tongue of a giant serpent.

Part VIII
Cleverness and Stupidity

·69· *The Mirror*

• WANG THE THIRD was a stupid man. One day his wife wanted him to buy her a wooden comb and, being afraid that he would forget it, she pointed at the narrow moon crescent in the sky and said, "Buy me a wooden comb, but it must be just like the moon in the sky."

A few days later, the moon shone full and round in the sky. Wang the Third remembered what his wife had told him and, since his purchase was to be as round as the moon, he bought a round mirror and took it home.

The moment his wife saw it, she stamped on the ground, fled back to her parents' house, and said to her mother, "My husband has taken a concubine."

The mother-in-law looked into the mirror and said with a sigh, "If only he had chosen a young woman! Why did he take such a hideous old hag?"

Later they brought the case before the district judge. When he saw the mirror, he said, "How dare you people, when you have a quarrel, dress up just like me! It's unbelievable."

·70· *The Living King of Hell Dies of Anger*

• THERE WAS A LANDLORD who exploited the farmers so much that they all called him the Living King of Hell.

The landlord owned seven mou [about one acre] of land at the foot of the eastern hill, which he rented out to a farmer. This tenant was diligent, worked very hard on his field, and when he had paid his rent after the harvest, he still had some surplus for himself. When the landlord saw that the tenant had some surplus, he became angry and tried to figure out how it would be possible to get all the rice of this farmer.

One day, wrinkling his brows, he developed a plan and had the tenant brought before him. Then he told him, "Next year you do not have to pay rent. We will just simply divide the harvest evenly. Do you agree?" "Very well," answered the farmer obediently. "All right," said the landlord smilingly. "My half is the upper half, and yours is the lower half." "Yes," said the farmer.

When, next year, the time for the partition of the harvest came, the Living King of Hell came joyfully to the field. But when he looked, he drew cold air into his mouth: the whole field had been planted with taro. He regretted his words, but because he had made the agreement there was nothing for him to do but angrily to take the worthless leaves of the taro home.

When he was home, he planned again to strip the farmer of all his harvest. He had him brought to his house, and said, "Next year we will again divide the harvest evenly; but I will take the roots, and you the stalks." "All right," said the farmer happily.

When the landlord came to the fields at harvest time the next year, he saw that the whole field had been sown with wheat. He became extremely angry, but since he had made the agreement he could not back out of it. So there was nothing to do but silently take the roots home.

He still did not give up. He thought to himself, "The last two times I could not strip you, but next time I shall." When he had found a good method, he had the farmer called again, and told him: "Next time at harvest I want to have both ends, and you can get the middle." "All right," said the tenant, and he left undisturbed.

When the next harvest time came, the landlord was sure he could strip the tenant of his harvest. But then he discovered that the tenant had grown only popcorn, and there was nothing on both ends of the stalks. Without a word he went home. He was so mad that he could not sleep for a number of nights, and soon he died.

·71· *Money Makes Cares*

• CH'EN PO-SHIH was a famous rich man in Ch'üan-chou about one hundred years ago. He had so much money that he was al-

ways busy investing it, lending it, and receiving and paying out
taxes. From morning to night he never had a moment's peace. He
had little time to eat—he never had dinner till late at night.

His wife pitied him for all the worries he had, and kept saying
to him, "Look after yourself. Please don't slave yourself to death."
Ch'en Po-shih agreed with her, but he did not know how to avoid
his work.

His neighbor, Li the Fourth, was as poor as a church mouse. As
a laborer, he earned only three hundred coins a day; but that,
with the one hundred and eighty that his wife managed to gain
through her energy and thrift, was sufficient to keep them alive.

Li was an industrious man, and it was usually evening before
he stopped work. Then he went home, gave his wife the money
he had earned, and worried about nothing else. If he was in a
good humor he sang songs to a flute or a mandolin, and that was
his only amusement.

The sound of his playing and singing was borne across to the
house of Ch'en Po-shih, but Ch'en was too busy to pay any attention to the strains of the mandolin or the flute, or even to hear the
carefree talk of his two neighbors. He was going through his bills
with his debtors or tenants, and till far into the night he had no
time for food.

His wife, however, was saddened by the gay sounds. After the
people had gone and Ch'en was eating his evening meal, the
sound was still to be heard. His wife said to him, "Listen, Li
sounds so happy, although he is so poor. We are so rich, and yet
we are never happy."

"Have you never heard the proverb, 'The penniless man has
plenty of time'?" asked Ch'en. "He can be gay, because he is poor.
It would be quite easy to make him quit singing. We need only
give him some money." "If you do that, he will be happier still,"
answered his wife. "Wait till tomorrow," said Ch'en. "If you still
hear him singing, I will admit that I was wrong."

Next morning Ch'en sent a servant to ask Li to come to his
house. Li did not dare to refuse, and appeared at once. "How
have you been getting on lately?" asked Ch'en. "Oh, sir, we have
been neighbors for so long you must know what I do. Working
for other people, one has no time to wonder whether one is well

or badly off," answered Li. "Exactly," said Ch'en. "You will never earn much as a laborer, and since as old neighbors we more or less belong together, I have thought of something for you. I will give you five hundred pieces of silver, which you can use to start a promising business. You can take the money with you; you needn't come back later to repay it." With these words he handed Li the five hundred pieces of silver.

Never having dreamed of such an offer, Li could only stammer out, "Many thanks for your kindness." Then he took the money and rushed home in a wild state of excitement to tell his wife all that happened. Now he no longer went to work.

The power of money is really uncanny. After Li had received the silver, he did nothing but wonder how he could use it to the best advantage. He could find no completely satisfactory solution. In the evening he arrived an hour late for dinner, which he gulped down quickly. Naturally he had no time for singing or playing; on the contrary, he groaned and sighed, and tossed about on his bed all night without getting a wink of sleep.

Ch'en and his wife listened very carefully that night to hear what neighbor Li did, but there was no sound of music. "Was I right?" Ch'en asked his wife, and his wife smilingly admitted he had won his bet.

For two nights Li could get no sleep. On the morning of the third day he was so exhausted that he could hardly stand or sit, but just sleepily rolled about in bed. Suddenly the deity of luck appeared before him, and said, "Money makes cares. Think of that, and bother no more about it."

Li understood at once and, leaping out of bed, he hurried over to Ch'en's house and returned the money just as he had received it. "Well, Li," asked Ch'en, "have you any plans?" "No, I have no plans," answered Li. "I am here today to give you back your money, and to thank you for your kindness." Placing the money in Ch'en's hand, he left the house.

Li felt as though a weight had been taken off his heart. He went home and slept the whole night through. The next day he went out to work, and in the evening the sound of his singing and playing was heard in Ch'en's house.

A few years later Ch'en himself became poor, but the singing and playing of Li still continued.

• THERE WERE ONCE two friends of approximately the same age who loved one another very much. Whenever they did anything or ate anything, they always did it together. Later one of them became ill and died. The other one was very upset, and soon he too fell ill and died like his friend.

After their death they became a two-headed phoenix with four legs and two wings; their bodies had grown together, so that wherever they went they were always together. They collected food in the woods every day or ate fruit from the trees.

One day a hunter with his gun went hunting in the forest and saw how this bird ate fruit in the trees: one head picked a ripe fruit but, instead of eating it, gave it to the other head to eat. When the hunter saw that they loved one another so much, he could not bring himself to shoot the bird.

The hunter told everybody about the double-headed bird. Quickly the story spread until finally, I do not know how, even the king heard about it. He sent a hunting official into the forest to catch the bird. When this official came into the forest, he searched for a long time without finding the phoenix. But one day, early in the morning, he saw the bird eating fruit in the top of a tree. He took his gun and aimed but, before he could fire, the double-headed bird had gone to another tree. When he took aim the second time, the bird again flew away. And so it went several times. The hunter was helpless, and since it had now grown late he could do nothing but sadly go home with his head down.

At home he pondered a long time until finally he thought of a plan. Day and night he wove a great many nets, and then he went into the forest before dawn and put the nets on some branches where fine ripe fruits were growing.

When it became light the double-headed phoenix flew to the tree to pick some fruit, and the nets entangled its feet so that it could not fly away. As soon as the hunter had trapped the bird, he immediately presented it to the king.

The king kept the phoenix in a very fine cage and every day fed it the best of fruits as well as other food and sugared water. Although the phoenix was detained in the cage, its two heads still loved one another as before; they ate together, drank together. When the king saw that they loved one another so much, he became very jealous and devised a plan to separate the two heads so that they would become two phoenixes. He now gave food only to one head and not to the other. But as soon as the one which received the food saw that the other had none, it did not eat anything at all, no matter how much they tried to force it.

Many such attempts failed. The king became very angry, and cried, "This phoenix does not obey me at all." He sounded the gong and called all his ministers to the court. "Whoever among you succeeds in separating the two heads of the phoenix so that they become two living birds will receive half my kingdom." A high official said, "If Your Majesty keeps your word, I will undertake this job. But you will have to allow me to take the bird home. Within a month I can achieve this task." The king granted him this wish and reaffirmed his promise in front of all his high officials. Then he gave the bird, together with the cage, to the official.

At home the high official hung the cage under the overhang of the roof, and every day fed the bird the best of food. All day long he sat in front of the cage and observed how the two heads ate together. In his heart he kept thinking of how he might divide the two heads so that he could get half the land, as the king had promised. After he had thoroughly studied the bird for a few days, he found that once each day the two heads were turned for a short while in opposite directions. He thought to himself, "This must be the way to separate them from one another."

The next day, when he saw that the heads turned away from each other, he quickly went to the head next to him and said into its ear, "Tsh-tsh-tsh." Then he immediately went back into the house. When the other head turned back, it asked, "What did the official tell you?" The first head said, "He said something, but I did not understand a word."

And so it went, the second day, and the third day. As soon as the two heads of the phoenix were turned away from one another, the official went to the head to which he had spoken the first time, and said, "Tsh-tsh-tsh." Then he immediately went back into the house. The other head always asked, upon turning back, "The official always tells you something; tell me about it." But the head which had listened to the words of the man really could not tell his beloved other head what he had said, and could only answer, "He said something, but I did not understand a word." Then the other head began to be suspicious, and said, "I guess the official plans to kill me. Why do you not tell me honestly what he said?"

For many days the official continued to repeat his "tsh-tsh-tsh" into the ear of the one head when the two heads were turned away from one another, and then he always went quickly into the house. The other head always asked, "What did the official tell you?" His companion always gave the answer, "He said something, but I did not understand a word."

Eventually the head which did not hear the talk of the official began to believe less and less in what his companion said. So they began to quarrel. Finally, once when they were quarreling very bitterly, they pulled strongly and the flesh which connected them in the center tore apart, so that the one phoenix became two.

When the high official saw that the two birds were separated, he was extremely happy. Immediately he took them to the king and asked for half the king's land. But the king said, "Do not hurry. Make your request again slowly."

After that, whenever the high official mentioned his request, the king always had flowery words and clever sayings by which he silenced the official. Finally, the man got nothing. Even the hunter who had captured the double-headed phoenix did not get any reward from the king.

·73· *The Donkey in Kuei-chou*

· THERE ARE NO donkeys in Kuei-chou. Once a man brought one up the river on a cargo boat; but on his arrival he saw that it could not be used in the high mountains, and so he set it loose. A tiger saw it, and was terrified by the enormous beast, which he thought must be a god. He hid in a wood to observe it. After a while he approached a little nearer, but the donkey pretended not to notice anything.

The next day the donkey brayed, and the tiger ran away in a terrible fright, thinking that the donkey was going to bite him. He was still afraid when he went up and looked at it again, but it did not seem to have many tricks.

Gradually he became used to the braying. He went nearer and nearer, now in front, and now behind, but did not yet touch it. Day by day he became braver, until at last he gave it a push. At this the donkey could no longer contain its anger and lashed out with its leg, much to the delight of the tiger, who now knew that the donkey had no other means of defense. He leaped on to its back, tore open its neck, and ate it.

A donkey looks so big that one thinks that it must be very strong; it brays so loud that it must be very powerful. As long as it did not display its powers, the savage tiger did not dare attack it and eat it; but when it displayed them, its doom was sealed.

·74· *The Rat and the Ox*

· THERE WAS ONCE a deity living among men—I forget exactly at what time—who wanted to find twelve animals for the zodiac in order to name the years.

He had already placed the dragon, the snake, the tiger, and the hare when the rat and the ox began to quarrel about which was the bigger. Naturally, the body and the appearance of the ox was much larger; when it heard the claims of the rat, it shook its horns and shouted, "Everyone knows that I, the ox, am big and immeasurably strong. How can a rat that only weighs a few pounds dare to compete with me? I call it ridiculous."

The sly and cunning rat merely laughed coldly at the boasts of the ox, and said, "Everyone is conceited about his own size and capabilities. That is no standard. We must bend to the judgment of the majority. It is true that I am only a poor little rat, but I will measure myself with you today."

Fearing that the battle of words between the ox and the rat would develop into a serious quarrel, the deity quickly interrupted. "Naturally a rat is not as big as an ox. But since he won't believe it, we must trust to the decision of the crowd. That is the just way to decide. I suggest that you think the matter over and then go out and hear the people's verdict." The ox agreed at once to the suggestion of the deity, since he thought that his victory was assured.

The rat, however, pretended to be in despair and sunk in gloom. He said, "I must be a little bigger before I can appear before the people."

Seeing the rat so disheartened, the ox thought that, whatever happened, the rat would still be much smaller than he, and he agreed to its doubling its size. He himself did not bother, because he was already one hundred times bigger than the rat.

When the rat had grown, they went out into the town. "Look! Never before have I seen such a big rat. It is incredibly big." From the moment they left the house until their return, they heard on all sides exclamations of wonder at the size of the rat; but no one looked at the ox, because people see oxen every day, whereas they had never before seen such a large rat.

The stupid ox had fallen into the rat's trap, but it did not realize that it had been tricked—it merely thought the people had no eyes. Since it had lost, it had no dignity left, and had to resign the first place to the rat. From that time the rat became the first animal in the zodiac.

·75· Why Does Li T'ieh-kuai Have a Wounded Leg?

• MANY PEOPLE say that the immortal Li T'ieh-kuai was once an ordinary man. One day he bought some garlic in the street and put it in his bag, which he carried over his shoulder.

He was passing a temple of the earth deity when he saw several immortals eating red pills of immortality. He wanted to eat some too, but could think of no way of arranging it. Suddenly he had an idea. He tapped his bag and said to the immortals, "The pills that you are eating are too small; just look how big my pills of immortality are. I will help you eat your little ones, and then you can have some of my big ones."

Seeing the pills in his bag, the immortals invited him to come and eat with them, and Li shoved the pills into his mouth with both hands. All the while he was laughing to himself, because he could not laugh openly with his mouth full. Soon all the little pills were gone, and the immortals said to Li, "Now let us have your big pills." Li opened his bag, dumped his garlic out, and said with a laugh, "Make a good meal now."

The immortals were not annoyed at being deceived, but climbed onto a cloud and flew off to the mountain of the volcano. Having eaten the red pills, Li T'ieh-kuai was able to go with them. When they arrived at the volcano, the immortals flew very high. Li, being only a beginner, could not reach great heights, and he lost one of his legs, which was burned off in the fire. That is why he has a wounded, festering leg.

Other people say that when he was young he was very poor, and his mother ordered him to go into the hills every day to collect wood. The wood that he collected, however, was sufficient for only one day, which caused his aunt to say, "What are we going to burn when it rains?" One day it really did rain and there was no wood in the house. His aunt cursed him, "Lazy devil!" she said, "today we will use your foot as fuel."

Now Li T'ieh-kuai had already learned some tricks from the immortals in the hills. So he went to the fireplace, sat down, and stuck his foot into the fire, which blazed up much brighter than with wood. When his aunt saw him, she shouted out, "Are you mad! I was only joking when I said you ought to stoke the fire with your foot; I didn't mean it seriously." At the same time she pulled his foot out of the fire. But that was a grave mistake, because the bottom part of the leg fell off and naturally became infected. If his aunt had not pulled it out, he could have taken it out when the food was cooked and his leg would not have even been singed. The aunt used the burned-off leg to brush up the cinders.

·76· *The Mother of Heaven*

• ONE DAY the ruler of heaven had some important business in a distant part of his realm, which would keep him busy for three days. He therefore transferred all his duties to the old mother of heaven, and asked her to look after everything in his absence. "But for these three days you must grant man's every wish," he warned her. The mother of heaven smilingly nodded in agreement.

She left her palace, mounted a cloud, and traveled everywhere to attend to the wishes of men. As she was passing a river, she heard a man say, "Heavenly Father, send wind. If a wind blows, I can sail away." She ordered the wind to blow and went on her way.

Soon she arrived at a large orchard where she heard someone calling, "Heavenly Father, please tell the wind to stop. If it goes on any longer, all my pears will fall." This was too much for the mother of heaven, and she returned to her palace.

The next morning she set off again, and heard an old voice saying, "Heavenly Father, send rain. If it rains, I can sow my beans." She sent a heavy rain, which lasted all day.

But in the evening on her way home, she heard a young girl say with a sigh, "Heavenly Father, please send fine weather. Otherwise all the ginger I am drying will rot." The mother of heaven could bear it no longer, and with a groan she returned to her palace. During the third day she kept to her room.

In the evening the ruler of heaven returned from his journey, and she told him all that had happened and begged him to forgive her. He said generously. "It isn't very difficult. You must send a strong wind to blow on the rivers, and a gentle breeze on the pears. Rain must fall during the night in order to sow beans, and the sun shine during the day to dry the ginger."

The mother of heaven understood at once, but asked with a smile, "Why didn't you tell me before?"

The Two Earth Deities

· IN A CERTAIN DISTRICT there was a deity of the earth on the southern mountain and another on the northern mountain. Being stationed in such out-of-the-way places, they had not received incense or any other form of sacrifice for a long time, and both were on the verge of starvation.

One day the earth deity of the southern mountain saw a young cowherd go past his temple. Without a moment's hesitation, the deity stretched out his hand and stroked the boy's body several times.

On arriving home, the boy began to burn all over his body, and he became very ill. His family were distracted with worry, but suddenly they heard a voice saying from the boy's mouth: "I am the deity of the southern mountain. I have come to drive away the illness, which has been caused by the mountain spirits. If you go to the temple of the earth deity and cut a piece off the camphor tree in front of it and give it to the boy to drink, he will be cured."

The people all cast themselves to the ground when they heard that the earth deity was present. The father of the boy, following the deity's directions, cut off a piece from the camphor tree, boiled it, and gave it to his son to drink. A quarter of an hour later the invalid had recovered.

The next day the family sent a pig's head, five beasts of sacrifice, and various other gifts to thank the deity for his favor. The deity was overjoyed at the success of his plans, and sent a servant to invite the deity of the northern mountain to dinner.

On receipt of the invitation, the northern deity hurried across at once. At the sight of the choice meal, his mouth began to water; he begged his host to tell him by what means he had acquired such a repast. "A man cannot always stay poor," said the southern deity proudly. "One needs only to think out a plan." "Do come to the point and tell me how you did it," said his guest. "Don't be in such a hurry; I will tell you later. We are terribly hungry now." During dinner, the southern earth deity told the whole story to his guest, who noted every word so as to imitate him and have some luck himself.

By a fortunate chance, a cowherd went by the temple of the northern deity on the following day. The deity stroked him several times as he had been told, and he noticed that the boy received a terrible shock.

The boy ran home and became very ill, whereupon the deity said, "You must go to the temple of the earth deity of the northern mountain, cut a piece off the camphor tree near by, cook it, and give it to the sick boy to drink."

The father naturally rushed off to the temple but, although he searched everywhere, he could find no camphor tree behind the temple. He stood dumbly wondering what to do, when he remembered that the image itself was made of camphor wood. He decided, therefore, to cut a piece off the deity; but, thinking that it would be too painful in front, he lifted up the deity's dress and cut a bit off his buttocks. This he boiled and gave to his son with the greatest success—the boy became well at once.

Unfortunately, this man was desperately poor. He could scarcely earn his daily bread, so that it never occurred to him to offer a sacrifice to the earth deity. The deity, however, thought that they were evil people; not only had he received no benefits, but he had even been injured by them. The more he thought about the matter, the angrier he became.

Finally he decided to vent his ill-humor on his neighboring deity. He hobbled over to his temple, where the deity looked at him in surprise and then said, "I have not seen you for a long time, brother. How changed you are!" The northern god did not even take the time to sit down, but immediately launched into an account of his misfortunes.

The southern deity was not at all sympathetic, and laughed till his sides ached. "Ha! Ha! You must be careful what kind of family you choose. If you never even thought about that, you cannot have remembered that there is no camphor tree near your temple. If one is so stupid and gets injured, there is no reason for blaming it on someone else."

·78· Chu the Rogue

• CHU, THE GOOD-FOR-NOTHING, was a regular rascal, prepared to play pranks on all and sundry. One day the sun was blazing in the sky, and he called out, "Sunshine P'usa, I never sent for you. How dare you come uninvited into my room! I will complain to Yü huang-ti." The sunshine P'usa was very frightened by this threat, and said, "Please don't complain. There is a pot of silver in front of your house—you can take that." When Chu really found a pot of silver, he no longer shouted accusations at the sun.

The next night the moon was shining, and he said to it, "Moonlight P'usa, I never sent for you. How dare you enter my house without permission! I will complain to Yü huang-ti." "Please don't do that," said the moonlight P'usa in a terrible fright. "Take the pot of gold behind your house and say no more about it." After he went and dug up the pot of gold, Chu the Rogue kept silent.

One day he went into the temple of the plague deities. "You are jumbled together in threes and fours," he said to them. "You are certainly bad men. I will complain to Yü huang-ti." But the plague deities were not so meek as the sun and moon gods. When they heard Chu's disrespectful words, they complained to Yen-lo-wang, the king of hell.

Yen-lo-wang happened to be in the judgment hall at this moment, and he sent the bee spirit up to earth to find this wicked man. But Chu was very clever, and pasted paper over all the holes in the doors, walls, and windows. He left only one small hole, which he covered with a pig's bladder. Therefore, when the bee spirit arrived, it searched in vain for some opening until it came upon the small hole. "I've been trapped!" it cried, as it found itself inside the bladder. Chu chortled with glee.

When Yen-lo-wang realized that the bee spirit had been gone for several days without returning, he ordered the one-legged spirit to go up to earth and catch Chu. Unfortunately, Chu also knew about this, and filled his house with prickly things and sat down in the middle of the thorns. The one-legged spirit found Chu sitting in his house doing nothing, and dashed in. The thorns stuck in the spirit's foot and, being unable to run away, he was taken prisoner by Chu.

Yen-lo-wang soon noticed that the one-legged spirit also failed to return and, mounting his thousand-league horse, he went together with Oxhead and Horseface to the house of Chu. Chu knew of his coming in advance, and gave his wife exact orders about what to do. With a smile on her face she went to greet Yen-lo-wang and invited him to dinner.

After the meal Chu took an old water buffalo out of the stable. When he mounted the animal to ride down to the underworld, as he had arranged with Yen-lo-wang, his wife hung two glowing arrows on the animal's back, so that the buffalo, maddened by the sudden pain, rushed away so fast that Yen-lo-wang's thousand-league horse could not keep up with it.

Yen-lo-wang called out to Chu to stop, and then asked him, "What kind of buffalo is that? I never knew that they could run so fast." "It is a thousand-league buffalo," answered Chu without turning a hair. Yen-lo-wang was very surprised, and begged Chu to allow him to try it. Chu agreed, but warned him, "My buffalo knows only its master. It only runs fast with me." "Is there nothing to be done to make it think I am you?" asked Yen-lo-wang. "Perhaps it would be deceived if you put on my clothes," answered Chu. He gave his clothes to Yen-lo-wang, who put them on and got on the water buffalo, which refused to move a step. Chu, however, was seated on the thousand-league horse and dressed in Yen-lo-wang's clothes.

He gave the horse a blow and soon arrived in hell, where he placed himself on to the throne, and said to the rakshasas and other small servant ghosts, "Chu the Rogue is following me on a water buffalo. Beat him the moment he arrives."

The spirits did not know that the man on the water buffalo was the king of hell. They did not ask his name, but pulled him off his mount and thrashed him, until Oxhead and Horseface arrived and explained what had happened. Mad with rage, the king of hell climbed onto his throne and ordered the little spirits to heat the caldron of oil for Chu to be boiled in.

When the spirits brought the oil, Chu asked them, "Do you want to become rich?" When they all asked him how it could be managed, he continued, "You see, Yen-lo-wang is a stupid man. You need only a few pints of oil to boil one man. I suggest that you leave enough oil to roast me and then sell the rest. Won't you become rich then?"

The little spirits were very pleased at this idea, and sold the spare oil at once. Just at this moment the order came to boil Chu. Anxious to show their zeal, the spirits cast him into the caldron. But he did not cry out, because he held himself up on one side with his head and on the other with his feet; although Yen-lo-wang went on stoking the fire, he could not boil him to death. In despair he ordered the spirits to drag him to the Yin-Yang River and leave him there to freeze to death.

On the bank Chu called out as loud as he could for someone to ferry him across. There was a carp in the river, who was so sorry for Chu that he offered to carry him to the upper world himself. Chu looked at the carp, and thought, "What a fine carp! I must catch it and sell it for wine." He called out, "Brother carp, please tell me how I can cross over." "It's very simple," answered the carp. "You get on to my back, and I will carry you across." "But your back is so slippery," said the rascal. "I am afraid of sliding off. I don't think I dare go, unless you agree to a suggestion of mine. I shall tie a rope round your body and hold one end myself. Then I won't drown if I fall in."

The carp allowed itself to be bound, and Chu rode safely over the river with the rope in one hand. But when he arrived in the upper world, he dragged off the poor carp and sold it to buy wine.

·79· *The Kitchen Deity*

• WHEN ON EARTH, the kitchen deity was a miserably poor mason who was fated to remain poor all his life. Therefore the harder he worked, the worse he became, until at last he had to separate from his wife and marry her off to another man.

One day he was engaged to do some work by the man who had married his former wife. The mason had no idea who she was, but his wife still used to think about him. Since it was not possible to call to him, she thought she would help him in a secret manner.

He was still very poor, but her new family was fairly rich. So she baked some sesame cakes, in each of which she hid a piece of money. When the mason took his leave, she sent him these as a gift for the journey without mentioning a word about the money. He, however, being destined never to have any money, naturally was unable to keep these unexpected riches.

On his way home he went into a small teahouse to rest, where another customer saw his basket full of cakes and asked to be given one to taste. The mason handed him one, and the other man found the money inside. He talked to the mason, and eventually persuaded him to sell them for a small sum.

The mason was born under an unlucky star, and thought he was doing a good bit of business by getting some money for the cakes. And so in this way he wasted everything that his wife, out of love, had given him.

Later he discovered that his wife had sent him cakes filled with money, all of which he had disposed of. He thought to himself, "I am fated to live my life in poverty. What is the point of continuing?"

And he took his own life. But the ruler of heaven took pity on his miserable existence and appointed him deity of the kitchen in recognition of his goodness and honesty.

Notes
to the Tales

PART I

THE ORIGIN OF HUMAN, ANIMAL, AND
PLANT CHARACTERISTICS

·1· *Why Men Are So Bad*

Stories about the exchange of hearts and the accompanying change of character are fairly common in Chinese short story literature, but they seem to be rather rare in present-day oral traditions.

Motif A1384, "Origin of evil inclinations."

Not in Eberhard, Typen. *Text from Shao-hsing, Chekiang province.* Min-su *No. 75, p. 39.*

·2· *Why Are There Cripples on Earth?*

P'an-ku, as the primeval being or as creator, occurs in Chinese literature from the third century A.D. He seems to have been connected with southern Chinese aboriginal societies. The most common legend about him is that the world and the beings on earth were created out of his body and his limbs.

Motif A1338, "Origin of physical defects."

Eberhard, Typen No. 70. *Text from An-p'ing in Ho-pei province.* Lin Lan, Min-chien chuan-shuo, *I, pp. 7–8.*

·3· *Whence Came the Ox?*

Motif A2515.1, "Why ox is draft animal."

Eberhard, Typen No. 77, *with only two texts. Text from Weng-yüan, Kuang-tung province.* Ch'ing-shui, T'ai-yang ho yüeh-liang, *pp. 15–16.*

·4· *The Ti-tsang Bodhisattva and the Ox*

Yü huang-ti (Jade Emperor) is the highest deity in popular religion; the Ti-tsang P'u-sa (Ksitigarbha bodhisattva) is traditionally the deity of hell. His cult began to gain popularity in China during the T'ang era. The center of the cult was in An-hui province; however, from a very early time, Ti-tsang had close connections with Buddhist communities in southern Korea.

Motifs A2515.1, "Why ox is draft animal," and Q560, "Punishments in hell."

Eberhard, Typen No. 79, with four texts. Text from Sung-chiang, Kiangsu province. Lin Lan, Kuai-hsiung-ti, pp. 7–8.

·5· Pocket Crabs

Only three modern texts of this tale have been recorded; no earlier text is known.

Motif A2312.3, "Origin of dents in crab's shell."

Eberhard, Typen No. 2. Text from Kuang-tung province. Lin Lan, Hsiang-szu-shu, pp. 83–84.

·6· Why Does the Cock Eat the Millepede?

The millepede is one of the five poisonous animals which can be used to make the ku poison (see also Nos. 42 and 52). Attempts are usually made to exterminate them on the fifth day of the fifth month. The cock is their principal enemy.

Motifs A2281, "Enmity between animals from original quarrel," and A2426.2.18, "Origin and meaning of cock's cry 'cock-a-doodle-do.'"

Eberhard, Typen No. 1. Another text is in Eberhard, Volks-märchen No. 1. Text from central China. Lin Lan, Min-chien chuan-shuo, I, pp. 43–44.

·7· The Origin of Opium Smoking

This story is also told in China about tobacco or the betel plant. All these stories are typical of south China. The oral tradition of both India and Japan contains variants of this tale. In the former, it is usually told of the betel nut; in the latter, generally of tobacco. Indians of both North and South America also tell similar tales about the origin of these two narcotics.

The motif of reincarnation in a plant growing from the grave is frequently found in Western variants of the Cinderella tale. Rather than the fairy godmother, it is often a bush or tree springing from the mother's grave which provides Cinderella with clothes and carriage. Chinese variants of the Cinderella story have *neither of these motifs; instead, the spirit of the mother resides in a cow who assists Cinderella. See No. 66 for a text and discussion of the Chinese Cinderella tale.*

Motifs, A2691.4, "Origin of opium," and E631, "Reincarnation in plant (tree) growing from grave."

Eberhard, Typen No. 88, with texts, all modern. Text from Lien-ch'eng, Kuang-tung province. Min-su No. 13/14, pp. 35-37.

·8· The Origin of the Carrot

This tale connects the carrot with the pious Mu-lien (Maudgal-yâyana). According to popular belief, Mu-lien later became Ti-tsang, the ruler of hell. The first part of the tale refers to the very popular story of the sinful mother who is saved from hell by her pious son. This is the topic of many pious tracts and numerous theater plays. The connection of Mu-lien with the radish (or carrot) probably comes from a pun: Mu-lien's personal name in Chinese popular tradition is Lo Pu; this is close to lo-p'u, the radish

Motif A2611.05, "Parts of human or animal body transformed into plants."

Eberhard, Typen No. 89. Text probably from central China. Lin Lan, Hsiang-szu-shu, pp. 3-5.

·9· Where Does Rice Come from?

A detailed study of Asian tales about the origin of rice has been made by Toichi Mabuchi in Asian Folklore Studies, XXIII (1964), 1-92. Concentrating on tales found in the insular areas of eastern and southeastern Asia, Mabuchi concludes that tales in which rice and other grains originate from the corpse of a deity probably represent the oldest stratum of tradition. In more recent texts, rice and other grains are acquired directly either from heaven or from the netherworld; in some instances they come as a gift, in others they are stolen. Mabuchi did not deal with the tales of mainland Asia. The tale given here would seem to partake of both his classifications of rice as a gift from heaven and rice from the body of a deity.

Motifs are A2615.2, "Plant from mother's milk," and A1423.2, "Acquisition of rice."

This tale is related to Eberhard, Typen No. 86. Text from Weng-yüan, Kuang-tung province. Ch'ing-shui, T'ai-yang ho yüeh-liang, p. 28.

· 10 · The Dog and the Rice

See the note to No. 9, above, for a discussion of other Asian tales about the origin of rice.

The bringing of an original rice plant by an animal, which is then rewarded with food, is found in Motif A2435.3.10.1, "Why rat may eat rice." In this motif, so far reported only from India, the rat brings the original rice plant from a pond. In the present text from China, the rat's place is taken by the dog. Motifs A2545.3, "Why dog eats first," and A1423.2, "Acquisition of rice," are also applicable.

Eberhard, Typen No. 86. Seven variants have been collected. Text from Szu-ch'uan, Sui-ning. Lin Lan, Hsiang-szu-shu, pp. 77–78.

PART II

LUCK AND GOOD FORTUNE

· 11 · Goldhair Becomes Minister

This tale is popular not only in China but also in other parts of Asia and throughout Europe, and is known in Africa. Negroes in many parts of the New World tell variants or episodes. Readers of Grimms' famous collection will be familiar with the German story of the sham doctor from which Type 1641 takes its name.

Children with brown or even blond hair are not rare in China. The reason may be a vitamin deficiency rather than a racial trait.

The paternal uncle is traditionally the person who has to take over the education of an orphaned nephew. "Barbarian" is a general term for any non-Chinese, but is most usually applied to Mongolian or Turkish tribes of central Asia.

Type 1641, Doctor Know-All *Eberhard,* Typen *No. 190, with fourteen texts. No early examples of this tale have been found in China. Text from central China. Lin Lan, San-chiang-chün, pp. 98–102.*

·12· A Jar Full of Ants

This tale is known since at least the fifth century A.D. The central motif is the forecast that a treasure is predestined for a certain man; a thief will never get it. Usually the gold or silver turns into snakes when the wrong man tries to take it.

This tale has been collected in twenty variants in Japan and eight in India. A Japanese version is No. 44 in Folktales of Japan, *a companion volume in this series.*

Type 834A, The Pot of Gold and the Pot of Scorpions. *Eberhard,* Typen *No. 176 has seven variants. Earlier variants are in Eberhard,* Volksmärchen *No. 113. Text from Chekiang province. Lin Lan, San chiang-chün, pp. 63–64.*

·13· The Discovery of Salt

The Chinese phoenix (feng-huang), *is a mythical animal quite different from the phoenix in Western mythology. It is a symbol for the empress, and in general is a lucky omen. Additional characteristics of the phoenix are detailed in the note to No. 72, below.*

Motif A1429.4, "Acquisition of salt."

Eberhard, Typen *No. 73 has only two modern and no early texts. Text from Shao-hsing, Chekiang province. Min-chien, I, No. 12, pp. 71–72.*

·14· The Journey of the Silver Men

In this tale the interest centers on the principle that fate determines whether a person becomes rich or remains poor. It is curious that in this story no one becomes suspicious upon seeing eight men traveling together, since eight is a symbolic figure. The popular belief in the Eight Immortals might well have raised suspicion that our eight travelers were the immortals in disguise.

Motif N101, "Inexorable fate."

Eberhard, Typen *No. 177; Eberhard*, Volksmärchen *No. 114.*
Text from central China. Lin Lan, San-chiang-chün, *pp. 106–108.*

PART III

TALES OF LOVE

·15· Faithful Even in Death

This is one of the most common Chinese tales, and is the subject of a great number of theater plays. Most of the plays, which have existed at least since the Ming era (1368–1644), take up only one or two incidents of the tale—either the life of both heroes in school or the visit of the boy to his schoolmate—and usually leave out the ending. The transformation into a rainbow is not typical of this tale type, but it can and does occur in several other stories. Since the rainbow in China has long been connected with sexual intercourse, a number of different tales offer a sexual explanation of the rainbow's origin.

Motifs K1837, "Disguise of woman in man's clothes," T81, "Death from love," and A791.9, "Origin of rainbow: transformed butterflies (souls of lovers)."

Eberhard, Typen *No. 212, with eleven texts. Text from central China. Lin Lan*, Min-chien chuan-shuo, *II, pp. 44–52.*

·16· The Faithful Lady Meng

This story is widely known in all parts of China, mainly because it has furnished the theme of many famous plays since the Ming era. Ku Chieh-kang and his colleagues have traced this story back more than twenty-five hundred years and have shown its changes over the centuries. It is indeed one of the earliest stories of Chinese folklore. The Great Wall, constructed by the cruel emperor Ch'in Shih Huang-ti in the third century B. C., was incorporated into the plot of the story after it was already a well-formed tale about faithfulness to a fallen husband.

Most modern texts of the story do not have the introductory part concerning the supernatural birth of the girl; this motif is an intrusion from other tales.

*According to old custom, a girl lost her reputation if she was
seen undressed by a man. This is the reason why, in many texts,
she forces a young man to marry her after she found that he had
observed her in the bath. These texts then usually go into much
detail about the dangers of her trip to the border. Meng Chiang is
extraordinarily chaste, although she cannot possibly have been
much in love with a man whom she had to force to marry her. In
some early versions, the dangers of the trip consist of various
monsters and goblins. The final part of our text really belongs to
the tale of Han P'eng (Typen No. 211), also a very early tale
and a close variant of the latter half of our story here.*

*The motif of the foundation sacrifice to insure the stability of a
new building or wall is very old in European tradition. It is
found, for example, in the Arthurian legend. This motif is also
known in Japan and India. It appears again in this collection in
No. 60 where a foundation sacrifice is demanded to insure the
successful construction of a furnace.*

*Motifs S261, "Foundation sacrifice," and T211.2, "Wife's suicide
at husband's death."*

*Eberhard, Typen No. 210. Text from central China. Lin Lan,
Min-chien chuan-shuo, II, pp. 39–43.*

·17· The Infection

*Although no text earlier than 1800 is known, the tale is built
upon an actual folk custom: the ritual defloration of girls. The
story is also founded on the belief that if a girl has leprosy or
venereal disease, she can be cured only by giving away the disease
to the first man with whom she has relations. Ritual defloration
is known widely in south China, southeast Asia, and the Ti-
betan-Chinese border areas (see Hirosato Iwai, in Toyo Bunko
Memoirs, No. 7), often being connected with Buddhist ceremonies. In China this custom is known only in the southern coastal
provinces. It is found among non-Chinese aboriginal tribes, who
also follow the custom of pre-marital freedom until the end of the
first pregnancy. They regard the second child as the first "real"
child.*

*Related motifs are T182, from "Death from intercourse," and
B511.1.2, "Snake creeps into man's mouth and heals him."*

Eberhard, Typen *No. 197; Eberhard,* Volksmärchen *No. 124.*
Text from Kuang-tung province. Min-chien, *I, No. pp. 45–49.*

·18· The Amazing Adventure of a Scholar

This tale seems to have a history of more than a thousand years in China. In popular belief, monkeys have their own kingdom and their own king. One of the most famous classical novels of Chinese literature—Hsi-yo-chi (Monkey's Pilgrimage)—has a monkey king as the central hero. In the early medieval period, monkeys were already linked to the theater; monkey players traveled around the market places and gave performances.

The motif of the man who involuntarily lands in the bed of the daughter of a high dignitary is known from theater plays. The marriage of a lowly hero to a girl of very high rank, often against her father's will, is one of the most nearly universal motifs in folk tradition. This motif, L161, is shown in the motif index to occur in no less than thirty-eight separate tale types.

Motifs D2135, "Magic air journey," and L161, "Lowly hero marries princess."

Eberhard, Typen *No. 183. Earlier texts are mentioned in Eberhard,* Volksmärchen *No. 116. Text from Chin-hua, Chekiang province.* Lin Lan, *San-ko yüan-wang, pp. 41–46.*

·19· Husband and Wife in This Life and in the Life to Come

Although the Orpheus-like introduction of this tale is rare in China, it corresponds very well with popular beliefs about life in the netherworld. Below the earth there are numerous hells, each one with a special king. In these hells a great number of men are employed, and these men have their households and wives. Dead persons do not recognize relatives or former acquaintances, and are like goblins. By touching any piece of metal such as a coin, they can regain their memory. The episode of the girl who has held a coin in her closed hand from the time of her birth, and who opens her hand only when she has met her former and at the same time future husband, is prominent in this tale. This motif is found in Buddhist stories in the short story literature.

*Sprung from the universal desire to preserve the marriage rela-
tionship beyond the bonds of death, the Orpheus motif is popular
in the oral tradition of many peoples. The Indians of North
America used this element in numerous tales. Ann Gayton in
"The Orpheus Myth in North America," JAFL XLVIII (1935),
263–93, made a thorough study of the theme in the northern
half of the New World. An older work of 1895, but still a
valuable reference source, E. Maass's Orpheus, views the myth
in a world-wide context.*

*Motifs F81.1, "Orpheus," T589.5, "New-born child reincarna-
tion of recently deceased person," and H100, "Identification by
matching parts of divided token."*

*Eberhard, Typen No. 144. Text from central China. Lin Lan,
Hsiao Chu Pa-chieh, pp. 31–35.*

· 20 · *The Mason Wins the Prize*

*The introductory part of our text is common to many tales. In
popular Buddhism, "western India" or "India in the west"—the
country where the real Buddha lived—and "western heaven"
—one of the paradises in which a Buddha is living—are used in-
terchangeably; the term Hsi-t'ien can mean both. The last section of our tale, in which the emperor sees the woman's picture
and falls in love with her, also occurs independently (Typen
No. 195). Both tales are old, but are not normally connected as
in our text. Variants of the last section are popular in Japan
where episodes are found in the eighth-century Nihongi; for a
good example collected in modern times, see No. 48 in Folktales of Japan, a companion volume in this series.*

*Type 461, Three Hairs from the Devil's Beard, is found here.
Our text differs from the European counterparts of this famous
tale in the introduction and conclusion, but the principal element of the story is similar to the worldwide tradition. The latter section contains elements of Type 465, The Man Persecuted
Because of His Beautiful Wife. Here we find motif H1381.3.1.1.1,
"Quest for bride for king like picture he has seen."*

*Eberhard, Typen No. 125, with eleven texts; Eberhard, Volks-
märchen No. 83. In the latter work some of the sources of this*

famous story are studied, especially the connection between the tale and the classical novel Hsi-yo-chi (Monkey's Pilgrimage). *Text from Shao-hsing, Chekiang province.* Shao-hsing, *pp. 72–79.*

· 21 · The Stone of the Beautiful Maiden

This is a text collected by Chinese Communist folklorists. I have the strong suspicion that this tale has been extensively edited, probably so much so that the original form is now unrecognizable. The text strongly stresses those values which Chinese Communists want to instill in their citizens. Although the tale starts out with the motif that the prince intends to choose a bride by throwing a ball at the selected girl, the prince dislikes all upper-class girls. The wise old man tells him that only lower-class girls are good. But all his privileges and all his power cannot bring him into contact with the common people. Finally, he comes to the conclusion that a union between upper and lower classes is impossible. He decides to become a member of the lower class, so that ultimately he would be worthy of marrying a lower class girl. The story in this form runs counter to all traditional Chinese social and cultural values.

Motif T91.6.2, "King (prince) in love with a lowly girl," and A972.5.6, "Hole in stone caused by weapon of warrior.".

Text from Yün-nan province. No place name is given, but it is said that the text comes from members of the partly assimilated Pai tribes; these are probably of Thai origin. Source: Yün-nan ko-min-tsu min-chien ku-shih hsüan, *pp. 73–74.*

PART IV

SUPERNATURAL MARRIAGES

· 22 · The Pretty Little Calf

Although this tale contains motifs which are known from other folktales in China, especially Typen No. 53 and 43, it seems to be a unit by itself. Typen No. 43 contains an incident about a frog-child which is similar to the one about the calf-child found here.

Motifs *K2110.1*, "*Calumniated wife*," *E611.2.3*, "*Reincarnation as calf*," and *D721*, "*Disenchantment by removing skin (or covering)*."

Eberhard, Typen No. *33*. Text from Kuan-yün, Kiang-su province. Lin Lan, Yün-chung-ti mu-ch'in, pp. *14–20*.

·23· The Bank of the Celestial Stream

This is one of the most common Chinese tales. It is used to explain the origin of various constellations and the Milky Way. It also often explains the rain which tends to fall on the day of the festival of the seventh day of the seventh month (rain and rainbow cover the meeting of the lovers) or the disappearance of magpies on that day (they form a bridge for the couple to cross over the celestial stream). It is, however, fairly clear that originally this was a swan maiden tale. The astral motifs seem to be an addition. The story appears in an early form in the second century B.C. as an astral tale; the swan maiden theme emerges somewhat later.

The festival of the seventh day of the seventh month has been adopted by Japan, where it is known as the Tanabata festival. The folktale given here about the heavenly maiden and her lover who meet on that day has also been taken over by the Japanese, who consider it one of their best-loved stories. For a good variant, see No. 23 in Folktales of Japan, *a companion volume in this series. The episode of the obstacle flights is found in No. 19 in the same volume.*

Motifs *A761.3*, "*Stars as transformed lovers*," *A778.3*, "*Milky Way as a river*," *D672*, "*Obstacle flight*," and *K1335*, "*Seduction (or wooing) by stealing clothes of bathing girl (swan maiden)*."

Eberhard, Typen No. *34*. Additional historical materials are noted in Eberhard, Volksmärchen No. *21*. Text from Kuan-yün, Kiang-su province. Lin Lan, Huan-hsin-hou, pp. *53–57*.

·24· The Dark Maiden from the Ninth Heaven

Although closely related to the swan maiden tale, this folktale as a separate entity has a long history in China. It occurs many times in short stories from the T'ang period (A.D. 618–906) on.

The heroine, Chiu-t'ien hsüan-nü, is a popular deity who appears in a number of theater plays before 1600. In one play, she revives a faithful wife who had been murdered; in another, she teaches the hero the magic art of fighting (see Ch'ü-hai I, 598 and II, 824–25).

Heaven is believed to have nine stories; this concept antedates the Christian era and was a part of astronomical theory in the Han period.

New Year's is the greatest Chinese festival, and everyone tries his best to prepare an elaborate feast. There are special New Year's markets, usually close to famous temples in the cities; in these markets, books and paintings are often found, which are used for the New Year's decoration of the houses or as gifts.

The sin which is committed by heavenly beings and punished by temporary exile to the earth is often that of having had erotic feelings, but in some instances it is a simple violation of some ceremonial rule. Our text is not explicit on this point. The motif as such recurs continually in Chinese short stories, dramas, and novels.

The idea of a portrait of a beautiful woman coming to life seems to be Oriental, but is closely related to a motif popular in European tradition, T11.2, "Love through sight of picture," in which the lover searches until he finds his beloved whose portrait he possesses. This motif has appeared in No. 20 in this collection. A Japanese tale embodying elements of both motifs is No. 43 in Folktales of Japan.

Motifs Q431, "Punishment: banishment (exile)"; D435.2.1, "Picture come to life," and T111.2, "Woman from sky-world marries mortal man."

Eberhard, Typen No. 36; Eberhard, Volksmärchen No. 23. Text from San-yüan in Kuang-tung province. Lin Lan, Chin-t'ien-chi, pp. 45–51.

·25· The Pig That Warms the Ocean

This narrative is composed of several tales which often occur separately. This first part is the story, well known and widely spread in China, about the Muslim who discovers a treasure

(Eberhard, Typen *No. 169, with thirty-seven texts; the type is known since the T'ang era). The second part—the marriage to the daughter of the dragon king—is* Typen *No. 39, which is equally well known, with thirty-five variants, the earliest again dating from the T'ang era.*

Tales about an undersea dragon kingdom which is visited by a mortal are popular in both China and Japan. Other Chinese tales in this collection in which the undersea dragon kingdom appears are Nos. 27, 45, 46, 47, 64 and 65. One of the best-known Japanese tales, that of Urashima Taro, follows this theme. See Nos. 11, 32, and 40 in Folktales of Japan *for Urashima Taro and other tales featuring a dragon kingdom. Some of the Japanese tales may well have been borrowed from China, but as yet no genetic relationships have been proved.*

Motif B580, "Animal helps men to wealth and greatness." The second part of the tale is Type 465, The Man Persecuted Because of His Beautiful Wife.

Text from Kuan-yün, Kiang-su province. Sun Chia-hsün, Wa-wa-shih, *pp. 107–119.*

·26· Why the Horns of Cattle Are Curved

No direct parallels of the bent horn motif from other parts of China have been collected, but the present text falls into the group of tales common in China, which explain various animal characteristics. Pavilions made entirely of horns probably do not exist, but I have seen in Nepal temples and pavilions which were almost completely covered with horns. A trace of the cult of water buffaloes widespread in south China, can probably be found in this tale. The word for "cow" and that for "buffalo" are the same in Chinese.

The motif of magical conception from the eating of food which has been in contact with a supernatural being is found throughout the world. A famous instance is that found in Greek legend where this motif is connected with the birth of Perseus. Thompson in The Folktale, *p. 340, notes that the magical conception motif is known in the oral tradition of nearly all American Indian tribes except those of the Southwest. The theme is a favorite narrative element in India, and appears in other Chinese tales than the one given here; see* Typen *Nos. 51 and 60.*

Motifs T511.3, "Conception from eating vegetable," and A2326.3.4, "Why buffalo's horns are bent."

Text from Yün-nan province. Sung Che, Yün-nan min-chien ku-shih, *II, pp. 96–99.*

·27· The Witch's Daughter

Although only four variants of this story type have been collected in China, the tale is extremely popular in northern and eastern Europe. More than one hundred variants have been collected in Finland alone. Much of the setting of this tale goes contrary to Chinese culture. A man would not usually give away his sons, and a young man normally does not go to live in the house of his bride, although this does occasionally occur. Other elements of the tale are thoroughly Chinese: the descent to the dragon kingdom; the allusion to the Monkey King, who appears as Wu-k'ung, the hero of the classic sixteenth-century novel Hsi-yo-chi *(Monkey's Pilgrimage) and the use of the wedding drum.*

Type 313A The Girl as Helper. In addition to this type, Motifs B571, "Animals perform tasks for man," and E37.1, "Failure to resuscitate because of premature disturbance of members to be left in cask for certain time," are prominent here.

Eberhard, Typen *No. 46. Text from Kuan-yün, Kiang-su province. Sun Chia-hsün,* Wa-wa-shih, *pp. 135–148.*

·28· The Marriage of the City Deity

Stories about marriage to a deity are found in China as early as the fourth century B.C. It is not known how long the Chinese have worshiped city gods, but such local deities are mentioned in texts from about 500 A.D. on. Ceremonies like the one described in our text are still celebrated in Taiwan and were once common throughout south China. One of the main attractions of these celebrations was theater plays performed to please the deity. Marriage to a deity is considered to be a dubious honor, since it means physical death; but it establishes a special relationship between the deity and the family of the bride which is advantageous for the family in their social relations with the rest of the village or town as well as in their religious relationships to the otherworld.

Frequently in Chinese variants of this tale the supernatural visitor is identified by a needle and thread fastened to his garments before he leaves his lover's bed. This incident occurs in No. 29 in this collection. This motif is related to H119.2, "Needle left in garment of husband by abducted wife as sign." The needle and thread identity test is popular in Japan. Keigo Seki has made a thorough study of the Japanese tradition of this motif, in Studies in Japanese Folklore, *pp. 267–88. Seki traces the story back to the eighth-century* Kojiki, *and states (p. 285) that the tale was introduced into Japan from China and Korea some time before the beginning of the seventh century.*

Motifs T111.1, "Marriage of a mortal and a god," and H117, "Identification by cut garment."

Eberhard, Typen No. 109, with eight variants. Earlier texts are discussed in Eberhard, Volksmärchen No. 71. Text from Chiehyang, Kuang-tung province. Min-chien, II, No. 1, pp. 33–34.

·29· *The Son of the Turtle Spirit*

The turtle has two opposing symbolic meanings in Chinese folklore. On the one hand, he is regarded as obscene, as a symbol of the penis; on the other hand, he is a divine animal, representing the deity of the North Pole. Our text connects the story of the relations of a girl with a supernatural being or an animal with stories about geomancy (Typen No. 173). The first part often occurs in theater plays and in short stories; the second part is found mainly in short stories and in oral tradition (see also Nos. 33 and 34).

The note to No. 28 discusses Japanese variants of the first half of this tale, that part dealing with the marriage to a turtle and his discovery by tying a thread to his garments.

Motifs B604.2.1, "Marriage to turtle," and Q111, "Riches as reward." A related motif is H119.2, "Needle left in garment of husband by abducted wife as sign."

Eberhard, Typen No. 112 has more than thirty variants of this tale. Eberhard, Volksmärchen Nos. 73 and 74 has additional texts, and traces the early history of this tale. Text from Sung-chiang, Kiangsu province. Lin Lan, Hui Ta-wang, pp. 105–117.

· *30* · The Wife of the Monkey

Tales about monkeys or apes marrying women are widespread in central and south China as well as in Tibet, and are very old (see discussion in Eberhard, Volksmärchen No. 79a). Our story is only one of many which explains the bare red buttocks of some monkeys. The singeing of the monkey's buttocks on a hot stone as an explanation of their present redness is also found in Japanese tradition. No. 41 in Folktales of Japan *contains this motif.*

Motifs B601.7, "Marriage to monkey," and A2411.1.5.1.1, "Why ape has red back."

Eberhard, Typen No. 119, with eleven texts. Text from central China. Lü Tung-pin-ti ku-shih (small edition), pp. 84–88.

· *31* · The Bear's Husband

This tale is known from the eighteenth century and also appears in modern collections. Early texts do not have a bear as a wife but a native woman, as discussed in Eberhard, Volksmärchen No. 80. Our text is interesting as one of several examples of a connection between an existing clan, a cult, and a folktale. The hero, Wang P'ing, is not otherwise known.

The common motif of human-animal marriage, B600, usually deals with the forced marriage of a girl and a beast. In having the bridegroom abducted by a female animal, our tale here is somewhat unusual. The well-known European tale of the Bear's Son, Type 301, The Three Stolen Princesses, *elements of which are included in Beowulf saga, tells of the capture of a girl by a bear and the subsequent birth of a supernaturally strong son. Motif B601.1, "Marriage to bear," is specifically applicable to our tale.*

Eberhard, Typen No. 121, with six variants. Text from Yang-hsin in Shan-tung province. Shan-tung min-chien, I, pp. 24–25.

PART V

PERSONS WITH MAGIC POWERS

· 32 ·   *The Magic of the Mason*

This story is known from texts as early as the eighteenth century, but elements of it are much earlier. Craftsmen are believed to have a secret book, the Book of Lu Pan, *in which magical tricks are written down. Lu Pan, the patron saint of the carpenters guild, is supposed to have lived before 300 B.C. and to have been the inventor of a number of technical devices. In early texts he is already connected with magical tricks.*

Motifs N135, "Objects effect change of luck," and Q42, "Generosity rewarded."

Eberhard, Typen *No. 100, with eighty-nine texts. Discussion in* Volksmärchen *No. 62. Text from T'ang-ch'i, Chekiang province. Ts'ao Sung-yeh, II.*

· 33 ·   *The Tale of the Turtle Mountain*

This tale has early variants in the short story literature and has circulated steadily to the present time. At its core lies the belief in geomancy—that is, the belief that some features of the earth and nature influence the fate of people and their descendants. The selection of grave sites with favorable geographical traits was in the hand of geomancers, who often delayed burial for years. A high percentage of all lawsuits in traditional China arose from fights over such sites, mutual claims, or violation of tombs illegally or legally built. Human interference with nature can destroy favorable sites, as is true in this tale. Belief in geomancy militated strongly in traditional China against the construction of railways and roads which altered the character of the landscape and often caused tombs to be relocated. See Nos. 28 and 34 for other tales about geomancers.

Motif E754.3, "Burial in certain ground assures going to heaven," and N134, "Persons effect change of luck."

Eberhard, Typen *No. 174, with fifteen texts;* Eberhard, Volksmärchen *No. 108–111. Text from Chao-ch'ing in Kuang-tung province. Lin Lan, Sha-lung, pp. 100–5.*

· 34 · The Geomancer

This is a widespread story typically Chinese in form. It is connected with geomancy, and also with the belief that an emperor is entirely different from other humans. The advice which the father in this story gives to his sons violates all rules of filial piety, and because of this violation the plan ultimately fails. The chamber pot is an unclean object which should not be used in any ritual. In the tales it is often employed to prevent the thunder god from striking an intended victim. A similar function is exercised by the bushel on the roof of the house.

The future emperor appears in this story first in the form of a dragon; later, the dragon symbolizes the emperor. During the Manchu period (1644–1911) and earlier, astrologers were active in studying the sky and other phenomena of nature in order to discover impending catastrophes and calamities. Their prognoses were often used as a means of criticizing the emperor and to inducing him to change his behavior.

See Nos. 28 and 33 in this collection for additional stories which deal with the work of a geomancer in finding an auspicious grave site. The headnote to No. 33 discusses geomancy.

Motifs J154, "Wise words of dying father," and M370, "Vain attempts to escape fulfillment of prophecy."

Eberhard, Typen No. 172; Eberhard, Volksmärchen No. 107. Text from central China. Lin Lan, Tung-hsien mai-lei, pp. 92–95.

· 35 · The Empress of Heaven

The T'ien-hou (empress of heaven) is one of the most famous deities along the Fukien coast of China. She has long been connected with the Lin clan. Her cult spread over south China together with the dispersion of the Lin and allied clans, and she even had temples among the Chinese in California. The legends about her life differ, but cults devoted to her worship were in existence as early as the twelfth century.

Motifs R138, "Rescue from shipwreck," and E721.2, "Body in trance while soul is absent."

Eberhard, Typen No. 152; Eberhard, Volksmärchen No. 98. Text from Te-ch'ing in Kuang-tung province. Ch'ing-shui, T'ai-yang ho yüeh-liang, pp. 21–23.

· 36 · The Monk with the Bag

Pu-tai ho-shang (Monk with the Bag) is believed to be a rein-carnation of Mi-lo (Maitreya), the Buddha of the Future. According to early tradition, he lived on Mount Szu-ming near Feng-hua (Chekiang) and died on the third day of the third month A.D. 917. He was already deified by the twelfth century if not earlier. His figure is often found in temples; he is popularly called the Big Belly Buddha. His life story and other legends are found in F. Lessing, Yung-ho-kung, I, pp. 21 ff. Lu Pan is the patron saint of the carpenters, and appears in many legends as a supernatural helper.

Motifs D1641.4, "Forest cleared by magic," and V411.5, "Treasure given away by saint miraculously restored."

Eberhard, Typen No. 186, with variants from numerous regions of China. Further early texts are mentioned in Eberhard, Volksmärchen No. 118. Text from Feng-hua, Chekiang province. Lin Lan, Huan-hsin-hou, p. 45–48.

· 37 · The Festival of Pouring Water

This tale is much more typical of southern and western Asia than of the Far East. It serves as an explanation of a folk festival which has similarities with the Indian holi festival. In India, people pour colored water over one another in the main ceremony. There are also close resemblances to the so-called "cold water festival" held in the spring and introduced—so the sources clearly say—from the Near East into China, where is was popular in the T'ang period (A.D. 618–906). This festival has been found in central Asia and in Iran; it is an Iranian New Year's festival. I am not aware of texts or reports from Yün-nan province about the existence of the festival described in this story nor about the way it is celebrated today, but documentation for Yün-nan province is so poor that this lack of information proves nothing. However, since this is a text collected in Communist China, it should be accepted with caution.

The motif of unique vulnerability, Z311, "Achilles heel," is found throughout the world, particularly in the Near East and India, but is comparatively rare in China. The motif of the rolling skull is widely known in all parts of south China and southeast

Asia (see Eberhard, Volksmärchen No. 75). The motif index does not contain a reference to the rolling skull motif in precisely the form it is found in this tale, but does list D1549.7, "Murdered man's head will cause earth to burn or sea to boil: must be carried about." Until now this motif had been reported only from India.

No close parallel in Eberhard, Typen. Text from Yün-nan province. Sung Che, Yün-nan min-chien ku-shih, II, p. 93–95; reprinted with minimal changes in Yün-nan ko-min-tsu min-chien ku-shih hsüan, pp. 200 ff.

· 38 · Kung Yeh-ch'ang Understands the Language of Birds

The hero of this tale is regarded as a disciple of Confucius. Early texts give the hero the power of understanding the language of the birds. The tale given here is a recent variant. For the introductory episode about the immoral snake girl and the virtuous Kung, the closest parallels are found not in China but in the Near East, in the cycle of stories about Shahmeran, the king of snakes. The tests to which Kung is later subjected also have their closest parallels in the Near East. On the other hand, the story of the strange bird which has to be fed red-hot nails is known from other Chinese texts of the medieval period.

Motif B217.1.1, "Animal languages learned from eating serpent."

Eberhard, Typen No. 8 has four texts. Text from Shao-hsing, Chekiang province. Min-chien, I, No. 12, pp. 100–3.

· 39 · First Discuss the Price When the Pig Is Dead

Popular concepts about the various hells and the life there, and about the way in which persons are reborn in different shapes, are present in this folktale. All these motifs also appear in short stories, for example, the man who visits a friend in the netherworld, and the person who takes a good-looking dress without knowing that it is an animal skin. The basic idea of the sinner who is reborn as an animal is, of course, Buddhistic.

Motifs F81.1.2, "Journey to land of dead to visit deceased," and E611.3, "Man reincarnated as swine."

Eberhard, Typen No. 145, has only four texts, one from the early nineteenth century. Text from Ch'üan-chou, Fukien province. Ch'üan-chou min-chien, I, pp. 97–100.

PART VI

HELP FROM SPIRITS AND DEITIES

·40· *Lü Tung-pin as the Patron of Barbers*

This tale is typical of many tales about patron saints of Chinese guilds. It strongly suggests the cycle of anecdotes about Alexander the Great and his barber. As yet we know of no early text of this folktale in China. Emperor Chu Hung-wu ruled from 1368 to 1398.

Motifs K1811, "Gods (saints) in disguise visit mortals," and V211, "Miraculous healing by saints."

Text from Fu-chou, Fukien province. Min-su No. 78, p. 65.

·41· *The Spirit*

According to popular belief, persons who drown in rivers or lakes become ghosts who have to remain there without hope for reincarnation until they can find a replacement. They tend, therefore, to entice other persons to commit suicide in the water. In the more common form of this tale, the ghost who refrains from drowning his friend or any other person is made a deity as a reward for his good heart.

Cormorant fishing is typical of the whole coastal area of south China. The birds are half tamed, and return to their masters. Rings placed around their neck prevent their swallowing the large fish they catch, and these the fishermen take.

Motifs F420.5.1.7.5, "Water-spirit gives mortal fish," and F420.5.1.5, "Water-spirits work as servants for mortal but disappear when compensation is offered or origin suspected."

Eberhard, Typen No. 132 has the more typical form of this tale, in which the fisherman advises the ghost not to kill another person. Text from southern China. Lin Lan, Huan-hsin-hou, pp. 39–43.

· 42 · *The Little People*

This tale is based upon a belief characteristic of south China and connected with magic beliefs surrounding the ku *poison. Ku is usually made of several poisonous animals, and can be used for different kinds of black magic, among them love magic. On this whole complex, see Eberhard,* Lokalkulturen im alten China, *II, pp. 134–60, in which the connection of this magic with human sacrifice is discussed.*

Beliefs in helpful household spirits of various kinds are popular in many places throughout the world. Such beliefs are widespread throughout Europe, particularly in the north. A whole section (Nos. 61–66) of Folktales of Norway, *a companion volume in this series, is devoted to house spirits.*

In Japan, numerous spirits or kami *are believed to be resident in various parts of the house and its outbuildings, but are not thought of as performing household chores. No. 43 in* Folktales of Japan *tells of storehouse deities which leave because of mistreatment.*

Motifs under F480, "House-spirits," are applicable here. The acquisition of the spirits in this tale suggests Motif F481.0.1.3, "Cobold acquired by placing food for him in a certain place," reported from Lithuania.

In general, this tale belongs to Eberhard, Typen *No. 114, but in some forms the variants are close to* Typen *No. 64. See especially Eberhard,* Volksmärchen *No. 39, in which this type is further analyzed. Text from Ching-ting, Fukien province.* Minsu *No. 13/14, pp. 8–9.*

· 43 · *The Wang-liang's Magic Cap*

The cap or cloak which makes its wearer invisible is a popular motif in folktales throughout the world. In Europe this element frequently appears in variants of Jack and the Beanstalk *(Type 328,* The Boy Steals the Giant's Treasure*). Japanese and Indian tales containing the Tarnkappe motif are often very similar to the Chinese tale given here.*

Chinese names starting with an "A" indicate persons of low social status.

Motifs *D1361.15*, "*Magic cap renders wearer invisible: Tarn-kappe*," and *K359.1*, "*Theft by means of magic invisibility.*"

Eberhard, Typen *No. 64*, with nine texts. In Eberhard, Volks-märchen *No. 39*, texts from as early as the T'ang era are discussed. Text from Shao-hsing, Chekiang province. Min-chien, II, No. 7, pp. 5–7.

·44· The Fairy Grotto

Most of the eighteen known texts of this tale are early, with the earliest probably coming from the fifth and sixth centuries. The heroes in the present text are two men who are believed to have lived in the second century A.D. and to have experienced this adventure in the T'ien-t'ai Mountains of Chekiang province. Their adventure, it is said, made the mountain famous as a retreat. Later, Buddhists took over the mountain and built many monasteries on it.

This tale contains some of the elements of the widely known Japanese story of Urashima Taro, No. 32 in Folktales of Japan. The supernatural passage of time and the receipt of a magic object with which to regain access to the enchanted world are themes common to both tales. Also, the death of the hero after misusing or mislaying the magic object appears in both traditions. Japanese scholars have long debated the extent of Chinese influence on the tale of Urashima Taro. Most of this discussion centers on Buddhistic elements in eighth- and ninth-century Japanese variants, and remains largely a matter of speculation. No rigorous comparative study of either the Japanese or Chinese variants has been made.

The principal motif is *D2011*, "*Years thought days.*"

Eberhard, Typen *No. 103*; Eberhard, Volksmärchen *No. 65*. Text from central China. Lin Lan, Kui-ko-ko, pp. 31–33.

·45· Hsiang Meets the Dragon King

The persons mentioned in the text below are members of some of the oldest leading clans of Hu-nan province. To some degree this story and similar ones published in the same collection reflect the impact on the native clans of Chinese settlers and the subsequent

Chinese administration in the area. This text was collected in Communist China, and exhibits some of the values which the regime likes to stress. The popular rebel is a Robin Hood who helps the poor but fights the upper class. The ruler has no understanding of the suffering of the common man, and feels his power threatened. The name Lieh-ko-nai is not explained in the text; obviously it is the personal name of the hero. But personal names of more than two parts and of this specific structure are non-Chinese. By implication, we may assume that the hero belongs to a native tribal group.

This tale and the previous one bear a superficial resemblance to the Rip Van Winkle story, but lack the element of an extended sleep.

Motif D2011, "Years thought days."

Eberhard, Typen No. 103. Text from Hu-nan province. Source: Sung Che, Hu-nan min-chien ku-shih, pp. 29 ff.

· 46 · The Wild Goose Lake

This story is closest to Typen No. 40, but has significant differences. In all examples of that type there is a hero, whereas here there is a heroine. The element of the magic key which is hidden and well protected is rare in China, but typical of the Near East and southern Asia. The importance given to folksinging, on the other hand, is typical of many different tribal groups throughout southern and western China. In this tale the custom is connected with a folk festival. I do not have other information about a festival in Yün-nan which is celebrated on the twenty-second day of the seventh month. The typical one is a torch festival on the twenty-fourth day throughout Yün-nan.

The absence of confirming information does not a priori throw doubts on the authenticity of this text, but it should be kept in mind that it was collected by Communist Chinese and that it happens to stress values which they regard as extremely important: in a critical situation, men are helpless but a girl can accomplish the task. She is willing to sacrifice herself for the welfare of the community. Although a poor, lower class girl, she has such qualities that even the daughter of the king is inferior to her. She

*is so conscious of community welfare that she does not show in-
terest in wealth at all, in spite of her poverty. Practically all these
traits run counter to traditional Chinese values.*

*Motifs F776, "Extraordinary gate," F886.1, "Golden key," and
K341, "Owner's interest distracted while goods are stolen."*

*Text from Yün-nan province. No place name is given, but it is
attributed to the I tribes of Yün-nan, a partly assimilated group
probably of Thai origin. Source:* Yün-nan ko-min-tsu min-chien
ku-shih hsüan, *pp. 75–77.*

· 47 · The Bridge of Ch'üan-chou

*The bridge of Ch'üan-chou, which still spans the Loyang River,
is one of the most famous engineering works of ancient China
and is the subject of many novels, short stories, and theater plays.
In the form presented here the tale is obviously a composition of
numerous stories, most of which are known in the literature from
the late fourteenth century on. The individual parts of this tale
occur in many other areas of China in connection with other
bridges.*

*Our text contains numerous allusions to legends and other be-
liefs. The ruler of heaven, theoretically the highest deity of the
pantheon, is here clearly identified with the deity of the north
star. The tortoise and snake are his symbolic animals, and are
commonly represented in reliefs or sculptures found in temples
throughout China.*

The rank of professor (chin-shih) *indicates a man who has
passed the highest state examination. It is believed that this high
earthly honor is also recognized by spirits and ghosts. Several
texts report that there were examinations even in hell and heaven.*

*Hsia Te-hai, the drunkard's name, means "can go into the sea".
Predictions made on the basis of an explanation of a written Chinese character were a common way of reading oracles, and many
literary stories in short story collections deal with this idea.*

*The eight workmen were, of course, the Eight Saints or Im-
mortals of popular belief. Lü Tung-pin is one of them. Chess
playing is a suitable leisure time occupation for saints; many tales
contain this motif.*

The use of the foot as firewood is also a common motif in Chinese tales, usually of Buddhist character. This motif appears again in tale No. 75, with disastrous results. The use of one's legs as firewood is found in India under Motif D2161.3.3.1, "Witch burns her child's legs for wood then covers child with sheet and child is whole," but has not been reported from any other area.

If a monk like I-po died in a truly Buddhist way—while sitting with crossed legs—his body was often wrapped in burlap and covered with lacquer, producing a statue of the monk.

It is one of the duties of the earth deity to watch hidden treasures, if these have an owner. In a number of stories, a stranger is allowed to borrow from such a treasure until the real owner has grown up; then the borrower has to return the money to the owner. K'ang Chin-lung (K'ang gold dragon), in testing Li Wu, behaves as Taoist saints often do in order to find out whether an adept is really serious.

The family names of the principal heroes of this story are the family names of a group of famous Fukienese clans. These clans still identify themselves with the bridge and the stories about it.

Motifs D1258.1, "Bridge made by magic," and H984, "Tasks performed with help of saint."

Eberhard, Typen No. 101 and 102; Eberhard, Volksmärchen Nos. 63 and 64. Text from Ch'üan-chou in Fukien province. Lin Lan, Sha-lung, pp. 60–67.

·48· The Faithful Official

In most cases the available texts of this tale are very early, the earliest going back to the first century before Christ. The story is still alive today, usually being told as a local legend. The idea that there are oxen in the water may refer originally to water buffaloes rather than to oxen. Iron animals or other objects made of iron are believed to be in rivers in order to hold the river within its banks. This whole complex of river and iron is typical of south and central China and occurs only rarely in north China. The self-sacrifice of the governor is in accord with Confucian principles of good government.

Motif S264, "Sacrifice to rivers and seas." Compare also S267, "Flood stopped by sacrifice of boy and girl."

. .*Eberhard*, Typen *No. 93, and Eberhard,* Volksmärchen *No. 52, have many similar tales, mainly from central and western China. Text from Hsüan-ch'eng, An-hui province. Lin Lan,* Min-chien chuan-shuo, *II, pp. 95–97.*

· 49 · The Water Mother

No early texts of this tale have been found, although the cult of the Water Mother has been traced back to the Sung era. The Water Mother (Shui-mu niang-niang) *is a well-known deity, but is no longer popularly worshiped (see H. Doré,* Recherches, *Vol. X, p. 796–98; Vol. VI, p. 4, p . 128, p. 132–33; Vol. XVII, p. 4).*

Elements of Type 565 The Magic Mill, *which is often found in Europe, particularly in Scandinavia, appear in this tale. The magic mill story is known in Japan in a form very close to its European counterparts. A variant is No. 39 in* Folktales of Japan. *The disastrous misuse of magic objects by jealous relatives forms the theme of No. 65 in the present collection.*

Motifs C762.1, "Tabu: using magic power too often"; and D1652.0.1, "Magic object causes thing to become inexhaustible."

Eberhard, Typen *No. 63; Eberhard,* Volksmärchen *No. 38. Text from Nanking, Kiang-su province.* Min-su *No. 11–12, pp. 48–51.*

· 50 · The Tiny Temple of the City Deity

The basic theme of this tale is the mutual responsibility of deities and human beings. It is the duty of the local deity to give rain; if he does not do so, the people can put him under pressure. It is also the duty of a local official to care for the welfare of his subjects. Our text does not say why the local deity did not procure rain, but we can guess that there was an order from a higher heavenly authority which he could not override. That the Jade Emperor (Yü huang-ti) finally gives rain, speaks for this explanation.

The localities which are mentioned are well known in Hangchou. The Ch'ing (Manchu) dynasty came to an end in 1911.

Motifs A162, "Conflicts of the gods," and D2143.1.3, "Rain produced by prayer."

Eberhard, Typen *No. 185, with six texts. Text from Hangchou, capital of Chekiang province.* Min-chien, *I, No. 6, pp. 4–11.*

PART VII

KINDNESS REWARDED AND EVIL PUNISHED

· 51 ·   The Tiger General

Seven variants of this tale have been collected from various parts of China. The earliest text is from the fourth century (Sou-shen chi 20, *p. 1a, from central China*). *In this story, the midwife receives venison every day as a gift from the grateful tigress. Motifs found in this tale occur often in both ancient and modern short stories.*

There was a temple for the Five Tiger God in Peking at the beginning of this century, but it is not known whether that deity had any relation to our story. The motif of the trial of the tiger is often found in popular plays and short stories.

Tales about animals being rescued from pain and later showing their gratefulness are of world-wide distribution. Probably the best known is that of Androcles and the lion. The tale given here about a midwife's son being rewarded with a bride finds a parallel in Dorson's Folk Legends of Japan, *pp. 143–44. In the Japanese tale a blacksmith helps a wolf give birth, and later marries a beautiful woman who proves to be the wolf in disguise. There is another story about a grateful wolf as Tale No. 7 in* Folktales of Japan, *a companion volume in this series. See No. 67, below, for the story of an ungrateful wolf.*

Motif B387, "Tiger grateful for woman assisting tigress as midwife."

Eberhard, Typen *No. 17. The variant given here is probably from central China. Lin Lan,* Huan-hsin hou, *pp. 9–12.*

· 52 ·   The Gratitude of the Snake

Typically Chinese is the trip of the young man to the imperial examinations, a motif which permeates Chinese drama, short stories, and novels as well as folktales. The snake and millepede belong to the five poisonous animals which traditionally are connected with the festival on the fifth day of the fifth month on which they are magically killed or exorcised. For this see also Nos. 6 and 42 in this collection.

In tales about grateful animals, the snake often plays a prominent role. There seems to be considerable dramatic interest in a situation in which the snake, generally the object of aversion, proves itself to be a real friend of man. The snake appears again as a grateful helper in Nos. 38 and 53 in this collection. A popular folktale about a grateful snake is No. 29 in Folktales of Israel, a companion volume in this series.

Motif Q51, "Kindness to animals rewarded," B524.3, "Helpful snake protects man from attack," and B264.4, "Fight between snake and millipede."

Eberhard, Typen No. 18 has thirteen texts. Text from Hangchou, Chekiang province. Lin Lan, Chin-t'ien-chi, pp. 1–10.

· 53 · The Greedy Minister

The earliest documentation for this tale and for the proverb "The snake eats the minister," which is often used as the tale's title, is discussed in Eberhard, Volksmärchen No. 14. According to this study, the basic theme of this tale may have been prevalent in China long before the Christian era. Many modern texts replace the pearl by a piece of liver—snake's liver is regarded as a powerful medicine.

The bureaucratic setting of our text, with the emperor, the chancellor, and the state examinations, is typical of Chinese tales and occurs even in the early variants. The man who has passed the highest examination (chin-shih; here called professor) is immediately given a high executive post.

Motif B103.4.2.2, "Snake vomits jewels," and Q272, "Avarice punished."

Eberhard, Typen No. 19, with six texts. This is another tale about the fine sense of justice and gratitude ascribed to snakes. See Nos. 38 and 52 in this collection for other tales dealing with this motif. Text from Wu-ch'ang in Hupei province. Lin Lan, Niao-ti ku-shih, pp. 82–87.

· 54 · The Man in the Moon

Stories about a grateful bird furnishing the seed of a squash, gourd, or pumpkin in which treasure is later found are popular in

Korea and Japan as well as in China, but do not seem to have been noted elsewhere. As in our story here, these tales usually conclude with the disastrous consequences of a greedy person's attempt to duplicate the good fortune of his neighbor.

This tale has not been found in any early Chinese sources but references to the markings on the moon are found at a very early date. In addition to the cinnamon tree, the Kuang-han kung (Palace of Boundless Cold), and the cock as markings on the moon, we often find references to the hare, frog, or toad.

Speculation as to what has brought about the peculiar markings on the moon's face has occupied people throughout the world. In addition to the motif-index reference given below, Thompson lists under A751 more than thirty separate motifs accounting for the moon's markings.

Motifs D1463.2.1, "Magic pumpkin furnishes treasure," Q2, "Kind and unkind," and A751.1, "Man in moon is person thrown or sent there as punishment."

Eberhard, Typen Nos. 24 and 25, with nine variants.

Text from Ch'ao-chou, Kuang-tung province. Lin Lan, Chint'ien-chi, pp. 53–57.

·55· *The Gossiping Animals*

This is one of the most popular stories about animals, and has been known in China since at least the fifth century. Type 613, The Two Travelers (Truth and Falsehood) of which this story is a variant, is known all over the world. Fifty-four variants have been recorded in Germany alone, Turkey reports twenty-one, and India sixteen. Christiansen concludes, after an exhaustive study (FFC 24, 1916, The Tale of the Two Travellers), that the folktale is of Oriental origin.

There are of course many types of magic remedies found in the various versions of the tale. The pill made of dirt is a common motif in Taoist stories; it is usually one of the Eight Immortals who offers such a medicine. The pills are rejected by the unelected, and accepted by those who have been called to the faith.

Motif N452, "Secret remedy overheard in conversation of animals (witches)."

Eberhard, Typen No. 28, with twenty texts. Text from central China. Lin Lan, Kui-ko-ko, pp. 18–21.

· 56 · The Butcher and the Vegetarian

According to Buddhist belief, a butcher is a sinner because he takes the life of innocent animals; therefore one cannot be a good Buddhist unless one is a vegetarian. This story, told in the vein of Buddhist exempla, shows that outward behavior is not an indicator of real piety. Our text refers to the Taoist saint Lü and his fight with Pai Mu-tan (Miss White Peony), a prostitute with whom he has started a flirtation, a story which is found in various literary forms before 1600 and which provided the plot for a number of theater plays. The end of our text contains a motif which in a slightly milder form is common, and recalls an adventure of the secondary hero in the novel Hsi-yo-chi (Monkey's Pilgrimage): a man meets one or several girls in a house in the wilderness; he is invited in and flirts with the girl(s). The next morning he finds himself in a tomb, and often dies of terror or exposure.

The motifs in our text are T332.1, "Woman sent by deity to tempt self-righteous anchorite," and Q415.3, "Punishment: man eaten by worms (snake)."

Eberhard, Typen No. 126 has only two texts. Text from P'u-chiang in Chekiang province; Lin Lan, Chin-t'ien-chi, pp. 65–69.

· 57 · Lü Tung-pin Tests the Ascetic

Tales of this type occur in China before the sixth century A.D. Lü is one of the Eight Immortals of Taoist theology, and can be replaced by other immortals in this tale. He is also the patron saint of barbers, as is related in No. 40 above. Usually, it is his friend Li T'ieh-kuai who has a festering leg. Lü often only has a festering wound or requests that he be scratched to relieve his itching.

Motifs D2161.4.17, "Magic cure by licking," and H1573.1.2, "Loathly deed performed as evidence of Christian virtue." The latter motif appears in Irish mythology, where it is associated with Christianity; in our tale we have the same concept expressed in Taoist terms.

Eberhard, Typen No. *106, with seventeen variants. For early texts see Eberhard, Volksmärchen No. 69. Text from Weng-yüan, Kuang-tung province; Ch'ing-shui, Hai-lung-wang-ti nü erh, pp. 84–85.*

· 58 · *The Dissatisfied Benefactor*

The basic theme of this tale—how the saints probe the sincerity of their followers—is more than a thousand years old in China. In our text, the names of the saints are not mentioned, but most probably the storyteller thought of Lü Tung-pin and Li T'ieh-kuai, a pair of friends who belong to the set of eight Taoist saints. The well of wine, too, is often found in other Chinese stories. It is usually destroyed by the greed of the owner. The water-to-wine transformation motif, beside being the first miracle reported to have been performed by Christ, occurs in the folk tradition of numerous countries. German, Greek, Irish, Icelandic, and Spanish sources are mentioned in the Motif Index.

Motifs H1565, "Tests of gratitude," D477.1 "Transformation: water becomes wine," and Q338. "Immoderate request punished."

Eberhard, Typen No. *106, with seventeen variants. Early texts are discussed in Eberhard, Volksmärchen No. 69. Text from Feng-hua, Chekiang province. Lin Lan, Ts'ai-hua-lang, pp. 31–35.*

· 59 · *The Wicked Rich Man Who Was Turned into a Monkey*

This tale has not been found in this form in early Chinese texts, but the fact that as many as fourteen close variants are known in Japan suggests that it has a fairly long history.

The behavior of the rich man violates the rules of Buddhism and Taoism. Taoist saints often take the form of beggars to examine the moral qualities of a believer. Most commonly, it is Lü Tung-pin who appears as a beggar, but Li T'ieh-kuai (Li, with the iron crutch) can take his place.

Before modern times, many families had slave girls. These were girls from poor families, to whom the buyer paid a price—a down payment for future services of the girl. The girl was then a servant in the house until the time for her marriage arrived. The owner had to arrange a marriage and pay the costs of the dowry for services received. Not all these girls were badly treated. Often, had they not been sold, they would have died or would have been left to die, since poor parents were frequently unable to feed another child. Girls who were sold could find a much better husband than if they had grown up with their parents.

Motifs D1337, "Magic object makes beautiful or hideous," and Q551.3.24, "Punishment: Transformation into monkey."

Eberhard, Typen No. 81. Text from Feng-hua in Chekiang province. Lin Lan, Ts'ai-hua-lang, pp. 36–40.

· 60 · The Sacrifice of the Maiden

The motif of the sacrifice of a human being in connection with a new building, wall, kiln, or smithy is very old in China. Archaeological excavations have proved that in the Shang era (before 1050 B.C.) human beings were buried under the foundations of palaces. Numerous texts as late as about A.D. 1000 report such sacrifices as historical facts in connection with buildings and installations. From the Sung era on (after A.D. 960), this motif occurs mainly in accounts that tend to report rumors or in folktales. See the note to No. 16, above, for a full discussion of this theme.

Motifs S261, "Foundation sacrifice," and K1612, "Message of death fatal to sender."

Text from Chü-hsien in Chekiang province. Min-chien, II, No. 10, pp. 332–34. Eberhard, Typen No. 99 has twelve texts from the coastal areas of China.

· 61 · The Mynah Bird

This story is reminiscent more of Indian than of Chinese tales. The motif of the animal which is hidden behind a deity and speaks as if the deity itself had spoken is found in two ancient Indian collections: the Malalasekera (a collection of Buddhist myths) and the Panchatantra. It may have been through these sources that it entered China and lodged in Chinese literary stories.

This text was collected in Communist China, and strongly stresses those values which today's regime likes to stress. The plasterer—a man of the lower class—is an honest, good man. The employer—a member of the upper class and a governmental official of the old regime—is a thoroughly bad character. The bird is faithful, and helps the poor man in his work. To get the bird for himself, the official makes illegal use of his power. He does this purely to satisfy his own whim—he has no other gain to expect. He not only cheats the poor worker but has him beaten unmercifully as well. His servants—for instance, the cook—are as cruel as the master. But in the end, the honest and good worker is rewarded and the corrupt official publicly punished and humiliated. Just as landlords in 1948 were forced to make public confessions of their crimes, so here the official has to confess. He is also stripped of his beard, a symbol which indicated his social status. A version of this tale has now been found in Taiwan. This version (by Ts'ao Chi-Fei, sent for publication to the editor of the Hsin-sheng pao *newspaper; not yet published by December 1967) leaves out the poor plasterer and has only the magistrate who punishes the bird because it had dirtied his desk and who suffers later the revenge of the bird.*

Motif K1971, "Man behind statue (tree) speaks and pretends to be God (spirit)." No direct parallel in Eberhard, Typen. *Text from Yün-nan province. Sources:* Yün-nan ko-min-tsu min-chien ku-shih hsüan, *pp. 26–29.*

·62· The Helpful Animals

No early texts of this tale have yet been found. In some Chinese variants, the tale explains the hatred between cats and dogs, as is true in many instances of this tale from countries other than China. This folktale is popular in eastern Europe, the Near East, India, and Japan as well as in China. Forty-five variants have been collected in Russia alone.

Type 560, The Magic Ring.

Eberhard, Typen *No. 13, with nine texts. Text from Kuan-yün, Kiang-su province. Lin Lan,* Tu-chiao hai-tse, *pp. 92–96.*

·63· The Tale of Nung-kua-ma

Although this folktale is widely known in China, I have not yet found an early text. Since the tale is most probably influenced by stories from India, it can be predicted that early Chinese texts will some day be found. Thompson and Roberts, in Types of Indic Oral Tales, *lists some twelve Indian variants. Nung-kua-ma is a local word, which is not found elsewhere in the literature.*

Variants of this tale are distributed throughout the world. It is especially popular in northern Europe. A representative Japanese variant is No. 6 in Folktales of Japan, *a companion volume in this series.*

Types 130, The Animals in Night Quarters, *and 210,* Cock, Hen, Duck, Pin, and Needle on a Journey.

Eberhard, Typen *No. 14 has twenty-six texts, mainly from southern China. A full text is also published in Eberhard,* Volksmärchen *No. 9. Text from Weng-yüan, Kuang-tung province.* Min-su *No. 15, pp. 42–48.*

·64· Tales of the San Kuan

Although in general tales of this type are widely known, the particular tale given here is more famous than others. The introductory part of the classical sixteenth-century novel Hsi-yo-chi (Monkey's Pilgrimage) *is built upon the first part of this tale. The principal hero in this novel is Hsüan-tsang, the monk. Since he lived in the T'ang era (A.D. 618–906), he is often called the "Monk of the T'ang Empire" (T'ang-seng). This name has been explained as "floating monk," because of the similarity in pronunciation with "T'ang monk."*

The complete folktale is the subject of numerous theater plays, which usually concentrate upon the first part of the story. It is localized at Golden Mountain (Chin-shan), a rock in the Yangtse River where drinking water could be found. This rock and the monasteries there played an important role in Chinese Buddhism. The Yün-t'ai (Cloud Terrace Mountain) is another famous mountain with many monasteries.

The latter part of the tale appears in another classical novel, Investiture with Divine Rank, (Feng-shen yen-i). *Chiang Tzu-ya,* the main figure in this novel and again in numerous early theater plays, is said to have lived in the eleventh century B.C.—that is, some 1,700 years before the monk Hsüan-tsang. This episode of the tale explains the origin of a popular deity, San Kuan (Three Officials), who has been known locally since at least the twelfth century. According to some traditions, San Kuan is not one but three persons—the officials controlling sky, earth, and water. The final part of the tale clearly refers to the Ming era of about A.D. 1500. At that time, large sections of the coastal population of southeast China were relocated in the interior because of continuous attacks by Japanese pirates and secret collaboration between the pirates and local officials. Stories about treacherous ministers, who caused such inequities without any real reason, are common today along the coast.

The popular element of the journey to the dragon kingdom reappears in this tale. See the note to No. 23 for a discussion of Japanese variants of the underwater dragon kingdom tales.

Motifs B375.1, "Fish returned to water: grateful," S331, "Exposure of child in boat (floating chest)," and D812.7, "Magic object received from dragon king."

Eberhard, Typen No. 58 and 39. A discussion of this tale is in Eberhard, Volksmärchen, pp. 153–54. Text from the Yün-t'ai Mountain in Chekiang province. Lin Lan, Chin-t'ien-chi, pp. 19–31.

·65· The Wishing Stone

The undersea dragon kingdom is prominent in this tale as in the preceding story. The receipt of a magic object from an underwater being, and its subsequent misuse by a greedy relative, forms the plot of a number of Asian folktales. Additional Chinese tales containing this motif can be found under Eberhard, Typen No. 61 and 62. A Japanese tale in which this motif is prominent is No. 22 in Folktales of Japan, a companion volume in this series.

The loss of a magic object through greed is of course a worldwide motif. The story of the goose that laid the golden egg is probably the one most familiar to Western readers; the golden goose story was also known to the ancient Greeks, and appears in

*India in both the Panchatantra and the Jātaka collections. See No.
49 in this collection for another Chinese tale in which a magic
object is misused with disastrous results.*

*Motifs D812.7, "Magic object received from dragon king,"
D1470.1.1, "Magic wishing-stone," and D877, "Magic object loses
power by overuse." Also present are elements of Motifs L0–L99,
"Victorious youngest child."*

*Eberhard, Typen No. 40. Text from Kuan-yün, Kiang-su
province. Sun Chia-hsün, Wa-wa-shih, pp. 149–159.*

· 66 · Cinderella

*The Cinderella story is undoubtedly one of the most popular
folktales in the world. In China, elements of the Cinderella tale
can be found in texts of the T'ang era (seventh to tenth century); in the West variants can be found in the narrative tradition of every European country.*

*Two extensive studies have been made of the tale. In the first
study, made in 1893, Marian Cox was already able to utilize some
345 variants. Anna Birgitta Rooth, in her study of 1951, had
nearly three times that many at hand. On the basis of her exhaustive analysis, Rooth concluded that the Cinderella story must have
originated somewhere in the Middle East and spread both east
and west from there. There are still gaps, however, in the distribution of the tale, and the precise relationship between the Chinese and European redactions has not yet been demonstrated.*

*Two companion volumes in this series contain tales of related
interest: No. 38 in Folktales of Japan, and No. 48 in Folktales of
Israel.*

*Eberhard, Typen No. 32, with references to eleven texts. The
tale is often very close to Typen No. 31, and in fact the second
part of our tale belongs completely to Typen No. 31. Text from
P'an-yü, near Canton, Kuang-tung province. Lin Lan, San-ko
yüan-wang, pp. 70–80.*

· 67 · The Great Flood

*The major part of this tale—that of the rescue and marriage of an
abducted princess—is closely related to a folktale long popular in*

Western tradition, The Quest for a Vanished Princess, *Type 301A. Elements of this tale type are found in Herodotus' reworking of Greek mythology and in the saga of Beowulf. The flood episode is of course popular throughout the world. The escape in a boat constructed according to directions received from a supernatural being is similar to the Genesis account of the deluge.*

The ungrateful wolf in this tale finds a parallel in the well-known early Chinese story, Chung-shan lang (The Wolf from Chung-shan) *about a rescued wolf who threatens to kill his benefactor. This story contains elements of Type 155,* The Ungrateful Serpent Returned to Captivity. *Variants of Type 155, with either a serpent, bear, or lion as the thankless animal, have frequently appeared in European exempla. The tale of the treacherous animal is found in Aesop and is also popular in India.*

Stone lions are typically found in front of temples and offices; they protect the building against bad spirits. It is possible that this custom is of Near Eastern origin.

"His Excellency Wang" (Wang Yüan-wai) is a title which is customarily used in theater plays and popular literature with the connotation of a rich man in retirement.

The festival of the ascent of the dragon on the second day of the second month is celebrated in many parts of China. It indicates the coming of spring rain, since the dragon produces rain when roaming around in the sky.

The long introductory episode of the flood contains Motifs Q42.3, "Generosity to saint (god) in disguise rewarded," D474.9, "Eyes of stone lion become bloody," A1021, "Deluge: escape in boat," and B360, "Animals grateful for rescue from peril of death." The remainder of the tale is very close to Type 301A as mentioned above.

Eberhard, Typen *No. 47 for the flood story; further discussion in Eberhard,* Volksmärchen *No. 28. The second part of the story belongs to Typen No. 122, which deals with the rescue of a girl from an ogre's cave. Text from Chang-ch'iu, Shan-tung province.* Shan-tung min-chien chuan-shuo, *I, pp. 37–60.*

·68· The Story of the Serpent

The earliest texts of this tale usually refer to the periodical sacrifice of a maiden to a river deity; the sacrifice takes the form of the marriage of the girl to the deity. In this form, the tale was known before the Christian Era. As in the text given here, many variants contain Buddhistic elements. Some medieval Chinese texts report such tales as historical facts in connection with heretic Buddhist sects or local Buddhist cults. Because it emerges pure from dirty water, the lotus is a flower endowed with a great deal of Buddhistic symbolism.

In many popular Buddhist sects the believer does not attempt to enter nirvana, but first to enter the western paradise.

The gunpowder and quicklime in our tale are innovations. Early texts have the official either personally enter the water and fight the spirit or send the priests into the water to announce the sacrifice. By so doing, the official abolishes the heretic cult.

The familiar three score years and ten of Western tradition, perhaps influenced by the allotted life span mentioned in the Bible, contrasts with the sixty-year span shown in this and in another Chinese tale, The Life Span of Men, Eberhard, Typen No. 71. The figure of sixty years as the maximum life span appears also in Japanese tales: see No. 53 in Folktales of Japan, in this series.

Motifs S140.1, "Abandonment of aged," and D965.6, "Magic lotus plant."

Eberhard, Typen No. 95 has twelve texts from central and northern China. Variants are also found in south China. Text from central China; Lin Lan, Huan-hsin-hou, pp. 49–52.

PART VIII

CLEVERNESS AND STUPIDITY

·69· The Mirror

This tale is found in China as early as the T'ang era (A.D. 618–906). Cognate stories are well known in Japan. A variant similar to the one given here is No. 55 in Folktales of Japan in this *series. The story is known also in the United States and in England.*

Motif J1795, "Image in mirror mistaken for picture."

Eberhard, Typen 57, No. 3, with ten texts. Text from P'ing-hu in Chekiang province. Lou Tse-k'uang, Ch'iao-nü, pp. 88–89.

·70· The Living King of Hell Dies of Anger

This folktale is well known in India and Japan and throughout Europe and North America, but no Chinese text other than this one is known to me. It should, however, be kept in mind that this text is found in a collection from Communist China, and that it strongly stresses values which today's China likes to stress. The landlord behaves like an evil king and is thoroughly exploitative. His only interest is to squeeze the last penny out of his tenants. The tenant is good and clever, and by his cleverness he cheats the upper class. No similar tales known to me from pre-Communist China depict landowners as completely evil. In the pre-Communist tales it is rare to find the common farmer depicted as being better than anyone of another class. Exploitation of the kind described in the text given here was not known in the older tales; agreements of the kind described would in traditional stories be made between a clever man—often a scholar—and another man of the same or even lower (not higher) social level. There is a strong suspicion that the tale has been thoroughly changed, if it is a folktale of Yün-nan at all.

Type 1030, The Crop Division.

Text from Yün-nan province. No place name is given, but the story is said to come from the Pai tribes, a strongly assimilated tribal group, probably of Thai origin. Source: Yün-nan ko-min-tsu min-chien ku-shih hsüan, pp. 115–16.

·71· Money Makes Cares

The central theme of this tale occurs in a theater play of the Ming era (A.D. 1368–1644) in which a detective discovers a thief: a boy who has always been singing suddenly stops singing after he has the money. Tales of this type appeared in Europe in the Middle Ages in collections of exempla. A variant is No. 66 in Crane's The Exempla of Jacques de Vitry.

Motif *J1085.1,* "*The happy friar becomes unhappier as he re-ceives ever more and more money.*" *This motif also forms Type 754,* The Happy Friar.

Eberhard, Typen *No. 204 has only this one text. Text from Ch'üan-chou, Fukien province. Wu Ts'ao-ting,* Ch'üan-chou min-chien chuan-shuo, *I, pp. 84–89.*

·72· *The Two-Headed Phoenix*

Although two-headed animals are not uncommon in Chinese mythology, the phoenix is commonly conceived of as a pair; the male (feng) *and the female* (huang). *The phoenix is regarded as a bird of good omen, a symbol of the empress. It appears again in No. 13 in this collection.*

This text is one which, in my opinion, is very strongly revised by editors in Communist China, if not invented by them. The story stresses all the values which the present regime commends: the hunter is basically good; the king is envious and cruel, and cheats even his own servants; the ministers are cunning and evil. The common man, symbolized by the phoenix, is strong and vir-tuous if left alone. But the evil members of the upper class try their best to instigate mistrust and hostility among the common people; as soon as they succeed, they have power over the com-mon man.

Motif K2131, "*Trickster makes two friends each suspicious of the other's intentions,*" *is prominent here. This motif is found in Ireland, India, and Africa as well as China, but has not been re-corded in any intermediate countries. The specific use of whisper-ing to destroy friendship is found in motif K2131.3,* "*Woman de-stroys men's friendship by pretending to whisper to one.*" *This motif has been reported from India.*

No direct parallel in Eberhard, Typen. *Text from Yün-nan province. Sung Chê,* Yün-nan min-chien ku-shih, *I, pp. 129f. Re-printed with minimal changes in* Yün-nan ko min-tsu min-chien ku-shih hsüan, *pp. 202 f.*

·73· *The Donkey in Kuei-chou*

The outline of the story is close to Typen *No. 3. No modern texts of this story seem to have been recorded. As noted in the discus-*

sion of Typen *No. 4, in* Eberhard, Volksmärchen, *this tale seems to have originated in India.*

Motif K2324.1, *"Ferocious animal frightened by ass braying."*

Eberhard, Typen *No. 4. Text from southern China.* Liu Tsung-yüan hsien-sheng chi (Collected Works of Liu Tsung-yüan) *from the eighth century A.D.*

·74· *The Rat and the Ox*

Eberhard, Typen, *does not mention this fairly common tale, but it belongs with tales like* Typen *No. 6 which attempt to explain the Chinese zodiac. Japan has borrowed the Chinese system of zodiacal animals, and explanatory tales involving a clever rat are also popular there. Curiously enough, the Western zodiac seems to have given rise to no tales such as these. Two references in the motif index under "Zodiac" are to Middle Eastern tales, but neither of them contains explanatory motifs.*

Motif K80, *"Contests in other physical accomplishments won by deception."*

Text from Fukien province. Lin Lan, Hsiang-szu-shu, *pp. 96–100.*

·75· *Why Does Li T'ieh-kuai Have a Wounded Leg?*

Li T'ieh-kuai (Li, with the iron crutch) *is one of the Eight Immortals. It is usually in connection with Lü Tung-pin that he becomes an immortal. Several theater plays, from the fourteenth century on, treat the Lü-Li friendship. In the most popular legends, Li wanted to travel around, so he left his earthly body under the care of his disciple. But when he was away for seven days, the disciple got worried and buried the corpse, so that Li, upon his return, had to find a suitable body. He could find only the body of a beggar with a festering leg. See Tale No. 47 for another story containing the motif of legs used as firewood.*

The appearance of the volcano in the version given here is unusual. Stories about volcanoes are rare in China—there are no such mountains in China proper.

Motifs D1346.7, *"Pill of immortality,"* and D1531.2, *"Magic pill gives power of flying." The latter part of the tale contains Motif C940, "Sickness or weakness for breaking tabu."*

The first part of this tale belongs to Eberhard, Typen No. 107, and the last part to Typen No. 184. Text from central China. Lin Lan, Min-chien chuan-shuo, II, pp. 70–71.

·76· The Mother of Heaven

The ruler of heaven (T'ien-chu) here has the same name as the Chinese equivalent of God in Catholic Christianity, but he is the husband of T'ien-mu (mother of heaven), a deity about whom little is known. I have only one text from 1453 from Hsin-hui in Kuang-tung province, in which T'ien-mu plays a dominant role.

Motif J2465, "Disastrous following of instructions."

Text probably from central China. Lin Lan, Kua-wang, pp. 59–61.

·77· The Two Earth Deities

According to texts from the T'ang era, this tale seems to have first been Buddhistic, then became identified with various indigenous deities. Legendary tales which show deities or saints in ridiculous situations or portray them with undesirable character traits are fairly common and are not a product of modern times. In popular religion, deities were nothing but officials. They were of higher rank than officials on earth, but were nevertheless beings with much the same character traits as humans.

Motifs D2161.4.10, "Disease cured by same thing (person) that caused it," and J2415, "Foolish imitation of lucky man."

Eberhard, Typen No. 164 has four modern and one early text; in Volksmärchen No. 104, texts from the T'ang period are mentioned. Text from southern China. Lin Lan, Huan-hsin-hou, pp. 4–8.

·78· Chu the Rogue

This story has not yet been found in texts dated before 1800, but its main episode—the account of the man who defies death—can be found in earlier sources. Usually the hero in such stories is P'eng-tsu, a sort of Chinese Methuselah. The satirical beginning of our text is not unique; religious folktales are often told in a slightly mocking tone.

A P'u-sa *(bodhisattva)* is in Chinese folk religion a Buddhist deity. Jih-kuang *(sunshine)* and Yüeh-kuang *(moonlight)* are well-known figures of Buddhist religion. They have counterparts in Indian Buddhism, but in China, where they are known since at least the fourth century A.D., they are also connected with popular Taoism. Yüeh-kuang is in early folk belief a messianic figure, whose reappearance on earth was predicted by apocryphal texts.

Yü huang-ti is in folk belief the emperor of all deities, both Buddhist and non-Buddhist. This deity is more recent than the two bodhisattvas; it has become prominent only since the eleventh century.

The Wen-shen *(plague deities)* are very numerous, and are usually represented as triads in folk temples. Their cult is strongest in coastal central and south China. On the island of Taiwan, of four thousand temples studied, eight hundred were devoted to these deities.

The hells in folk religion are highly organized and bureaucratized institutions. Normally there are ten hells with up to 135 sub-hells. Yen-lo-wang *(King Yama)* resides in the fifth hell, and not in the first or judgment hell. The king of hell has many servants; one of them, Huo-wu-ch'ang *(life is not eternal)*, has to catch the soul of the condemned person and bring the soul down to hell. Huo-wu-ch'ang can adopt different shapes; sometimes he is a one-legged creature. Belief in one-legged beings is more typical of southern than of northern China.

Niu-t'ou *(Oxhead)* and Ma-mien *(Horseface)* are two policemen in hell, standing by the main judge. Popular prints depict them with animal heads on human bodies. A raksha is another type of employee in hell.

One of the most famous punishments in hell is the caldron of oil; the ice hell too is well known. The Yin-yang River, usually called the Nai-ho River, separates this world from the netherworld. A bridge as wide as a hair goes over it, and this is the reason why Chu prefers to ride on a carp, which is a fish of good luck.

Motifs D831, "Magic object acquired by trick exchange," and B184.1.1, "Horse (mule) with magic speed."

Eberhard, Typen *No. 156 has nine texts. Text from Ju-kao in Kiangsu province. Lin Lan,* Chin-t'ien-chi, *pp. 99–107.*

·79· *The Kitchen Deity*

The deity of the kitchen (Tsao-wang) is one of the most popular deities of Chinese folk religion. A picture or figure of it is above every hearth and is the object of special worship about the twenty-fourth day of the last month of the year. It is believed that the deity will leave at that time to report about the family to the higher authorities in heaven. Many families cover the mouth of the figure with honey or sugar so that it can tell only sweet things about the family.

Literary sources mention a number of instances in which men became so poor that they had to sell their wives; this motif occurs also in theater plays. The woman becomes the concubine of an older man.

Motif N351, "Money (treasure) unwittingly given away." The present tale is related to Type 841, One Beggar Trusts God, the Other the King, *in which each beggar is given a loaf of bread, with the loaf of the second being filled with gold. Not knowing the nature of the loaves, the beggars exchange them. This folktale is found scattered throughout Europe, the Near East, and India. Tales close to this Chinese variant are popular in Japan.*

Eberhard, Typen *No. 177, has two texts which form a special subtype. Text from central China. Lin Lan,* Min-chien chuan-shuo, *II, pp. 90–92.*

Bibliography

This bibliography contains only books and journals which are mentioned in the headnotes or cited as sources. The Chinese characters for nearly all of the works in Chinese can be found in my *Typen*. A bibliography of texts of Chinese folktales to 1935 is found in my *Typen* and *Volksmärchen*. A bibliography of recent folkloristic literature in Chinese is in preparation.

AARNE, ANTTI, and THOMPSON, STITH. *The Types of the Folktale: A Classification and Bibliography.* ("Folklore Fellows Communications," No. 184.) Helsinki, 1961.

CH'ING-SHUI. *Hai-lung-wang-ti nü-erh* (The Daughter of the Dragon King of the Sea). Canton, 1929.

———. *T'ai-yang ho yüeh-liang* (Sun and Moon). Shao-hsing, 1933.

CHRISTIANSEN, REIDAR THORWARD (ed.). *Folktales of Norway.* Trans. by Pat Shaw Iversen. Chicago, 1964.

COX, MARIAN ROALFE. *Cinderella.* Publications of the Folk-Lore Society XXXI, London, 1893.

CRANE, THOMAS FREDERICK. *The Exempla of Jacques de Vitry.* Publications of the Folk-Lore Society, XXVI. London, 1890.

DORÉ, HENRI. *Recherches sur les superstitions en Chine.* 18 vols. Shanghai, 1911–1938.

DORSON, RICHARD M. *Folk Legends of Japan.* Rutland, Vermont, and Tokyo, 1962.

———. editor, *Studies in Japanese Folklore.* Bloomington, 1963.

EBERHARD, WOLFRAM. *Lokalkulturen im alten China.* 2 vols. Leiden and Peking, 1943.

———. *Typen chinesischer Volksmärchen* ("Folklore Fellows Communications," No. 120.) Helsinki, 1937.

———. *Volksmärchen aus Südost-China, Sammlung Ts'ao Sung-*

yeh ("Folklore Fellows Communications," No. 128.) Helsinki, 1941.

GAYTON, A. H. "The Orpheus Myth in North America." *Journal of American Folklore*. XLVIII (1935), 263–93.

GRUBE, W. *Feng-shen yen-i, die Metamorphosen der Götter*. Leiden, 1912. This is a German translation of *Feng-shen yen-i* (Enfeoffment of Deities). A popular novel probably of the 18th century, compiled on the basis of earlier texts. Author unknown.

JEN-MIN WEN-HSÜEH CH'U-PAN SHÊ (ed.). *Ch'ü-hai Tsung-mu T'i-yao* (Abstracts of Plays in the "Sea of Plays"). 3 vols. Peking, 1959.

———. *Yün-nan ko-min-tsu min-chien ku-shih hsüan* (Selection of Folktales from all Ethnic Groups of Yün-nan). Peking, 1962. A number of texts in this collection are taken from the work of Sung Chê.

KAN PAO. *Sou-shen-chi* (In Search of the Spirits). Collected probably during the fourth century.

LIN LAN. *Chin-t'ien-chi* (The Golden Frog). 2d ed., Shanghai, 1930.

———. *Hsiang-szu-shu* (The Tree of Mutual Love). Shanghai, 1934.

———. *Hsiao Chu Pa-chieh* (Little Chu Pa-chieh). Shanghai, 1932.

———. *Huan-hsin-hou* (After the Exchange of the Heart). Shanghai, 1931.

———. *Hui Ta-wang* (Great King Ashes). Shanghai, 1933. This is a re-edition of *Hsiao Chu Pa-chieh,* above.

———. *Kuai-hsiung-ti* (Unusual Brothers). Shanghai, 1932.

———. *Kua-wang* (King Melon). Shanghai, 1934.

———. *Kui ko-ko* (Brother Ghost). Shanghai, 1932.

———. *Lü Tung-pin ku-shih* (Stories about Lü Tung-pin). Peking, 1925. (This is the so-called "Little Edition").

———. *Min-chien chuan-shuo* (Folk Traditions). 2 vols. Shanghai, 1930–31.

———. *Niao-ti ku-shih* (Tales about Birds). Shanghai, 1925.

———. *San-chiang-chün* (Three Generals). Shanghai, 1932.

———. *San-ko yüan-wang* (Three Wishes). Shanghai, 1933.

————. *Sha-lung* (Sand Dragon). Shanghai, 1931.

————. *Ts'ai-hua lang* (The Flower Picker). Shanghai, 1930.

————. *Tu-chiao hai-tse* (The One-Legged Child). Shanghai, 1932.

————. *Tung-hsien mai-lei* (The Saint Tung Sells Thunder). Shanghai, 1932.

————. *Yün-chung-ti mu-ch'in* (The Mother in the Clouds). Shanghai, 1933.

LIU TSUNG-YÜAN. *Liu Tsung-yüan chi* (Collected Works of Liu Tsung-yuan). 8th century. Edition: Sih-pu pei-yao.

LOU TSE-K'UANG. *Ch'iao-nü ho kai-niang-ti ku-shih* (Stories about the Clever and the Stupid Girl). Shanghai, 1933.

————. *Shao-hsing ku-shih* (Stories from Shao-hsing). Canton, 1929.

MAASS, E. *Orpheus*. München, 1895.

MABUCHI, TOICHI. "Tales Concerning the Origin of Grains in the Insular Areas af Eastern and Southeastern Asia." *Asian Folklore Studies*, XXIII, No. 1 (1964), 1–92.

NOY, DOV. (ed.). *Folktales of Israel*. Trans. by Gene Baharav. Chicago, 1963.

ROOTH, ANNA BIRGITTA. *The Cinderella Cycle*, Lund, 1951.

SEKI, KEIGO. (ed.). *Folktales of Japan*. Trans. by Robert J. Adams. Chicago, 1963.

SHANTUNG PROVINCIAL POPULAR EDUCATION OFFICE (ed.). *Shantung min-chien chuan-shuo, ti i chi* (Folk Traditions from Shan-tung. Collection No. 1). Chinan, 1933.

SUN CHIA-HSÜN. *Wa-wa-shih* (The Baby Stone). Shanghai, 1930.

SUNG CHÊ. *Hu-nan min-chien ku-shih* (Folktales from Hu-nan). Hong Kong, 1961.

————. *Yün-nan min-chien ku-shih* (Folktales from Yün-nan) 2 vols. Hong Kong, 1961.

THOMPSON, STITH. *The Folktale*. New York, 1951.

————. *Motif-Index of Folk Literature*. 6 vols. Rev. ed. Copenhagen and Bloomington, Ind., 1955–58.

THOMPSON, STITH, and ROBERTS, WARREN E. *Types of Indic Oral Tales*. ("Folklore Fellows Communications," No. 180.) Helsinki, 1960.

TS'AO SUNG-YEH. *Ts'ao Sung-yeh Collection*. A manuscript collection in 7 volumes, collected in and around Chin-hua (Che-kiang) by Mr. Ts'ao with the collaboration of school students. The Chinese original was lost when the Berlin Anthropological Museum was destroyed during World War II. A German translation is in the hands of W. Eberhard. Publication of this translation is in preparation.

WU CH'ENG-EN. *Hsi-yo-chi* (The Monkey's Pilgrimage). A popular novel, probably of the 16th century. An English translation is: WALEY, ARTHUR, trans., *Monkey*. New York, 1943.

WU TS'AO-TING. *Ch'üan-chou min-chien chuan-shuo* (Folk Traditions from Ch'üan-chou). 3 vols. Ch'üan-chou, 1931–3.

Index of Motifs

(Motif numbers are from Stith Thompson, *Motif-Index of Folk-Literature* [6 vols.; Copenhagen and Bloomington, Ind., 1955–58])

A. MYTHOLOGICAL MOTIFS

Motif No.		Tale No.
A162	Conflicts of the gods	50
A751.1	Man in moon is person thrown or sent there as punishment	54
A761.3	Stars as transformed lovers	23
A778.3	Milky Way as a river	25
A791.9	Origin of rainbow: transformed butterflies (souls of lovers)	15
A972.5.6	Hole in stone caused by weapon of warrior	21
A1021	Deluge: escape in boat	67
A1338	Origin of physical defects	2
A1384	Origin of evil inclinations	1
A1423.2	Acquisition of rice	9, 10
A1429.4	Acquisition of salt	13
A2281	Enmity between animals from original quarrel	6
A2312.3	Origin of dents in crab's shell	5
A2326.3.4	Why buffalo's hornes are bent	26
A2411.1.5.1.1	Why ape has red back	30
A2426.2.18	Origin and meaning of cock's cry 'cock-a-doodle-do'	6
A2435.3.10.1	Why rat may eat rice	10
A2515.1	Why ox is draft animal	3, 4
A2545.3	Why dog eats first	10
A2611.5	Parts of human or animal body transformed into plants	8
A2615.2	Plant from mother's milk	9

B. ANIMALS

B604.2.1	Marriage to turtle	29
B103.4.2.2	Snake vomits jewels	53
B184.1.1	Horse with magic speed	78
B217.1.1	Animal languages learned from eating serpent	38
B264.4	Fight between snake and millipede	52
B360	Animals grateful for rescue from peril of death	67
B375.1	Fish returned to water; grateful	64
B387	Tiger grateful for woman assisting tigress as midwife	51
B511.1.2	Snake creeps into man's mouth and heals him	17

Motif No.   *Tale No.*

B524.3	Helpful snake protects man from attack	52
B571	Animals perform tasks for man	27
B580	Animal helps man to wealth and greatness	25
B600	Human-animal marriage	31
B601.7	Marriage to monkey	30

C. TABU

C762.1	Tabu: using magic power too often	49
C940	Sickness or weakness for breaking tabu	75

D. MAGIC

D435.2.1	Picture comes to life	24
D474.9	Eyes of stone lion become bloody	67
D477.1	Transformation: water becomes wine	58
D672	Obstacle flight	23
D721	Disenchantment by removing skin	22
D812.7	Magic object received from dragon king	64, 65
D831	Magic object acquired by trick exchange	78
D877	Magic object loses power by overuse	65
D965.6	Magic lotus plant	68
D1258.1	Bridge made by magic	47
D1337	Magic object makes beautiful or hideous	59
D1346.7	Pill of immortality	75
D1361.1.15	Magic cap renders wearer invisible	43
D1463.2.1	Magic pumpkin furnishes treasure	54
D1470.1.1	Magic wishing stone	65
D1549.7	Murdered man's head will cause earth to burn	37
D1531.2	Magic pill gives power of flying	75
D1641.4	Forest cleared by magic	36
D1652.0.1	Magic object causes thing to become inexhaustible	49
D2011	Years thought days	44, 45
D2135	Magic air journey	18
D2143.1.3	Rain produced by prayer	50
D2161.3.3.1	Witch burns her child's legs for wood	47
D2161.410	Disease cured by same thing (person) that caused it	77
D2161.4.17	Magic cure by licking	57

E. THE DEAD

E37.1	Failure to resuscitate because of premature disturbance of members to be left in cask for certain time	27
E611.2.3	Reincarnation as calf	22
E611.3	Man reincarnated as swine	39
E631	Reincarnation in plant (tree) growing from grave	7
E721.2	Body in trance while soul is absent	35
E754.3	Burial in certain ground assures going to heaven	33

F. MARVELS

Motif No.		Tale No.
F81.1	Orpheus	19
F81.1.2	Journey to land of dead to visit deceased	39
F420.5.1.5	Water-spirits work as servants for mortal	41
F420.5.1.7.5	Water-spirit gives mortal fish	41
F480	House-spirits	42
F481.0.1.3	Cobold acquired by placing food for him in a certain place	42
F776	Extraordinary gate	46
F886.1	Golden key	46

H. TESTS

H100	Identification by matching parts of divided token	19
H117	Identification by cut garment	28
H119.2	Needle left in garment of husband by abducted wife as sign	28, 29
H984	Tasks performed with help of saint	47
H1381.3.1.1.1	Quest for bride for king like picture he has seen	20
H1565	Tests of gratitude	58
H1573.1.2	Loathly deed performed as evidence of Christian virtue	57

J. THE WISE AND THE FOOLISH

J154	Wise words of dying father	34
J1085.1	The happy friar becomes unhappier as he receives ever more money	71
J1795	Image in mirror mistaken for picture	69
J2415	Foolish imitation of lucky man	77
J2465	Disastrous following of instructions	76

K. DECEPTIONS

K80	Contests in other physical accomplishments won by deception	74
K341	Owner's interest distracted while goods are stolen	46
K359.1	Theft by means of magic invisibility	43
K1335	Seduction by stealing clothes of bathing girl (swan maiden)	23
K1612	Message of death fatal to sender	60
K1811	Gods in disguise visit mortals	40
K1837	Disguise of woman in man's clothes	15
K1971	Man behind statue speaks and pretends to be god	61
K2110.1	Calumniated wife	22
K2131	Trickster makes two friends each suspicious of the other's intentions	72

Motif No.   *Tale No.*

K2131.3   Woman destroys men's friendship by pretending to whisper to one   72

K2324.1   Ferocious animal frightened by ass braying   73

L. REVERSAL OF FORTUNE

L0-L99   Victorious youngest child   65

L161   Lowly hero marries princess   18

M. ORDAINING THE FUTURE

M370   Vain attempts to escape fulfillment of prophecy   34

N. CHANCE AND FATE

N101   Inexorable fate   14

N134   Persons effect change of luck   33

N135   Objects effect change of luck   32

N351   Money (treasure) unwittingly given away   79

N452   Secret remedy overheard in conversation of animals   55

Q. REWARDS AND PUNISHMENTS

Q2   Kind and unkind   54

Q42   Generosity rewarded   32

Q42.3   Generosity to saint in disguise rewarded   67

Q51   Kindness to animals rewarded   52

Q111   Riches as reward   29

Q272   Avarice punished   53

Q338   Immoderate request punished   58

Q415.3   Punishment: man eaten by worms (snake)   56

Q431   Punishment: banishment   24

Q551.3.4   Punishment: Transformation into monkey   59

Q560   Punishment in hell   4

R. CAPTIVES AND FUGITIVES

R138   Rescue from shipwreck   35

S. UNNATURAL CRUELTY

S140.1   Abandonment of aged   68

S261   Foundation sacrifice   60, 61

S264   Sacrifice to rivers and seas   48

S267   Flood stopped by sacrifice of boy and girl   48

T. SEX

T11.2   Lover through sight of picture   24

T81   Death from love   15

T91.6.2   King in love with a lowly girl   21

T111.1   Marriage of a mortal and a god   28

Motif No.		*Tale No.*
T111.2	Woman from sky-world marries mortal man	24
T182	Death from intercourse	17
T211.2	Wife's suicide at husband's death	16
T332.1	Woman sent by deity to tempt self-righteous anchorite	56
T511.3	Conception from eating vegetable	26
T589.5	New-born child reincarnation of recently deceased person	19

V. RELIGION

V211	Miraculous healing by saints	40
V411.5	Treasure given away by saint miraculously restored	36

Z. MISCELLANEOUS MOTIFS

Z311	Achilles heel	37

Index of Tale Types

(Type numbers are from Antti Aarne and Stith Thompson, *The Types of the Folktale* [Helsinki, 1961])

I. ANIMAL TALES (1–299)

Type		Tale No.
130	The Animals in Night Quarters	63
155	The Ungrateful Serpent Returned to Captivity	67
210	Cock, Hen, Duck, Pin, and Needle on a Journey	63

II. ORDINARY FOLKTALES (300–749)

A. Tales of Magic

Type		
301	The Bear's Son	31
313A	The Girl As Helper on the Hero's Flight	27
328	The Boy Steals the Giant's Treasure	43
461	Three Hairs from the Devil's Beard	20
465	Man Persecuted Because of His Beautiful Wife	20, 25
510	Cinderella	66
560	The Magic Ring	62
565	The Magic Mill	49
613	The Two Travelers	55

B. Religious Tales (750–849)

834	The Pot of Gold and the Pot of Scorpions	12
841	One Beggar Trusts God, the Other the King	79

D. Tales of The Stupid Ogre (1000–1199)

1030	The Crop Division	70

III. JOKES AND ANECDOTES (1200–1999)

1641	Doctor Know-All	11

General Index

Abandonment of child, 147

Abduction: of newborn child, 41; of maiden by evil spirit, 166–67

Aborigines: of south China, 199; non-Chinese, 205

Accidents, lucky, 13, 14, 15

Accusation, false, 76

Achilles heel as motif, 217

Advice: from scholar, 25; from deity, 110; from son of Dragon King, 149

Aesop, 236

African tradition, 202, 239

Alexander the Great, 219

American Indian tradition, 200, 206, 211

Ancestors, interment of, 75–77

Androcles and the lion, 226

Anger, 5, 16, 26, 174; caused by deceitful wives, 43; deity's eyes red from, 150; as cause of death, 153, 180

Animals: as guardian of treasure, 102; take revenge on eavesdropper, 129; poisonous, 220; of iron, 225; zodiacal, 240

Ants: as helpers, 57, 172; saved from flood, 164

Appointment secured by trick, 104–5

Arthurian legend, 205

Asian tradition, 201, 202, 205, 217, 222, 234

Astrologers, 216

Augury from written character, 105

Baldness magically cured, 49

Bad luck, 74, 136

Bamboo: supernatural, 24; reincarnation as, 159

Banishment. See Exile

Barbarians, 14

Barbers, patron saint of, 219

Bargain, deceptive, 80–81, 180

Battle between snake and millepede, 123

Bear as husband of girl, 214

Beard as symbol of status, 232

Bed, enchanted, 60

Bee, ghost of, 192

Beet as magical food, 53

Beggars, 26, 27–29; Taoist saints as, 230

Beheading, 16

Benefactor, mysterious, 162

Beowulf, 214

Betel nut, 200

Betrayal of secret, 116

Bird: eats red-hot nails, 86; washes in boiling oil, 86; steals crop, 127; captured, 139; visits master in prison, 139; accuses magistrate, 140; speaks as deity, 140

Birth: from pumpkin, 24; supernatural, 24; mysterious, 53

Blood from severed head, 83

Bones: of helpful animal saved, 157; sight of, causes death, 161

Book of magic, 215

Boot as coffin, 95

Bribe to deity, 243

Bride: brings good fortune, 46; celestial, 46; from portrait, 46; of deity dies, 62; abducted by tigers, 119

Bridge: of copper, 129; to paradise, 129; local legends of, 223; to netherworld, 242

British tradition, 205

Brownies. See Elves

Buddha: Laughing, 80; Big Belly, 217; of the Future, 217
Buddhistic belief, 218
Buddhistic elements in tale, 221, 242
Buddhistic literature, 206
Buddhistic myths, 232
Buddhistic tale, 241
Buddhism, 229, 230; popular, 207; Chinese, 233; Indian, 242
Bureaucratic setting as typical, 227
Burial, propitious, 66
Bushel as protection, 216
Butcher as sinner, 229
Butterflies, 204
Buttocks, burned, 68

California, Chinese temples in, 216
Calf: as reincarnated child, 41–43; as bridegroom, 42
Cap: brings about reincarnation, 87; of invisibility, 96
Capture by monkey, 29, 67
Carp: as supernatural being, 149; as steed, 194, 242; as symbol, 242
Carpenters, 73; patron saint of, 215, 217
Carrot, 8, 9
Cat: recovers magic object, 142; killed by woman, 143
Caves, 29; as entrance to other-world, 97, 99
Ceremony, Buddhist, 205
Chamber pot as protection, 216
Charity as virtue, 130, 133
Cherry branch, magic properties of, 56
Chess playing, 55, 97, 223
Chiang Tzu-ya, hero of novel, 233–34
Child: expelled from home, 27; attempts to murder, 41–42; searches for father, 54; supernatural, 79–80; saves family, 80; abandoned in river, 147; found by monk,

147; finds mother, 148; finds father, 149
Ch'in Shih Huang-ti, Emperor, 24–26
Chinese culture, tale contrary to, 212
Chinese tradition, influence of, on Japanese, 221
Ch'ing-shui, 199, 216, 230
Chin-shan, 233
Christian tradition, 230
Christianity, 229–30
Christiansen, Reidar Th. (Norwegian folklorist), 228
Chun-shan Lang, 236
Cinderella: motifs in, 200–201; studies of, 235
Cinnamon tree, in moon, 127
Clan names: used in tales, 221; given to heroes, 225
Clans in tales, 214
Class conflict in tales, 222
Clay, men created of, 3
Cloud as evil spirit, 165
Cloud Terrace Mountain, monasteries of, 233
Clown, hero as, 151
Clue, thread as, 64
Cock: horned, 5; enemy of the millepede, 6; attacks evildoer, 127; in moon, 127
Cock's crow, reason for, 6
Coffin, theft of, 76
Coin: restores memory, 32; as token, 33
Comb, 179
Communist folklorists, 208
Communist text, 208, 217, 222
Communist values in tales, 222
Complaint of workmen, 73
Concealment in tree, 128
Conception, magical, 53, 211
Concubine, 243
Confucianism, popular, 242
Confucius, hero disciple of, 218
Constancy as virtue, 21–24

Cormorant fishing, 219

Corn, 180

Cow: steals rice, 5; steps on crab, 5; as helpful animal, 43–44, 156–57; killed by stepmother, 157

Cowherd as hero, 43–44

Cox, Marian R. (English folklorist), 235

Crab: betrays secrets, 5; finds cow stealing rice, 5; reason for mark on back, 5

Creation legend, 3

Creation of man, 3

Cruel stepmother, 156

Cruelty, 134; of goblin, 82; to daughter-in-law, 112

Cults: popular, 199; of water buffalo, 211; in tales, 214; of Water Mother, 225; Buddhist, 237; of plague deities, 242

Cure: found in dream, 7; by snake, 29; by shaving, 91

Cursing, 23, 26; of benefactor, 3

Custom, folk, 205

Dead in netherworld, 31

Death: from love, 23; warning of, 27; caused by deity, 62; magically induced, 74; of magic animal, 77; from shock, 161; from anger, 180; as requirement of marriage, 212

Debt, canceled, 130

Deceptions: lazy hero poses as doctor, 13, 14; fatal, 37; monstrous birth, 41; feigned illness to accomplish murder, 42; rich man disguised as cook, 50; bridegroom eaten by tiger, 56; of monkeys, 58–59; of ogre, 59–60; enchanted food, 60; lime as medicine, 68; in bargains, 80–81, 180; hero falsely accused of murder, 85; of emperor by minister, 104; monster ambushed, 145–56; heroine drowned, 158; substituted bride, 158; false accusation, 184; in

order to steal, 188; of spirits, 193; of carp, 194

Defloration, ritual, 205

Deification, 217; of humans, 80, 150; of ghost, 219

Deity: as messenger, 44; enjoins peace, 44; of sea, 69; of fire, 80; of hairdressers, 91; appointed, 98; as ruler of heaven, 103; appears in dream, 110, 114; in chains, 114; abused, 114; of city, 114; disguised as monk, 116; as beggar, 134; of kiln, 136; of luck, 182; chooses zodiacal animals, 186; transfers duties, 189; causes illness, 190; heals, 190; as heroine, 210; local, 212; highest, 223; with human traits, 241; in triads, 242; messianic, 242; of plague, 242

Disappearance: of girl, 67; of house, 130

Discovery of secret, 93

Disenchantment: by donning bridal robes, 42; by hiding portrait, 46–47

Disguises: woman as man, 21; as cook, 50; man as monkey, 58–59; deity as young man, 62; as barber, 91; saints as workmen, 105–6; deity as monk, 115; immortal as beggar, 131; deity as beggar, 134; pirate as merchant, 147; dragon king's son as carp, 147–49; serpent as flower, 175; as lord of hell, 193

Doctor, sham, 13

Dog: as grateful animal, 3; as bringer of rice, 10; recovers magic object, 142; killed by woman, 143

Donkey: frightens tiger, 185; killed by tiger, 185

Dorson, Richard M. (American folklorist), 213, 226

Dragon: lacks horns, 6; provides water for moat, 51; of mud, 65; killed, 78; in grave, 78; causes

Dragon (*continued*)
flood, 111; as helper, 170; in underground otherworld, 170; zodiacal, 186; undersea kingdom of, 234; produces rain, 236

Dragon king: invites peasant to visit, 48; promises reward, 48; daughter of, 49; gives bed of white jade, 58; in underground palace, 99; dwells in sea, 142; restores lost treasure, 142; daughters of, 149; rescues merchant, 149; as helper, 152; requests music, 152; gives magic object, 153; journey to, 234

Drama, folk motifs in, 210

Dream: of cure, 7; how to prevent flood, 111; advice given in, 114

Drought, 100, 113

Drowned become water spirits, 219

Drunkard as messenger, 105

Dumbness as punishment, 5

Dwarf, helpful, 92

Earth: influences man's fate, 215; deity of, 224

Eastern European tradition, 212, 232

Eavesdropper, 15; learns valuable secret, 128

Egg, snake's, found by schoolboy, 124

Eight as symbol, 203

Eight Immortals in tales, 229, 240

Elves, 93–95; dowery of, 94; eat humans, 94

Emperor: of heaven, 4; assigns task, 120; confers title on hero, 120; as dragon, 216

English tradition, 238. See also British tradition

Entrance to other world, 98

Envy: of rich man for poor neighbor, 50; inspires imitation, 126

Escape: from pursuing monkeys, 59; from monkey, 68; from bear, 69

Etiological endings: origin of crab's markings, 5; origin of cock's crow, 6; origin of rice, 9, 10; origin of celestial bodies, 43-44; reason for appearance of moon, 127; explaining zodiac, 187

Etiological tales, 3, 6–8, 38, 55, 83, 103, 214

European tradition, 202, 205, 207, 214, 220, 235, 236, 238, 243

Evil spirits of river, 103

Examinations, imperial, as folktale motif, 223, 226, 227

Execution, 16

Exempla: Buddhist, 229; medieval, 238

Exile, to hell, 4. See also Punishment, nature of

Exorcism of five poisonous animals, 226

Extortion, 192

Eyes: reddened, 68; sealed, 68

Fairy: as bride, 43–44, 51; loses clothing, 43; raiment of, restores magic powers, 44; guards supernatural cave, 97; in moon, 126

Fairy godmother, 200

False accusation, 109

Fatalistic ending, 61

Fate: prevents wealth, 195; determines wealth or poverty, 203

Feng-huang. See Phoenix

Feng-shen yen-i (novel), 233–34

Ferryman, 17

Festival: on thirtieth day of seventh month, 5; burial, 25–26; of New Year, 29, 45; of sacrifice, 136; of second day of second month, 170, 236; of July seventh, 209; folk, 217; Indian, 217; of Tang period, 217; spring, 217; of May fifth, 226; of ascent of dragon, 236; of twenty-fourth day of last month, 243; of kitchen deity, 243

Fidelity, 25–26

Filial piety, rules of, 216
Finger substituted for carrot, 9
Finnish tradition, 212
Fire, deity of, 80
Firewood from human limbs, 224
Fish: origin of, 26; bite monster, 146; curative properties of, 147; weeps, 147
Fishing with cormorant, 219
Fisherman: walks on water, 92–93; catches treasure, 141
Fishmonger: helps conquer monster, 144; refuses to aid heroine, 157
Flight: from netherworld, 32; of saint and prostitute, 129; on a cloud, 188
Flood: occurs yearly, 110; prevented, 111; caused by magic object, 113
Flower vase turns into maiden, 49
Folk cure, 205
Folk custom, 26, 205
Folk medicine, 205
Folk singing, 222
Folksong as lure, 110
Food: mysteriously prepared, 45, 49, 154, 159; magical, 53; enchanted, 60
Fool as hero, 127
Fortune teller, 136. See also Geomancer
Foundation sacrifice, 25, 205, 231
Frog in moon, 228

Gardner as ogre, 59–60
Gayton, Ann (American folklorist), 207
Geomancer accused of theft, 76
Geomancy, 213, 216; folktales about, 215
German tradition, 202, 228, 230
Ghost: of wife, 31–33; of millepede, 123; cooks for rescuer, 159; resumes human form, 159; of bee, 192

Girl: as scholar, 21; as helper in hero's flight, 60–61; bought for sacrifice, 136; sale of, 231
Goblin king, 82
Goose lays golden egg, 234
Governor deified, 110
Grateful animals. See Helpful animals. See also under specific animal
Grave: opens at prayer, 23; violated, 24; of mother, 200. See also Tomb
Grave site: favorable, 64, 215; chosen by geomancer, 77, 215
Great Wall, 24, 25, 26
Greed, 8, 93, 133, 155, 180
Greek tradition, 230, 234
Grimm collection, 202
Guardian spirit, 25
Guild of carpenters, 215
Guitar played by hero, 153

Hair as weapon, 82
Hare: as supernatural creature, 97; zodiacal, 186
Harvest saved from drought, 103
Haunted room, 123
Healing: magic, of tree, 127; by holy man, 131
Hearth god, 243
Heaven: ascent to, by dragon, 6; return of bride to, 46; of nine levels, 210
Hell, 206; deity of, 199; in folk belief, 218; in folk religion, 242; king of, 242
Helpful animals: sparrow, 67; assist in destroying wild beasts, 120; restore lost treasure, 142; killed, 143; bite invading monster, 145–46. See also under specific animals
Heretic cults, Buddhist, 237
Hermit: as helper, 56; tested, 131
Hill: as grave site, 75; in shape of turtle, 75

Holy man eaten by snakes, 131
Horns: on temple, 211; pavilions of, 211
Horse with extraordinary speed, 193
House, magically built, 154–55
Household spirits, 220
Housekeeping by elves, 94
Hsi-yo-chi, 206, 212
Human sacrifice, 25, 231
Humans become deities, 98, 195
Hunger, 4, 91; assuaged by stone, 170
Huns, 24
Hunter traps phoenix, 183

Icelandic tradition, 230
Identification: by tokens, 62, 213; of mother by child, 43
Identity test, 213
Ill luck. *See* Bad luck
Illness, 27–29; feigned, 42
Image taken for picture, 179
Imitation: leads to disaster, 87–88; of hero by envious person, 126; foolish, 190
Immortality, 24, 26
Immortals, Eight, 203
Imprisonment: by monkey, 67; by bear, 69; of ghosts, 192
Ingratitude, 132–33; of man, 3
Injury from interruption of magic act, 188
Indian tradition, 200, 203, 205, 212, 218, 220, 223, 228, 231, 232, 234, 236, 238, 239, 243
Inspector: of earth, 150; of heaven, 150; of waters, 150
Invisibility: from wearing ogre's skin, 96; from cap, 220
Invulnerability, 82
Iranian tradition, 217
Irish tradition, 229, 230, 239
Israeli tradition, 227

Jade Emperor, 119, 225
Japanese tradition, 200, 203, 205, 207, 209, 211, 213, 214, 220, 221, 225, 228, 230, 232, 233, 237, 238, 243
Jātaka (collection of Indian Tales), 235
Jealous wife kills sparrow, 159
Jealousy of other wives, 41
Jih-kuang, 242
Journey: to hell, 8; magical, 29; to bottom of sea, 48; to seek fortune, 151
Judge of hell, 242

Kami, 220
Key: stolen, 102; as motif, 222
King: assigns task, 184; fails to give promised reward, 184; promises reward, 184. *See also* Emperor; Ruler
King of snakes, cycle of stories about, 218
Kitchen god, 243
Knife, as magic object, kills bride, 61
Korean tradition, 199, 213, 228
Ksitigarbha boddhissttva, 199
Ku Chieh-kang, 205
Kuan Yin, 107; as bestower of rice, 9
Kuang-han Kung, 228
Kuei-chou, 185, 240

Lake opened with key, 101
Landlord, 238
Laughter, 36, 37
Laziness, 13
Leg: burned in volcano, 188; used for firewood, 188
Legend: Arthurian, 205; of goddess, 216; local, 225
Leprosy, 205
Lessing, F., 217
Letter sent to dragon king, 105
Li T'ish-kuai, 230
Li T'ie-kuai, 240
Life span, traditional, 237

Lin, clan of, 216

Lin Lan (collector), 199–201; 203–7; 209–10, 214–17, 219, 221, 223, 225–32, 234–35, 237, 240–41, 243

Lion: as helpful animal, 35; devours boy, 56; predicts flood, 163; as protector, 236; of stone, 236

Literature: third-century, 199; fourteenth-century, 223; folk motifs in, 233; role of popular tradition in, 236

Lithuanian tradition, 220

Liu Tsung-yüan, 240

Love magic, 220

Love sickness, 21, 23

Lover: hidden, 30; as star, 44

Lotus: as way to western paradise, 174; as Buddhist symbol, 237; mysterious, 237

Lou Tse-k'uang, 238

Loyang River, 103

Lu Pan, patron saint of carpenters, 215, 217

Lü Tung-pin, 131, 223, 230, 240

Luck: bad, 74, 136; changed, 74

Lucky: accidents, 13–15; discovery of salt, 16

Maass, E., 207

Mabuchi, Toichi (Japanese folklorist), 201

Magic: learned from immortals, 188; black, 220

Magic flight, 44

Magic formula, 87

Magic objects: silver men, 17; dress, 43–44; cowhide, 44; hairpin, 44, 49; ring, 44; weaving shuttle, 44; portrait of girl, 45–46; banner causes sea to part, 48; flower vase, 49; pearl divides water, 51; pot produces silly things, 52; cherry branch, 56; from pearl, 56; iron rod, 56; golden fork, 58; lime, 58–59; needle, 58–59; oil, 58–59; flying knife, 60–61; ship, 73;

sword, 76; snake's liver, 85; obtained from ogre, 95; stolen by spirit, 95; accidentally destroyed, 96; lost by gambler, 96; offered as gambling stake, 96; skin of ogre's face, 96; given by fairies, 97; reed, 97–98; lost, 98; key, 101; wand, 112; misused, 113; ladder from pumpkin vine, 126; Palace of Boundless Cold, 126; pumpkin seed, 126; golden cinnamon tree, 127; sword, 129; from saint, 135; handkerchief, 135; pot enriches owner, 141; box, 149; wishing stone, 154; dress, shoes, and horse from pot, 157; paper ship, 163; lost, 234

Magic occurrences: real birds from paper ones, 51–52; conception, 53; trip to moon on pumpkin vine, 126; tree healed of ax stroke, 127; rat doubles in size, 187

Magic powers: resumed, 46; of supernatural wife, 49–52

Magician as builder, 81

Magistrate: attempts to buy speaking bird, 138; confesses crimes, 140

Magpies form a bridge, 209

Maiden: as helper, 58; gives magic objects, 58

Malasekera (collection of Buddhist myths), 232

Manure collector helps conquer monster, 144

Marriage, 31; forced, 25; to reincarnated wife, 33; to monkey, 67; to animal, 67, 214; to deity, 212, 237

Mason, 73; becomes deity, 195

Master, cruel, 134

Memory regained, 32

Merchant rescued by son of dragon king, 149

Message, fatal, 137

Messengers, of hell, 192

Messianic deity, 242
Methuselah, Chinese, 241
Middle Eastern tradition, 235
Midwife: male, 13, 14; assists ti-
  gress, 119
Mi-lo, 217
Min-chien, 220
Ming era, 204, 205, 234, 238
Millepede, hostile to snake, 123
Ministers, treacherous, tales about,
  234
Miracles, 230
Mirror, 179
Mistake, fatal, 137
Mistaken identity, 179
Misunderstanding, 15; due to speech
  impediment, 160
Moat, magically produced, 50
Modesty, 21
Monasteries, 233
Money: as source of worry, 181;
  given to poor man, 181; in cake,
  195
Mongols, 202
Monk, 8, 174; as beggar, 80, 161; as
  designer of bridge, 106; disguised
  deity, 115; finds child, 147; as
  helper, 162; as hero, 233; float-
  ing, 233
Monkey: burned, 68; escape from,
  68; unwittingly betrays secret,
  128; as hero, 206; in theater, 206;
  kingdom of, 206
Monkey's Pilgrimage. See Hsi-yo-chi
Monster invades house, 145-46
Moon, 179; fairies in, 126; palace
  in, 126; as place of exile, 127;
  boy in, 127; cinnamon tree in,
  127; reason for appearance of, 228
Moralistic endings, 24, 26, 29, 52,
  78, 125, 131, 134, 141, 156, 180,
  195
Mother, greedy, 8
Mother-in-law, cruelty of, 112
Mountain, golden, 233

Mouse helps recover magic object,
  142
Mu-lien, 201
Murder of supernatural lover, 64
Muslim as treasure seeker, 47
Mynah bird as helper, 137
Myth, Buddhist, 232

Nature influences man's fate, 215
Near Eastern tradition, 217, 218,
  222, 232, 236, 243
Negro tradition, 202
Netherworld, 206; visited, 218. See
  also Other world
New World tradition, 202
New Year, 29; festival of, 45; ac-
  counts settled, 94-95; Iranian, 217
North Pole, deity of, 213
North star as highest deity, 223
Northern European tradition, 212,
  233
Norwegian tradition, 220
Novel: classical, 206, 207, 229, 233-
  34; folk motifs in, 210, 223
Nudity, 25
Number, as symbol, 203

Obscenity, symbol of, 213
Ogre: in netherworld, 32; wang-
  liang, 95, 220
Oil merchant refuses aid, 157
Opium, 200; origin of, 6-8
Oracle from written characters, 223
Origin: of ox, 4, 5; of fish, 26; of
  culture item, 83; of festival, 83
Origin tales. See Etiological endings
Orphan, 13
Orpheus motif, 206
Other world: western, 34, 129; en-
  tered with magic formula, 87; re-
  turn from, 99; underground, 167.
  See also Netherworld
Ox: as messenger, 4; sent to help
  men, 5; builds house, 54; of iron,
  110; quarrels with rat, 186-87

Pai tribes, 238

Palace: built by poor man, 46; magically produced, 49; of Dragon King, 99; in moon, 126; of crystal, 149; of dragon king, 149; of harmony, 150. See also Magic objects

Panchatantra, 232, 235

P'an-ku, 3

Parrots give advice, 101

Patrilocal residence, 212

Patron saint, 229; of merchants and ships, 80; of kiln, 136; of carpenters, 215, 217; of guilds, 219

Peacock gives advice, 101

Pearl: water-dividing, 51; of iron, 56; as reward, 125

Peddler helps conquer monster, 143–45

P'eng-tsu, 241

Perseus, 211

Phoenix: as lucky omen, 15, 239; indicates treasure, 15, 16; two-headed, 183; as symbol, 203

Picture, emperor enamored of, 36

Piety, 8, 9

Pig: ocean-warming, 47; as reincarnated child, 88

Pill: of dirt to cure illness, 128; of immortality, 188; of dirt as Taoist motif, 228

Pirates: throw passenger overboard, 147; Japanese, 234

Plasterer as hero, 137

Plowing, 4, 5

Poison, Ku, 220

Poisonous animals: exorcised, 226; snake and millepede, 226; the five, 226

Policemen of hell, 242

Popular belief, 203, 206, 219

Popular religion, 243

Pot of paper, 93

Poverty magically induced, 74

Prayer: for favorable wind, 69; for rain, 114

Predestined treasure, 15, 203

Promise: broken, 14, 116; fulfilled, 116

Prophecy, made and fulfilled, 161–64

Proverbs, 87, 181, 227; Thai, 82

Pun on personal names, 201

Punishment, nature of: dumbness, 5; to grind rice, 41; death, 16, 43, 95, 145–46; exile from heaven to earth, 46; swallowed by snake, 84, 125, 131; execution, 91; beating, 98; exile to moon, 126–27; devoured by wild animals, 129; transformation into monkey, 135; sacrifice of child, 137; imprisonment, 138, 139; bird to be eaten, 139; shaving beard, 140

Punishment, reason for: transmitting wrong message, 4; betraying secrets, 5; treasure concealed from emperor, 16; monstrous birth, 41; deception, 43; fault committed, 46; lying, 85; clumsy shaving, 91; theft from elf, 95; impertinence, 98; greed, 125, 126, 137; eavesdropping, 129; use of magic object, 135; careless work, 138; refusal to sell pet, 139; taunting magistrate, 139; crime, 140; invading woman's home, 145–46

Purification with water, 83

P'u-sa, 242

Quest: for precious objects, 34; fulfilled, 35; for key, 101

Rabbit. See Hare

Railroads, building of, in China, 215

Rain, 209; prayed for, 114; produced by local deity, 225

Rainbow, 209; origin of, 21–24; as symbol, 204

Raksha, spirits of hell, 193

Rat: quarrels with ox, 186–87; as

Rat (*continued*)
trickster, 187; doubles in size magically, 187

Recognition: lack of, 31, 79; of son, 43; by token, 160, 173

Regret causes sleeplessness, 7

Reincarnation: as plant, 7; as new-born child, 33; as calf, 41–43; as bird, 86; accidental, 87; as pig, 88; of pirate as minister, 150; mother as cow, 156; of heroine as sparrow, 158–59; as bamboo, 159; as two-headed phoenix, 183; as animal, 218; of sinner, 218

Religion: popular, 199; folk, 242

Resuscitation: by deity, 3; of dog, 3; of man, 3; attempted, 61; by killing pig, 88

Reward, nature of: dog given food, 9; official post, 14; official position and riches, 16; whatever is requested, 48; money, 65, 146; appointment as earl, 86; acquittal of false accusation, 110; life saved, 123; snake's pearl, 125; magic seed, 126; bride, 128, 158; immortality, 131–32; magic handkerchief, 135; gold or bride, 166; half of kingdom, 184

Reward, reason for: bringing rice, 9; delivery of child, 14; finding treasure, 16; stopping sea from boiling, 48; burial, 65; performing difficult tasks, 86, 184; hospitality, 110; rescue, 122–23; kindness, 125; disease cured, 126, 128, 131; cure of wound, 131; charity from recipient, 135; return of daughter, 166

Rice, origin of, 9, 10

Rice broker refuses to aid heroine, 157

Rip Van Winkle, 222

River: celestial, 44; association with iron, 225; of other world, 242

Robin Hood, 222

Rock: flying, 38; in Yang-tse River, 233

Rod of iron, 56

Rolling head, 83

Rooth, Anna B. (Swedish folklorist), 235

Ruler of heaven, 44

Russian tradition, 232

Sacrifice: foundation, 25, 205, 231; human, 25, 94, 136–37, 231; to husband, 26; of daughter, 136–37; ineffective, 137; to river deity, 237. *See also* Human sacrifice

Sailors aid in escape, 69

Saints, 223; as workmen, 106; as trickster, 107; patron, 217, 219; Taoist, 224, 230; test followers, 230

Salt, discovery of, 15, 16

San Kuan (twelfth-century popular deity), 234

Scandinavian tradition, 225

Scholar: girl as, 21; as hero, 125, 226; aids heroine, 157–58

Search: for husband's bones, 25; for sacrificial victim, 25; for dead wife, 31; for beautiful woman, 36; for bride, 37; for father, 54; for missing daughter, 67; for thieving bird, 127–28; bird searches for master, 139; for mynah bird, 139; for parents, 148

Secrecy enjoined, 92, 114

Secret: elicited by lover, 82; discovered, 93; betrayed, 116

Seki, Keigo (Japanese folklorist), 213

Self-sacrifice: to prevent flood, 110; as Communist virtue, 222–23

Serpent as lotus, 175. *See also* Snake

Sexual freedom, pre-marital, 26

Shahmeran, 218

Shang era, 231

Shao-hsing, 218

Shape shifter, 242
Ship of clay, 74
Shipwreck, 69
Shoe, lost, 62, 157
Short stories, 213; literary, 199; Buddhistic, 206; folklore in, 215, 218, 223
Sight restored, 153
Silver, men of, 17
Sinner, 229
Site, auspicious, 75
Skin of ogre, 96
Slaves: mistreated, 134; in China, 231
Snail, golden, 109–10
Snake, treasure transformed into, 15; cures disease, 29; rewards peasant, 85; tamed by scholar after rescue, 121; freed, 122; hostile to millepede, 123; forfeits life to save master, 123; as scholar's pet, 124; eats holy man, 131; bites monster, 146; saved from flood, 164; as helpers, 172; zodiacal, 186; girl as, 218; as symbol, 223; as grateful animal, 227; liver of, as medicine, 227
Snake catcher helps conquer monster, 144
Snake minister: killed by peasant, 84; reincarnated as bird, 85
Snake princess punished by snake king, 84
Sorrow as cause of death, 153
Soul catcher, 242
Spanish tradition, 230
Sparrow: as helpful animal, 67, 171; reincarnation as, 158–59; kept in golden cage, 159; saved from flood, 164
Spendthrift, 13, 17
Spying, 30, 93; by jailer, 139
Stepsister drowns heroine, 158
Storm maims people, 3
Stutterer, utterances of, misunderstood, 160

Suicide, 107; becomes water spirit, 219
Sun Chia-hsün, 211, 212, 235
Sung era, 225, 231
Sung Che, 212, 217, 222, 239
Supernatural abilities: monk with second sight, 161; understanding bird language, 218
Supernatural beings: wang-liang, 95, 220; as monk, 147–48
Supernatural lover, 63
Swallow as grateful animal, 125–26
Swan maiden tales, 43–44, 210
Sweets as bribe, 243
Swine as helpers, 56–57
Sword, magic, 129

Tanabata, 209
T'ang era, 220, 233, 238
T'ang-seng, 233
Taoism, 229, 230
Taoist motif, 228
Taro, 180
Task: put down rebellion, 14; bring dragon pearl, 34; bring shell of turtle spirit, 34; bring golden-haired lion, 34; assigned by father-in-law, 34; accomplished with supernatural help, 49–52; build moat, 50; provide water in moat, 50; provide hedge of trees, 51; fill wood with birds, 51; sow linseed, 56; collect sown seed, 57; find concealed witch, 57–58; bring bed of jade from dragon king, 58; bring drum of monkey king, 58; cut bamboo, 59; build temple, 81; translate bird language, 85–86; feed headless bird, 86; destroy wild beasts, 120; to heal, 131; straighten hemp, 156; separate grain, 156, 171, 172; retrieve shoe, 157; fatal, 160–61; transfer gold from one room to another, 172; divide two-headed phoenix, 184
Temple, burned, 80

Temptation of hermit, 229

Tests: understanding bird language to prove innocence, 85–86; by saints, 132–33; of charity, 133; ingratitude, 133; for true bride, 160

Thankless animals, 236

Theater plays, 29–30, 201, 204, 205, 206, 210, 213, 221, 229, 233, 234, 238, 240; monkeys in, 206; as part of ceremony, 212; folk motifs in, 223, 243

Theft: of drum from monkeys, 59; by invisible man, 95, 96; from elves, 95; by spirit, 95; of key, 102

Thief, 238; confounded, 15

Thirst, 53

Thread as clue, 64

Three Officials. *See* San Kuan

Throne, lotus, 174

Thunder prevented, 216

Tiger: devours boy, 56; kills child, 85; abducts bride, 119; helped by human midwife, 119; rewards midwife, 119; appears as witnesses, 120; drives away wild beasts, 120; unwittingly betrays secret, 128; frightened by donkey, 185; kills donkey, 185; zodiacal, 186; as deity, 226; as grateful animal, 226

Time distorted, 98, 99, 221

Ti-tsang P'u-sa, 4, 201

Toad in moon, 228

Tobacco, 200

Token: brings recognition, 33; given by maiden, 169; of identification, 213

Tomb, made for snake, 124

Tortoise, as symbol, 223

Tracts, religious, 201

Traits, human, ascribed to deities, 241

Transformation: treasure to snakes, 15; silver men to humans, 17; dress to butterflies, 23; bamboo to rainbow, 24; monkey to human, 29; child to calf, 41; by shedding animal skin, 42; calf to young man, 42; witch to peach, 57–58; noodles to snakes, 60; peach to witch by biting, 58; turtle to man, 63; entrails to snake, 103–4; entrails to tortoise, 104; man to fish, 107; saints to beggars, 132–33; wine to brandy, 133; water to wine, 133; man and woman to monkeys, 135; deity to mortal, 212; water to wine, 230

Treacherous companion, 169

Treasure: buried, 15; predestined, 15, 203; kept for rightful owner, 108; sold, 195; guardian of, 224

Trickster, 194 *See also* specific animals

Turkish tradition, 228.

Turks, 202

Turtle: as hero, 62; in mountain, 75–77; symbolic meaning of, 213

Underground entrance to other world, 98, 99

United States tradition, 238

Unpromising hero, 13, 29, 33, 44, 47, 65, 98, 108, 120, 128, 130, 153, 161, 194, 206

Unpromising heroine, 53, 156

Values, Communist, 208, 238

Values, traditional, 208, 238

Vegetarianism, religious, 229

Vendor. *See* Peddler

Venereal disease, 205

Volcano, 240

Vow: to marry a certain person, 22; fulfilled, 69, 110; not to marry, 80

Waiter gives advice, 31–32

Wall destroyed by weeping, 25

Wang-liang, 95, 220

Wastrel. *See* Spendthrift

Water: ability to walk on, 92; cannot be crossed by supernatural creature, 94; ceremony of pouring, 217

Water buffalo: swallows child, 41; as steed, 193

Water carrier as helper, 48

Water Mother, 225

Water rat helps recover magic object, 142

Water spirit: walks on water, 92; departs when discovered, 93; as ghost of suicide, 219

Well: in other world, 31; of wine, 133

Wen-shen, 242

Wheat, 180

Wife: mistreated, 6–7; reincarnated, 33; discovers secret, 93; predestined, 206; sold, 243

Wine, well of, 133

Wishes granted, 189

Witch as ogre, 56

Wolf: unwittingly betrays secret, 128; saved from flood, 164; as treacherous animal, 166; eats mother, 166

Woodcutter: assists tiger, 119; as hero, 167

Workmen: complain of food, 73; perform task in miraculous manner, 105

World tradition, 206, 207, 214

Yang-tse River, 233

Yin and Yang, 3

Yüeh-kuang, 242

Yü-huang-ti, 199, 225

Yün-t'ai, 233

Zodiac: animals of, 240; explanatory tales of, 240

Although folktale themes are an important part of Chinese literature, the scientific collection of folktales began in China only with the nationalist movement which followed World War I. Many facets of Chinese life and culture are revealed in these stories of city gods and magicians, thieves and beggars, serpents and tigers, treacherous ministers and dutiful sons in an ever changing panorama of rural and urban folk tradition.

"This collection of 79 stories is drawn from Eberhard's 1937 landmark work, 'Chinese Fairy Tales and Folk Tales,' supplemented by six newly-translated tales from Communist China. Historical notes for each tale and indexes of motifs, and types add to the book's usefulness."
—*Library Journal*

"With his continued interest and the knowledge of a specialist, Professor Eberhard has made this book of interesting tales indispensable to the student of Chinese folklore literature."—Li Chi, *Public Affairs*

"Eberhard is an outstanding scholar and Sinologue . . . The notes are extensive; the bibliography excellent."—*Choice*

The University of Chicago Press